BEAUTIFUL
Storm

BEAUTIFUL STORM

Copyright © 2024 by Katherine Jay

Cover image by Wander Aguiar Photography LLC

Cover design by © Books and Moods

Editing by Happily Editing Anns

CONTENTS

AUTHOR'S NOTE

This book contains subject matter that some people may find triggering. A list of the main potential triggers can be found on Katherine's website.

https://www.katherinejayauthor.com

Please note, triggers are not listed here to avoid spoilers for the book.

STORM PRODUCTIONS PRESENTS

BEAUTIFUL STORM'S SOUNDTRACK

So Beautiful by Pete Murray
End Game by Taylor Swift, Ed Sheeran, Future
All Of Me by John Legend
Fall At Your Feet by CYRIL, Dean Lewis
Belong Together by Mark Ambor
Don't Stop Me Now by Queen
The Man by Taylor Swift
Lego House by Ed Sheeran
Whatever It Takes by Imagine Dragons
Falling Like The Stars by James Arthur
Gonna Love You by Parmalee
I Can't Fall In Love Without You by Zara Larsson
Nervous by Gavin James
What Ifs by Kane Brown, Lauren Alaina
Faded by Alan Walker
Don't Let Me Down by The Chainsmokers, Daya
Easy On Me by Adele

AVAILABLE NOW ON SPOTIFY

For all the readers who love their book boyfriends a little bit cocky, a little bit sweet... and a whole lot OBSESSED... Enjoy!

And for those of you thinking about giving someone a second chance... or third... make them work for it. It will be worth it in the end.

PROLOGUE

AMELIA – AGE TEN

Most boys were put on this earth to be annoying, but Luke... Luke was born to make me laugh.

"Do Hulk next," I call out, kicking my legs behind me as I lie on the grass, watching Luke try to play football acting as different comic book characters.

"Hulk? You got it." He growls, pretending to rip off his clothes but trips over the ball as he throws himself around, falling on his ass, sending us both into fits of laughter.

"Hulk is definitely my favorite." I grin when he stands and jogs over.

"I think I'm done," he says with a huff as he joins me. "It's getting dark anyway, and you know what that means."

"I don't want to go home." I pout before rolling over and staring up at him.

"Why? Aren't you hungry?" His brows furrow and I can't help but laugh again, even though I'm sad. Typical Luke, always thinking about food.

"I am hungry. But my parents are acting weird."

"Weird, how? Mine are always weird. Have been since I was born." He shrugs and I immediately shake my head.

"No, not that kind of weird. They keep shushing each other when I enter the room, and Dad's going out a lot more."

"Oh."

"Yeah."

"It's probably nothing." He sits down beside me, tossing the ball on the grass between us. "Sometimes adult things don't make sense."

"Maybe. Can you promise me something?" I sit up and spin around to face him, crossing my legs as I wait.

"Anything." He turns my way but stays on a slight angle so his big legs don't get in the way. "You know that."

"When we're adults," I begin, ignoring him when his lips twitch. I always tell him it's better to be a kid and now, I'm asking him to think about being an adult. "When we're adults," I repeat, "let's not be weird."

Luke bursts out laughing before his face drops and he turns serious again. "Deal. But Ace, you're already weird." He bites back a smirk when I reach out and shove him over.

"I am not."

"Nah, you're not. You're perfect."

Shaking my head, I stand up and brush myself off, staring down at him now lying on the grass, almost exactly like I was. "Can you promise me something else?"

"Yep."

"No secrets."

"That's easy. I tell you everything."

"*Promise.*"

"Okay. I promise. No secrets. Now can we go home to eat?" I giggle while he stands, wrapping his arm around my shoulder. "I really need some food."

"Yeah, okay." I roll my eyes. "But only because you're annoying when you're hungry."

Luke snorts before pinning me with a concerned expression. "Are you going to be okay? Going home? Want me to come?"

"I'll be fine. Adults are always weird, right?"

"They sure are."

🏈 🏈 🏈

Age Eleven

Dear Diary,

It's been 76 days since I last saw Luke Bennett and I'm still hurt by what he did. He was supposed to be my best friend. I don't think I'll ever forgive him.

Love Amelia J. Rosenberg

Age Twelve

Dear Diary,

Today was a good day until Luke ruined it.

I got an English award for my short story and was called up to the front of the class. Then Luke got an award for physical education and said that winning for sports is better than winning for English. Of course, everyone cheered.

I wish I could change schools.

Love Amelia Rosenberg

Age Fourteen

Dear Diary,

A new kid named Preston started at our school today and he winked at me. Melody said that he liked me, but I don't know. We just met. He is so dreamy. He has blond hair and ocean blue eyes. The best thing is that he doesn't play football. He likes music. We'd be perfect together.

Luke wasn't happy about Preston's arrival but too bad. He's just jealous that now there's someone hotter than him at school.

I'm going to try and talk to Preston tomorrow.

Love, Amelia

. . .

Age Fifteen
Dear Diary,

I'm finally a freshman. If only me and Preston had more classes together. Instead, I'm stuck with Luke in four of them and Preston only one.

On the plus side, Preston and I started working at my mom's garden center over the summer break and Mom said she might keep us on during the year. That means we'd get to spend time together after school. Alone. As long as she doesn't find out I like him.

And maybe if no one else is around, he'll finally sing me the song he's been writing.

Love Amelia

Age Sixteen
Dear Diary,

I don't know what happened. It was supposed to be a bit of fun...but it all went wrong and now I might be in trouble.

I can't talk about it and I definitely can't write it down. I'm so lost.

Amelia

Age Seventeen

I can't believe it! Preston asked me to Prom. It was

one of the most romantic things anyone has ever done for me. He gave me flowers and he wrote me a song. MY OWN SONG.

Only I still don't know what that means. We spend all our spare time together but he's never made a move. Is this his way of telling me he likes me?

Amelia

Age Nineteen

It's been a month since I saw Preston, and I'm not going to lie, I'm struggling. He was touring for our two-year anniversary and while he sent me roses and another love song he'd written for me, I was a mess. I am a mess. How do people do this long-term? How are we going to do this long-term? Music is his dream. If all goes to plan this is the first of many tours to come. And who knows how my filmmaking will go. I want to take on the world.

I miss him so much. Amelia.

Age Twenty One

We did it. We got engaged. Preston proposed to me backstage at a music festival, just the two of us. It was his first big tour and when I surprised him in the audience, he ran off stage to find me.

Spending time apart is never going to be easy, but we love each other and I know we can make it work. Amelia.

. . .

Age Thirty

I've been putting everything I can into this marriage but it's not working. Preston is great. Always has been. But our spark is dwindling. Maybe it's been that way for a while now. We barely have sex anymore, not that we had it regularly to begin with, but at least there was intimacy. Now, I can't remember the last time we held hands.

I shouldn't be complaining... After all, he supports my dreams and we're making beautiful magic together with his music and my storytelling. The music videos I've directed for him have propelled him to stardom and he's taking me along for the ride.

We still laugh together. We have fun. I'm his muse. I never go without.

Objectively, he's the perfect husband. But we're both so busy and...

I need a break.

Age Thirty Two

I fucked up. It's been years since I wrote about him but I couldn't leave this out.

I slept with Luke. I was trying to move on and I stupidly slept with a man I despise.

And now I'm pregnant.

Send help.

CHAPTER ONE

AMELIA – AGE THIRTY-TWO

TWO MONTHS EARLIER

It's time to get back out there. Let's hope I know what the hell I'm doing. If I'm honest, I'm terrified.

I tap my foot against the leg of the chair and mindlessly stir my espresso martini. The same drink I've been staring at for the last hour. *I don't even like coffee...yet somehow, I'm addicted to the smell and thought this would be a good idea.*

"What about *him*?" my friend Hayley says as she sits down beside me, immediately knocking back the remainder of her drink, pointing to the fit-looking man in a business suit busting a move on the dance floor. "He looks like he could *satisfy some needs*," she adds when he thrusts his hips.

"I'm not having sex with some random guy." I huff out a laugh and roll my eyes.

Not to mention, I've never really been attracted to well-groomed businessmen, and lately, I've found myself drawn to men who are a little more rugged. But I digress. "Just because I'm single—"

"Okay." Hayley cuts me off as she lovingly squeezes my leg, knowing all too well the rant I was about to launch into. "I get it. I won't suggest..." Something catches her eye and she trails off, peering over my shoulder with a giddy smile replacing her sympathetic expression. "What about a guy you *do* know?"

"What?" I foolishly spin around to find Luke Bennett, infamous tight end for the San Francisco Storm football team swaggering our way. Yes, he's more of the *rugged* type I was referring to, despite currently wearing a suit, but he's also a former friend. One I'd prefer to keep in the past. Actually, I'd *prefer* he didn't exist.

I don't want to notice the way his lips lift in a half smirk as he raises an eyebrow as if to say "I see you watching me"—ever the cocky asshole that he is—and I don't want to notice his mocking wave before his smirk turns into a scowl. I don't want *anything* to do with him.

"Ugh, I'd rather sew myself shut," I mutter under my breath as he turns away.

"Amelia, geez. That's not a visual I need when I'm only two drinks in."

My eyes flash to Hayley's and I can't help but laugh. "Oh...but more drinks and it would be fine," I joke, shaking my head at the woman who has recently become my rock.

Hayley stares at me, deadpan, or maybe a little confused. "Yes. No issues."

It might be the alcohol coursing through my veins after Hayley insisted my first drink should be a shot, or the need to prove to Luke that I'm having fun, but either way, I throw my head back and laugh out loud. *God, I love her.* She came into my life at the best possible time after moving to America with her actor boyfriend. They'd met when they starred together on an Australian soap opera, and when he was cast in a sitcom to be filmed here in San Francisco, she followed in the hope that she'd get her big break too.

Long story, short... I was working as an assistant at the studio where they were filming and we met waiting in line at the cafeteria. It took half a cup of coffee for her and three bites of a donut for me to convince us we were going to be friends, and we've been close ever since, bonding over the harsh world that is the film and television industry, along with our love of sports.

Although I'm still trying to figure out how Aussie Rules works.

That aside, what really cemented our friendship is that both our relationships imploded at the same time. Hayley caught her douchebag boyfriend cheating on her with his co-star, and I made the hardest decision of my life by suggesting my husband and I take a break. Safe to say, he wasn't happy about that request, and our marriage ended shortly after.

Hayley got back on the horse right away, or horse rider in her case—literally riding a cowboy within days of her breakup—while I've been taking my time. I wanted to let my heart heal a little first. I'd been in a relationship since I was seventeen. I needed a break. For me. But now...

"What's wrong with Luke I-could-melt-your-panties-with-one-look Bennett?" Hayley says, cutting into my thoughts, her eyes following Luke as he walks toward his teammates at the bar. "He's hot...he doesn't like strings...at all—he'd probably let go of a balloon if you gave him one—and he has the body of a god." Her eyes flash to mine, catching me looking in his direction. "If nothing else..." She grins. "He's nice to look at, and his experience might mean you learn a thing or two."

What? My gaze shifts her way and I frown. "*Or* he could be lazy in bed knowing he can move on to the next girl before the night's through."

"True. That's a possibility but it's not what I'm hearing around the traps."

"What traps? What does that mean?" I raise an eyebrow and scoff. "Is that another Aussieism?"

Hayley frowns as she tucks her long blonde hair behind her ears. "You don't say that here?"

"Nope."

She hums to herself. "Then yes." She nods, straightening up in her seat. "Yes, it is. It basically means it's not what I've been hearing. Point is...he's a good option."

"I can't."

"Why? You love football."

"Nah," I lie. "I'm more into hockey men..."

Hayley shushes me with a gasp. "No, you're not. We don't play favorites when it comes to football or hockey men. You can't bullshit me."

"Ugh." *I'm going to have to tell her.* "I—"

"You're a relationship girl, right?" She cuts in before I can speak. "You don't want your next relationship to be shadowed by the fear that he's a rebound guy. And you said so yourself—you and Preston had a vanilla sex life. It's time to put yourself out there. Fuck the no-strings guy that you know will be great in bed. Then search for your soulmate later."

A little part of me comes to life as she speaks. Yes, I said that. I said our sex life was vanilla, but at the time I was okay with that. Now I want to try more, and it makes sense to try it with someone I can easily walk away from. But it has to be someone else.

"If I were to take your advice...and I'm not saying I am...yet. But Luke is not the right choice. I've known him for years, and if I'm being honest, I wouldn't cry if he was hit by lightning."

Hayley laughs out loud, her twinkling eyes moving in the direction of the obnoxious players as they chant by the bar. "Poetic considering he plays for Storm."

I bite back my smile as she grins from ear to ear. "Point is..." I say, using her words to tell her I mean business. "I'd rather stab him while he slept than let him touch me." *Again.*

"Okay." She claps her hands together, her eyes lighting up like it's Christmas. "*One.*" She raises a finger. "I need that story. And two." Her second finger lifts. "Hate sex is highly underrated. It could be *exactly* what you need."

"I'm not having hate sex."

"Why?"

I try to take her seriously but the deep furrowed brow and confusion set in her features makes me burst out laughing again. "Because..." I begin confidently, but pause. "Because..." *Jesus. Why is hate sex a bad idea?* "I don't know. Let's talk about that *after* I have some mind-blowing *feelingless* sex first."

"Deal. We'll revisit this conversation tomorrow." She nods and I laugh again, her confidence and positivity always bringing a smile to my face.

After one more glance toward the football players, I ignore the way my chest tightens at seeing Luke after all this time and steer the conversation in another direction. I'm not going to sit here and pretend he's not God's gift to women because I'd be lying to myself. That man is fine. But I am more than capable of pushing that from my mind simply by remembering what an ass he is. And the hurt he caused me. It does the trick every time.

"We need to dance," I say, straightening my crimson dress as I stand, hoping by some miracle it's suddenly less revealing. "I'm never going to find someone if I remain tied to my chair." I'm not completely conceding to her mission to find me a one-night stand, but if I keep drinking without moving, I'm likely to start making bad decisions.

"I agree," Hayley nods. "But...we?"

"Yes. You're coming with me. I need at least three songs before you disappear with some guy."

"Three?" Her eyes scan the room, undoubtedly searching for said guy, her lips pursed as she considers my request. "Okay. I can do that." She bounces on her toes as she stands. "Let's go." She knocks back her drink and straightens her shoulders before grabbing my hand to lead me to the dance floor. "We've got this."

I laugh as I'm dipped back until the tips of my fingers brush against the floor, and when I'm lifted again, my new friend, Chase, whispers in my ear. "And that's how it's done."

I give him an impressed nod but hold back my smile, making him work for it.

"Ahh, like that, is it?" He chuckles. "What more do you want?" His eyes narrow, jokingly trying to read my mind. "Flowers." He clicks his fingers. "Every woman wants flowers."

He's been trying to "woo" me—his word, not mine—for the last thirty minutes and I'm surprised to say I'm enjoying it. In fact, tonight has turned out to be much more fun than I expected.

When I mentioned I wanted to try a dating app, Hayley insisted on taking me out first and dragged me to the hottest new bar at the Westerly hotel. She said I should try things the old-fashioned way. And she may be right. It's not hard to imagine how a night of passionate dancing would be enough to consider taking someone home—or in my case, taking someone to a room upstairs since I'm spending the night here at the hotel. Only, I'm not convinced I'm that type of person.

"I actually loathe the giving of flowers," I admit with slightly clenched teeth. "My ex used to bring them home every time he had bad news or after he'd been gone for an extended period, and now just the thought of them makes me shiver."

"Noted." Chase cringes. "No flowers. But also... What a dick."

I laugh but Preston wasn't a dick. *Back then.* He was a great husband, and he hated that he was always leaving me alone. He assumed he was softening the blow. He wasn't; he was actually making it worse.

Chase and I continue to dance, with him whispering ideas in my head, each one more impressive than the last but still doing nothing to light a fire inside me.

There's not even a spark.

After a few more minutes, I catch Hayley's eye and she smiles proudly. Despite promising me only three songs, she's still dancing close by, keeping an eye on me like I'm a lost child. And maybe, when it comes to this one-night stand business, I am.

I'm generally strong enough to take care of myself, but I have no idea what I'm doing here. And Hayley knows it. Still, I wink back pretending to be more in control than I am and give her a nod of approval for the guy she's dancing with. A guy I swear I've seen on a billboard somewhere advertising men's cologne...or was it underwear... or is he that new golfer?

Here in the darkness, surrounded by the strobe lights and outfits that cost more than what I make in a year, he could be whoever he wanted to be. Maybe he's famous, or maybe he's no one at all. And that's what worries me. Not the fame thing—that actually goes against a guy when it comes to me—but the fact that anyone can fake it. Even me to a point. I'm flirting and giggling like I'm a sure thing, but I'm not. I'm still undecided. And as soon as Chase figures that out he'll drop me like I'm hot, forcing me to keep up the charade until I've made up my mind. Just like everyone else here.

"I've got it," Chase says suddenly, snapping his fingers as he cuts into my thoughts. He waits until our eyes lock before delivering his line devoid of sarcasm. "How about I take you out back and rock your world?" *Yep, he really just said that.*

"Excuse me?" I pull away, my gaze puzzled as I wait for him to laugh and tell me he's joking. *Please, please be joking.* He bounces his eyebrows similar to how Hayley did and I cringe. *Not a joke then.*

"Does that ever work?" I ask seriously. I know I'm sort of here for exactly what he's proposing, but surely, people don't talk like that.

Chase laughs. "Surprisingly, yes."

"So this is all part of your act? The nice guy wooing?"

Chase's previously friendly expression morphs into a cocky grin, and I get my answer. *Though, wasn't I doing the same thing—acting?* God, this is hard. I work in the world of make-believe, and toward the end of my relationship with Preston, we were both playing pretend.

For once, I want something to be *real*, even if it is only a one-night stand. *Is that too much to ask?*

Chase's friend returns from the bar and I use the distraction to make an escape. "I'll be back," I yell over the music, already backing away. "I'm going to the bathroom."

Hayley stops dancing and leans in as I squeeze past. "Want me to come with you?" she asks, her brows furrowed at the confusion on Chase's face. I get it—despite the blatant ploy to get in my pants, he's been fun. I shouldn't be walking away.

"Nah." I shake my head. "You keep dancing. That guy is smoking."

"Right?" She bites her lip as he wraps his arms around her, waving me off when I walk away. I may need a breather, but that doesn't mean I have to ruin her fun.

The line for the bathroom is relatively short, but it gives me enough time to think, and... *What the hell am I doing?* Thinking is my problem. It's a one-night stand, for fuck's sake. I shouldn't be thinking; I should be living in the moment. Enjoying myself and letting the night flow. So what if he's faking it? As long as he gives me a very real orgasm and helps me get over my reluctance to get back out there, why should I care?

Mind made up, I fix my hair and stand tall, ready to lose my mind and have fun. After straightening out my dress, *again*, I confidently stride back to the main room, ready to make a move.

It's my time. I deserve this.

I've just reached the dance floor, my eyes searching the sweaty masses, when I'm spun around and a familiar body blocks my view.

Luke.

"Ugh." I don't bother to hide my groan.

"You dodged a bullet," he says, his gaze drifting over my shoulder as he smirks.

"What do you want, Luke?" *For over ten years I've managed to avoid him and now...*

"I'm saving you from humiliation."

Stepping back, I fold my arms over my chest and pop my hip, smiling when Luke's eyes flash to my cleavage. "Eyes are up here, asshole."

"You know what, *Joy*? Dance away. As you were." He spins me back around before I have the chance to outwardly react to my nickname. God, I hate that name. He started calling me that when our friendship first began to crumble, reminding me that of all the students at our school, he alone knew me intimately. I despised my middle name—Joy—preferring to call myself Amelia J, and he used that against me. He said it was fitting, since I was such a *joy* to be around.

As a twelve-year-old, the sarcasm still dripped from his words.

I shiver when he moves to stand beside me, his hands barely touching my arms as he repositions me, putting Chase directly in our line of sight. And he's sucking face with someone new. *Great.*

I smile like it's no big deal. There's no one to blame but myself. I may have told him I'd be back, but I know my expression screamed "you blew it, buddy."

"Oh well." I step out of Luke's grasp. "You win some, you lose some." I shrug when in reality... *I am not cut out for this.*

"Told you," Luke gloats, his smug expression boring into the side of my face.

My smile widens while I mentally flip him off, imagining myself slamming the heel of my stiletto down onto his foot. Then, satisfied with that visual, I walk away, beelining to the bar to buy myself some time.

But of course, Luke follows behind me, never one to let something go.

"Go away, Luke," I call out over my shoulder, hoping he can hear me over the noise. "I've had enough of douchebag strangers for one night."

"So we're strangers now?" he rasps into my ear, making me jump as his breath warms my skin, with him *much* closer than I thought he was.

"We haven't seen each other in *years*," I say without turning around, refusing to give him any more than I have to. "And we haven't spoken for longer than that. So yes, I would consider you a stranger."

I keep walking, as if I don't know him, but he doesn't take the hint, and when I reach the bar, he settles in beside me, casually resting his elbows on the counter. His biceps bulge and my stupid traitorous eyes flash to the strained muscles, noting the hint of a tattoo peeking out from below his rolled-up shirtsleeve. My heart races, and for some messed-up reason that can only be explained by a complete lapse in my sanity or maybe alcohol, I picture him pressing me against a wall as I squeeze my legs shut, silently cursing Hayley for putting the idea in my head.

"But I tried to help you," Luke responds with a raised eyebrow, as if he knows *exactly* what I'm thinking, and I hate that he usually does. At least, he used to.

"Oh please." I huff, keeping my cool. "You wanted to be there to witness my embarrassment. Sorry to disappoint you, but I'm *fine*. I don't *need* anyone's help. Especially yours."

"Yeah. You made that clear," he snaps out of nowhere, startling me.

"What?" I shake my head before I continue. I'm supposed to be ignoring him. True, that's harder with the sudden venom in his tone, but still, I need to try. I can't let him get to me.

The server comes over, and I use that as my excuse to turn away. "I'll take a cider, please," I say with a warm smile. "Whatever you have closest to you."

He reaches below the bar and grabs me a bottle from Australia, making me giggle, before handing over the card reader and smiling. The second I've paid, I turn to walk away, preemptively readying myself to give Luke one last scowl.

But he's gone. He disappeared without a trace. And I'm alone. Just like I wanted.

I stay by the bar, my back against the counter as I slowly sip my cider, and after finishing, I move back to the dance floor, swaying on the edge until I'm ready to call it a night. My heart's not in it anymore. Not that it really was to begin with.

I want to move on. I do. But the thought of starting over after all this time is a little crippling and really freaking annoying. I was married. We talked about having kids. And now I'm getting offers to have my world rocked in a parking lot. *Oh, how my life has changed.*

"It doesn't have to be a bad thing," Hayley whispers, clasping my hand as she sidles up beside me.

"Huh?"

"You have a defeated look about you. But single life is supposed to be fun. Instead of looking at it like you've lost something, take a leaf out of my book."

"You mean a page?"

"Nope."

I laugh, gesturing for her to keep going.

"What I'm trying to say is that being single is a *good* thing. Embrace it."

I stare at her for a second, letting that idea sink in. I loved Preston, but I lost myself along the way. Being single gives me the chance to find myself again. To finally live the life I always wanted. On my terms. "You're right. I'm looking at it all wrong."

Hayley's eyes light up just like they did at the mention of hate sex earlier. "So can I find you—"

"Not tonight," I cut her off. "But I'm going to look at this whole *single thing* differently from now on. I promise."

"Okay. I'm calling that *progress*. Talk to you in the morning then?"

"After my massage."

"Deal."

She gives me a tight squeeze before making her way back to her man, laughing when he lifts her into the air.

I can do that. I'm a strong, confident woman, and I can be carefree and wild. Just like Hayley. I know it. I'm going to be.

Tomorrow anyway.

Tonight, my bed's calling me. I'm done.

The music fades as I walk away, and I can't stop my growing smile. Life doesn't have to be trying. All I have to do is be more positive. Tomorrow's a new day.

I tap my foot in time to the music as I wait for the elevator to arrive, and as the doors open, I'm met with a group of attractive men, all dressed in business suits, making me giggle to myself. Hayley would be in her element right now. And maybe with this new outlook on life, I need to think about men differently, too. What's wrong with a man in a suit? Especially if it's only for the night.

They're deep in conversation until they spot me and pause, all eyes flashing my way. "Going up?" one of the guys asks with a relaxed smile and sparkling green eyes, making me grin in return. *Guess I can see the appeal.*

"I am. Thank you." The guys move back to give me some space and I step inside.

A wave of relief washes over me as the doors begin to shut, bringing me one step closer to my new beginning.

"Busy night?" I ask, reaching out to press the button for my floor at the same moment a hand juts through the gap in the doors, startling me as they fly open again. *Jesus Christ.*

Silence falls over the space, and when the owner of the hand reveals himself, I hold back a groan as Luke slips in, immediately moving to my side.

"What are you doing?" I ask, my teeth clenched as I peer over my shoulder, my smile back in place.

"I'm calling it a night," he says, wrapping an arm around my shoulder, his fingers dancing across my skin. "I couldn't bear to think of you alone in our bed, so I'm coming with you. *Surprise.*"

Surprise? Wait. What?

CHAPTER TWO

LUKE

Amelia Rosenberg. Amelia *Joy* Rosenberg. I roll her name around my mind, matching her stare as her cruel dark eyes bore into mine. This girl...this *woman*. It's been years and yet, seeing her rattled feels like a victory.

"Don't worry your pretty little face." I bop her on the nose, enjoying the way she crinkles it in disgust. "I'm not missing out on too much fun." I'm completely bullshitting because I'd much rather be out on that dance floor than stuck in here. But it's too late now. I may as well make the most of it.

The elevator chimes as Amelia attempts to subtly shrug me off, but when none of the guys move, her eyes flash to the floor number. "Oh, sweetie." She smiles brightly, keeping her voice bubbly as she walks through the doors presumably realizing it's her stop. I move to follow but she turns at the last second, placing her palm on my chest. "Don't be silly." She giggles, lightly shoving me back inside. "You should keep partying. Drink your little heart out. I insist."

Nice try, but unfortunately you're stuck with me. "Not happening, my love. My *Joy*." I grab her hand and pull her against me as I step out, waving to the men behind us when I'd rather flip them off. "Night, gentlemen."

Amelia doesn't protest as we move, but the second the doors close, she turns on me, ripping her hand from my grasp. "What the hell are you doing? Why are you here?"

"I'm reluctantly walking you to your door," I say truthfully, my tone laced with boredom as I signal for her to continue on her way.

Her brow furrows and she eyes me curiously before releasing a whiny little huff and stamping her foot in protest, drawing my attention to her legs. "You say that like I'm making you follow me."

Ah. Maybe because your actions are. "Just walk," I groan, as my gaze makes the journey back to her face, lingering momentarily on the way her deep-red dress clings to her body.

"I don't need to walk," she snaps, perhaps to get my attention. "I'm here." She points to the door behind her making me huff out a sarcastic laugh. *Of course it's the room closest to the elevator.* "You can fuck off now," she adds like I'm wasting her time.

I don't want to be here anymore than she wants me to be. I was walking past, minding my own goddamn business when I saw her stepping into the elevator with a group of guys I know to be bad news. I tried to keep going —I *really fucking* tried—but I couldn't let her unknowingly walk into trouble. Yes, she drives me insane, and I'm not ashamed to admit, I've pictured her downfall many times before, but I don't need that kind of guilt on my conscience. It would mess with my good vibes. I'm not that guy.

Instead, I saved her ass. *Again.*

And this is the thanks I get.

"Go inside, Amelia," I grate, unmoving.

She pouts, and I'd probably find it endearing if she wasn't so goddamn annoying.

"What do you think I'm trying to do?" she says. "You're still here."

God, do I have to explain it to her? "I'm not leaving until you walk through that door and lock it behind you."

"Ugh." She folds her arms over her chest and frowns. "Why do you care?" Her voice holds strong but there's something new in her expression. Curiosity maybe.

I step forward mimicking her stance, forcing her backward until her ass hits the door. "*Why* are you being so stubborn?"

Amelia's shoulders drop and she bites her lip, drawing my gaze as she brutally tugs on the pink flesh. "Why do you always bring out the worst in me?" she asks, her voice barely above a whisper. I open my mouth to remark but she holds up a finger to silence me. "I'm not a mean person," she continues. "But with you... Ugh." She groans from the back of her throat and it almost sounds sexual. Especially when she adds, "The things I can picture doing..."

My eyes widen as my cock twitches, forcing me to bite back a grunt. *No. Nope. Not happening. There are plenty of women downstairs. And that is not what she meant.*

I clench my teeth as unwanted visuals swirl through my mind. Amelia on her knees, her lips wrapped around my cock as she sucks me dry. Amelia naked against a wall, her legs spread as she palms her breasts. Amelia bent over a table... *Jesus.*

"Go *inside*, Amelia. *Now*. Before..." I trail off, shaking my head.

"Before what?" she challenges, her eyes locked on mine as she stares me down, her gaze pushing me to answer.

My hands tighten into fists as I fight my natural instincts. I'm about to tell her to forget it, but she innocently bites her lip again, and fuck, I swear her pupils dilate.

"Before. What?" she repeats slowly, her voice breathy as she steps forward trying to inch me back.

And I'm *done*.

Fuck it. "This."

"Wha—" Grabbing her face in my hands, I silence her words with my mouth, sending us both stumbling into the door. A feeling of déjà vu hits me but I push it from my mind. That was another time, another Luke.

Amelia's lips part, undoubtedly to yell at me, but when I caress her tongue with my own, she melts into me before grabbing my waist and pulling me closer.

The air between us shifts as our mouths mold together, our lips moving in sync, our breathing shallow.

I press into her, and she welcomes me, her grip on my waist tightening as she slowly rocks against me, her movements creating a friction I do not need right now. But fuck if I can stop it.

My cock hardens as I sink my hands into her thick brown hair, eliciting a soft mewl from her lips. I'm acutely aware that we shouldn't be doing this, but right now, the only thing that concerns me is getting Amelia to scream my name, and it all starts here.

I suck her bottom lip into my mouth and tilt her head, deepening the kiss and stealing her breath as she gasps. Dropping my hand to the hem of her dress, I bunch the material beneath my fist and groan. *What I wouldn't give to taste her.*

My grip tightens as I consider my options, but Amelia speaks first, cutting into my thoughts.

"Do you want to come in?" she rasps against my lips, her stare confident when I pull back to look at her.

I think about it for all of two seconds before I lift an eyebrow and nod. "About time."

Amelia's eyes narrow but before she can sass me, I cut her off. "Open the door, Joy. Unless you want to come right here. Right now." *I am not messing around.*

"Jesus."

She roots around in her pocket before finally producing the key to her room and opening her door, dragging me over the threshold. The mood changes the second we're inside, and I almost laugh at the tension hovering between us. *Who knew it was still there.*

"I never thought the alpha thing would work for me," Amelia says, almost incredulously, before her gaze lifts to mine. "But God, that was hot."

"Thank you." I smirk as I remove my jacket, letting it drop to the floor. "Though I never thought I'd win you over so easily."

Her face drops and she forcefully shoves me away. "Fuck you," she retorts, making me chuckle.

"And she's back." I kick the door shut behind me before stalking toward her, sinking one hand into her hair as the other settles at her waist, giving her a squeeze. "I like the snarky version of you. She keeps things interesting."

Amelia opens her mouth, but just like in the hall, I cut her off with a kiss, instantly swirling my tongue around hers, consuming her as I crowd her.

She moans against my lips before her head falls back and her entire body shivers. *She's unequivocally mine in this moment and she doesn't even know it.*

Wrapping my fingers around her hair, I hold her head in place as I kiss a path along her neck, sucking the heated flesh into my mouth, listening to her breaths quicken as her body begs for more. But just when I think she's letting me take control, she reaches out and palms my shirt, curling her fingers until her nails bite through the cotton. Marking me. Making me hurt.

I swallow back a groan and continue kissing her, refusing to give her the satisfaction of knowing she affects me.

While I can say with absolute certainty that *this* was not my intention when I followed her, I'm not complaining. Amelia may be the last person I ever expected to bed, but I can't pretend she hasn't aged beautifully. And who am I to turn down a good time?

She's—

"Where did you go?" she whispers, her voice holding back a giggle as she draws my attention, her hands roaming before she starts undoing my buttons, tugging me forward when I don't answer.

"What?" I tighten my hold on her hair, pulling her head back as my lips meet her neck again, sucking the flesh below her ear.

"You stopped...moving," she says breathlessly, her skin pulsing beneath my touch. "Did you...ah...space out a little?"

I drop my hand from her side and reach beneath her dress, skating my fingers along her thigh, feeling her body shake as I move toward her center. "I was thinking about how naive you are," I lie. "Getting into an elevator with a bunch of guys you don't know?" When my hand meets her panties, I waste no time running the tip of my finger along the edge of the satin... teasing... loving when she clenches in anticipation.

"You were...thinking?" Amelia tries to sass me again, but despite locking me with her intense stare, her voice comes with a breathy sigh, making me chuckle. "Bad idea," she continues, finally snapping out of her daze and ripping the shirt from my shoulders like it pains her, her gaze moving to my bare chest. "Did that hurt?" she asks, her voice no longer wavering.

"Thinking?" I raise a brow as she reaches out to touch me, the tips of her fingers gently stroking my abs. "No, that doesn't hurt." Dropping her hair, I grab her free hand and raise it above her head, pinning her against the wall as I lean in. "Not as much as touching you does."

Giving up the teasing, I run a finger through her pussy, holding back my groan when I find her dripping for me.

Amelia sucks in a breath but smiles wide, pretending she's unaffected.

"Oh, I'm sorry." She fakes a pout but I see through her shameless attempt at keeping her cool. "Should we stop?" She drags her nails across my skin, only pausing when the tips of her fingers dip below my waistband.

"Just try it," I growl, my cock pulsing when she immediately undoes my belt, not bothering to argue as she works to release my cock. *This woman.*

With her focus on my pants, I continue to tease her, swirling my finger around her clit, holding her in place as she wriggles and gasps. Her movements quicken and I can't stop my lips from curling into a smile. There's something particularly satisfying about knowing she feels the same. Knowing how affected she is. Like me, she can't walk away now that we've started something.

I'm ready for more, but when she still hasn't released me, I struggle not to laugh. "Are you fighting with my zipper?" I pause, knowing I'm the one distracting her. "Don't worry, not everyone is perfect."

"Nobody is perfect, asshole. Least of all you. Less talking. It's easier to pretend you're someone else."

"Ouch." I huff out a laugh before rubbing my fingers across her entrance, making her entire body jolt. "Did—"

"If you insist on using that mouth," she says, cutting me off, her eyes meeting mine in challenge as she lets go of my pants, "I have some suggestions."

Damn, Amelia. "Dirty talk. I like it." *A lot.*

Before she has a chance to say anything else, I drop to my knees and curl my fingers around her panties, dragging the silky material down her legs. With her wet thong on the floor, she holds her knees together as though shy all of a sudden, but I don't let her dwell on it. Instead, I grab her leg, lifting it to my shoulder as I open her wide, leaning in to lick her. Slowly.

And God, it's good.

She tastes like that first deliciously satisfying lick of an ice cream you thought you'd never be able to eat.

I'm not going to pretend I've never pictured this moment, but it's been years. Good things *do* come to those who wait.

I lick her again and her whole body shakes, but it doesn't feel like one of those this-is-incredible shakes, more of an I'm-going-to-fall shake. *Has she never had sex against a wall before?*

"I've got you, Amelia." I put her at ease. "You won't fall. Just enjoy it."

The tension in her legs releases, and I smile to myself. She can tell me she hates me as much as she wants, but she just admitted she trusts me without a single word.

After giving her a few seconds to settle, I spread her with my fingers, and flatten my tongue against her soaked center before lavishing her with attention.

Finally getting my fill.

I lick, I tease, I nibble on her clit, doing all that I can to elicit those cries. And God, does she deliver.

She's a writhing mess above me, struggling to take in air, gasping for pleasure, and I'm desperate for more. I want her screaming my name. I want her to remember me every time someone else attempts to make her feel half as good as I do. *Am I cocky?* Fuck yes, but it's not without the knowledge that I'm right.

I don't know how long I spend devouring Amelia's pussy, but as her breathing picks up speed, I know she's close. Her legs shake again, but I hold her still, keeping her steady so she can focus on her needs. On the pleasure I'm giving her.

She cries out, rolling her hips against my face a few times before stopping abruptly, a rushed apology leaving her mouth.

"Fuck, no," I admonish. "Don't ever apologize. Take what you need. Ride my face. Suffocate me. I want to *feel* you when you come for me."

I suck her clit into my mouth as I mix things up, pumping two fingers inside her. A high-pitched mewl escapes her and she involuntarily bucks into me. But instead of pausing this time, she continues her movements, finally seeking her pleasure.

"That's it, Amelia. Take it. Fuck my face. Hard."

"Jesus, Luke," she moans, her voice higher than usual. "What are you doing?"

"I'm making you feel good. Stop thinking. It's not good for anyone."

She pauses again, but this time when she starts moving, I sense a shift. And God, do I like it. Sinking her hands into my hair, she pulls at the strands, locking me against her as her hips pivot in rhythm.

Doing as asked, she fucks my face with abandon as my cock throbs in my pants, begging for action. But it can wait. She needs to finish at least once to ensure she's ready for me.

I swirl my tongue over her clit and she lets out a high-pitched gasp, forcing me to bite back a groan. Curling my fingers inside her, I brush against her wall as my tongue continues, working her until her body convulses, her walls tightening as she calls out in ecstasy. "God, fuck. Yes."

That's it, Ace. Almost there.

She cries out again and... *Fuck, did I just think of her as Ace?*

I continue my ministrations as her orgasm hits, her center pulsing against me as her ragged breaths fill the air between us. She's a beautiful mess while I pretend I wasn't thinking about the nickname I gave her when we were friends, as opposed to the name I bestowed her *after* she decided she was too good for me.

She grabs my hair, the wall, her breasts, anything she can hold on to as her high overwhelms her, bringing my attention back to the present, her frantic moans hardening my length.

I snap out of my thoughts and focus on her sounds, reading her needs until her breathing slows and I remove my hand, holding her still in case she can't stand on her own. "Are you satisfied?" I ask, looking up at her from my knees, taking in her flushed cheeks and tangled hair.

"Not even close," she lies, her lips twisted into a mischievous grin as her breath rushes from her mouth.

"Amelia. Amelia. You are so goddamn beautiful it hurts." I chuckle under my breath, squeezing her thighs beneath my palms. "If only you weren't always such a pain in my ass."

Amelia's eyes widen but she recovers quickly, giving my head a shove. "A little orgasm isn't enough to change me," she rushes out, dropping her foot to the ground before stepping away.

"Maybe not." I laugh. "But we're not done yet. Get on the bed."

CHAPTER THREE

AMELIA

Who the hell am I? And what is he doing to me? Ignoring the fact that Luke called me beautiful, I roll my eyes in protest and wait for what he does next.

He groans as he stands, before huffing out a laugh and effortlessly throwing me over his shoulder, eliciting a squeal as he spins me around, rushing across the room.

When we reach the bed, Luke tosses me onto the mattress and grips my ankles, while I bite back a moan. I work hard on remembering who I am, but I struggle to think of anything other than the man in front of me as he pulls me toward the edge, completely obliterating my previous notions on sex. I liked vanilla. I *loved* vanilla.

But this is something else entirely and I'm *losing my mind.*

After spreading my legs, Luke wastes no time settling himself between them, swirling his tongue through my heat until I cry out again.

Digging my nails into the bed, I claw at the sheets...needing something to keep me grounded. This isn't me. At all. But God only knows why I'd want to be me right now when I'm enjoying this too much. It's addictive.

"Are you ready for more?" Luke asks, his voice penetrating my thoughts as he stands up, and I instantly miss his touch. While I'd love nothing more than to quip back with some smart-ass response, we're beyond that, and I'd do just about anything for "more" right now.

"Yes," I rush out, sitting up to grab the back of his neck, pulling him onto the bed, unable to meet his stare as I whisper, "I need you inside me. *Now.*" I've never been more hungry for it.

Luke groans and I swear his length throbs against me as he grabs my chin and forces me to look at him. I barely take a breath before he crushes his mouth to mine, completely devouring me as he groans again, the vibrations sending a spark straight to my core as I taste myself on his lips.

The kiss is messy, rushed, passionate, and so goddamn intoxicating I don't think I'll be able to break away. But Luke does, and when he releases me from his hold, he lifts to his knees, giving me the perfect view of his abs as he palms his cock over his pants. "Jesus, Amelia. Don't look at me like that."

"Like what?"

"Like you want me."

"I don't want you," I say honestly, because that's not what I'm craving. "I want what you're about to do to me...and I'm going to need you to hurry it up."

His lips pull into a smirk as his eyes light up, staring as though I just gave him the ammunition he needs to take me down. *And maybe I did.* But I'm in too deep to care.

Without a word or smart-ass response—which is a little unnerving—Luke gets off the bed and slowly removes his pants. I sense his gaze on my face, but my eyes stay firmly locked on his chest, letting myself enjoy it while I can. He really is a stunning specimen of a man. Such a pity he knows it, acting like he's selflessly letting all women reap the benefits.

Although, I suppose he is.

As I stare, I picture his abs tensing while I lick a path across his perfectly rigid muscles, and it's not until he clears his throat that I'm snapped out of my thoughts. He steps out of his briefs and I lift my gaze, meeting his eyes when he stands tall. "Your turn," he says, crawling back on the bed, slowly running his hands up my legs until he reaches the hem of my dress.

My skin tingles with his touch, and my body warms at the intensity of his stare.

"This is new," he muses as he points to my chest, his other hand palming my leg. "The Amelia I remember wouldn't have her tits out like this."

I internally flinch but hold my gaze. "Don't do that," I scoff, though he's not wrong. I've been dressing differently since I ended my marriage. But I've been doing it for me, not other people. And this one's further out of my comfort zone. "Don't pretend you know me. I'm not that girl anymore."

"Oh, I know. You may have hated me back then, but you were never this feisty. I like the new you."

Once again ignoring his slight compliment, I raise an eyebrow and change the subject. "Do I need to undress myself or do you want to do it?"

"Decisions. Decisions." Luke runs his finger across his bottom lip, making me bite down on mine as my breath quickens. "How about you do it," he decides. "Let me enjoy the view."

With my pulse racing, I rise to the challenge and grab his hand, making a show of removing it from my body before clasping my hands around my hem. With painstakingly slow movements, I lift to my knees and drag the material along my skin, gliding my dress over my head. I'm supposed to be teasing him, but the second I remember my panties lying somewhere on the floor on the other side of the room, my core pulses, picturing his expression as I expose myself.

With my dress off, I toss it on the bed, and it's not until I reach for my bra that I finally let myself glance Luke's way. Our eyes meet and I almost gasp at his expression. The way he stares at me is primal. There's a fire in his eyes that makes my heart pound out of control...like he wants me more than air...as though he'll die if he doesn't get another taste.

And no one has ever looked at me that way.

God, he's good.

Now I know what he meant when he told me not to look at him like I want him. It's hard to take.

Dropping my gaze, I remove my bra and throw it in the direction of my dress as my insides twist into knots. I'm naked and exposed and more vulnerable than I've ever been before, but I've also never felt so alive. Luke grabs my clothes and tosses them to the floor before moving closer and crowding my space, forcing me to fall back onto the bed.

Without a word, he squeezes my breasts before running his hands along my skin, his palms burning a path as they glide down my body, only stopping after he's wrapped his fingers around my ankles.

Lifting my legs, he pushes my knees against my chest before spreading them wide and moving to settle between them. He's exposing me more than I'd usually be comfortable with, but despite my rapid heartbeat, I welcome it.

My breath catches as Luke stares at me for a beat before releasing his grip on one ankle and reaching for his length, drawing my eyes to his cock for the first time.

And he's sheathed.

How long was I stuck in my head?

"You're so ready for me," he rasps, his eyes once again locked on my center. "And fuck, I'm ready for you."

Am I ready? I swallow a lump in my throat because now that it's happening, I'm not so sure.

Leaning forward, Luke lines himself up with my entrance, and when his tip presses against me, I clench around him. Since I've only been with Preston, I don't have a lot to compare to, but it's not hard to see that he's longer than Preston was. And definitely thicker.

As if sensing my nerves, Luke rolls his thumbs over my clit, making me forget all my troubles as a spark ignites inside me, my body instantly relaxing while I focus on his movements. *God, he's so good at this.* And yes, I say God, because he deserves some credit for his creation.

My head falls to the bed as a new tension builds low in my belly, and I'm about to demand Luke's mouth again when he pushes an inch inside me. I cry out as it burns, but there's a pleasure to the pain that makes it all worth it.

"Jesus Christ," he groans between his teeth. "You are so fucking tight."

An irregular sex life will do that to a person, but I'm not about to say that. "Just...ah...give me a second." I wait for his impatient groan, but he shocks me when he pauses, his eyes locked on mine.

"Take what you need. Move when you're ready. There's no rush."

What? Don't be a gentleman now, Luke. I can't handle that.

I nod slowly and take a deep breath, letting the tension go while Luke teases me with his fingers, his movements lighting up my entire body. And I want more.

After wrapping my legs around him, I roll my hips and dig my heels into his back, pulling him closer as he slips farther inside me, sinking deeper until he's buried to the hilt. And this time the burn is like fireworks. Like a new high I never knew I was chasing and—

"Oh God."

"Fuuuck. Yes. Can I move?"

"Please. Yes." *Don't make me beg.*

Luke rocks his hips, starting a gentle rhythm as I adjust to having him inside me. But the second I push back, showing him I'm ready, it's on.

We thrash around, slamming into each other as the pressure increases between my legs. His fingers bite into my skin and I welcome the pain, all of it adding to the moment. To the intense feeling working its way through my body.

Wrapping my arms around his neck, I pull at his hair, loving the way he groans at my touch before crashing his lips to mine, instantly swirling his tongue in my mouth.

We find our rhythm, and it doesn't take long for the tension to build in my middle again, but my orgasm sits just out of reach. I've only ever been able to come with a finger, and I doubt this will be any different because—

"*Holy shit.*"

Luke lifts my hips, changing the angle as he drills into me and *my God.* The pleasure intensifies and I'm just about to beg for more when he pulls out of me and rubs his length over my clit before slowly pushing back in. My body jerks as he repeats his movements, and on his third go, he has me flying over the edge, crying out his name as my release consumes me.

"Fuck, Amelia. *Jesus.*" Luke pumps harder, clenching his teeth as I buck against him, meeting his fervor. "Yes."

He lets out a guttural groan before his body shakes and his cock pulses inside me, giving me another burst of this new ecstasy.

Our movements slow and when my body starts to relax, Luke stills inside me, unmoving while my heart slams against my rib cage.

Time slows, and I'm not sure how long it's been when he lets out a soft groan and drops onto the bed beside me, curling his arm around my waist, his fingers dancing across my stomach.

Goosebumps coat my already warm skin and I have to bite back another satisfied mewl. That was epic. There is no other way to describe it. Hayley was right. His experience does work in my favor. In everyone's favor. There was nothing lazy about that. It was heated and intoxicating and so goddamn passionate.

But it was Luke. *Shit.*

This is what he does. He's practically a professional.

Clearing my throat, I jump up and search for my clothes, ignoring the fact that my insides still pulse from the best sex of my life. "Thanks for the service," I say, trying to hide as I wriggle into my thong. "I trust you can let yourself out."

Luke chuckles as he stands, and I catch sight of his Adonis body, my eyes drawn to the deep grooves that run in a V, guiding my gaze toward his thick, dangerous weapon. *Ugh. What is wrong with me?* True, it should be considered a weapon with the way it just broke me, but I'm over thirty; I shouldn't be thinking this way. And I definitely shouldn't be imagining all the ways I'd like him to continue to destroy me. *Dammit. Why does he have to be Luke?*

"Want a picture to remember me by?" he asks, and I mentally curse myself, knowing he's just caught me staring.

"The awful image I have burned into my brain is more than enough, thank you. But I appreciate the offer." I turn away, grabbing my bra and dress from where they landed on the floor, ignoring Luke when he chuckles again until a string of curses flies from his mouth.

"Fuck. Fucking fuck."

"What's the matter?" I ask. "Did you just fall in love with me?" I laugh to myself until Luke falls silent, drawing my attention. "What happened?"

He points to his cock before pointing to the condom on the bed, confusing the hell out of me. "Um…"

"It *broke*, Amelia. It *fucking* broke."

I stare at him as the color drains from his face before bursting out laughing.

"It's not funny," he says. "You need to—"

"I'm on the pill." I stare at him until he looks my way. "You can stop panicking. Surely this isn't the first time something like this has happened to you. Considering how much you get around."

Luke's entire body deflates but he still manages to roll his eyes before muttering, "Thank God."

I roll my eyes right back, then turn around and continue to dress until his presence fills the space behind me. "Tell me, Amelia"—he trails off as though waiting for me to react—"will this little interaction of ours make it into your diary? Will it be accompanied by a photo?"

"What?" *The. Hell.* I flinch but catch myself before turning around, keeping my expression passive when I face him.

Luke suppresses a smirk, seeing through my facade, and I tense. "Oh, sorry. Was it supposed to be a secret?"

That little asshole. Ugh. He knew about my diary? How is that possible? And for how long?

"Why are you here, Luke?"

"Have you already forgotten you invited me in?"

"No, I meant...I thought I cut you from my life *years* ago."

Luke winces. At least I think it's a wince, but when he laughs a little sardonically, I'm not so sure. "You thought you cut *me* out?" He scoffs. "I was glad to see you go."

"Then why talk to me at all tonight?" I throw my hands in the air and spin around, storming toward the door.

"I saw you and couldn't help myself." He pulls on his shirt but leaves the buttons undone, letting it hang from his ripped body as he picks up his jacket, trying to mess with my head. And it's working. "I wanted to talk to the woman that's continued to affect my life *years* after she left it." *Huh?* "Then I couldn't walk away when you stepped headfirst into trouble."

"I, what?" I'm not asking about the trouble, as he alluded to that before. But...what did I do to affect him?

"You almost cost me my football career," he answers my silent question. "Multiple times. It was years before I stopped having to explain myself."

"Your football career?" I huff out an incredulous laugh. *That's it?* "Are you kidding me, Luke? You almost cost me *my life.*"

"Bullshit." Luke huffs before shaking his head as though I'm exaggerating. And I wish I was. "That didn't happen or I'd have known about it. Your beautiful temple was unharmed."

"Unharmed?" He can't be serious. I went to the hospital for smoke inhalation. I still get bronchitis occasionally, which I *never* had before that fire. To this day, I still have no idea why the police let me off while Luke got in trouble, but I've always known better than to question it out loud.

Luke stares me down, his serious expression never wavering. He honestly thinks he did nothing wrong. "You know what? Never mind. I'm okay now." I open the door and smile. It takes a lot to ignore the fact that he called me beautiful a second time, but I'm proud to say I push the information out of my mind. It's been a long time since I cared what Luke thought about me—over ten years—and I'm not about to start again. "Goodnight, Luke." I step aside and gesture for him to leave. "I'd say it was a pleasure, but it wasn't."

"Feeling is mutual, but I appreciate you scratching an itch." He buttons his pants as he walks but stops when he reaches me, his expression full of something I can't quite decipher.

"I should have said this a long time ago," I say, pinning him with a glare. "If you ever see me again, pretend you don't know me. I'm done."

"Works for me. Bye, Amelia." He stares into my eyes as he delivers his parting message and a shiver runs through me, waiting for more. But after shaking his head, he walks away, beelining for the stairs instead of waiting for the elevator, never once looking back.

"Good riddance," I say as he turns the corner, not loud enough for him to hear me, but enough to be satisfied I made the last remark. *Good riddance.*

And what the hell was all that?

I'm not sure how long I lie on the untainted side of the bed staring at the ceiling, but it feels like I've barely closed my eyes when my alarm goes off.

I curse the heavens until I remember the massage I booked and the world is good again. That's exactly what I need. A moment to myself. A moment to forget life and focus on my body. While not focusing on the fact that it hurts in all the right places and feels *so* good it's already craving more. My body...not me...*it*. It's a physical response, nothing more, and I have no doubt it would be the same with someone else.

I refuse to believe that was a Luke thing.

Plenty of guys have experience. I just have to find someone else to set my body on fire. Then I'll forget all about last night.

Like it never happened.

Just a blip on my radar.

A moment that changed me, sure, but a single moment all the same.

Nothing more.

Because no matter how alive Luke made me feel, he's still *Luke*, and any chance of a relationship—sexual or otherwise—burned along with the memory of the last time I ever genuinely cared for him.

And that fire still haunts me.

So no. There's no going back. They're called one-nightstands for a reason. And this one is staying in the past.

CHAPTER FOUR

AMELIA – AGE SIXTEEN

> *Dear Diary,*
> *I don't know what happened. It was supposed to be a bit of fun...but it all went wrong and now I might be in trouble.*
> *I can't talk about it and I definitely can't write it down. I'm so lost.*
> *Amelia*

"Truth or Dare."

"Dare." I'm not stupid enough to choose "truth." I've seen people's truths get used against them. One of the girls on the yearbook committee actually snuck someone's truth into last year's edition. The kids at this school are brutal.

I chance a quick glance around the dark room, mentally running through all the potential dares this old mansion has to offer. And there are loads of them. They could make me spend time alone in what this town believes is a haunted barn or have me permanently mark my name on the wall, evidence that I've been here if the cops ever get sick of us throwing parties.

Though, I say "us" loosely because while my peers have been coming here for years, this is my first time. All because I overheard one of my so-called friends telling her boyfriend I was too chicken.

I can handle a lot of things, but being talked about behind my back is my own personal nightmare. It's the reason I'm so friendly to everyone, always *making sure people have no reason to talk about me. Keeping people on my side.*

Except for Luke. That ship sailed long ago.

A laugh draws my attention back to the circle just as my challenge is set. "You have to spend an hour locked in the attic with…" She trails off with a smile and ugh. One of those dares. I set my gaze on the group, holding back my reaction. I have no doubt I could talk to anyone here, and if they don't want to talk, I'm good with silence too.

"An hour with…" Brianna repeats herself, taking her time and driving me crazy, though I don't let on.

"Come on, the suspense is killing me." I mock, pretending to be excited.

Brianna stares at me smugly before her gaze lifts to something behind me —or more specifically someone—and then announces a name like she's announcing it at an awards ceremony. "The man. The God. Luke Bennett."

An involuntary groan rips from within me and I don't bother hiding it. She says "The man. The God" but what I hear is… "The self-absorbed. The competitive. The overconfident and annoying. Luke Bennett." And he wasn't supposed to be here. At least, that's what my friend told me.

"Come on, Joy." Luke speaks from behind me, his cocky tone making me cringe as he calls me by the nickname I hate. "I'm game if you are."

God, where did he come from? And how long has he been here?

I jump up and dust myself off before turning to face him, my expression neutral while he grins. "Let's go," I say with confidence, keeping my voice upbeat as I hold back my disdain. People know we don't get along, but they don't need to know just how much he affects me.

Wolf whistles and cheers ring out as we walk away, but I don't look back. Luke, however, joins in on the fun, acting like he's about to have the time of his life. And I can say with absolute certainty that's not the case. I want nothing to do with him.

We walk up the stairs, and it's not until we're out of earshot that I finally break my silence, being sure to keep my voice low so it doesn't reach the guy assigned to follow us. "I thought you'd be too cool for one of these parties," I say as we hit the first landing, keeping myself one step ahead of Luke.

"Half the team is here, so I'm here." He shrugs, no big deal, but I sense there's more to it. Not that I ask; instead, I fall quiet again.

"I see you're still in some kind of one-sided competition with me," Luke scoffs, not bothering to hide his feelings as he grabs my shoulder, startling me.

I stop suddenly and almost lose my footing when I spin around to face him, waving him off when he leans forward to help me. "That's crazy," I say, shaking off his hold. "I don't know what you're talking about."

"Sure you do." He moves ahead, taking the stairs two at a time. "It's been happening for years."

"What has?" I proceed with denial.

He waits until he's reached the next landing before turning around to face me, his expression pinched as if to say, "are you kidding me?"

"You..." He points my way. "You've been trying to beat me at everything since we started middle school. Do you think I haven't noticed the excitement you get when you receive a higher score on a math test, or the snicker that escapes you when I mess up a presentation?"

"You're delusional," I snap. "If I snicker it's because it's nice to see the high and mighty fall. And I'm excited because I'm happy and proud."

"The 'high and mighty'?" He scoffs before shaking his head and taking a step back when I reach him, raising his hands in the air as he lets me pass, making a show of not touching me. Like I'm poison.

"Yes." I roll my eyes. "People like you who think you're above everyone else."

"I think that?"

"Don't play dumb."

"Whatever."

He rushes ahead again, making it to the top landing in a few steps, but pauses before walking through the door. I assume he's going to wait and slam it in my face, but he surprises me by opening it when I arrive and holding it there until I walk by.

I almost thank him until he leans in close, whispering as I move past. "And now you have to spend an hour with the likes of me. However will you cope?"

His breath sends a shiver down my spine but I hold still, refusing to show him he affects me. "Easily," I say confidently. "Because as you alluded to, I'm competitive and I always win."

"Alright then... Ladies first." He pins me with a stare, pointing toward the ladder dropping down from the attic, and I internally grimace. I don't

want to be the first up there, but I also don't want him to know that I'm scared of what we'll find, and I'm about to give in until I remember.

"No way. I'm wearing a dress. You're not getting a peep show. You go first. And you." I spin around to find our supervisor, David, standing behind us, his arms folded and a bored expression in place. "You stay by the door."

"I have no interest in your panties, Amelia," David says as he gestures toward the ladder. "Can you both hurry up?"

Luke groans before stepping onto the bottom rung and huffing out a breath. "I'll see you up there."

He climbs slowly, each step putting me a little more on edge until I'm not sure what's worse—spending an hour with Luke, or spending an hour stuck in a dusty old attic.

And it takes all of two seconds for me to find out.

A *shiver runs through me as the cold night air seeps into my bones. I was wrong. There is nothing easy about this dare. I'm confused as to why everyone talks about the barn being haunted, when this attic looks like something straight out of a horror movie. Dusty ancient furniture, a strange-looking box that's begging to be opened, and a random door that leads to God knows where but is too small for any regular-sized human to fit through.*

Yet, none of that's what has me rattled. It's the tiny space and the darkness.

I've never been claustrophobic, but there's something about being locked in here with stifling air that's making me extremely uncomfortable.

Not to mention, I'm here with Luke.

As if the mere thought of him compelled him to speak, he steps forward. "How long has it been since we were last alone together? Four, maybe five years." He stretches his arms before sitting on an old chair and laughing when a puff of dust shoots into the air. "It's not exactly my idea of a good date, but it'll do."

I'd usually snap back with a smart-ass response, but the longer I'm here, the more uncomfortable it is, and I can't bring myself to answer. Something doesn't feel right, but I can't put my finger on what.

Luke falls silent, and I hate that it draws my gaze. I may not be able to see much in the darkness, but it's impossible to miss the whites of his eyes as he stares at me.

"What's wrong?" he asks after a beat.

"Nothing." I suck in a sharp breath. "I'm fine."

"You're not fine." He stands and walks over to where I'm leaning against the wall, stopping a few feet in front of me. "Amelia, what's wrong?"

The more he asks, the more an irrational panic runs through me until I'm struggling for air. "I don't know what's going on. But I can't..." Breathe.

"Do you want out? I'll tell them you can't handle it."

What? "I can handle it. I'm just..." I try to suck in another breath when a strange noise booms in the silence, making Luke's brows furrow.

"Amelia, you need to quit."

"I can't."

"Why are you being so stubborn?"

"Because no one quits. And I don't want them to start talking about me again."

Luke's eyes widen before he curses quietly. "People always quit. They just get new dares."

"I can't." I shake involuntarily and blow out a shallow breath, hoping he didn't notice. But he did.

"Amelia."

"No." My breathing increases to an alarming rate, and I'm no longer sure if it's the attic that has me rattled or the thought of going back down to the group before the time is up. But either way, I'm struggling.

"Shit." Luke hisses and my eyes flash his way to find him stalking toward me. "Look at me, Amelia." He grabs my face in his hands, his eyes boring into me as mine fight to focus. "I need you to take slow, deep breaths. Can you do that?"

"What?"

"Breathe in." I breathe in.

"Breathe out." I breathe out.

"Now repeat that again."

I do as asked a few more times and the panic subsides, but when I'm finally able to concentrate again, Luke's still staring at me, his own gaze full of concern.

"I'm okay," I whisper as my heart races. "Thank you."

"Good." Luke blinks, snapping out of his stupor. "Do you want to go down?"

"No."

He smiles but doesn't release my face, and my breath picks up speed again, this time for a different reason.

"Luke, what are you doing?" My eyes bounce between his as he drops a hand to my waist and huffs out a breath.

"I have no idea, but I can't seem to step back."

My breath hitches, while deep in the back of my mind there's a voice screaming at me to remember who this is. That we're not friends anymore. But I just saw a side of him I haven't seen in years, and it's blocking my common sense to the point that I want him to kiss me.

Luke brushes a hair away from my face and my heart slams in my chest, trying not to focus on his eyes locked on mine as though he's staring into my soul in a way only he ever has.

"Ace," he whispers, my old nickname rushing from his lips like it's escaping after years of being held back, and then, before I can process it, his mouth is on mine and he's kissing me.

Luke Bennett is kissing me.

His lips gently caress mine, before his tongue sneaks out, seeking entry, and I panic. I've never been kissed before. What if I do it wrong? What if—

He nibbles on my bottom lip and I gasp, my lips parting to let him in. And then my instincts take over, matching his intensity. Our tongues swirl, his hands roam over my body, and he's eliciting sounds from me that I've never heard before.

As if feeling for the first time, every one of my senses heightens. My skin tingles where he's touching me, his smell makes me euphoric, and the taste...

I'm a mess of chaotic thoughts and butterflies but enjoying every second as he possesses my mouth, taking everything I have to give.

"Luke," I moan against his mouth, and he groans in return.

"Fuck, Amelia."

"Fire!" A voice breaks into my mind, and I spring away, confused until the words register.

Fire?

The voice calls again and I panic. "We have to go."

Luke stares at me for a second before he snaps out of his daze. Glancing down at his phone, he shakes his head. *"Ten minutes to go. Are you really going to fold? The next dare is guaranteed to be worse."*

"What?" I stare at him dumbfounded, my mind racing and my lips still tingling from his kiss. *"Luke, there's a fire."*

He crosses his arms over his chest. "A challenge is a challenge." He turns away but not before his face drops. What the hell is going on?

"You're being ridiculous. This is crazy." I rush to the door, my panic increasing until I'm hyperventilating again.

"Help!" I call out. *"Please. David?"*

Luke's low laugh filters into the air. "It's a joke, Amelia. Can you smell any smoke?"

"Why would anyone *joke about a fire?"*

"I don't know." He throws his hands in the air. "To piss off the couples hooking up."

That makes no sense, but I wouldn't put it past some of these kids, and as I concentrate, he's right—I can't smell anything.

"Are we calling it quits or are you going to take the risk?" Luke bounces his eyebrows and a negative energy settles in my stomach.

"Did you plan this?"

"Are you staying or going?" He ignores my question, making me nauseous.

"Staying." I drop down to the wooden flooring, securing my arms around my chest, unsure whether I should be angry or embarrassed. "Were you part of this?"

"I'm here, aren't I?"

"No, I mean...is this your *dare as well?" I want to ask if someone dared him to kiss me, but I can't bring myself to say it.*

Luke opens his mouth to answer just as someone screams in the distance.

"Answer me. Is that part of your—"

"Shh." Luke cuts me off as he steps closer, seemingly on alert, and it's then the smell of smoke permeates the air.

"Luke?"

"That wasn't supposed to happen."

"What?" I wait for him to laugh. Pray *for him to laugh but he doesn't. "Luke, please tell me this is a joke."*

"It's not."

Oh God.

"We have to go. Jesus! Why didn't we leave?" I race back to the door of the attic as Luke peers out the window, frustratingly taking his time. "What are you doing? Come on." I pull on the handle but it doesn't budge. "Oh God. Did they lock us in? Luke, are we locked in?"

My panic rises as I violently shake on the handle. "Help! Someone help!"

No one answers, so I turn to yell at Luke, but the sound of sirens echoes through the air, cutting me off.

Luke curses under his breath while my heart stops. It's real.

"Oh God, oh God. Are we going to die? This is all your fault."

Luke's eyes flash to mine, his expression full of anger. "No one forced you to be here, Amelia. And your freak-out isn't helping. I need to think."

To think? Shit. We're stuck.

The door rattles from the other side and we both freeze. "We have to go," David calls out. "The police are here." He opens the door and we both rush to climb down, but the second we're at the bottom of the ladder, Luke takes off in the opposite direction.

"Luke, wait," I call out, but he doesn't slow.

"Stay with David," he yells back at me. "He'll get you out." And then he's gone.

He set me up, made me feel alive, and then left me.

How could I be so stupid? Nothing has changed.

CHAPTER FIVE

AMELIA – PRESENT DAY

I did it. I finally made it. And this time, I did it on my own. Now let's hope I don't mess it up.

"Everything okay?" Hayley asks when I meet her inside our regular cafe, after taking a phone call out front. I keep my lips sealed for as long as possible, but when her brows furrow, I can't stop my giddy smile.

"Brighton Productions wants me to start on Monday instead of next month. They've got a new project they said I'd be perfect for."

After years of working my ass off for minimal or no pay, I've finally landed my dream job as a television director. Me. A director. Of real things. That I get paid for.

I'm still in shock, but I'm sure it'll sink in once I start. Which is *Monday*. I'm so freaking excited, I could squeal. But I won't because I'm in a packed cafe and I don't like attention.

Hayley, however, squeals for me. "Gahhh. That's amazing, Ames. I knew they wouldn't keep you on 'light duties' as you called it. I'm so proud of you." She jumps up and rushes to my side of the table, giving me a hug.

"Thank you for sending the positive vibes into the universe. It probably got me the role."

"Positive vibes didn't do that. *You* did. Have you forgotten I've seen your work? Those music videos you made for Preston *all* went viral. And the ideas you told me you were pitching to the production company? Utter perfection."

"Thank you," I repeat, smiling shyly. "I needed that. I've been nervous."

"I noticed." She squeezes my shoulder. "But you shouldn't be. I'm still pissed Preston hasn't paid you for your work. If he had, maybe you wouldn't have put so much pressure on yourself when looking for a job. He owes you big time for his success."

"I know. And so does he." *At least, he used to.*

"Really? Because from where I'm standing, he's reaping the benefits and riding the train toward the high life, while you're barely making ends meet in a tiny one-bedroom apartment."

"In fairness, my apartment may be small, but I live in one of the best areas of San Francisco. I'm close to the beach, walking track, the studios and—"

"Okay, you're not *that* hard done by, but still..."

"I know what you're trying to say, but I like that I did this on my own. And the next step is LA."

Hayley and I have been talking about moving to LA for months now, but our plans never get further than that. *Talk.*

That's about to change though, because if all goes to plan, I'll be moving with Brighton Productions, and Hayley will be coming with me.

"Yes, you can do it alone," Hayley continues. "And it's great that you did. My point is that you could be sharing in his riches." She pouts while I huff out a sigh. *There goes my good mood.*

"We never really talked about that. It wasn't about the money." *I never considered the possibility that we'd lose ourselves in the process.*

"It wasn't about the money because you were married. It was a given. Actually, you're still technically married. You could claim it."

I burst out laughing, ignoring the looks I get from other diners. "Have I ever told you I love the way your mind works?"

"You have."

"I'm not going to take money from Preston after walking out on our marriage."

"He owes you. And you didn't walk out. He forced your decision."

"Maybe so. But I'm the one that filed the divorce paperwork. I'm the one that left. I'm just waiting for him to sign."

Hayley falls silent. She hates the fact that Preston took advantage of my guilt, but I'm moving on.

"Don't worry about me, Hayley. I'm going to make my own money. Lots of it." I wink. "I don't need his help."

"Boss woman." She bites back a grin but it shines through, as does her proud expression.

"Thank you. For everything. Now, it's time to celebrate. I'm going to be a director. On Monday."

"Yeah you are." Hayley laughs and we keep chatting until we've finished our drinks, then make plans to head out to a bar. Despite the little detour in my happiness at the mention of Preston, I'm still high on life and deserve the celebration. I've been working my ass off for this—mostly without pay —and after several rejections, with the majority of companies refusing to look at my work because it comes without references, I finally have my shot.

And I'm going to prove that they made the right choice. I may not have taken the traditional route to this role, but I never stopped working and this is all I've ever wanted. They'd be hard-pressed to find someone more dedicated than I am.

It's my time to shine. And party. It's my time to let loose.

Within reason.

Something wakes me the next morning, and my head pounds as my mind drifts into consciousness. "Ugh," I groan. *What the hell happened last night?*

The sound starts up again, and realizing it's coming from my bedside table, I blindly reach out to make it stop. I've just located the source when something or *someone* smacks me in the face. *"Jesus."*

I startle before rolling over at the same time Hayley gasps. "Ouch. Fuck. I'm sorry. Ugh." She covers her eyes with her hands. "My head."

"What about *my* head?" I ask, rubbing the side of my forehead that just met her palm.

"I thought I was home. Wait, I *am* home. You're at my place. I was trying to stop the ringing."

Ringing? That was a phone?

Sure enough, the ringing starts again and we both collectively groan. "Make it stop," Hayley pleads before burying her head under her pillow, drawing my attention to her bed for the first time. *Well there you go. We* are *at her place.*

When I'm finally thinking clearly, I grab my phone to silence it but freeze when I find Preston's name.

"Preston's calling me," I say softly, a little shocked and a lot confused.

Hayley doesn't answer, so I whack the pillow until she pops her head out. "What was that for?"

"It's Preston."

Her eyes widen before she grabs my phone to check for herself, squinting as she tries to read the screen. "*Shit.* It is. Why would he be calling?"

That's what I want to know. "Do you remember any of last night?"

"Of course I do. I wasn't *that* drunk."

"Okay, good." I relax slightly. "I'm guessing I was, because I can't remember a thing. Did I mention Preston?"

As I ask, I scroll through my phone looking for any calls or messages I may have made but there's nothing. *Thank God.* I breathe out a sigh of relief and lie back down. "Did I do anything I shouldn't have?"

"Not that I can remember, but there's a couple of hours missing between us dancing and somehow getting back he—"

My phone rings again, cutting off Hayley's words as we both peer down at the screen. *Preston again.*

"Jesus, he's keen as mustard," Hayley says, the annoyance clear in her expression, her words making me frown.

"He's what?"

"You know... Excited. Enthusiastic. Eager to speak to you."

"Thank you and yes, he is. But why?"

"I don't know, and as much as I'd love to tell him to fuck off, it's going to annoy you until you find out. You're better off answering."

Ugh. I hate that she's right, but it will drive me crazy if I don't know.

"Preston?" I answer as Hayley lies down, tucking her hands under the side of her face as she closes her eyes. "What's up?"

"What's up? Amelia, I spoke to your mom. You did it! You got your dream role. Congratulations." *Dammit.* He's being nice.

"Thanks, Preston. I'm really excited. Nervous but excited."

"That's great. Well, not the nervous part... But you know you're talented, we all do...and...ah...it's good. This is good."

It doesn't sound good. In a matter of seconds, his tone went from enthusiastic and proud to completely unsure. "Preston, is—"

"Come home. I miss you and—"

"*What?*" I sit up straight, my fight mode activated. But I don't want to fight him. We've been through this before. "*You* told me to *leave*."

"No, I didn't. You walked."

"Preston, you gave me an ultimatum. Did you honestly expect me to stay after that? That's not how marriages work."

"You wanted a break!" His voice rises and I jump, thankful that he can't see me.

Taking a deep breath, I calm myself before responding. "All I asked was for a little time to find out who I was, if I wasn't your muse. I was losing myself. No, I'd already *lost* myself. And my mood was going to ruin us." I don't know why I'm telling him this *again*. We've talked about it at great length.

"I've tried, Amelia. I have, but I can't do this without you."

"Do what?" If he'd said this when I first walked away, I would have longed for him to tell me he couldn't do life without me. Then maybe it wouldn't have hurt so much. But I know better than that now, so when he says his next words, I'm not at all shocked.

"I can't write. I need you. I thought you'd come back. I thought you'd figure out we belong together, doing this. And you'd come back."

Jesus.

I close my eyes before slowly releasing a breath, and when I'm settled enough to open them again, Hayley's in my face shaking her head as she over exaggerates mouthing the word no. *Does she seriously think I'd go back?*

I roll my eyes and shoo her away just as Preston pleads again, a new angle this time. "I can make all your dreams come true, Amelia. People already love our music videos. Think about how famous you'll be when our fan base grows. It's happening soon. I can feel it."

"Preston."

"No, wait. I need you to seriously think about this. Because you do *not* want to get left behind. You'll regret it."

Oh great, so we're going through all the stages of grief right now. But in the wrong order. What's next?

"I refuse to believe we're over. It's not possible. We were perfect together and you know it. You'll be back. You're *nothing* without me."

Denial then. Oh, and anger. What in the—

"Give me the phone." Hayley stands in front of me, arms crossed over her chest, her expression positively raging. "Actually, fuck that. I'm going over there. Tell the asshole I'm on my way."

She stalks toward the door, her hair still messed from last night, her makeup smudged all over her face, and it warms my heart.

"Preston. I'm not coming back. Ever. Find someone else to use." I hang up before jumping to my feet and rushing over to Hayley, wrapping her in a hug as she unlocks the door. "You beautiful soul, you." I giggle. "Thank you. I appreciate you having my back."

She turns around, her smile proud. "You did good. But I wish you'd let me go."

"Why?"

"Because that guy deserves a good slap across the face, and I really wanted to be the one to do it. Unless you want to, of course."

"Thank you." I laugh again. "But I have a feeling his life isn't going to be all sunshine and rainbows, and that's enough for me. Though I do hate that he was talking to my mom."

"I wouldn't worry about that." Hayley waves me off.

"Why?"

"I'm pretty sure your mom called everyone she knows. She's excited for you."

My nose scrunches when a little rope knots itself around my heart, giving it a tug. *Dammit.* I asked her to stop doing that. It's been a week since I mentioned it, so I figured she'd listened. But if she hasn't, that will mean she called—

My phone rings right on cue and I groan, dropping it to the counter beside me.

"She *didn't*." Hayley groans on my behalf.

"She did, and I can't handle that right now."

I walk away as the name Damien flashes across my screen and an image of his smiling face flashes across my mind. "I'm taking a shower," I say, refusing to speak to the man otherwise known as my dad. I've reached my quota of dealing with estranged men from my past. I'm done.

I spend Sunday watching my music videos on repeat, hoping to remind myself of what I'm capable of. To acknowledge what my new bosses saw in me.

My plan was to build myself up so I could walk—no, stride—into my new workplace with the confidence to blow them away. And by Sunday night, I'm good.

But come Monday, my confidence is shot and I find myself rushing around—despite being early— and working myself into a sweaty mess.

"Excuse me," someone calls out as I walk past reception, pulling me to a halt. Apparently I've also become a rude person.

"God, I'm sorry." I stop, spinning around to walk back to her. "I'm Amelia. I just—"

"You're our new director," she says with a beaming grin. "We're so happy to have you here. I loved your music video for 'Is This All Life Is.' I've played it a hundred times."

My chest tightens with emotions as some of the tension leaves my body.

"Thank you,"—my eyes flash to her name badge—"Jennifer. Any gossip I need to know before I walk through those very expensive and very official-looking doors?" I'm not kidding; the doors look like they're made out of pure mahogany with solid gold trim.

Jennifer laughs. "So much. I could talk for hours. But don't let the doors fool you. It's a front. It's what they want you to see. At the end of the day, it's just wood." She lifts her shoulder in a half shrug and I instantly like her.

"Thanks. I needed that."

"You've got this." Her smile widens. "Don't let *anyone* tell you otherwise. You're talented." She glares at something over my shoulder, and I'm about to question her when we're interrupted by a grumpy-looking man in a well-pressed business suit who does not look in the mood for gossip. "I'll buzz you in," Jennifer tells me with a subtle eye roll. "Let's talk later."

I nod as I walk through the doors and into the elevator, hoping the man isn't coming inside. But no such luck. He follows me in, standing dead center, his presence filling the small space.

"Can you please press for level eight?" I ask instead of trying to reach around him.

"It's already done," he replies tersely, and... *Great*. He's going to my floor.

"Thank you." I smile politely but he's not looking my way. Nothing like an intimidating figure to increase my nerves on day one.

When the doors open on level eight, I follow the man through the halls, both of us walking through the glass door to the conference room. He sits down next to the head of the table, while I take a seat across from him, keeping my smile locked in place when he gruffly looks my way.

"Tom and Jim will be here shortly," a woman I don't know tells us as she pops her head into the fishbowl. "Can I get either of you something to drink?"

"Yes," the suit guy says, his eyes now set on his phone. "I'll take a cold-pressed drip coffee, strong, with a dash of caramel. A dash," he repeats and I internally wince at his tone.

The woman doesn't even frown before turning to me. "Is water okay?" I ask, noting the smallest hint of a smile.

"Of course. I'll be back with both."

She walks away and within a minute, the room fills and my new bosses arrive, taking a seat before they've said hello. Suit Guy nods and smiles, and they have some kind of silent exchange before one of the executives, Tom, clears his throat and launches into the meeting.

"We met with a couple of the big networks last week, and Susie's put together a filming schedule to ensure we meet our deadlines." The woman from before rushes in and places some documents down in front of each of us as another woman follows her in with a tray of drinks.

Tom ignores them both as he continues on. "Jake, we've got you on the Hallawell Project, and Amelia..." He trails off when his business partner, Jim, gets his attention. "I almost forgot. Everyone, this is Amelia. She's starting with us today. Can you all say hi?"

I smile as a collection of greetings comes my way, and Tom nods with a warm grin, easing more of my tension.

"We are very excited to have you on the team, Amelia," he adds, making my smile widen, forcing me to work hard not to let my giddiness show. *I'm a professional. I need to stay professional.*

"Tom isn't wrong," Jim says, smiling back at me. "Amelia's work on the Chasing Lies music videos is phenomenal, and if you haven't viewed them, I suggest you rectify that immediately. Susie can send you a link."

"Oh my God. Thank you," I blurt out, ignoring the discomfort in my chest at the mention of my ex's band. "I can't wait to start. I'm ready to get my hands dirty." I smile brightly and internally cringe. What was that? *So much for not letting the enthusiasm show. But how is this real?* Yes, it's what I've been working toward since I was a teenager, but I honestly didn't expect it so soon.

Jim smiles again, and a little part of me wonders if that's a good or bad thing. I thought production executives were supposed to be scary. "I'm not going to lie," he says—and *here it is,* I think— "as everyone here will tell you, some of our shows are bigger than others, and they may not be what you were expecting, but I can promise we have big plans for you. And first up is *Project Storm.*"

"*Project Storm?*" I ask, trying to remember all the projects I've been reading about since they offered me the job. I'm ninety-nine percent sure that *Storm* wasn't listed in the bible they gave me. I would have remembered that because, like now, it would have made me think of Luke and his damn football team. "It wasn't on the—"

"Are you kidding me?" Suit man stands as he cuts me off, his hands on his hips in anger. "I've been working my ass off here and you give the newbie *Project Storm?* You give *Project Storm* to a girl?"

What?

"Sit down, Jake," Jim demands. "There's a time and a place for this discussion and this isn't it."

Jake sits but his expression doesn't waver. Meanwhile, rather than take offense over something I've been fighting all my life, I ignore his sexism as my brain focuses on what's more important than some asshole's opinion of me... *What the hell is Project Storm?*

"Amelia will be heading up *Project Storm* because that's who we want," Tom says with pursed lips. "Her style is more suited to the fast pace of the show."

"What show?" I blurt out and then grimace. "Sorry. It just wasn't—"

"Ah, yes. It wasn't in your bible. It's a high-profile show that we've been keeping to ourselves. We've been granted access to the San Francisco Storm football franchise. Full access. And that means all the players, all the staff, and all that goes along with it."

"Wow. That's incredible," I say out loud, but inside I'm screaming, *"God-fucking-dammit."* Hayley is going to have a field day with this information. "And what's the angle?" I force a smile, while mentally banging my head against a wall.

What was I thinking sleeping with Luke? I don't even like him. I spent the better part of my childhood and teen years wishing he would disappear, and then I go and sleep with him. And now, in a sick twisted turn of events, I'm going to be working with him. *I'll repeat... Goddammit.*

Oblivious to my inner spiral, the creative director of the company, Patrick, launches into a speech about their early concept, and when he's done, his eyes lock on mine. "We're excited for your ideas once you've had a chance to process everything. This project could get us the exposure we need to break into the next level."

"I'm curious..." I hesitate before asking the first question that comes to mind. "Are the players all aware and happy about the full access you're planning?" Because I anticipate we'll have some push back from the team.

"Of course," Patrick says, though I can tell he's not so sure. "Why wouldn't they?"

"I don't know. Maybe because not everyone wants to be on TV."

Jake laughs out loud before shaking his head and turning to Tom. "This is what I mean. She's the wrong person for this job. The guys will love the exposure. Trust me."

CHAPTER SIX

LUKE

Our media liaison, Keeley, smiles as she finishes telling us all about *Project Storm* while I wait for the backlash. *Three, two, one...*

"No fucking way," my friend Dylan, one of our star wide receivers, protests. "I'm out." He walks away, grumbling about not wanting to be on camera, and I get it. He's never wanted the limelight. He plays because he loves the game, but if he could, he'd do without all the bullshit that comes with the job. In fact, I was ninety percent sure he was going to retire when his first kid was born, but then he surprised me and kept playing. But his family and privacy will always come first.

Me on the other hand... "I think it's a great idea," I say honestly. "Count me in. Just tell me where I need to be."

According to Keeley's big speech, the San Francisco Storm is set to feature in a new TV series showcasing the world of professional football players. It's not the first show to spotlight a football team and won't be the last, but from the way they're pitching the idea, it sounds like the first to be this intrusive. They've basically been given a backstage pass into our lives.

And it's great! I have nothing to hide...*anymore.*

"Thank you, Luke." Keeley giggles, and if I didn't know any better, I'd assume she was flirting. But I've been there, tried that, and discovered she does not mix work and pleasure. *Such a shame.* "We're not sure who they want to feature yet, or how it's going to play out, but I'm grateful for your enthusiasm. All I know at this stage is that it's happening, and the crew are coming in next week for a walk-through to discuss plans."

"Why the hell would the bigwigs agree to this?" Wyatt, our offensive tackle, asks under his breath, confusing me. I would have put all my money on this being his thing. "I mean, I'm all for it," he adds, making me grin, "but I'm genuinely shocked."

We all are, with the exception of Thomas, our quarterback, who suspiciously doesn't appear shocked at all. And if he already knows something, he and I are going to have words.

The meeting adjourns shortly after Dylan's walkout, and I rush to meet up with Thomas. "How long have you known?" I ask, catching him in the hall.

Thomas pauses, turning to face me. "What makes you think I knew?"

"Uh. Maybe the complete lack of surprise on your face when they announced it. You forget how well I know you." Thomas and I have been friends since high school, and now he's engaged to my sister. It's safe to say, I can read him.

He sighs as his shoulders drop. "They mentioned it last week, but I wasn't allowed to say anything. I was told in case they needed backup selling the idea." He shrugs like it's no big deal.

"Why would they ask you to do that? You hate the idea."

"What?" His eyes widen, making me burst out laughing.

"Come on. Don't bullshit me."

"Okay, fine. I hate the idea. The last thing I want is someone digging around in my private life."

That's what I figured. "Then why agree to help them?"

"I made a deal. I said I'd help if they kept me out of the spotlight. I'm more than happy to be featured when I'm here at the stadium, or for anything to do with the game, but my personal life is off-limits."

"Fair deal, but...do you really think you'll get much pushback?" *Other than Dylan who's probably thinking the same thing Thomas is.*

Thomas raises an eyebrow. "I can name a few."

"Well, I am not one of them. I have nothing to hide. Let them see it all." I spread my arms wide, letting the world know I'm an open book, laughing to myself. But when I glance back at Thomas, he has a strange look on his face, making me pause until I register what I said. "Shit. I didn't mean that you had something to hide. I—"

"Relax, I know. This expression,"—he waves his hand in front of his face—"is one of a man who does not want to *see it all* when it comes to you. Why does it feel like you're about to become famous for all the wrong reasons?"

I bark out another laugh while a knot forms in my stomach. "Because, my friend, I was born for this." And the past is firmly locked in the past. I'm sure of it.

"God, what have they done?"

I try not to focus on the tension in my middle as we walk together to the locker rooms, and with the team all abuzz with the news, I easily push it from my mind. Then the second we run out onto the field, my focus shifts to where it should be...football.

Pre-season has barely begun, but I can already tell it's going to be our year. When Thomas joined the team a few years back, the Super Bowl talk revved up, and since then, we've been getting stronger by the day. If it's going to happen, I'd put all my money on it happening this year. Which, now that I think about it, is probably why they're making a show about our team and why the bigwigs, as Wyatt called them, agreed to it. The networks get a boost to their ratings and we get more exposure. It's a win-win.

As soon as I get home after practice, I dump my bag in the hall and head straight for the sliding door leading out back. "Shadow?" I call out into the yard, listening for my energetic black Labrador retriever, smiling as I anticipate her bound around the corner.

Only I'm met with silence.

"Shadow. Where are you, pup?"

Silence again.

Turning around, I groan as I walk back into the house, collecting my phone on my way to the living room.

I know exactly where she is. That pain-in-the-ass sister of mine has pup-napped my dog *again*. She lived here for a few months, and now she thinks we're co-parenting or something, it drives me crazy.

I'll admit, I got Shadow on a whim, and sure, it took me a little while to get used to the commitment, but now she's my world. The only female I'll let sleep in my room. My lifelong companion. And I want her back.

I dial Lainey's number as I fall onto the couch.

"*Chipmunk*," I whine when she answers. "Have you taken Shadow again?"

Lainey groans at the new nickname I've given her before confirming my suspicion. "I have. When's the last time you walked her?"

"Yesterday."

"Yesterday? Bullshit."

"No bullshit. We went for a run along Edger's Beach. She helped me meet a—"

"I don't want to know about your hook-ups. And dammit, Shadow, you hustled me."

"Shadow hustled you?" I question her slowly, not bothering to tell her that I didn't actually hook up that time. It's more fun to make her squirm.

"She did. I walked over to say hi and she was all sad with her puppy-dog eyes gazing longingly out the window. I assumed she'd been stuck inside."

I try hard to hold back my laugh, but it bursts out of me. "Okay, yep. She most definitely hustled you."

"I know," she complains.

God, I love that dog.

"Anyway, we're almost back to your place. I'll be there in a minute. You're alone, right?"

I roll my eyes even though she can't see me. "Yes, Alice in delusionland. Would I be calling you if I wasn't?" She's under the impression that I'm never alone, that I have a girl with me twenty-four seven. And I guess she'd usually be right... if she hadn't stolen my dog.

Shadow's always with me when I'm home. As for the other girls... They come and go.

"Alice in delusionland. Really?" Lainey scoffs, her love for my ever-changing nicknames wearing thin. "You must be running out of ideas."

"Don't worry, I've got plenty more where that came from." Finding new nicknames for Lainey should be considered a full-time job, but I can't call it work because it's too much fun.

"You're lucky I know you do it out of love."

"Love? Yeah, right. I reserve nicknames for the people who annoy me the most."

"I'm here," she announces, ignoring me. "I'm hanging up." She hangs up before I can respond, and seconds later, Shadow comes racing toward me just like I expected her to do outside.

"Come here, gorgeous girl. How was your walk?" I drop to the floor and roll around with her, razzing her up as she licks me. "Did your aunt look after you?"

I sense Lainey watching us and when I look up she has an amused grin on her face. "If your women could see you now."

"They'd love it. Why do you think I got her in the first place?" It's true that I'm guilty of wanting Shadow because I thought she'd help me with the ladies, but I quickly discovered she was better than that. She's not just a show pony; she's my life.

"If only you could find a woman to love like you love that dog."

"That dog is the only constant love I need in my life. When are you going to listen to the fact that I'm happy?"

Honestly, I expected more from Lainey. She knows me better than anyone else. I'm not going to change.

"I know you're happy, Luke. And you know I'm usually the one to defend you when others try to set you up, but I'd love a sister."

"You've got Summer," I state the obvious. Summer is Thomas's sister and our teammate Dylan's wife.

God, our team is way too close for comfort.

"I do have Summer," Lainey admits. "But I want someone that will be forced to come to our family functions. With our parents. Someone to share in my misery."

Ahh. It all makes sense now. Mom and Dad just celebrated their fortieth wedding anniversary and Lainey struggled with it. While she's in a relatively good place with our family now, there were times it got a bit tense and the big events usually hit her hard.

"Well, aren't you the sweetest?" I joke to lighten the mood, knowing she won't want to talk about it. "Work on Ryan. You've got two brothers, remember? You've got a better chance with him."

Lainey blows out a breath as her phone rings, but when she looks at the screen, her expression instantly lifts and she smiles.

"It's Thomas." *Of course it is.* I've never seen anyone else elicit that expression. I love Lainey, and I love Thomas like a brother, but no one should place that much of their happiness in one person. It can't be healthy. "I'm going to go," she adds, walking to the door. "See you soon?"

"If not before, then I'll see you the next time you steal my girl."

"Looking forward to it."

"Oh, and Pink Barbie, if you're nice to me, I'll try and find someone to bring over for Thanksgiving." The next big family event. "Maybe I can find a fake date or something."

Lainey spins to face me as she bursts out laughing. "Thanks, bro. Love you."

"Yeah, yeah." *Now I just have to find someone that won't get too clingy.*

A week later, there's a strange energy in the air when I arrive at the stadium. It's not all doom and gloom, but it's definitely not the excitement I thought would be hovering after our first preseason win over the weekend.

"What's going on?" I ask Reed, one of our running backs. "There's a weird tension in the room."

Reed grimaces. "You just missed a very heated discussion between Zane and Easton." Zane's our rookie and let's just say he's a whippersnapper on and off the field, while our teammate Easton has a don't-be-a-dick policy. East and I don't speak that often. For obvious reasons.

"Damn. What did Zane say this time?" Poor kid just has to open his mouth around Easton these days.

"He wolf whistled at the crew."

"What crew?"

"The film crew. Where's your head this morning?" *Back in my bed where I should be... Wait.*

"The crew are women?" This show just got a lot more interesting—a female crew. Lucky for me. "Ouch. Motherfucker." I rub my arm where Reed just punched me. "What the hell was that for?"

"That was on behalf of all the women in the world. This isn't the fifties. Of course some of the film crew are women." He rolls his eyes, and I cringe.

"I didn't mean it like that. I knew there would be females, but when you said it, my mind went to an all-female *crew,* and oh, the possibilities..."

Reed laughs but I can tell he still thinks I'm a dick. "I'd love to spend a day in your mind."

"I bet you'd love to spend a day in my body too." I wink, making him laugh harder. He knows he's hot. He doesn't need my body to get the girls. He could rival a bodybuilder with the muscles he's working and he's just as pretty. But he needs to get out of his head. He's been in love with his best friend, Bria, for years.

"So, when do I get to meet this crew?"

"They're coming back at—"

A whistle blows, cutting Reed off, though none of the other players notice it, until...

"The whistle means *quiet,* people," Thomas's loud voice booms, and the rest of the team hush as Keeley jumps onto a bench seat to get our attention.

"I know you're due to have a meeting with the crew and the coaches soon, but I've been asked to set a few ground rules." Her gaze moves to Zane and I internally groan. I can already guess rule number one. That fucker just ruined it for the rest of us with one little wolf whistle.

"Rule number *one*. The crew are not here for your enjoyment. They're here to work and they're off-limits. That means no flirting, no exchanging of phone numbers, and definitely no dating." Her tone makes it clear that the term "dating" is actually her way of saying "do not fuck the film crew," and that puts a downer on things.

"And rule number two?" Zane asks, forever being his smart-ass self.

"I'm glad you asked, *Zane.* Rule number two is...don't be like Zane." The guys cheer and laugh, with those close to Zane patting him on the back. But of course, Zane smiles proudly. Keeley shakes her head and waits until the ruckus dies down before adding, "Let's keep the schoolyard antics out of the stadium and conduct ourselves in a professional manner. After all, you never know what might end up on the TV screens of your fellow Americans."

She announces a few more rules—but most of them are obvious things like "try not to swear on camera" and "check for cameras before getting naked"—and once she's done, we're called onto the field for a meet and greet with the crew.

I find it funny that Keeley mentioned schoolyard antics when this whole shebang could be compared to preparing us for a field trip. *Stay in line. Don't interrupt. Be on your best behavior. No touching the display... or in this case... no touching the crew.* Seems more trouble than it's worth, if I'm honest.

When we're all gathered on the field, Keeley once again steps up to the mic, and my eyes flash to our head coach. If he's not up there, then I'm almost certain he's not at all happy about what's going on. Which begs the question... Why *is* he going along with it during such a huge season for us?

"Before I introduce you to the team from Brighton Productions," Keeley begins, "I want to thank you all in advance for your participation. I'm excited about this new venture and can't wait to get started."

With our team lined up in workout gear, the production crew stand out in their business attire as they walk toward us. But through the bodies of people, one stunning figure shines brighter than the rest. My eyes drag up from her sky-high red stiletto heels, taking in her tight fitted pants—that would undoubtedly show off a perfectly sculpted ass—before moving up to her white, almost see-through blouse that dips just low enough to tease a little cleavage while not actually revealing anything at all.

I could stare at her body all day, but when I finally get a look at her face, I don't know whether to laugh or choke on thin air. "What the actual fuck?" *Amelia?*

It's safe to say, the no-dating rule isn't going to be a problem. At least where my dear "friend" is concerned.

CHAPTER SEVEN

AMELIA

Fuck.

I f I thought Luke was going to hate the fact that I'm here, I was dead wrong. I've never seen him so happy. And that makes things worse.

Why do I get the feeling he's going to enjoy this more than he should?

"Hi, Amelia, is it?" He squints as though trying to grasp a hold of a fake memory, and I roll my eyes. "I'm Luke. It's a pleasure to meet you."

He holds out a hand for me to shake, and I stare down at his palm.

After we were all introduced and the producers spoke about their plans, we were given the opportunity to mingle and get to know each other. I immediately headed toward Storm's head coach, Jonathan Pierce, but was intercepted by Luke on my way over to him.

"Well?" Luke questions me when I don't react with enthusiasm.

"Stay away from this one," one of his teammates warns me as he joins us, his gaze sincere. "He'll be in and out of your pants before you can say 'he has a cute smile.' Yes, he does, but that's how he gets you."

Luke bursts out laughing, slapping his teammate on the back. "That and my giant cock." He waggles his eyebrows, turning my way to catch me fake gag. "Don't listen to Carter. He just wants you all for himself. But unfortunately for him, you're off-limits."

Carter laughs as he walks away, leaving Luke and me alone, or at least, out of earshot of others.

I've had a week to mull over this project and my impending proximity to Luke, but it wasn't enough to quell the anger over the hand fate dealt me. I'm clearly being punished for my lapse in judgment after sleeping with him a couple of months ago, but while I'd give anything to remove myself from this unfortunate situation, I can't. It's my dream.

"So..." Luke begins, his gaze darting back to the rest of my crew before settling on me again. "This is what you do?"

"It is. And trust me when I say, I'd rather be on any other project right now."

"That's a shame. I was thinking you could work our little tryst into the show somehow. I'm sure it would boost your career."

"Ugh. We are not secret lovers. It happened once and it won't happen again."

"I'm just trying to help."

My jaw drops at his straight face. He really does think highly of himself. "How does that head of yours fit through the door?" I question, genuinely curious.

"With style." He winks while I mentally wince, embarrassed for him.

"Okay. Well, it was nice catching up with you, but I've got to mingle." I put on a fake smile and wave before stepping away, but he grabs my arm at the last second, pulling me to a stop.

"I trust you're not going to bring up certain things from our past," he whispers between clenched teeth, his happy demeanor gone, while I work hard to keep a straight face, my pulse racing.

"I have no idea what you're talking about," I lie before shaking myself free and walking away, my head held high, proud of myself for how I handled that little interaction. Especially considering his touch completely rattled me.

I haven't been able to stop thinking about our night together, and being in his presence again makes it hard not to picture his naked body. And he had to touch me. A vision of his huge palm wrapped around his throbbing length comes to my mind, and I picture him walking toward me, his piercing eyes locked on mine while he—

Goddammit.

It's such an unfortunate side effect to him being the title holder of the guy-who-gave-me-the-best-orgasm-of-my-life. Hayley tells me there are plenty of men out there that could make me feel that good, and that I'm comparing Luke to a low base, but I haven't really been in the mood to find out. At the moment, my job is the priority. I can worry about my sex life later, when I have the time to not just unpack my sex with Luke, but to also figure out why the sex with Preston wasn't as good. Was it me? If it was, I can't afford to let myself spiral.

I don't talk to Luke again during the meet and greet hour, but I sense his eyes on me whenever I'm close by. I, on the other hand, use all of my willpower to ensure I don't so much as glance in his direction. This is going to be hard enough without me wasting energy on negative thoughts. No, the less I see Luke, the better.

As I'm leaving the building, an unfamiliar voice calls my name, and I turn to find Thomas Kelly walking toward me. Considering he's the quarterback, I should have spoken to him tonight, but the producers were monopolizing his time. Thankfully I now have the chance.

"Thomas—"

"Amelia Rose, what are the chances?" A smile graces my face as I picture a fourteen-year-old Thomas accidentally throwing a football at my head. *My fault, not his.*

"Hi Thomas, it's been a while."

He smiles knowingly. "How have you been? I tried to catch up with you inside, but your producers love to chat."

"You've got to be a good communicator in their role. As do I, but the difference is that *I* know when to stop."

"On that note, you'll be the one making the big decisions on what makes it to the screen, right?" He grimaces, and I bark out a laugh.

"Are you nervous about something?"

"No, not at all. I've got my limits noted in my contract." He smirks while I laugh. *Good thinking.* "I actually think it's really cool that you're here," he continues, "directing this. I finally know someone famous."

"Umm. Hello. It's not nearly as cool as being the quarterback for one of the top teams in the NFL."

Thomas attended the same high school as Luke and I did, but was the year above us. I first met him the day he almost knocked me out. I dropped to the ground and he came rushing over to make sure I was okay. We had a nice easy chat that day, and if he hadn't been teammates with Luke, we may have become friends. But it wasn't meant to be. I'd vowed to stay away from the team.

Maybe I should have continued that vow all the way to now.

"Hardly," Thomas says, releasing a breathy laugh. "I just throw a ball around. You're the star. And I've got to say, it will be nice having a familiar face around when they're filming. I'm still a little on the fence as to whether or not I'm happy about the show."

I internally wince, but at the same time, I like his honesty.

"That's fair. From what I understand, they didn't exactly give you much notice."

"Oh, I knew weeks ago." He waves off my concern. "But we should be focused on our game. The Super Bowl is in our sights. The last thing we need is a distraction."

My nose scrunches. *I'm the distraction.* At least, the production is, and I'm officially the face of it. "I promise to try and be as discreet as possible during practice and on game days. The last thing we want to do is mess things up for you. But if we get this right, it could be amazing for the team. For exposure."

Thomas's eyes flash my way, and I curse myself for saying the wrong thing, until he smiles. "You're right. From now on, I'm going to embrace it."

"Oh yeah? Does that mean you'll let us glimpse a bit of your life outside of these walls?" I tease, comically clenching my teeth so he knows that I'm joking.

Thomas huffs out a laugh before shaking his head. "No chance. But good try."

Hayley stands up and waves as I scan the low-key bar we agreed to meet in after work. I smile apologetically, already running behind on my first day, but she just rolls her eyes, refusing to accept my concern.

"How was it seeing Luke again?" she asks the second I'm in earshot. "Was he an ass? A gorgeous ass but an ass all the same. Did you talk? Ooh, was there a heated moment? I bet—"

"Hayley!" I cut in. "I haven't even sat down yet."

"You're right. God, who am I?" She shakes her head with an appalled look on her face, making me laugh.

"We need to find you some work," I say as a joke, because she has way too much time on her hands.

"We really do." She nods multiple times. "I'm starting to seek out drama elsewhere."

"You've got an audition next week and I know you're going to smash it," I say, using her words. "After that, this won't be an issue."

"Yes, I'm good. Anyway, how was your first day at the stadium? Was Luke an ass?"

"Isn't he always? Although, he wasn't completely awful." *Until the end.* "And that's worse."

"Definitely. It means he's planning something diabolical."

"He's not a cartoon villain, Hayls." *God, I'm shortening her name now... am I becoming an Aussie?*

"Ugh, I need drama." Hayley groans before laughing. "Anyway, back to Luke. Let's hope he gets on your good side because he is definitely made for TV. That man has charisma for days."

"I don't want to hear that." I comically wince. If I could make the call to keep him out of the show altogether, I would.

"Sorry." She laughs again. "But it's true."

"Why'd I have to go and have sex with him?" I groan and drop my head into my hands as I pretend to cry.

"Because he's gorgeous. Maybe you should do it again."

"What? No." I giggle. "It's *Luke.* Did we have mind-blowing sex? Yes. At least I did. But is he still at the top of my shit list? Also yes. And I can't imagine that changing."

"But it could be hotter with him all... 'I hate you, but you're a goddess in bed.'" She puts on a deep gruff voice for Luke. "And you all 'I hate you too, but harder...yes, there.'" Her pitch rises and I can't help but laugh out loud.

"It's not happening."

"Sure it's not." She waggles her eyebrows and I groan again, knocking back the drink Hayley already had waiting for me. *This is all new for me.* I don't talk about my sex life. Then again, I'm still trying to work out who the real me is. So, what do I know?

The night flies by, but the later it gets, the more obnoxious my yawning becomes until I can no longer hide it. This day...no, this *week* has kicked my ass. From the early mornings to late nights of planning and then today answering question after question, I'm done.

"I don't mean to be a party pooper, but I'm freaking exhausted. I need to go home."

"It's only nine," Hayley teases but at the same time she stands. "I get it. You're a big-name director now. You need your beauty sleep."

"Ha. I wish. But I do need sleep. I can't believe how tired I am after my first production day." *I need to start looking after myself better. Now's the time to be on my A game.* "I promise I won't make a habit of this. It's just been a big week. I need to start eating better. Next time, be ready for an all-nighter."

Hayley snorts out a laugh but doesn't call me out on the fact that I have never been an all-nighter kind of girl. Instead, she kisses my cheek and pulls me into a side hug. "Sweet dreams, sweetie. I'm going to go and find me a man."

I look like garbage when I wake the next morning, but it's nothing a little makeup won't fix. On the drive home last night, I realized I could attribute all of my tiredness to stress. I felt the same exhaustion when I first left Preston. I know that once things settle down, I'll feel better, and it makes pushing through so much easier.

When I pull into the stadium parking lot at seven a.m., I find one of the guys from the team, Easton heading inside. A hint of uncertainty settles in my chest when I remember hearing his negative stance on the show, and when he fakes a smile and picks up his pace to get away from me, the feeling deepens.

So far, I've only had a handful of enthusiastic players, and if it continues to be that way, I'm going to struggle to make a decent production. The idea was that we'd focus on the entire team, not a few random players. That's been done. Many times.

And I need this show to be a hit.

I'm the first to arrive at our newly created Storm stadium office, but before I can dump my oversized bag onto my desk, the door swings open again. I lift my gaze to say hi to whoever it is, but am startled when it's Luke.

"Uh, hi?" I question, dropping my bag as he locks the door, my chest tightening at the sound of that little click. "Unlock the door, please. I have crew members arriving shortly." I smile, working hard to mask the nervous energy coursing through me until he turns the lock again, eyeing me curiously. "What do you want?" I ask, my voice curt.

He frowns before snapping out of it, his face suddenly neutral. "I thought we could have a chat."

"Okay." He walks forward and when he reaches my desk, I move around the opposite side, heading over to the makeshift kitchen they put in for us, making a show of pouring myself a coffee, even though I don't drink it. *I'm fine. Luke being here is fine.* "Chat away. How can I help you?"

"You know why I'm here," he rasps, standing right behind me, making me jump at his close proximity.

"I don't know—"

"Don't bullshit me, Amelia. I just want to know you're not going to use the fire to gain ratings."

"What?" I knew that's what he was alluding to, but now that he's said it out loud, I'm offended. "Why would I do that?"

"Oh, I don't know—to advance your career? *To help yourself.* Just like you did when you told the cops I might have had something to do with it."

"I didn't... That's... God, you have no idea what I went through." I know I shouldn't have mentioned his name to the police but I panicked. I didn't know they'd arrest him for it. "You were never charged. It's not a big deal. I don't know what you're worried about."

"I just want your word that you'll keep it to yourself."

"Or what?" I stare him down, trying not to appear shaken by the threat dripping from his tone. And when he doesn't say anything, I continue, needing to fill the silence. "I would have thought you'd love it. You'd be the star of the show. Or wait..." I fake a gasp and cover my mouth with my hand before whispering, "Are you worried it will ruin your reputation?" I exaggeratedly grimace. "I guess it wouldn't be a good look when people find out you set me up and then ran away when shit got real. Leaving me inside a *burning building.*" My heart races as the fire once again burns through my mind, but I subtly suck in a breath to calm down.

"You had David." Luke waves off my comments as though I've barely rattled him, but I don't miss the anger in his eyes. "You got out. You were fine. I sav—"

"I wasn't." I pause, refusing to rehash a part of my life long buried. While it's not the event that kicked off my hatred toward Luke, it definitely cemented it, and I'd prefer not to fall down that rabbit hole of emotions. He played me that night and then I let myself get dragged back into his world a third time when I slept with him. I should have learned my lesson by now. "I won't mention the fire. It's not exactly something I like thinking about."

"Good." Luke fakes a grin before leaning in close, his hard body pressed against mine as he enters my personal space, forcing me back until my ass is digging into the metal edge of the counter. "As long as you stay quiet, I'll be the perfect subject for the show. You want me to smile, I'll fucking smile." As if I need a demonstration, his expression easily morphs to give him a boyish charm, like he has a default setting ready to go, and it's completely unnerving.

"I'm sure we can keep this professional," he adds, his smile turning cocky once more. "That's what you want, right? Unless you were thinking about another night of fun."

As he whispers, his lips hover so close to my skin that I swear I feel his touch below my ear, sending an electric current through me. My heart pounds in my chest, threatening to break through my ribs, and I wish I could say it was due to the anger I hold and not because I'm imagining him settled between my legs.

"I can stay professional," I whisper back, my lips purposely brushing his cheek as I turn my head, hoping to rattle him even half as much as he's rattling me. "And I'll keep the fire a secret, but make no mistake." I shove him back and step aside, putting some much-needed space between us. "You will never be touching me again. That's a promise. They both are. In fact, let's pretend we don't have a past. We don't know each other. Period."

Luke raises an eyebrow before shaking his head with a laugh. "Works for me. Pleasure doing business with you."

He walks away, and I hold my breath until he's gone, my body deflating as soon as the door clicks shut again, the tension finally leaving me.

I take a deep breath, but I've barely had a chance to process what just happened when the door flies open again and our director of photography walks in, beelining straight for me.

"What's the plan for today, Boss?" he asks as he drops down into the seat opposite me, pulling out his notepad. "It's a day of observations, right?"

"Observations, yes," I rush out, hoping I don't appear too flustered while inside my heart is still racing. "We'll take some photos and... ah... After that we have a meeting with the coaching staff."

"Eh." Craig scrunches his face as though disgusted by the idea. "I'm not all that interested in another 'you better not get in the way' speech. Do they think we're stupid? I've been filming documentaries for years, some focusing on subjects that didn't know they were subjects. I can be discreet."

"I know you can. And I know you'll keep the crew in line. But they're nervous. It's a huge year for them, and they don't need any distractions." *Wow, look at me paraphrasing or maybe stealing Thomas's words.* I run the words through my head again. Thomas was right. They don't need us to take away from their efforts for the Super Bowl; they need us to be a part of it.

"On the way to the top."

"What?"

Shit, I didn't mean to voice that. I'm a little all over the place. "I was thinking out loud. Trying to find an angle for the show."

Craig stares at me, confused. "I thought we had an angle?"

"We did. We do. It's just an idea."

The network wants a day-in-the-life style show and I understand why that would appeal. Reality television is a moneymaker right now. Those real estate shows where they just follow the realtors around are killing it. But they're not entirely organic, and we can't script drama here at the club. Well, we could, but as a fan of football, I will never let that happen. *Even though the Storm isn't my team.* And even though, as Luke said, I have information on him specifically. I'd never share it. There has to be something better. Something more gripping. Something that only comes from following a team that just might make it all the way to the top.

We spend the next week mostly out of sight—planning, observing, choosing locations—so for the most part, I'm able to pretend Luke doesn't exist, mostly, except when I find myself daydreaming about our time together.

Damn him and his expert hands...and mouth.

When we're halfway through the second week of preproduction, it's time to start our one-on-one chats with the players, and I can't wait. The more I get to know them, the easier it will be to create a story and the more receptive they'll be to give me what I need. I'm excited to get into it, but I have one complaint—everyone *loves* Luke.

So of course, he's up first.

CHAPTER EIGHT

LUKE – AGE SIXTEEN

I pace my yard, my head reeling from the events of last night—from the fire—and I'm nauseous. What a fucking mess. It was supposed to be a fun night. A way to let off steam while also getting back at Amelia for the bullshit she put me through over the years.

The house wasn't supposed to go up in flames. I just wanted to challenge her. Nothing more.

A vision of the fire burns my retinas as another wave of guilt hits me.

Blowing out a breath, I run my hands down my face as someone opens the back door, drawing my attention.

Mom.

No doubt coming to check that I'm still here. That I haven't snuck away like I wish I could.

We stare in silence until she purses her lips and hits me with a look of disappointment before walking inside.

My chest tightens but I deserve it, and I understand where it's coming from. Her firstborn—the kid that's supposed to be smart—got himself arrested. I'd be disappointed too.

Only I didn't get *myself* arrested. That was all Amelia. While I put myself in the line of fire to help her—running directly to the police—she decided she'd screw me over when she got herself caught, and I'm fucked if anyone else speaks out. A lot of people are.

My muscles tense as I think about Amelia again. But instead of the deep hate I want to feel, my stupid mind replays our kiss and my traitorous heart races. What was I thinking? *Actually, I wasn't thinking. I was reacting, and for some reason, I couldn't stop myself. She's the only one outside of my family that I've ever felt protective of, and this time that led to dangerous territory.*

But never again.

I want to hate her. I've always wanted to hate her, but no matter how hard I try, there's something stopping me.

As I pick up my pacing again, waiting for my dad to get home from his business trip so he can give me a piece of his mind, my thoughts stay firmly locked on Amelia. On the feel of her lips pressed against mine. The taste of her. The moans. Her warmth.

In that moment, I wanted her. All of her.

But that feeling has well and truly passed. I will never touch her again.

Unless, of course, I get a chance to fuck with her like she fucked with me.

If that day comes, I'll bask in the glory.

CHAPTER NINE

LUKE

Amelia's resting bitch face is on point when I walk into the room, and I can't help but smirk as it slips into a scowl. It's not like I wasn't expecting this reaction after our moment in her office last week, but I couldn't leave it alone. I had to make sure she wasn't going to use the fire as a ratings grab. It would make a damn good story, but I have no plans of letting one stupid mistake takeover my life again.

I've already spent years haunted by that night and I thought I was finally free.

I raise an eyebrow and pretend not to care what Amelia thinks of me until I realize her expression isn't aimed my way. She hasn't noticed my arrival. She's glaring at some guy I don't recognize as he chats with Keeley on the other side of the room.

From my position by the door, I can see Amelia's leg bouncing under the table and hate that it has my hackles rising. She used to do that when she was anxious and I doubt that's changed. *Who the fuck is this guy?* And more importantly... *Why do I care?* She's more than capable of handling herself. I'm just here as the entertainment.

I clear my throat to get their attention and all eyes flash my way. "Luke, welcome." Amelia stands, gifting me with a warm smile, convincing me that something isn't right. She must really hate this guy if she's being nice to me, unless she's taking professionalism to the next level. "Please take a seat." She gestures to the chair in front of her. "Today we'll be joined by one of Brighton Productions' other directors, Jake. He—"

"Brighton Productions' more *seasoned* director, she means. I'm sitting in on today's session while I wait for my production to start next week. To help Amelia if she needs it. In case any of the guys prefer talking man-to-man. I'm sure you don't mind. You get it."

What a fucking douche. Who does this guy think he is?

"And if I do...*mind*?" I deadpan, folding my arms over my chest. No matter my feelings toward Amelia, sexism is bullshit.

The guy, Jake I think she said, stares at me for a minute before belly laughing out loud. "Good one. That's why everyone likes you. You're funny."

Yeah, and we'll see how funny you find it when I drive my foot up your ass. "That's me. The comedian. Amelia,"—I turn back to Amelia, directing my attention to her and her alone—"I'm ready to begin whenever you are."

Amelia's eyes widen but she recovers quickly. Apparently my hate for her isn't as deep as my hate for assholes that like to belittle their colleagues in front of others. It's a touchy subject for me since my sister went through some things in college, and I won't put up with it. *This is going to be fun.*

Amelia dives straight into the standard interview questions, asking me things I have no doubt she already knows the answers to as "the more seasoned director" huffs and puffs beside her.

"What age did you start playing football? Have you played anywhere else other than San Francisco? Do you have any siblings? What's your family like? Are there any family members that you'd prefer we didn't talk to?"

To the douche's credit, he keeps his muttering relatively quiet, but when Amelia announces we're moving on to more personal topics, he cuts in before she begins.

"If you have any skeletons in your closet that you don't want us to find, I suggest you disclose them now, or bury them *deep*. At the end of the day, this is a TV series and the producers want ratings."

My eyes flash to Amelia as she cringes. She's too nice for this. My secrets aside, I can't imagine her airing someone else's dirty laundry without permission. Although, I never would have thought she'd turn on a friend so easily, without telling *said* friend what they did wrong.

"I'm not worried about my skeletons," I say confidently, now that I have Amelia's word that she'll keep the fire out of the show. "Something tells me that even if your team of detectives or whoever discovers something they think is ratings worthy, you won't use it." I'm being a dick and pushing Amelia, but for some reason I trust her and this guy deserves it.

"Okay. I need to cut this off," Amelia says as if to prove my point. "Jake's trying to get you to spill your secrets by pretending we have investigators. This isn't that kind of show. If something comes up when we're talking to your teammates, or friends and family, then we have your permission to include it in the show. It was mentioned in the contract that you were incredibly quick to sign." She pauses as though giving me a moment to let her verbal jab sink in, but I smile and own it. I was quick to sign because deep down, I knew Amelia wasn't going to fuck me over before I confronted her about it. She can hate me as much as she wants, but I've got just as much dirt on her as she'll ever find on me. Only like her, I'd never use it. Unless she forces my hand.

"Anyway, Luke, I'm sure you have a clear conscience, so it's fine."

"Exactly." I grin. "So...hit me with the personal questions."

Amelia hesitates before she picks up the folder in front of her and begins reading. Her eyes briefly close, and it doesn't take much to guess what's coming next, so when she finally looks up, I almost laugh. She's about to ask me about my sex life.

"Are you okay with us discussing your...eh...sexual habits? It's not a secret you...ah...sleep around—"

"Stop, stop. *Amelia*. What the hell was that?" Jake cuts in, rolling his eyes, and he walks over and rips the folder from in front of her. My fists clench but I wait for him to finish. "I can't believe you got chosen for this project," he mumbles before standing tall. "Luke, let's chat openly instead of tiptoeing around things. I'm sure you know, there are some roles that women shouldn't be appointed to, and a television director is one of them. Especially the director of a football series. I'm sorry you've been put in this situation. Amelia, I'll take over from—"

"Like hell you will." I shove my chair back and stand up, anger coursing through me. Am I the poster child for equality? Hell no. I have my faults. But this blatant chauvinistic behavior is messed up. How are there still people that think this way? "I will only be answering to our perfectly qualified director, Amelia, *or* anyone Amelia wants me to talk to, and I will be advising my teammates to do the same. I know I'm a cocky asshole at times, but you are next level. Have you ever thought that maybe you didn't get this production because most of my teammates would tell you to fuck right off the second you opened your mouth? Hell, I know at least one that wouldn't hold back from punching you in the nose if he saw you treating anyone the way you're behaving now. If you think this is a boys' club, you are dead wrong." I finish my rant and turn to Amelia. "I'm going to go. Feel free to reschedule this interview when that *dick* has gone."

I move to leave, reaching the hallway as Amelia excuses herself to use the bathroom. It's safe to say she *won't* be heading left in the direction of the Ladies' room. No, she's going to—

"Luke, *wait*!" she whisper-yells right on cue, following me as I walk toward the locker room. I suck in a breath as I turn, preparing myself for her onslaught. "I didn't need you to defend me in there. I can take care of myself."

"I know. You're a strong, independent woman."

"Are you mocking me?"

"Not entirely. It's the truth, isn't it?" I shrug, giving her nothing. I knew this was coming the second I opened my mouth. But she can be as strong and independent as she wants; I don't care. I couldn't let that fucker keep talking.

Amelia opens her mouth to speak but closes it again and shakes her head.

"Am—"

"You don't know me, remember?" She cuts me off. "Start acting that way."

"What the fuck? I didn't do anything in there to suggest we had *any* kind of relationship, beyond a professional one."

"Are you kidding me?" she seethes, glancing down the hall before looking my way again. "Would you have defended a stranger like that?"

"Abso-fucking-lutely. That guy is lucky I didn't deck him. I will *never* tolerate bullying. No matter what form it comes in." An irrational anger wells inside me, but I smile to push it back down. It's got nothing to do with Amelia.

Amelia stares at me, almost in shock, and it makes my smile a little more real. Yeah, Amelia...there's so much you don't know about me.

It's a long, slow beat before she releases a sigh and nods. "Okay."

"Okay?" I question her. "So are we good now? Even?"

"What? No, we're not good. And it's not about getting even."

I start laughing before she's finished speaking. "Just messing with you. It's so much fun. Enjoy your day, stranger."

I walk away, leaving Amelia standing in the halls. And that's the last I see of her for the next few days with her spending her time in the interview room—thankfully without the douche.

So this is what an all-access pass looks like.

The chatter around the room is a mix of excitement and annoyance, and I don't have to look to know who sits in what camp. But while everyone is focused on what they plan to film, I'm focused on our director. Watching her in her element, as she flits around the room, oozing confidence as she always has, it's hard to look away. Jerkface should have seen her like this. I almost feel bad that I was her first interview—*almost*—because then maybe he would have. Of course, Amelia didn't want to discuss my sex life when she's a part of that history. She's a professional. Such a shame that dick misinterpreted it as lack of experience.

As I'm watching her, Amelia bends over to pick something up off the floor, and my gaze shifts to her ass. Today she's wearing a loose-fitting white tank top and a black skirt that should be considered too short for the workplace. Like she's taunting me. Trying to make me picture what's beneath that sliver of material. *Making me want her again.*

She's a goddamn smoke show.

It's not at all the Amelia style I remember, but then again, a lot has changed.

But...while I'm confident enough to admit she surprised me the night we were together, I don't go back for seconds. And with Amelia, I shouldn't have gone for a first.

Forcing myself to look away, I find I'm not the only one who's noticed her and my chest burns. Almost every guy in the room has his eyes in Amelia's direction and... *Fuck this.* I'm going over there to—

"Can you believe that's Amelia?" Thomas steps in front of me, making me jump.

"Jesus. Where did you come from?" I huff, glancing around the room. *I swear he wasn't here a second ago.*

Thomas rolls his eyes before laughing. "I've been behind you for a good ten minutes. Long enough to catch you staring at her ass. Too bad she's off-limits, huh? Although..." He looks away, seemingly lost in thought while my gaze finds Amelia again. "Didn't she marry that singer?"

"What?" I spin around so fast my shoulder slams into my teammate's, making him curse out loud, drawing unwanted attention our way.

Thomas chuckles to himself before the fucker walks away, letting his question hang in the air instead of providing me with that very important piece of information.

Is Amelia married? To Preston-fucking-Milford or was it Midford or Mitzford? *Not fucking important.* But how the hell didn't I know that? I slept with her. Fuck, does that make me an adulterer? Nooo, Amelia is the adulterer; I'm just the side piece. *God.* I groan out loud. *A side piece?* That sounds so much worse.

"You look pale," Keeley says as she approaches me, her face full of concern. "Everything okay? You almost knocked Richards over. Are you sick?"

"So *fucking* sick," I muse. I'm also pissed off. *How dare Amelia make me a fucking side piece.*

"*Shit.*" Keeley cringes. "Okay. Don't say anything. You know how it is. If people think there's an illness going around, they'll start to imagine they've got symptoms, and we can't afford for that to happen."

Despite not actually being sick, I stare at her deadpan. "Thanks, Keeley. I appreciate your concern."

Keeley giggles as she waves off my remark. "Oh, hush. I've seen you sick before and this is nothing like that. You're fine. But I'd still prefer you were gone. Go home. They're not actually filming today. Just setting up to see what angles work."

"They're in our locker room. What *angles* could they possibly need?" I ask with a frown before smirking at a visual of a camera aimed at my—

"Nope." Keeley laughs, cutting into my thoughts as though she just read my mind. "They're not going to be filming you naked. No one wants to see that."

"*Everyone* wants to see that, but that's not the point."

"It's fine. Go home. We'll be discussing it all before the film review session tomorrow."

"You're the boss." She's not, but I take her misinformed advice anyway, and head home after my shower, instead of hanging around to ask questions.

And with Thomas nowhere in sight since dropping his "Amelia is married" bomb, I need to find him. It's time I paid my sister a visit.

Lainey's arriving home as I pull up to the curb, and when I catch up with her, she's juggling a stack of books in her hands.

"Jesus. Let me take them."

"No, thank you. I'm good. I have to carry these around campus, so I can carry them here." She eyes me suspiciously before stopping and turning to face me. "Why are you here and why are you being nice?"

"I'm always nice."

"That doesn't answer my question."

"Do you know Amelia Rosenberg?" I launch into my question but pause. *Rosenberg*. She was introduced as Amelia Rosenberg. Thomas must be wrong. All that worry for nothing. "Never mind. I'm good."

I spin around to walk away, but Lainey kicks her foot out as if trying to trip me up. "You can't leave after that. The name sounds familiar but I don't know her. Should I?"

"Nope. All good." Amelia and I never hung out at my place, and Lainey's a few years younger so I doubt she'd know her, but I had to ask. *Now, I've changed my mind.* I'm out of here.

"Oh wait. Is she the girl that married Preston Milford?" *Dammit.* "The guy from Chasing Lies? I remember them being Heartwood High's musical claim to fame."

"Never heard of them." That's the truth. I have honestly never heard of Chasing Lies, but Preston I know.

Lainey barks out a laugh. "Of course you've never heard of them. I'll bet you think you're Heartwood's only claim to fame."

"Not true at all," I say. "What about Thomas?"

Lainey's laughter grows more obnoxious and I roll my eyes. "Luke,

Luke, Luke. I wish I had your self-confidence. But back to what's important. Who's Amelia to *you*?"

"She's nothing to me," I argue a little too quickly and Lainey knows it. She stares at me for a beat before lifting her shoulder in a half shrug.

"Mm-hmm."

Dammit, Lainey. I ignore the urge I have to correct her, knowing that's what she wants. Instead I walk ahead toward her door and when she doesn't follow, I turnaround to find her staring me down, her eyebrow perfectly arched.

"Are you coming?" I snap in a way only brothers can without getting a slap in the face. "You can make me a snack."

Lainey doesn't argue, but once we're inside, she dumps the contents for a sandwich in front of me while she makes herself a salad, a smug look on her face. We're mostly silent as we eat, but the second Thomas walks into the kitchen, her sisterly duties kick in.

"What's the connection between Luke and Amelia?" she rushes out before saying hi.

"What?" Thomas's eyes bounce between mine and Lainey's before he laughs to himself. "I don't know, Luke. What's your connection to Amelia?" He raises an eyebrow and I want to deck him.

"I have the same connection as *you*." *Sort of. Not really. But it will do for now as long as Lainey doesn't read too much into that if she finds out I slept with her.* "Amelia went to our school, and now she's working with the team."

"Oooh. So she's your next conquest?"

"Nope." I shake my head while popping the *p*. "I can honestly say that she is not. She's the director of the TV show they're making about the team. That's all. I was curious if you knew her."

"Sure. Okay. That makes sense," Thomas chimes in all nonchalantly, but I sense more coming after he pauses. "Except..." *There it is.* "You freaked out when I said she was married." His face lights up. "And—"

"I thought we were friends," I cut him off. "You're supposed to take that shit up with me before throwing me under the bus."

"You're right." He smirks as though I've just admitted I'm in love with her or something. "Ignore me. We'll talk later." He turns to Lainey and I punch him in the arm. Lightly, of course, because we need that arm if we want to win this year, but hard enough for him to complain.

Lainey lifts herself up onto the counter as Thomas approaches, making herself comfortable as she takes a bite of my sandwich. "You're not talking later." She shakes her head. "This just got interesting, and I'm going to change my earlier question. She's not your next conquest... You've already slept together and now you're worried about some guy that you claim you don't know hunting you down to beat the shit out of you. Am I right?"

Jesus. I wasn't worried about that before. And how the fuck did she so easily come to that conclusion? "You're half right. We did sleep together." Thomas's face drops. "*Before* either of us knew about *Project Storm*," I add for his benefit. He wouldn't be happy about me breaking the team rules. "But," I continue, "I'm not worried about an angry husband. I can take him. I'm pissed off that I didn't know. I'm no home wrecker."

"You're giving yourself too much credit." Lainey laughs at my expense. "Maybe she's allowed to sleep around while he's on tour. They might have some kind of arrangement, and you were merely a pawn in their little game."

"What the fuck?" Thomas and I say at the same time before looking at each other in confusion.

"Okay, so I've just finished reading a book like that. But it's not completely out of the realm of possibility."

"You know I'd never tell you what you can and can't read, Lainey," Thomas says, leaning against the wall, his eyes locked on hers. "As long as you know there will *never* be a third person in our relationship. You are mine and mine alone."

Lainey bites her lip while bile rises in my throat. "Goddammit. You're not fucking newlyweds; keep those moments to yourself."

"You're jealous."

"Nope. I'm appalled."

"Whatever."

Thomas chuckles while Lainey crosses her arms over her chest. She and I may be close, but I don't need intimate details about her relationship with my best friend. It's weird.

"So, back to *my* sex life," I say instead, bringing things back to the topic at hand.

Lainey scoffs, but before she can argue, Thomas cuts in. "What's the issue? So you slept with her. It's not the first time you've had to work closely with someone you've been with. Not to mention you've been trying to score Keeley since she started working with us last year. How is this any different?"

It's different because she played me, and I don't like being played. "You're right, it's not. I'm going to pretend it didn't happen like I do with everyone else. Thanks for the chat."

CHAPTER TEN

AMELIA

Why can't anything in my life run smoothly? It shouldn't be this hard. We've had our six-month cooling-off period. We've spoken about this at length. I just need him to sign the damn papers.

"Are you sure you don't want anyone to come with you?" Hayley asks from her comfortable position on my bed, in my tiny apartment, her face racked with concern as she watches me pull my hair into a messy bun.

"Anyone? Yes. You? No."

"What?" She sits up suddenly, her features morphing into an expression of mock horror. "What did I do?"

"It's not what you did that's the issue. It's what you want to do."

"Amelia," she whines, getting off the bed to stand by my side. "Please, please let me come. I just want to talk to him."

"With your fist?"

"*No.* I'm not that violent. A little slap maybe. But you can't say he doesn't deserve it. Did you forget I heard his voicemail?" *How could I have forgotten?* I've never witnessed her so angry on my behalf. "You know the one that went something like 'my pompous ass needs you to sign your brain and creativity over to me so that I can pass your ideas off as my own to finally stop feeling like the talentless hack that I am.'"

"I remember it. Only I remember it a little differently." I laugh at her antics. "And I take offense to you saying he's talentless. His angsty songs are amazing. But he keeps releasing pop stuff that's on trend."

"Just telling it like I see it."

She has a point. The stuff he's been releasing hasn't been great. But the message didn't exactly go as she described even if it was the same sentiment. Basically he said he'd sign the divorce papers with no pushback if I gave him my notes on all the ideas I had for his band's music videos, citing that since the ideas stem from the songs he wrote, he's entitled to them. He doesn't think I should be able to use them for any other purpose. It's an absolute joke, and while I have no intention of handing anything over, I agreed to meet him on the off chance that I could convince him to have a proper conversation. To stop and think about all that we've been through together and figure out a way to move forward without the hate he seems to have.

Hayley thinks I'm crazy. And maybe I am. But fuck if I'm going to let him get away with the bullshit attitude he's got at the moment. He's not the Preston I knew at all, and I want to get to the bottom of it. Not to mention, if we don't submit his divorce papers in the next few days, it's going to delay the process.

"I'm not trying to defend him, Hayley." She stares at me with her beautifully shaped eyebrows raised high on her forehead, calling me on my bullshit. "Okay, maybe I'm defending him a little, but if I don't, I feel stupid. If you truly believe he's such an awful guy, you must think I'm weak for marrying him."

God, where did that come from? My eyes well with tears, but I wipe them away as Hayley pulls me into a hug.

"No. God, no. I don't know him beyond what you told me after the breakup. And since then, he's been treating you like shit. My ex cheated on me back in Sydney. A few weeks before we came here. I knew he'd done it and I turned a blind eye so that he'd still take me with him. I was hoping the premieres or gossip magazines would get me noticed. I'm not telling you this because I think Preston treated you badly and you ignored it; I'm telling you this so that you know I have no right to judge anyone for their decisions and I never would."

"Oh, Hayley." I stand back and frown.

"No." She shakes her head and squeezes my arm. "I'm fine. But you... You're an amazing woman. And you definitely have a good head on your shoulders. You're driven and smart and strong. I have no doubt that you would have kicked Preston to the curb years ago if he wasn't good to you. I hate him for the way he's treating you *now*. Nothing about you or your past could make me think any less than the world of you. And I'm truly hoping you feel the same."

My eyes water for an entirely new reason before I squeeze Hayley in another hug. "I do. I feel the same. You're definitely stuck with me."

It's strange to think that my closest friend is someone I've only known for a year. I could have easily spiraled after my breakup, but Hayley kept me afloat and never once let me doubt myself. She's right... I haven't painted a very good picture of Preston since our breakup and because I was already doubting our relationship when Hayley and I met, I never really spoke fondly of him. But we had years of love. He *was* good to me for the most part. We changed so much. And now it's time we ended things once and for all.

Hayley pulls back, her eyes a little glassy from her own tears. "So I can come with you?" She smiles brightly, making me burst out laughing.

"Absolutely not."

I stand at the threshold, staring at the door of the apartment I once shared with Preston. Preston told me to let myself in, but while my key burns a hole in my pocket, I can't bring myself to use it. I should have given it back when we first broke up, but at the time, the thought never crossed my mind. Now, I'd do anything to be rid of them...him. Except what he's asking.

Preston's quick to answer when I finally knock, opening the door with a hesitant smile. "Amelia, hi," he says, dressed in my favorite pants of his. The pants that reveal a hint of his ankle...the pants I *always* complimented. I doubt it's a coincidence.

Ignoring his obvious attempt to make me feel things, I smile back, keeping my gaze above his waist. "Thanks for agreeing to talk. We should have done this properly in the beginning, instead of all our petty arguments. We're adults. We're better than that."

I hope.

A little part of me prays that since I put out into the universe that it's going to run smoothly, it will. What do they say, project a life you want?

Preston's brows furrow but he smiles through it. "Yes, you're right. We should have. It's good you're here now. Come in." He holds the door open and I pause after stepping inside, a stranger in what was once my sanctuary. I should be able to waltz on through like I own the place. After all, I know where everything is, yet I can't bring myself to take the first step.

"Lead the way," I say to Preston, watching as his nervous furrow deepens.

For fifteen years, this man was my world. Now he looks uncomfortable in my presence. And since I feel it, I can imagine I look the same.

"How are things?" he asks, most likely to fill the uncomfortable silence as we walk. "How's the new job going? Have you started any projects yet?"

"I have and it's going really well, but it's different to what I pictured myself doing."

"Are you allowed to talk about it?"

"Not yet. The plan is to announce it in January."

"That's great. I'll have to keep an eye out. Your mom said it was something like Bright Lights Productions?"

Goddammit, Mom. I really need to talk to her—again—about keeping my business to herself, or at least, keeping my business away from my ex and the man who used to be my father.

"Close enough." I smile.

We spend the next few minutes catching up on life. Preston tells me about his bandmates since I was quite close to them at one point, and I fill him in on my mom, though it doesn't take long to figure out that's pointless since he knows most of what I tell him. If our stilted small talk proves anything, it's that I never really had my own life before leaving Preston. I have no friends I can tell him about—he never got to know Hayley—and other than my new job, I have nothing else to say. It's like I'm two different people. The woman I was *with* Preston versus the woman I am *without*. And I much prefer the latter.

When our conversation dries up, I get to the point of why I'm here. "We should talk about the divorce."

"I told you; I'll agree to anything."

"If I give you my ideas."

"Come on, Ames. You owe me that much. You left and—"

"Stop. I'm not giving you my ideas. That's ridiculous. That's not how the world works. And even if it was, I wouldn't be handing them over."

"Then why are you here?" he snaps, the stress obvious behind his reaction, making me pause.

"What's going on, Preston? That voicemail...that wasn't you."

Preston stares at me for what feels like a lifetime, but just when I think he's going to argue, his entire body deflates.

"I don't know what I'm doing anymore," he whispers, his voice choked with so much emotion that my chest tightens. A sea of memories floods my mind of all the times we supported each other, but I try hard to block them out. Yes, we had our good times, but toward the end, it was all about Preston and his music. What I wanted no longer mattered, and I can't forget that. Not that I have the same feelings for him anymore, but I shouldn't feel anything for him. Even sorry. He did this. He broke us.

"I can't—"

"I'm creatively blocked," he cuts in, speaking louder this time. "And without my muse..."

"Don't. You've written plenty of songs without me."

"But they all suck and you know it. The new label we signed with continues to make changes to our style, and I can't keep up. I can't sing what they want me to sing."

"So don't."

"Come on, Amelia. You know it doesn't work that way. I'm a puppet. Do your cast members get to do what they want? Make their own rules?"

I know one that wishes he could, but in general... "No. They don't. But you must have known the control they had before you signed."

"Someone huge wanted to sign us. As if we could say no."

Ugh. I huff out a slow breath. I know he's right. I love football. Always have. But I never imagined my big break would be directing a football series. Only... *As if I was going to say no.*

"I get it. But that aside, I don't see how my ideas are going to help. Especially if you're not releasing those songs."

"They found us because of your 'Sideways' video. Our producer said it evoked an emotion in him that he hadn't felt from anyone else with a similar style. That it was unique."

"Okay." I speak plainly but inside I'm dying. San Francisco's biggest label signed Preston's band because of my video? That blows my mind. I knew I contributed to their success because that first video got millions of views which led to exposure, but I assumed the label had focused on the numbers. "I still don't—"

"I want to pitch them the ideas *with* the songs. As a package deal."

"What?"

"Think about it. If I sing one of my songs and then pitch the video idea, they might reconsider."

So basically, Hayley was right; he wants to pass my ideas off as his own.

"I can't. I'm sorry. They're my—"

"Please." He drops to his knees as he holds his palms together, begging me. "Please, Amelia. Just this one little thing and I'll sign the papers."

One *little* thing. He's delusional.

"Preston."

Tears well in his eyes, and my guilt sets in as a memory rears its ugly head. *You don't need to worry, Preston, because I'll always be here to help you.* I was so young and so naive when I said the words. But I said them.

"One idea." I finally break, hoping I don't live to regret it. "Tell me one song you want to pitch and I'll send you the idea I have for it." I had ideas for all his songs. I loved all his songs, until he started changing them when he was first signed to an indie label. He started changing them. Him. The indie label loved his early stuff. I get that a bigger label might want to control things, but he should have thought about that before breaking his indie contract.

Preston's eyes widen and a small smile pulls at his lips. Relief fills me until he opens his mouth. "What about three?"

Goddammit. Why can't this be easy? "One is my *only* offer."

"Amelia, you left me. I helped support you financially when you were studying. I was barely making ends meet, but I helped you."

"Did you love me?"

"What?"

"Did you ever actually love me?"

"Of course I did. I still love you. You're the one that left. What kind of a question is that? I wrote love songs about you."

Ugh. I know. But still... "One or nothing."

"Fuuuck. Fine. One. As soon as you send me the notes for 'Wicked Style,' I'll sign the papers."

Damn, he had to go and pick my best idea. An idea I could have used for a short film. "Sign the papers now and I'll send you my notes as soon as I get home."

Preston's teeth clench but he smiles. "Okay. Hand them over."

"I don't have them. You were served."

"Oh, right. I knew that."

He gets up and grabs an envelope from the desk across the room, and as he signs, I feel nothing. No regret but no relief either. I'm empty. And he did that. He made me feel that way. But at least now, I can try to move on. Hell, I can date if I want to. Not that I couldn't before, but it felt wrong.

Preston huffs when he's done, and when he hands over the paperwork —despite being the one that should be submitting them—I slide the documents into the envelope and seal it up, metaphorically closing the door on a huge part of my life. The package feels heavy in my hands, but I'm glad that it's done. I had to get them signed so I could feel whole again. Only, I don't feel any differently than before.

After a few parting words and the promise to send him my notes, Preston awkwardly hugs me goodbye, as if we ended on a good note. Then I leave.

It's done.

I'm divorced. Sort of. At least, I will be once I've filed the papers.

The emptiness remains as I walk to my car, but once inside, the reality of everything hits me at once and I shake uncontrollably, my mind whirring.

It's over. I finally get to start fresh.

But how do I even do that?

CHAPTER ELEVEN

AMELIA

How quick can one get a divorce processed? Because now that I have the signed papers, I'm willing to pay a ridiculous amount for a lawyer to get this done without issue. I need to be free because life just threw me another curveball.

Game two of Storm's pre-season ends with another win, and while the players go off to celebrate, I head back to my office to make notes. We weren't required at the game, but I wanted to get a sense of a game day for the players. I've experienced it from the sidelines, but never behind the scenes. And God, was it interesting, witnessing the way they get into the zone.

I've just sat down to type up my ideas when I realize I left my notebook in the locker room. *Of all the places.* Usually, I make notes directly onto my tablet. But when I'm around the guys in different levels of undress, I'm uncomfortable using a device. It's their private space and we're about to intrude on it with cameras. I don't want them to think I'm getting footage before I'm supposed to.

I check the time and make my way back to the rooms. I should be safe going in now because the guys would have left a while ago. But still, I don't take my chances, calling out as I enter.

"I'm coming in," I practically sing, laughing to myself when I don't get a response.

Once inside, it takes me all of twenty seconds to find my notebook, but when I turn to leave, I startle, finding Luke standing in the doorway.

"Looking for some 'dirty laundry'?" he seethes, catching me off guard. I'm used to his teasing but this is different. Still, I huff out a laugh and roll my eyes, holding up my notebook.

"It's none of your business," I snap back. "But if you must know, I left this behind." I wave the notebook back and forth.

"Right, okay." Luke huffs under his breath, shaking his head before walking over to his locker, seemingly more pissed off than usual. *And I can't let it go.*

"What's your problem this time?" I ask, popping my hip.

"You don't know me, remember?" He throws his comment over his shoulder. "Why do you care?"

"You're right. I don't care. I have no feelings...good, bad, or otherwise. I don't know why I asked." I move to walk past but he turns and stalks toward me, backing me into the lockers on the opposite wall.

"You had *a lot* of feelings when I was fucking you." His hands cage me in as he leans closer, until we're almost nose to nose. "Could I elicit those feelings now? Or do you need permission first?"

Permission? "What?" As I focus on his expression, his hand drops to my waist before sneaking under my top, his fingers setting my skin on fire. My breath hitches, but I hide it behind a cough as I subtly clench my legs. "I told you I'd never let you touch me again and that hasn't changed."

I bend to duck under his arms but he lowers himself until we're eye to eye again, and while he respects my wishes and drops his hand from my body, it doesn't matter. My skin still burns from his touch. There's no denying that he affects me. But it's all physical. My brain will win this time.

"Tell me," Luke asks, his breath warming my skin as he moves closer to whisper in my ear. "Is that something you want? Me not touching you. Or is it something you *vowed* to avoid? Because your reaction says otherwise." He leans back and his eyes drop to my heaving chest, distracting me from his strange words as I bite back a curse. Why is my body reacting to him?

"It doesn't matter," I huff out. "*Nothing* is happening between us again. Now please let me move." My heart races as I wait for him to respond, but it's not out of nerves. It's racing because my traitorous body wants what he's offering, only it doesn't change what we've been through. Or how much he hurt me.

Our one-night stand shouldn't have happened, and I refuse to let it happen again.

I stare at him in defiance until he finally nods. "As you wish." He steps back and turns away, leaving me alone and confused. *What the hell was that?*

My breathing quickens when he walks away, and as I straighten up, I'm dizzy. I try to move but when I do, I lose my footing, falling back against the lockers. "Ouch, dammit." *What is going on?*

Luke freezes by the door before his gaze locks on mine, a hint of concern set in his features. "Are you okay?"

"Yeah." I blink a few times before shaking my head. "I'm fine. I just lost my balance," I lie. I'd rather not talk to him about my personal problems.

"And you say you don't feel anything for me." He raises a challenging eyebrow until I roll my eyes. "Have a goodnight, Amelia." He chuckles. "See you around."

He disappears around the corner, and I sit down the second the door clicks shut, rubbing my head as I blow out a breath and try to make sense of what happened.

Does he want me? Or does he want to rattle me? Either way, why am I letting myself be rattled?

When I'm feeling better, I head to my office to work, and by the end of the day, I'm exhausted. Pair that with my dizzy spell and I'm worse than ever. I should be sleeping better now that Preston's signed the divorce papers. It's only a matter of time before it all goes through. So why am I so tired? It's like some invisible stress is draining the life out of me, and the one thing I can attribute that to is Luke. Having him close is getting to me. But I don't know how I can fix that.

M y knees bounce as I wait for my doctor. I'm no longer convinced that it's stress—there's something wrong. And I need to find out what before it affects my work. More than it already has. I can't afford this time off. Not now that I'm finally getting my chance.

"*Goddammit!*"

"Everything okay, Miss?"

Shit. Where did he come from? "Yes, Of course. Sorry. I was just talking to myself. All is good. Unless you count the reason I'm here and"—the nurse gives me a strange look—"never mind. I'm good. Thank you."

"Great. The doctor will be in soon."

"Thank you. Again." The nurse, whose name I didn't catch, disappears out of the room faster than he came, leaving me anxious again. *What's taking them so long?*

"Okay. Okay. I'm here." Doctor Roland walks in with a smile on her face. "Nice to see you again, Amelia."

"You too." I try to smile back.

She glances down at the file in front of her before looking up in concern. "I saw you a few months ago, so I'm guessing it's not an annual check-up."

"No, it's not. But it is something we've spoken about before."

"I'm listening." She maintains a straight face, but I know she's going to judge me.

"As we've discussed, I don't sleep well when I'm stressed and..."

"Yes."

"This is different. Some afternoons I struggle to keep my eyes open, and this time around I've been getting dizzy spells too."

Dr. Roland frowns a little as she flicks through some paperwork. "Has this been happening since our last visit, or more recently?"

"More recently. Last few weeks maybe. Right about the time I started my new job."

"Okay. Let me check the symptoms of the contraceptive we've got you on so we can rule that out. You're still taking it, right?"

"I am." Not that I have a sex life, but I take it like clockwork.

My legs bounce again as she types away at her computer, and I try to remember if my pill has ever affected me before, but I'd been off it for so long, I can't remember.

"Your pill doesn't explicitly list fatigue or dizziness, but that doesn't mean it's not the cause. How about we run a few tests, and if we can't find another reason, we can try swapping to a different option."

"Perfect." I sigh in relief. "That would be great."

I hadn't considered the pill being the issue. If that's all it is, I'll be laughing.

⚽ ⚽ ⚽

"You're pregnant," Dr Roland says as I stare at her wide-eyed. I heard her the first time but it's taking me a second to process it. I blink a few times with the words rolling around in my head, my expression undoubtedly marred with confusion.

"Sorry, what?" That can't be right.

"You're pregnant," she repeats for the third time, her lips pulled into a smile though I can tell she's holding back, waiting for my reaction.

"I can't be pregnant." I shake my head. *This is crazy.* "I'm on the pill." We just discussed that. "I…"

"You've only been on the pill for a few months. You likely got pregnant before you started."

Shit.

"I've…ahh…" My face scrunches as I admit the truth. "It's not possible. I was already taking the pill when I…" God, this is embarrassing. "I've only had sex once in the last six months, and it was after—" *Oh God. No. No. No. No. No.* The blood drains from my face.

"Amelia, are you okay?"

"No." My breath quickens and a fresh wave of dizziness takes over me, my fingers biting into the armrest of the chair as I fight to calm myself.

"Pregnancy doesn't have to be scary."

My gaze lifts to hers as I process what she's saying, what she's telling me. "I'm *pregnant.*" I'm pregnant with *Luke's* baby. "But how?"

"How long had you been taking the pill when you had sexual intercourse?"

"A week? Maybe two? I— Oh God." Realization hits me and I feel nauseous. "I… I… Is it bad? Have I hurt it? The baby. I didn't know." I suck in a deep breath, but it's pointless. I can't get any air. "I…I would have stopped taking it if I'd known. But I purposely kept taking it to skip my period so I had no idea and—"

Dr. Roland steps forward and tentatively squeezes my arm, cutting me off. "You haven't done anything wrong, Amelia. It's okay. The pill isn't always as effective in that first month and can also be affected if you don't take it at the same time every day or skip a day."

God, I can't remember. *Did I skip a day?* I guess it no longer matters how. It's happened.

"As for any distress you have for your baby... You should book an ultrasound to make sure the baby is healthy and happy, but there are generally no risks associated with taking the pill during pregnancy. It's not recommended, but it shouldn't be a cause for concern."

"Thank fuck." *Oh Jesus.* "I'm sorry. *Shit.* Ohh... I'm sorry again."

Dr. Roland laughs. "I've heard worse in my lifetime."

"Still, I'm sorry. What about eating and drinking? I haven't been careful with my food choices. I've had sushi. And while I'm not a huge drinker, I have been drinking."

"If the ultrasound comes back clear then none of those things are a concern. Just keep them in mind moving forward."

"Of course. What do I do next?"

"Going by your last mentioned period, I'd estimate you're about thirteen weeks along, but we won't know for sure until you've had an ultrasound." *Thirteen weeks? How the hell didn't I notice that?* "Here's a list of places we recommend." Dr Roland continues speaking, completely unaware of my internal freak-out, and I work hard to pay attention. "You should call as soon as possible as it can be hard to get appointments even if you're past the twelve weeks. But rest assured, there's no cause for alarm at this stage. While you wait, I suggest you look after yourself, rest, and drink plenty of water."

"Yes, definitely. I will." *Somehow...* around my fast-paced, always on my feet, demanding job.

I stand to leave, smiling despite being a little spaced-out.

"And Amelia?" Dr. Roland waves to get my attention, hitting me with her warm smile when I finally glance her way. "Congratulations."

Congratulations? "Thank you." *I'm having a baby.*

What the hell am I going to do?

Hayley's quick to her feet when I enter the waiting area, and I'm grateful she forced me to let her come. As I walk, she stares at my face, analyzing my expression, and her own face drops. "Fuck! What's wrong?"

"Can we talk when we get outside?"

"Okay, but you're freaking me out."

"Good, that makes two of us."

I pay for my appointment and rush out the door, making it two steps before turning around to panic. "I'm pregnant, Hayley," I blurt, almost knocking into her as she steps out the door. "I'm tired. I'm dizzy. I don't feel like myself. And yet that thought never crossed my mind. I can't be pregnant. I don't have time to be pregnant." My body shakes as reality sets in. *What am I going to do? What—*

Hayley grabs my shoulders to still me, before moving me away from the oncoming foot traffic. Despite standing in front of a busy medical center and pharmacy, I hadn't noticed a single person walk by.

"I thought you were on the pill?" she asks, never one to beat around the bush.

"I was. I *am*. But I'd only been taking it for a week or so when I..." I wave my hand as though that will explain what I mean, and when Hayley nods, I continue. "In short, it wasn't as effective as usual."

"*Bloody hell.*"

"*That* is an understatement." I start walking again, needing to move as my head swarms with questions.

"Don't hit me for asking, but didn't you wonder why you weren't getting your period?"

I shake my head as she moves into step beside me. "Nope, I was skipping them on purpose. They say it's a fake period when you're on the pill anyway."

"Shit. I do the same thing. How are you feeling about it all?" Hayley hesitates. "You just had the divorce papers signed and—"

"What's that got to do with anything?" I brush off her question. That's the last thing I need to be thinking about right now.

"I'm...ah...I guess I'm getting in early to say you don't need to go back to that asshole. We can work this out. I'll be there for you."

"What asshole?"

"Preston."

I come to a halt, and someone behind me curses when they almost bump into me, not that I care. I'm more focused on Hayley. "You think it's Preston's?"

"You don't?"

"No. I haven't slept with him for almost a year. It has to be Luke's."

"You didn't sleep with him that night you went over to collect the last of your things?"

"No. God, no. I would have told you that."

"*Shit*. But how can it be Luke's? Weren't you already on the pill by then?"

I cringe and turn away. "I didn't take it the first month I got it. I started a week or so before sleeping with Luke. And the condom broke."

"*Fuck.*"

"Yep."

"But also...maybe fate intervened. I mean how often does a condom break at the same time someone messes up their pill?"

"What?" *Is she serious?*

Hayley grimaces before shaking her head. "Never mind. We've got this." She clasps my hand as we begin walking again, giving it a squeeze. "What happens next?"

"Next..." I let out a long sigh.

I wish I knew. For years I tried hard not to get pregnant. Preston and I first had sex when we were seventeen. And while we didn't have sex often, I'd still panic every month, worried we'd somehow mess up. Then after we got married and while my career was stalled, the idea of getting pregnant lost the fear it once had. I got excited by the idea. Preston got excited by the idea, and we started trying. Or at least, letting it come naturally if it happened. Our sex life never changed, but we both knew there was a possibility of it becoming something.

Though, after a year, it still hadn't happened.

How can I have been having regular sex with someone, with my husband, and never have so much as a late period? But after one night with Luke... everything changes.

A pit forms in my stomach until I make the decision to look at this in a practical sense. To keep emotions out of it for now. "Next..." I say, my eyes meeting Hayley's. "Next, I have to arrange an ultrasound, then I have to sort out my life and try not to let this affect the Storm project."

"Sounds easy enough," Hayley lies, making me smile.

"Oh...and I have to tell Luke." *Smile gone.*

CHAPTER TWELVE

AMELIA

How do you tell a guy who only does one-night stands that he's going to be a dad? And more to the point, how do you deal with said guy being that dad when you want nothing to do with him. What did I do?

Three days after my life-changing appointment, I'm in my car in the stadium parking lot, feeling nauseous and staring at Luke like a stalker. I'm watching him go about his day while I sit here with a baby growing inside me and the power to change his world.

I work hard, trying to break my stare, but when his loud laugh filters through the air, it hits me in the chest. *I'm having a baby with Luke.*

My heart picks up speed and I find myself studying his every expression as he speaks, picturing a little boy with the same striking features, wondering if he'll be a little heartbreaker like his dad or go his own way, praying like hell that he's nothing like my own father.

A sharp pang settles in my stomach, and for a second I panic, until I remember it's the same feeling I get whenever I dwell on my dad abandoning us. His lies. For years, I blamed myself, thinking I wasn't good enough for him. And then Luke... my nausea intensifies and despite that being one of the symptoms of pregnancy, I know it's not that. I'm nauseous because my emotions are wreaking havoc on my stomach. I'm nervous to talk to Luke, anxious about my future, terrified of how my bosses will react, and annoyed that I'm giving Jake all the ammunition he needs to say, "I told you so." This industry is hard enough to crack, but at the same time... *I'm having a baby*. I need to get my shit together.

My eyes water but I smile through it. No matter what happens, at the end of this I'm going to have a baby. A baby. My world is about to change and that's a good thing. No matter how scary.

The vibration of my phone cuts into my thoughts as Luke walks inside, severing my trance. I take a deep breath before moving to answer, but when my gaze drops to the device locked in my hand, I freeze. *Damien*. My absent father. As though his ears were burning from my thoughts.

I stare down at his moniker while an image of his smile works its way to the forefront of my mind, the same smile I find staring back at me every time I look in the mirror. I may have my Mom's thick, wavy brown hair and small frame, but I've got my dad's coloring and facial features.

I used to think I was lucky. I had the greatest father. While my mom and I always fought, my dad was my hero. Right up until my elementary school graduation, when I learned the truth.

On what was supposed to be a happy day, I lost the two most important males in my life.

Luke being the second one.

My eyes water again and I swallow back the emotion. I've spent too many hours crying over that period of my life, and I've moved on.

And since the sight of his name makes me anxious, I'm seriously considering not telling my mom about the baby, knowing she'll likely run to tell Dad. The last thing I need is for my dad to try and worm his way back into my life, hoping for a second chance at being present.

I deserve better, and there's no way in hell I'd put my kid through that.

After canceling the call, I throw my phone onto the passenger seat before banging my head against the backrest and giving myself a pep talk. *It's time to focus, it's time to be professional, and it's time to get the hell out of the car.*

Taking another deep breath, I grab my things and throw open the door, not allowing myself a second longer to wallow. Having a baby is a *good* thing and it far outweighs the *bad*. I need to get over it. Wiping the tears from my eyes, I straighten out my dress and stand tall just as one of the players, Reed, steps into what I thought was my private bubble, making me jump.

"Are you okay?" he asks, his brows furrowed as he watches me.

I glance away, subtly wiping a hand over my face to clear up any stray tears. When I turn back to face him, I smile at his concerned expression. "Yes, thank you. I'm just tired."

"I saw you wiping your eyes."

Of course he did. "I promise. I'm fine. I was just thinking about something I read last night. A sad story. You don't need the details." I'm only half lying in this scenario—I did read a sad story about a couple who'd been together all their lives and died within a day of each other—but I wasn't thinking about that just now.

Reed eyes me suspiciously. From his interview and from talking with his teammates, I've come to learn that Reed is the caring guy on the team. The media even nicknamed him the Golden Boy. He's the guy that never puts a foot wrong and will protect his teammates at all costs. On and off the field.

And something about his expression tells me he just added me to his list. *God knows why.*

"Are you sure?" he pushes as if proving my point. "You were staring at your phone before you threw it on the seat. I'm going to go out on a limb and say it wasn't the phone that did you wrong." *God, how long was he watching me?*

"Wow. What made you choose football over investigative journalism?" The verbal dig is out in the world before I've thought it through, and I rush to cover my mouth, my eyes wide. "I'm sorry," I mumble behind my hand. "That was uncalled for. I do that when I'm stressed."

Reed stares at me for a second before he bursts out laughing. "I did it for the ladies. Football players get the girls. Whereas those journalists..."

"Not so much." I drop my hand, more at ease despite the fact that he's lying for my sake. He doesn't want the girls. Plural. He wants *one.* He's in love with his best friend. It was obvious from the way he spoke of her. But then his teammate Wyatt confirmed it.

"Not even close." Reed waggles his eyebrows and I join his laughter. "Are you heading inside?" he adds, pointing over his shoulder to the door Luke previously entered, making my heart clench.

"I am." *Unfortunately.*

"Okay, I'll walk you in. Maybe I can turn that frown upside down."

At that my chest heats and a warm smile spreads across my face. "You don't have to," I say honestly, waving a hand in front of my face. "Mission accomplished."

Now I just need to keep up the charade until I get the chance to talk to Luke. Easy-peasy. Right?

An hour later, some of the guys are on the field ahead of their next preseason game, while I'm on the sidelines making notes and taking photos, pretending I'm not anxious as hell.

I may be two pages in, but I have no idea what I've been writing because all I can think about is getting through this day so I can finally get this secret off my chest.

I exit out of my notes screen, ready to give in, when a to-do item pops up, reminding me I have to send Preston my music video idea. *Yay! Ugh.* If I don't do it soon he's likely to chase me, and I'd rather avoid future contact, especially now that I have more important things to contemplate... like being a mom.

After putting my tablet and camera away, I dig around my bag to find my ideas notebook and flip through the pages, looking for the specific song, as a wave of nostalgia hits me. Along with my journals, this book has been my biggest confidant since I was in high school—which means some of the ideas are hilarious. You could say not all my work stood the test of time. But when I come to the "Wicked Style" notes, I hold my breath as my heart races. I love this idea. But just like Preston himself, I need to forget it. After taking a photo with my phone, I rip the page from my book and shove it aggressively into my bag.

Am I giving in? Maybe. But I can't look at it like that. I'm doing this to cut Preston from my life, and in the long run, that's more important than a single idea.

A figure walks in front of me as I'm typing out my message and when I glance up, I spot Luke talking to the offensive line coach, laughing at something he says, once again making me picture a little boy or girl laughing the same, their little faces lit up in happiness.

My heart skips until Luke catches me staring, his smile replaced with a glare.

What the hell was I thinking?

Of all the people I could have slept with... Hell, a stranger would have been better. At least then we'd be starting with a clean slate. How can I share custody with Luke—if he even wants that—while the two of us hold so much anger toward each other. That's no way to bring a child into the world.

We need a truce. A ceasefire. An agreement. Something to ensure we're civil when it comes to our child. Our baby comes first.

No matter what.

I resist the urge to caress my belly and grab my tablet again to distract myself as Keeley drops into the seat beside me.

"Hi," I rush out with a smile, trying to appear put together when I'm very much not. "How are you?"

"I'm good. Sorry, am I interrupting? I wanted to talk about the schedule, but if you're busy..." She trails off, glancing down at my notes.

"No, you're fine." I shake my head and tuck a strand of loose hair behind my ear. "I was a little over note taking anyway."

"I understand that." Keeley giggles. "The guys are much more interesting in the locker rooms." She waggles her eyebrows, making me laugh as I raise a brow in question.

"God, I didn't mean it like that." She grimaces comically. "I'm clearly overworked and not thinking about my word choices. I'm in desperate need of a tropical vacation and a good lay if I'm honest. I need to relieve some built-up tension." I smile when she whispers the word "lay." It's not the word I would have used, but I like it. "You don't know anyone, do you?" she asks, anticipation set in her features. "I don't have the time to meet someone new."

"I wish I did," I say genuinely. Keeley's lovely; I'd definitely help her if I could. But what do I know about decent guys? "I'm guessing you don't want to go down the football player path?" I joke. Things could get awkward if she did.

Keeley scrunches her nose, giving me her answer before she speaks. "That's too close to home. Plus, one of the guys is my brother. We just don't publicize it."

"What?" I huff out a laugh. Not one person has let that slip.

"Oh, please don't mention that in the show."

I pretend to lock my mouth and throw away the key. "Your secret is safe with me. But can I know who it is?"

Keeley taps her fingers together as she lets out a giggle. "How about you guess? That would be more fun."

"Oooh. Okay. Let me think." I rub my chin as I study her features. She usually wears her long auburn hair straight, but today it's pulled up into a messy bun and I can tell that it's naturally curly. She has bronzed skin which makes me think she's Californian, and she has bright blue eyes, though that doesn't help considering I haven't paid enough attention to any of the players' eye colors. Except for Luke's. His deep piercing eyes always get me. It's been that way since we were kids. But I digress. *Dammit.*

I lift in my seat, pushing all thoughts of Luke out of my mind, and try to subtly scan the players on the field. My gaze finds Blake from special teams, his curly locks drawing my attention as they jut out from beneath his helmet.

"Blake?" I blurt in a rushed whisper but know I'm wrong when Keeley laughs. "Okay, what about..." I spot Nathan, remembering he's one of the few guys I don't know that also grew up in the Golden State. "Nathan! It's Nathan, isn't it?" Keeley doesn't share many resembling features with any of the guys on the team, so these guesses are baseless, but it's worth a shot.

She shakes her head, biting back a grin.

"Dammit. Okay. Wyatt, Dylan, Lawson, Miller."

"Nope. Nope. Nope, still wrong." Her smile lights up. She's loving this.

"Ugh." I pout. "I'll get there. So... your brother's the reason you avoid the team?"

"That and I've been burned by athletes before."

"Haven't we all?" A sigh escapes my lips before I can stop it and it draws Keeley's attention.

"Ooh...it sounds like there's a story there. I didn't mean to bring it up."

"No, no. It's okay. Mine's a little different. He was a friend. One of those situations where he became too cool for me."

"*Ugh*, that sucks. I hate those people." She squeezes my arm, giving me a sympathetic smile, and guilt hits over my white lie. Luke definitely changed when he started playing on a new football team, but he wasn't the one that walked out on our friendship. That was all me. He just led me to make that decision.

Keeley tells me about her experience with athletes, plural—they are definitely her type—and we pass the time chatting, not once discussing the schedule like we were supposed to.

I can understand why she wants to avoid football players. She mentioned they're the guys that hurt her the most, but if athletes are her thing, there are plenty of others out there. Hockey players for one. I wouldn't say no to Jesse Hastings or—*Oh God*, I can't think like that anymore. I'm going to be a mom.

"Are you okay?" Keeley asks, her voice dropping to a whisper again as she frowns. "You're a little pale."

"I'm okay. You just made me think of my own life and I fell into a hole. But I'm good now." It's going to take some time to really process the fact that I'm pregnant. I haven't seen the baby or heard a heartbeat. So, while it feels real, it also doesn't. "My story is long and for another time," I add, already comfortable enough to one day talk about it.

"It's a date." She laughs. "For now...it looks like they're done."

I lift my gaze as the guys jog off the field toward the tunnel, and my stomach knots knowing what I have to do. But while I have an urgent need to get this secret off my chest, now's not the time to talk to Luke. I know better than to throw a man off his game. No matter how much I dislike him, I'd never do that. No, it will have to wait.

But when did I go from hating Luke to merely disliking him?

Being the father of my child doesn't automatically give him bonus points. All he did was treat me to mind-blowing sex—that I still dream about daily—and break the damn condom. It's not— *The condom? We* broke it. Not me, *we*. There's a silver lining here. At least Luke can't throw the blame completely my way. If he gets mad, I can remind him of that tiny yet important piece of information.

But what if he doesn't get mad?

What if he ghosts me and refuses to acknowledge his child? Or worse, what if he has a family one day and our child gets left out, abandoned when they're old enough to understand what that means?

What if... *Jesus, I'm spiraling.*

I need to get this talk over with or God knows what kind of scenarios I'm going to conjure up.

As soon as the game is over, I have to talk to Luke. Let's hope the team wins. I need him in a good mood.

CHAPTER THIRTEEN

LUKE

We're celebrating another win as we exit the locker rooms, ready for a big night out. Preseason is almost done, and as suspected, we are killing it. The confidence I have leading into the regular season should be illegal. But fuck, am I certain this is our year.

"See you there." Reed waves over his shoulder as he beelines to the left while I head right, and I've just reached my truck when I remember Keeley asked to see me. *Dammit.*

Spinning around to rush back inside, I almost crash into Amelia where she stands behind me.

"Jesus." I grab her shoulders to still her before dropping them quickly and stepping back. "What are you doing?"

"Can we talk?" she asks, barely reacting to me almost knocking into her, making my body tense, automatically going into fight mode. *What did I do this time?*

"I'm supposed to be meeting—"

"Please," she rasps, making me pause.

"Okay, I have a minute." I've barely spoken a word to her since finding out she has a husband—information I easily confirmed with the trusty Internet. They've been married for years. I saw a grainy clip of them on stage after he proposed at a music festival. The caption read "If this isn't the most romantic proposal ever!!!!" Four exclamation marks. *Four!*

Amelia steps closer while my thoughts run rampant, and her eyes are wide like a deer. "Somewhere private."

Ouch. Now I know I definitely did something wrong. But fuck if I know what. It could be anything. I sneeze and this woman hates me for it.

"Private as in one of the meeting rooms here at the stadium, or..."

"Not here." She shakes her head.

Jesus. "Okay, what about my place? It's not too far from here. But I have to chat with Keeley for a minute first." Amelia's eyes widen before she glances around, probably checking if someone overheard me. "I promise to be discreet, if that's what you're worried about. I'll give you my address and we can meet there."

"Oh, it's not that... your place is great. Let me give you my number so you can text me the details."

After putting her number into my phone, she walks away without another word, and my eyes follow her until she gets to her car. The second she's out of sight it hits me. Someone found out about the fire. That has to be it, because what else could it be?

When I pull up at my house, Amelia's sitting on my top step with her knees pulled up to her chest, waiting for me, her arms wrapped protectively around herself. A tightness works its way into my chest. Whatever she wants to talk about is worse than I thought. And after working myself up on the drive over, I can't wait any longer.

I rush past her, making her jump as I open the door.

"Come on in. Let's get this over with," I say as she stands, and I motion for her to walk in ahead of me.

Amelia gulps but nods as she heads inside, and I note that her outfit is back to the casual style I'm used to. Effortless. Easy. Something you wear when you've got more pressing things on your mind. Kind of like when I throw on a hoodie or sweats. Although I've been told I still look hot dressed like that. It's a blessing.

I lead Amelia into the living room and sit while she remains standing. A beat passes before she starts pacing the floor, wearing a hole in my ridiculously expensive rug.

"Can you quit it?" I say, my eyes locked on the soft wool as she destroys it with her shoes. "Just tell me. So they found out about the fire. Big deal. You said you wouldn't use it, so I don't know why we need to talk about it.

You're not using it, right?" A trace of panic hits me but I ignore it when Amelia's eyes flash my way.

"What?" She stops pacing, staring at me as though I have two heads, her expression confused.

"Did you hear anything I said?"

"Honestly, no. But I can say with absolute certainty your whining is misguided."

"Oh, yeah?" I cross my arms over my chest as I sit back. "Then if it's not the fire, what is it?"

"The fire? Ugh." She rolls her eyes. "You're so far off base—"

"Spit. It. Out."

"I'm pregnant," she blurts...or maybe she spits just like I asked; I'm not close enough to tell. Either way I laugh somewhat inappropriately.

"Congratulations. Do you want me to force the team to cut you some slack or—"

"It's yours."

What? At that I laugh harder. Though I have no fucking clue why.

"Are you serious, Luke? You're laughing."

My phone lights up with a text but I ignore it. "Are you serious?" I counter with a scoff. "Or is this some kind of fucked-up joke or gold-digging situation?"

"Excuse me?" Amelia laughs this time but it's a little sadistic. "Do you honestly think I'd lie about that? I'd rather choose literally *anyone* else to be my baby's father. No matter how rich or poor they were."

She's offended but since it couldn't possibly cause more of a rift between us, I shrug. That ship sailed right under a bridge. May as well burn that fucker to the ground too. "What about your husband? Or do you sleep around because you're not fucking him?"

"What the hell, Luke?" Her fists clench at her sides and her gaze hardens. If I thought her glare was solid in the past, this one is five stars. But she lied to me. How do I know she's not lying now?

"Are you or are you not married?"

"I'm not..." She trails off as her shoulders drop and she lets out a long sigh. "I'm married." *Ding ding ding, correct answer.* "Technically," she adds. "But I've filed the paperwork for our divorce. We've been separated for over a year."

"Yeah, okay." I roll my eyes. "Then why is he still referring to you as his wife?" My teeth clench as I say the word "wife" and I curse myself for showing her that this is getting to me when it shouldn't be. I shouldn't care.

Amelia sighs again. "Until last week, Preston refused to sign the papers. He's all about the publicity these days, and maybe he thinks a divorce will be bad for his music. Especially since his latest hit is an upbeat love song. Either way, his decisions are his decisions, and he stopped caring about how that would affect me years ago."

Shit. My trusty Internet is not so trusty. I'm a dick. No wonder she hates me. And what the fuck, Preston?

"I'm sorry. I'm an asshole." I shrug. It's not an excuse, but we both know it's true.

"You really are," she seethes before throwing her head back and silently cursing the heavens. "But honestly, you being an asshole was never in question." My eyes flash to hers to catch her raising a brow in challenge, making me huff out a laugh.

"Nope. And since you already know that about me, I have to ask... Are you sure the baby is mine?"

Amelia closes her eyes before taking a deep breath and opening them again, pinning me with an expression that says, "you're a dick." And maybe I am, but I had to ask.

"Yes. I'm one hundred percent sure. Happy now?"

"Not exactly." This is not how I expected the rest of my day to go.

"I know it's a lot."

"You think?"

"Jesus, Luke. Would you shut up for a second? God, I was prepared for all kinds of negative responses but this is so hard."

My eyes fall to her stomach as she steps closer to say more, but I cut her off despite her telling me not to.

"I'm...gonna be a dad?"

She pauses, an argument ready to launch, before she huffs out a breath. "Yeah," she breathes out, the idea clearly not thrilling her. "Unlike you," she continues, using the "you" as a little slap to the face, "I don't fuck around, meaning I know with certainty that it's yours."

"Ouch." I fake a cringe though her words don't hurt me. I'm not ashamed of that part of my life.

"Don't act like you didn't deserve that," Amelia snaps, misinterpreting my response.

"You're right. I was an ass so you're being a brat. I get it. But now that's out of the way, apologies in advance for this."

"For what?"

I jump up and stalk out of the room before screaming at the top of my lungs. "Fuck. Fuck. Motherfucking. Fuck. Fuck."

I'm so loud, Shadow starts aggressively pawing at the back door, determined to break the glass so she can come to my rescue. I'd find it adorable if I wasn't numb. *I'm having a kid. I'm going to be a dad. To Amelia's baby.*

Holy shit.

I poke my head back into the room to find Amelia staring in my direction, a look of horror on her face. "I'm going to need a moment to process this." I gesture between the two of us and put on a fake smile. "But please stay. I won't be long."

Amelia nods but I don't wait for her to speak, turning away as she rushes out, "Okay."

How the hell is this happening?

Chapter Fourteen

AMELIA

I try to sit still while Luke's gone, but it's impossible with all the thoughts and feelings running through me. That could have gone better, but it also could have gone worse. I think. I'm a little confused. I was not expecting him to mention Preston, and I was not at all prepared when he did. Luke and I may not have been friends for years, but the hatred in his tone was something else entirely.

He was hurt.

He didn't like the thought that I'd deceived him somehow, and God, if that isn't hypocrisy.

Should I have told him to grow the fuck up and find me when he had calmed down? *Probably*. But I made a promise to put our child first and that's what I'm doing. I'm staying so we can have an adult conversation. I learned my lesson after Preston.

Maybe Luke and I should have talked about all our issues way back when, but what's done is done. Our baby is the only thing we need to discuss today, and I'm not leaving until he tells me to go.

Five minutes go past. Then ten and fifteen. And I'm just about to call out when Luke waltzes in, seemingly without a care in the world.

"Okay, I'm back," he announces. "So what happens now?"

What? I stare at him, my brows dipped in confusion. *That's it?* He disappears after screaming fuck multiple times and comes back all cool, calm, and collected.

"What happens now? What does that mean?"

Luke raises an eyebrow, suggesting I'm the one acting weird. "I thought that was obvious. You're pregnant. It's my baby. So, what's next?"

Huh? I blink a few times. I was ready for a range of emotions and reactions, but this wasn't on my bingo card. "I...ah...I have an appointment next week for an ultrasound. The first one. And that's when we'll know more specific details like size and due date."

"Good, good," Luke says calmly. "Text me the details and I'll be there. Do you have a specific doctor you'll be seeing? Do you know what hospital you're going to? Some have private suites, right? We'll definitely want one of those."

"Luke—"

"I'll chat with Dylan. I'll bet he and Summer had a private suite—"

"Luke, stop. Please." I stand and take a step toward him, but he moves around me and walks closer to the armchair in the corner of the room. Not that he sits. He just hovers. "My insurance doesn't cover any of that," I continue, wishing more than anything that wasn't the case.

"That's fine." Luke waves me off. "Mine does."

He starts to pace, but when I tell him it doesn't work that way, he spins around in shock.

"Why the hell not? It's my baby."

"Yes, but until the baby is born, it's based on my insurance."

Luke shakes his head like that piece of information is meaningless. "Okay. So, you need better insurance."

"We all need better insurance." I huff out a laugh. *Isn't that a dream?*

"I don't," he gloats. "My insurance is amazing."

I put on a smile, hoping it will stop me from showing him how I really feel. "We're not all star football players," I grate.

"No, you're not. But lucky for *you*, I am." He finally sits down before pulling his phone from his pocket. "How much does it cost to upgrade you? Or can I just pay for everything without insurance?"

"What?" *Did he really just say that?* "Are you out of your goddamn mind?"

"Too much? Fine. Call your insurance company and let me know the additional cost to upgrade. I'll send you the money. Our baby deserves the best."

I stare his way, and if I wasn't working so hard to maintain my composure, I have no doubt my jaw would have dropped. "Who are you?"

"What does that mean?" He has the nerve to be offended.

"Barely thirty minutes ago you thought I was a gold-digging whore and now you're throwing money at me?"

"I never said that."

"You kind of did."

"I never used the word whore."

I raise an eyebrow and frown. "It was implied."

"Okay. I was in shock. You caught me off guard. You had me worked up thinking I was a side piece and—"

"You what?" A side piece? I burst out laughing. I bruised his ego. *I knew it!* But now is not the time to celebrate that win.

"Never mind," Luke continues. "Point is, I said the wrong thing. It's not the first time someone has tried to convince me I'm a dad, but I never expected it from you."

"Ugh." I cringe at the thought of that. Picturing all the little Lukes out in the world. *Once again... of all the people I could have slept with.* "I didn't need to know that, but does our baby have any siblings?"

Luke chuckles, though my question is no joking matter. "Not that I'm aware of. They were all faking it."

"Why don't I trust that answer?"

"You're going to have to." Luke shrugs. "It's the only answer I've got. So back to the insurance..."

I let out a sigh before running my hands down my face. "I appreciate the thought, but you can't just pay to upgrade it."

"Let me look into it."

"Sure. But you won't—"

"Let me try."

I reluctantly agree despite it being a lost cause. I already considered it. I've scoured the Internet, checked out all the possibilities. I even looked into quick money making opportunities. Bank loans. Switching insurance companies. Everything. But at the end of the day, none of it mattered because no one would upgrade my pregnancy coverage until after a twelve-month waiting period and that was a few months too late. Yes, I found some that were closer to ninety days, but the coverage wasn't much better than what I had. For what Luke's proposing, I'd have to wait.

We fall silent again, but while he's not saying anything, I can sense his mind whirling. And I get it. It's a lot for him to take in without processing time. He deserves time to think, but I have to give him some credit for how he's taking it.

"I should go," I say, giving him his time. "It's been a long week. I'm tired and I'm sure you could use a moment."

Luke stares at me, unmoving, and a panic sets in. *Is this what a Luke Bennett breakdown looks like?*

"Luke, are you okay?"

"Far from it," he rasps before shaking his head. And the next time he looks at me, the confident Luke is back. "None of this is about me...or you. It's about the baby. All you need to know is that I'll be there for it. I want to help. Just let me know what you need."

I nod as I rush out a thanks with no idea what else I can say to that. In fact, I have no idea what to say about any of this. I was prepared to fight and defend myself. Like I had to in the beginning. But Luke...he didn't even ask me how it happened. This rational version of him is unnerving.

I grab my bag from the table and walk toward the front door. As I move into the hallway, a noise at the other end of the house draws my attention, making me freeze. *Is someone here?* All this time, I assumed we were alone. I spin around to find a beautiful dog at the back door, paws up on the glass, staring in my direction, like it's watching me. And when Luke steps into view, it bounces around playfully.

Something about the dog's happiness eases my mind. Maybe Luke isn't as closed off to feelings as he leads people to believe.

"I'm coming, pup," he calls out, laughing at the dog's reaction. "Just give me a moment." He turns back to face me and I see it. For the first time since we were kids, I see genuine love in his eyes. The love he used to project when talking about his little sister, no matter how annoying he thought she was. The love he used to project when promising me he'd always have my back.

At that thought, the warmth inside me subsides faster than it came, making way for a deep pit to form, and I hate that I'm questioning things but... "Can we really do this? Considering everything between us."

Having a baby with Luke doesn't change what he's done... What I've done... How can we possibly do this without fucking it up?

"Plenty of people co-parent that don't get along. It's all about showing up for your kids." His eyes flash to mine, and I see the moment he regrets what he said. "Fuck, Amelia. I didn't mean—"

"Forget it." I brush it off. "That was then. This is now. And you're right. Plenty of people do it and so can we. I'll see you at work, and I'll let you know when you're needed."

Without another word, I walk away, refusing to peer back at him until I'm settled in my car, Luke's words running on repeat in my mind.

"It's all about showing up for your kids."

Something my dad didn't do.

I guess that's one less thing for me to worry about, because at least Luke knows that.

Even if it's the very thing that tore us apart in the first place.

CHAPTER FIFTEEN

AMELIA – AGE ELEVEN

> *Dear Diary*
> *When my grandpa first gave me this book, he told me to fill it with all the things I loved about the world and I thought it would be easy. I had so many things to say. But then he died. My gut reaction was to burn every last page until my mom gave me a letter he'd written me, telling me it was his time and that he was happy. He was still filling his pages with love. In Heaven.*
> *I made a promise that day to continue to smile and I kept that promise right up until yesterday. When my dad and my best friend made me break it. And now I don't know what to write. I don't have anything good to say.*
> *But I'm trying.*
> *Love always, Amelia Rosenberg*
> *x*

I stare at the door, my fingers curled into the silk of my dress. The dress I bought especially for Dad because it's the same olive-green color as my eyes —his favorite color.

"Fifth grade, can you *please* take your seats. Your parents will be arriving soon." My nervousness builds as our principal attempts to shush the room, and when none of the students listen, I know we have about three seconds before—

"Students! Seats. Now. Or I will *not* be opening these doors and you'll remain elementary students for the rest of your days."

I roll my eyes at her awful attempt to scare us. No one will believe—

"Can she do that?" One of the kids panics behind me, making me giggle. I guess I was wrong.

We all settle slowly, and when the last student finally sits, the crowd falls silent as a teacher moves to open the door.

I watch with giddy anticipation as one by one our parents enter the hall, all dressed up for our graduation. And it finally hits me... I'm about to be in middle school. I won't be treated like a child anymore. I'm almost a teenager. The step before an adult. And I can't wait.

My mom waves when she notices me staring, and I quickly wave back, though my eyes immediately flit to the adults entering behind her. Searching.

My friends' parents arrive, as do other classmates', and Luke's family. But the one person missing is the one person I'm looking for. My dad.

When everyone's inside, they close the doors and I turn to face the stage, internally folding into myself as I fight to hide my emotions.

He didn't come. He promised and he still didn't come.

The ceremony begins and I can sense my mom's eyes boring into the back of my head, but I refuse to look her way. I don't need her sadness.

I should have known better.

I could tell something was wrong.

The night goes on and I barely move from my uncomfortable folding chair other than to receive my certificate, faking my smile as Mom and my classmates cheer.

After the formalities are done, the chairs are moved to create a makeshift dance floor, and my stomach knots at what's coming. Of course we'd be the only school on the planet to have this stupid tradition.

I hide away as best I can, turning down the few guys that ask me to dance, and when our principal makes the announcement I've been dreading, I freeze.

"Now, finally, the father-daughter, mother-son dance."

My classmate Vicki shoves her chair to the floor and runs away in a huff, drawing attention, and I feel for her. Her dad left when she was young, and she told them several times this was a bullshit tradition. I should have agreed, but I was too caught up in my own feelings, naively believing my dad would never let me down.

A few other kids stay seated, unfazed to be missing out. While I bite my cheek to stave off the tears.

He promised. And he let me down.

As the song plays, I smile at my friends and laugh when their parents embarrass them, but inside I'm dying.

He's been missing more and more lately, always working, prioritizing his need for a promotion over his only child. Over me. And I accepted it. But that was before he broke his final promise. Now I'm not so sure.

When the song's over and the regular music resumes, Luke walks my way, and a genuine smile lights up my face.

My rock.

The one person that really knows me.

Since I haven't seen him dancing tonight—other than when his mom forced him—a little part of me hopes he's here to keep me company.

"Luke, I—"

"Aww." His friend cuts me off with a fake little pout, appearing out of nowhere. "Daddy didn't make it? Such a shame."

He laughs out loud, before continuing on his path while I'm left stunned. Where did that come from? Luke's friends have always been nice to me. Luke made sure of that. But this guy is new. He's one of the football players on Luke's team, and we haven't really spoken.

I turn back to Luke and catch his eyes widen as his gaze bounces between me and his friend. He opens his mouth to speak and my pulse races, knowing he always defends me. But when his friend calls out, he follows without a word, shattering my already broken heart.

My eyes water again and I run to the bathroom, sliding into a stall as the first tear falls.

I'm ready for this day to be over.

I needed him. Both of them. And I don't know what to do now.

CHAPTER SIXTEEN

LUKE

A melia walks away, and I stare into space for what I'm certain must be hours. Despite appearing calm after my meltdown, I'm still struggling to process what she said, and no matter how hard I think about it, it doesn't feel real.

"I'm going to be a dad. A father. A parent. Somebody's old man. A pappy." *Nope*. Saying it out loud doesn't work either. "*Jesus*."

Of all the people in all the world, it had to be her. Amelia. The girl I once thought would be my friend forever. The girl I cared about more than anyone else until she decided she was too goddamn good for me. Amelia Joy *Fucking* Rosenberg.

The woman I can't seem to stay away from even though it pains me.

Why does she have to be so goddamn beautiful and sassy? That combination gets me every time. She drives me insane with her secrets, and her diary, and for thinking she has any right to hate me when she's the one that got me arrested.

If I'd just kept it in my pants, I wouldn't be in this mess. My life wouldn't be headed in a completely new direction. I wouldn't be a soon-to-be dad. And yet, as those thoughts enter my mind, my heart clenches, because...I wouldn't change a thing.

I have never wanted to be a dad. But now, I don't exactly hate the idea.

I just have no clue what the hell I'm supposed to do.

We talked about Amelia's next step, but what about *me*? Am I meant to pretend it's not happening? Or start preparing my house? Can I tell anyone? Does that twelve-week thing still exist? Do people still wait? God, when is she twelve weeks? When is she due? How long have I got?

I'm going to be a dad.

There's going to be a junior Luke or Amelia running around next year. Okay, maybe not *running* next year but soon and... *Jesus*. Why does that make me shiver?

There weren't supposed to be *any* little Lukes in the world. *Ever.* I worked hard to prevent that. It wasn't part of the plan.

"I can't look after myself."

Shadow barks and I pause my inner spiral to check that she's okay, but when I find her chasing a ball around the yard, I resume my panic. I'm going to be a dad. A Dad. I don't know the first thing about being a dad. I know I don't want to be like *my* dad. Sure, he was fine but he had his faults and—

"What's going on?"

"Holy shit, Lainey." I spin around, clutching my chest as my heart races. "Where did you come from?"

"The door." Lainey points to the door behind her, but her eyes remain firmly locked on my face, her expression doing nothing to hide her concern. *God, what did I say? What did she hear?*

"So what? You let yourself in?" I grab the water bottle I abandoned next to my gym bag on the floor and squirt some into my mouth, needing a distraction.

"I knocked." She shrugs. "What's going on?"

"Nothing. *Nothing*. I'm nervous. The season is starting soon and as I'm sure you know we've got some high expectations on us this year and—"

"Wow."

"Wow? Lainey, now is not the time for you to be giving me shit." I smile in the hope that it eases her mind but it doesn't.

"Who's giving you shit? You always put on a front, but I know you get nervous at the start of every season, and I know you're not the cocky asshole you always claim to be. But that's the first time you've actually admitted it to me." Her face lights up at the prospect of me opening up to her and my heart jolts. *Dammit.* In this case, it's a lie. But how do I tell her that unless I give her something real?

"Lainey—"

"Let me guess. You don't want to talk about it?" Her tone is teasing but her face drops a little.

"It's not that. I..." *God, what do I say?* "I want to talk to you about it, but can we do it another time? I love you but I've had a weird day, and I'd rather talk to you about it when I have a clear head." And when I know I'm allowed to officially tell people. *Why didn't I ask that question?*

"Yeah. Yeah. Okay. I'll just grab Shadow and go then?"

"What?"

"Shadow? Thomas said you were all heading out, so I'm here to walk her."

Goddammit. I completely forgot I'd suggested that. "Right. Sorry. I wasn't thinking. Thank you."

How the hell can I go out now? How can I sit around and drink when my mind is spinning? I'm going to be a fucking dad.

"Luke?"

"Huh?" I snap out of my thoughts to realize Lainey asked me a question.

"Are you okay?" she asks, her expression tense.

"Never better." I smile. "Why?"

"Because you spaced out."

"Whoops, what can I say... I thought you were leaving." I lift my hands in a what-are-you-gonna-do motion and smile again.

"Are you sure?"

"I'm *fine*. Did you want something?"

"I asked if you were bringing someone to the wedding."

What? Why would she ask that?

Lainey and Thomas are getting married after the Super Bowl; why does she need to know now? Either way, I won't be bringing anyone. I don't do dates and— *Actually, will I have a baby then?* I don't know the exact date, but with some quick mental math, I'm thinking it has to be close.

"Well?" Lainey asks when I still don't answer, stuck in my head again.

"No date," I rush out, forcing another smile. *But there might be a baby. Hope that's okay? Surprise, you're going to be an auntie!*

As we prepare for the regular season, our practices ramp up, meaning I barely see Amelia during the next week—other than once or twice

in a director's capacity. But that doesn't stop me from messaging her. Often. Assuming that's what I'm supposed to do.

> Luke: Is everything okay?

Amelia: Yes, why wouldn't it be?

> Luke: I don't know, I'm just checking in

Amelia: You don't need to do that. I'm fine

> Luke: I'm not worried about you

Amelia: Jackass

Despite her saying she doesn't need me, I still can't help myself, making my messages a daily occurrence.

> Luke: Are you getting enough food? Enough rest?

Amelia: Excuse me?

> Luke: I know you're here. Your car is in the lot but I never see you. It's not healthy to sit at a desk all day

Amelia: I'm fine.

> Luke: ...

Amelia: The baby is fine too

I laugh, but as I read the word "baby," a new energy settles inside me.

One I can't really explain because I haven't felt it before, but the urge to tell Amelia about it is strong.

Of course, I don't.

On day five of what I'm calling the post-baby-news haze, I arrive at the locker rooms to find a text from Amelia and my heart seizes. Without bothering to take off my gear, I check the message and burst out laughing.

> Amelia: I caught the end of practice today. Are you taking enough vitamins? You're getting older. You need to keep on top of it if you want to maintain your peak performance

The fucking sass on this woman.

> Luke: I'm a natural, Joy. It's all about a balanced diet and the right exercise program. Those rookies have nothing on me

> Amelia: God, you're full of it

I smile as I throw my phone back into my bag, but just like always, the weird feeling returns and my happiness fades. I have no clue what I'm doing. But doing nothing doesn't sit right. I hate the unknown, and right now, nothing is certain.

Shaking off my thoughts, I remove my shoulder pads, just as Reed sits down on the chair in front of me.

"You've been off all week, and I was voted the guy who should talk to you."

"What?" I scoff. "I haven't been off. My game is on point. I'm killing it out there."

"Not out there." He points in the direction of the field. "I mean in here." He waves his hands around the room. "You're usually chatty, and loud, and goddamn annoying, but at the moment..."

"A friend of mine just found out his girlfriend is pregnant," I tell him, and it feels good to get it off my chest. Sort of. "He's freaking out because she's got shitty insurance while his is amazing. And he doesn't know what to do."

"Mm-hmm. And that has you worried, why?" He eyes me suspiciously.

I let out a long sigh. "Okay. Fine. The guy isn't a friend. He's my brother." *Jesus.* My eyes widen. *Why the hell did I say that?*

Reed curses under his breath. "Wow, okay. That makes more sense."

"He's kind of panicking which is making me panic."

Reed nods, his protector mode switching gears while I picture him punching me when he finds out the truth.

"I know he's young," he says thoughtfully. "Just a rookie this year..." I nod though he's not really watching me. "But." He pauses and I lean in. Has he thought of something I missed? "Why doesn't he marry her? If they're together and having a b—"

"The fuck did you say?"

"*Jesus.* Not everyone wants to be a bachelor all their lives. You said it was his girlfriend. I'm assuming he's not about to leave her because she's knocked up. To me, it's the obvious answer."

"He's too young."

"He's having a baby. That tends to make someone grow up pretty fucking quickly."

Nope. Not happening.

"Luke—"

"Just how long have you been planning your wedding to Bria?" I cut him off and cringe, instantly regretting my words.

Reed's fists clench as he glares my way. It takes a lot to rattle Mr. Positive. But we all know never to mention his feelings toward his best friend, Bria. I shouldn't have said it. "Don't be a dick," he fumes. "Pass on my advice or don't. Whatever."

"I'm sorry," I say genuinely. I seem to be saying it a lot. "I'm not thinking straight because I'm worried about her." *The baby.*

"Her?" *Jesus.*

"Yeah." *Fuck.* "Ryan's girlfriend."

Reed eyes me for the longest beat before nodding. "I get it. I knew there was a caring soul under that tough exterior." He smiles and I relax. "But sometimes you need to think before you speak."

"Noted." A thousand times over. "Are we good?" I ask, just in case. Best I don't fuck up any relationships in my time of need.

"Yeah, we're good."

I smile as he leaves, and when I'm done getting changed, I have another text waiting for me.

> Amelia: In case you forgot, the ultrasound is tomorrow at 9:15am. If you want to come. I sent you the details a few days ago

And just like that, shit gets real.

> Luke: I'll be there

I just don't know if I'm ready for it.

CHAPTER SEVENTEEN

LUKE

I'm fifteen minutes early for Amelia's ultrasound appointment, and as I stand in front of the old, run-down clinic, I realize arriving early was a bad idea.

It gives me too much time to think. To panic. I should have taken my time this morning, had a long shower, and cooked myself a decent breakfast. But the second I finished my workout, I was antsy. Rushing for no reason.

While I've never been to a pregnancy ultrasound before, I've seen enough TV shows and movies to know they're a big deal. And the idea of that scares the hell out of me.

This situation is strange enough without adding a shared, intimate moment. But I can't not be there. It wouldn't feel right.

At nine fourteen, Amelia still hasn't arrived, and my panic grows.

Am I at the right place? I wouldn't be upset if I wasn't because this place has definitely seen better days, but I said I'd show up, and that's already a touchy subject for her. I don't want to fuck it up first go, because let's face it, I'm going to mess up at some point and I'd prefer it was further down the track, when I've already proven myself a little.

God, who the hell am I?

This kid already *owns* me.

My phone buzzes in my pocket, and I halt my pacing. *When did I start pacing?* Shaking off my thoughts, I rush to check it and find a message from Amelia.

Amelia: I'm up next. I guess I'll see you later today

What the hell? Did she give me the wrong address?

I hit call on her name and take a deep breath so I don't snap at her when she answers. She's a pain in my ass but she's also carrying my child, so I guess I should be nice to her. *Within reason.*

Amelia answers with a gruff hello, almost forcing the words to fly out of my mouth, but I remain calm. "I'm out in front of the address you gave me. And I've been here for fifteen minutes. Where are *you*?"

"I've been inside for twenty."

"What? Where's your car?" I turn around to search the parking lot again, but it's definitely not here.

"Um, it doesn't matter. Can you come in? We're up next." Before I can answer, she rushes out a "please" and a little tension leaves my body.

"Yep, I'm on my way." I hang up and open the door just as a heavily pregnant woman steps out.

"Oh, thank you," she says with a smile. "Good timing."

A young girl follows behind her, gripping the back of her dress as she dances along, and when they step out into the sunshine, she jumps excitedly. "Can we call Dad? He said to call as soon as we were done."

The woman's smile widens, projecting so much warmth my chest tightens. That's not in the cards for us. Instead, we're welcoming our child into an already broken home. And I know with absolute certainty that Amelia would never have wanted that. This must be killing her.

I continue to stare after them as they walk hand in hand, until Amelia whisper-yells behind me.

"Luke. We have to go in."

"*Coming*," I sing as I jog to catch up with her, only slowing when I fall into line, taking her in. Today she's in black yoga pants and a loose-fitting tee. Her wild hair is braided loosely down her back, with random strands poking out at all angles. I find myself staring until she starts clenching and unclenching her hands nervously.

"It's going to be fine," I whisper as I step closer. I have no idea if that's true, but I have an urge to put her mind at ease. Like I'm reverting back to the kid that used to do anything he could to protect her, and forgetting all the shit that's happened over the years.

"What?" Amelia asks as she jumps, obviously not hearing me approach.

"I said it's going to be okay. Great even."

She puts on a smile, but while it's clearly forced, she shakes out her hands before folding them over her chest and nodding, a little tension of her own dissipating as we walk to the exam room.

And I take it as a win.

After a quick introduction, Amelia's directed to the bed, while I hover awkwardly by the door, unsure of my place.

"You don't have to stand over there, Dad. Come on in. I'll grab you a seat."

Dad. *Dad*? Jesus. Saying it myself is one thing, but hearing it out of a stranger's mouth is an entirely different ballgame...and I prefer football.

The woman, who I think is named Jill—I can't remember because I was too busy assessing the equipment—moves a seat next to Amelia's head and gestures for me to sit.

I rush out a thanks as I do as I'm asked, then meet Amelia's gaze, her wide eyes doing nothing to hide her feelings. This is weird. We both know it. There's no other way to put it. I'm in a clinic, with Amelia, waiting to see our baby.

What the hell is this life?

"Okay, shall we begin?"

Amelia and Jill chat about timing and how she's feeling while I smile and nod. I'm certain I'm paying attention but the next thing I know, Amelia's tee is tucked under her bra and the waistband of her pants is being rolled down. I avert my gaze, because this part is personal, but when Jill laughs, I find myself glancing back to see why.

"You're going to want to focus this way," she says with a mocking tone, like she's speaking to a child. "I promise it's not scary. Just watch the screen if the rest of it *concerns* you."

"Concerns me?" The way she says "concerns" makes it sound like the sight of Amelia's stomach disgusts me. And that's not it. At all. I'm respecting her goddamn privacy. "I'm good. Don't worry about me."

She smiles before squirting thick jelly-like stuff onto Amelia's still-flat stomach, making her hiss. "Sorry, it's a little cold. I promise you'll forget all about that in a second."

"It's fine. I just didn't know what to expect."

"Are you ready?"

Amelia rushes out a yes, while my head screams *no*. This is something I *never* thought I'd be ready for. But I can't exactly say that out loud.

I'm still as she lowers the rod excruciatingly slowly toward the gel, my heart pounding so hard I'm surprised no one can hear it. I feel everything in those seconds—not just my rapid heart but also the blood pulsing through my veins, the buzz of the lights ringing in my ears, the energy surrounding me—yet my eyes don't move from Amelia's stomach, watching as Jill swirls the rod around, spreading the gel where she needs it.

I'm completely mesmerized until a new sound permeates the air, and my eyes flash to the screen. "What's that? Is that bad?" I ask, my chest so tight, I'm terrified of having a heart attack.

Jill laughs, but Amelia appears just as shell-shocked as I am. "That's the heartbeat," Jill says casually. "I thought I'd start with that since you're both new to this."

"The heartbeat?" I turn to Amelia at the same time she gapes my way, a sheen of water coating her eyes as mine tingle. "That's—"

"Our baby," she finishes for me, her voice so choked with emotion it cracks.

"I love this part of my job," Jill interrupts. "Ready for more?"

All eyes move back to the screen as Jill talks us through what we're seeing, and I stare in awe, my voice trapped in my throat.

Amelia and Jill continue to chat throughout the appointment, but I don't say a word because nothing feels right. There's nothing in my head big enough for this moment.

When she's done, Jill wipes Amelia's stomach and smiles. "Congratulations, Mom and Dad, you have a healthy—and I'm going to say happy—baby. Would you like a photo?"

"Yes, thank you," Amelia says, while I remain silent.

Then as Amelia gets up and straightens out her clothes, she says thank you and goodbye, on behalf of both of us, and I still can't speak.

A million thoughts rush through my mind as we walk toward the reception desk, and when Amelia hands over her credit card, a pit forms in my stomach. Doesn't her insurance cover this? Why is *she* paying if it doesn't? Shouldn't that be me? I need to talk to her about how this is all going to work and how we're going to split the costs. *Jesus.* The costs are the least of our worries. *We have to share custody.* We're going to need two of everything the same so he or she doesn't notice we're constantly shipping them off from one place to another.

This is so much more complicated than I imagined.

Amelia hurries outside ahead of me, letting the door shut instead of holding it open, and it narrowly misses smacking me in the face. I'd call her out if she wasn't marching away from me, seemingly annoyed until she spins on a dime to face me, her expression matching my awe. "Did that really just happen?"

I have no idea what just happened, but it was magic and I—

Her face drops and she shakes her head. "Are you going to say *anything*?"

I open my mouth to speak but nothing comes out because I don't know what the hell I'm supposed to say. Amelia stares at me for the longest beat before rolling her eyes and scoffing. "Okay, then. I'll see you at work."

I stay in my messed-up stupor as she storms off in the opposite direction, and it's then I remember she doesn't have her car, and I snap myself out of my daze. "Wait!" I call out.

She stops instantly, waving her hands around as she turns. "So you're finally going to speak?"

"Just get in my truck." I wave a hand toward my Chevy and wait for her scowl. But instead, her eyes widen.

"*What?*"

"I'm not letting you take a bus, *Joy.* Come on, I'll take you home." *Did she honestly expect me to watch her go?*

"How do you know I'm taking the bus?" she sasses. "Maybe I'm going to meet a friend."

"Are you?"

"No."

"Then get in my truck."

Amelia folds her arms across her chest and taps her foot, unimpressed, until I add "please" and put on my cheesiest smile, once again gesturing toward my beast parked on the other side of the lot.

We stare at each other, locked in some kind of standoff until finally, "Okay. Fine," she says as she gives in. "Because it'll be faster. Can you drop me at the stadium? My car's there."

"Yep, that's where I'm headed." I smile, but God, is it going to be this hard every time I try to do the right thing? I get that she's perfectly capable of doing this on her own, but why make it harder than it has to be?

Holy shit. When did I become the rational one of the two of us?

I'll give her the benefit of the doubt today because we just went through something life-changing, but it's going to suck if she keeps arguing every time I try to help.

Unless...

An idea I'd refused to acknowledge pops back into my mind, and I can't deny that it's kind of perfect, no matter how crazy it is.

I let the idea play out as we walk in silence until I'm certain it's the right choice.

It has to be. It solves all our problems. *Thank you, Reed.*

Keeping my mouth shut, I wait until Amelia's settled in the passenger seat—so she can't run away—then before starting the ignition, I hit her with my thoughts. "I've decided we should get married."

CHAPTER EIGHTEEN

AMELIA

This might be an exact repeat of an earlier entry but...
Fuck.

We what?

My seatbelt flings back as my gaze snaps to Luke, waiting for him to burst out laughing. One, two, three seconds pass and he doesn't so much as smile, making me panic. "I... You... Tell me you're joking."

"Nope."

"Nope?"

"I'm not joking."

What in the world? I take a deep breath as he stares at me in challenge, and while my instincts scream at me to tell him to fuck off, there's a small part of me that needs to know his thoughts, otherwise it will drive me crazy thinking about it.

"Okay. I'll hear you out. Why?"

Luke smiles but it's not his usual cocky grin, and my insides churn because of it. I glance away, uncomfortable, and lock eyes on the photos in my lap. Our baby. My heart clenches as a small smile pulls at my lips.

I'd walked out of the ultrasound with my mind blown, my heart full, and these photos in my hand. Photos I could have spent hours gazing at no matter how hard it was to believe there was a tiny human growing inside me. After the initial awe, I couldn't shut up with my reactions, gasping, oohing, and aahing any chance I got. Luke, on the other hand, hadn't said a word since the heartbeat, leading me to imagine so many crazy theories in my mind—he was freaked-out, he changed his mind, we broke him. But no, he had other things rolling around in his head.

A goddamn *marriage* proposal.

What?

He's silent again as I clear my thoughts, and when I glance back his way, he's staring at me.

"I need you to pay attention," he says slowly, probably worried about startling me, and he should be. I'm ready to run away screaming.

Instead, I smile. "I'm all ears."

"Good." He nods. "That ultrasound wasn't as bad as I thought it was going to be considering how run-down the building was." He rolls his eyes as though it was awful, but rather than snapping at him, I let him continue. "And Jill was nice and all—maybe a little too bubbly—but the thing is, I'm not waiting another ten weeks to see our baby again. And I'm not leaving the delivery to chance based on whatever hospital we can get on your insurance. I want to know the doctor I'm trusting with my child. I want all the bells and whistles...and I want to be able to arrive at a building and not stress because it looks like it's about to fall down."

"Wow. Look at you and your firm grip on reality." *Sarcasm is better than anger, right? Because I'd much rather be angry.*

"I've got the means, Amelia. I'm not going to pretend otherwise. I told you. Nothing but the best for my child."

"*Our* child."

"Nothing but the best for *our* child."

I'm not sure what to say next, but his calm and serious demeanor is freaking me out. He wants to get married? The guy that undoubtedly left a naked woman in his bed to meet me here...wants to marry me.

My mind whirs as he leans his shoulder against the backrest of his seat and angles his body to face me, making sure I know he's completely in this. Giving me his full attention. Telling me this conversation is important to him. His dark eyes bore into mine as he waits patiently, perhaps hoping I'm going to catch up with this thought process, while I'm still a long way behind.

"And you think that if we get married, we can use your insurance?" I ask slowly. That much I gathered, otherwise, this makes less sense.

"*Yes*," he practically cheers as though it's the most obvious thing in the world. "I've researched it. And while I may not be able to change *your* insurance without waiting periods, I can change mine." *Jesus.* He's really thought this through. Here I was thinking he was randomly throwing the idea out there. "If we do it now," he continues, "we can have the full gold class service before you're halfway."

Gold class service? God, as nice as whatever that is sounds, he's crazy. We can't get married.

"I've survived perfectly fine without riches and so have you. I'd never let anything happen to our baby regardless of money. This isn't a good idea."

"Why?"

"So. Many. Reasons." But let's skip the obvious ones—how much we can't stand each other—and instead go with the most important. "For one, I'm not breaking the law."

Luke's brows furrow. "Who's breaking the law?"

"We would be. You know...by pretending to be married." I whisper the last part in case someone overhears us, making Luke chuckle.

He leans in conspiratorially. "Again. Who's pretending? For it to work, we'd *actually* have to be married, *Joy.*" He throws out my nickname as though I'm ruining his fun and he's right. I'm not going to make this easy. I can't. "We'd make it official," he adds. "That's not breaking the law."

He doesn't get it. "It would still be fake. Marriages are supposed to be about love, and surely this isn't new information for you when I say there is no love here."

"Come on, Amelia. Arranged marriages happen all the time. Where's that love?"

Dammit. He has a point, but... "I still think it's a bad idea. I'm not even divorced yet."

"For fuck's sake." For the first time since starting this conversation, a hint of his frustration slips through Luke's facade. "I'll fix that too."

"Money doesn't fix everything."

"No, it doesn't. But it can fix *this*."

"You're making it sound like *I'm* the situation."

"You are. You're the one stopping this."

"And you're an asshole."

"I thought we established that was never in question."

I pause, running out of excuses. This is insane. I just walked away from my marriage; the last thing I want to do is fall into another one.

"I'm not marrying you."

I can't, can I?

"Don't be so selfish. This is the perfect solution to all my worries."

"Your worries. Not mine."

"You'd seriously turn this down because of your feelings toward me? What if something happens? You'll never forgive yourself for not having better care."

"*Jesus*, Luke. Don't say stuff like that." My heart races now that he's put that idea in my head.

"Marry me and you won't have to worry."

"Luke—"

"Is it because I didn't get down on one knee?" He opens the door of his truck and jumps out before dropping to the ground and glancing back at me. "Amelia Joy Rosenberg," he begins and I panic, my gaze darting around the parking lot to make sure nobody is watching.

"Please get up," I whisper-yell, but he ignores me. *God, what is he doing?*

"Would you do me the honor of becoming my wife?"

"No."

"She said yes!" He stands up and cheers, pretending to accept some nonexistent congratulations from well-wishers while I thank God no one's around. "Thank you. Thank you," he gushes. "Yes, yes, we're going to have a wonderful marriage. Oh, what a lovely thing to say."

"*Luke.*"

"Yeah." He drops the act immediately and gives me his full attention again.

"Please get in the truck." I don't bother hiding my frantic tone.

"You're making this way bigger than it needs to be," he says, as he sits down and closes the door behind him, cutting off the air supply. At least, it feels that way. "To paraphrase someone I know..." he continues as I stare at him, "'I'd rather choose *anyone* else to marry.' But this is the hand I was dealt, so work with me here."

"You're so funny. I—"

"I'm just trying to protect you." His voice rises, his words hitting me in the chest as they cut off what was about to be a smart-ass comment about the bachelor getting married. And when he adds, "I'll do whatever it takes," my heart stops and a tightness fills my chest.

Luke's eyes widen as though he didn't mean for that to come out of his mouth, but it was the right thing to say, because while it doesn't solve all our issues, when it comes to this, it changes everything. He smiles uncomfortably and for a moment I see the young boy I thought I'd follow to the ends of the earth. My protector, my friend. I want to believe he's still in there, but there's so much hurt between us I'm not sure we can fix it, and he's not the only one to blame.

The only way any of this is going to work is if we put our baby first, just like he said.

"If I do this—*if*—we'll need to set some rules."

"I wouldn't expect anything less." His cocky composure settles back into place as though he's won, and while it pisses me off, I don't argue. Instead I let out a slow sigh.

"I need you to pay attention." I throw his words back at him, and rather than make him laugh, his face drops and he nods.

"Thank you. First rule...no feelings."

"That won't be an issue."

"Agreed, but it had to be said." Luke nods as I move on. "Next, no telling anyone. And I mean *anyone*."

"Ah." Luke grimaces. "That's not going to work. Yes, we need to keep it quiet around certain people, but we have to tell *someone* in case we need to corroborate our story."

"*Goddammit.* Okay, I'll tell my friend Hayley, but that's it."

"Fine by me."

"Who are you going to tell?" I ask, hesitantly.

"Not sure yet. I'll decide on a case by case basis."

"*What*?" My heart races again. Why am I considering this idea? It's ludicrous.

"I won't tell anyone connected to you," he adds, noting my freak-out, though it doesn't ease my mind.

"We work together, Luke. We went to school together. Your parents know who I am. Who's left?"

"You worry too much. I'll keep it quiet. What's next?"

"No sex," I blurt out, and my cheeks heat as I continue. "We are *never* going there again."

Luke laughs to himself, and I hate the way it makes me squirm. "You didn't have to say that either. It's a given."

"Okay, good. And last, no fucking around with anyone else. If you're my husband, you don't stray." Luke's face pales and it's my turn to laugh. "Did you honestly think I was going to marry you, tell people about it, and then be fine when you continue your fuck-boy ways?"

"I can be discreet."

"You can be discreet? *Ugh*. Deal's off. In fact, I lied—the baby isn't yours. Forget I ever mentioned it."

"Fine," he huffs before his lips curl into a smirk. "That won't be as hard as you think, but you're a brat, you know that, right?"

"Believe it or not, while the idea of forcing you to keep it in your pants gives me so much joy, I didn't suggest it to piss you off. I suggested it to protect myself and our child. The last thing he or she needs is to be born into scandal. You're not the only one that cares."

Luke nods, and I sense he's about to say something but my phone rings, cutting him off. I'm torn when I glance at the screen. On one hand, this is an important conversation that we need to finish, but on the other hand, it's my boss and I can't afford to piss him off with the bomb I'm about to drop.

"It's work." I cringe. "I should get this. We've got our first day of filming tomorrow, and I was supposed to be in the office by now."

Luke's eyes flash to the time before he curses. "Say no more. I'm due at the stadium now anyway." He starts the truck but turns to face me before reversing out of the parking space. "Leave the arrangements to me. I'll let you know when I need something."

Our eyes stay locked for a beat before he smiles and looks away.

My mind spins on the drive with so much to unpack from the last couple of hours. It's strange enough to process the fact that I'm growing a baby inside me, a healthy little human that will be out in the world in less than six months. But then this...

I'm not sure my heart can take anything else.

Did I really just agree to marry Luke?

***

"**L**uke!" *I scream his name as he disappears out of sight, sending my pulse skyrocketing. He's leaving. He's actually leaving.*

"Come on. We have to go." David grabs my hand and we run down the stairs, only making it to the next level before the smoke overwhelms us. "We have to get out using the second-story balcony," David says, the panic clear in his voice. "It's too dangerous to go down."

I nod as I cough, covering my mouth with my arm and following him to the master bedroom, helping him break through the door.

My chest aches and I sweat while shaking the handle, praying it will open. "Please, come on. David, what do we do?"

"Step back."

A broken chair smashes into the glass and it shatters in seconds, the noise drowned out by the sound of the flames.

David pushes the sharp glass away before crawling out and moving toward the edge, his voice a distant echo as he waves at me to follow.

I'm scared. My body shakes as I watch him disappear over the edge. But I can't will myself to move. My lungs tighten as I struggle to take in air, and when my vision blurs, I jump into action.

"Come on, Amelia. You can do this."

Closing my eyes, I climb over the railing and find a tree branch to step onto, my heart frozen in my chest until my feet touch the ground.

Voices filter through the air and I take off in a run, as fast as my tired legs will allow. I pause when I make it safely into the tree line, but barely get a moment of respite before I'm coughing again, this time uncontrollably, a second wave of panic running through me. I'm going to need help.

I can't be near this. It could ruin my chances of getting into college. Mom will call my dad. She'll use this as a way of getting back into his orbit. And I can't handle that again.

I suck in a frantic breath and turn around, slamming straight into a hard chest. A police officer. I'm doomed.

"Come on," he says, his tone soft but his eyes full of annoyance. "Let's get you to a medic."

My panic increases and—

My alarm goes off at four thirty and I wake with a start, my heart slamming in my chest. When I last checked the time, my mind was still reeling at two a.m., but I must have fallen asleep at some point because the annoying tone erupting from my phone definitely woke me from the depths of nothingness, and now I feel like death.

I swear I was dreaming about something, but the imagery sits just out of reach in my mind. Though I can still feel how it affected me. Only I can't dwell on it.

Today's the day. The crew are setting up, the players have been briefed, craft services are ready to go. Within hours I'll be calling "action" for my first ever prime-time job.

And I'm a goddamn mess.

As if it wasn't difficult enough having to function knowing I was pregnant and hadn't announced it yet, I now have my impending nuptials to agonize over. Am I crazy for considering it? Maybe. But Luke's reasoning was good, and like him, I want to protect this baby. I want to do "whatever it takes," even if that means marrying a guy I can't stand to be in a room with.

I wish I could start over—reprogram myself so I can't access all the memories of our past—then maybe this would be easier.

I know that he's trying. I've seen the change in him since I told him I was pregnant, but we've tried to mend our friendship before—at least I thought that's what we were doing—and I walked away from that far worse.

There's a strong possibility we're not meant to be friends.

But co-parents don't have to be friends; they have to be civil and understanding, willing to negotiate, compromise, talk things through. As long as we can do that, we can make this work.

My phone buzzes across the wood of my side table, and I grab it to silence what I assume will be a follow-up alarm, but instead I find a message from Luke. It's a photo of a director's chair that's poorly edited to include my name. *And dammit if it isn't cute.* Until I read the accompanying text.

Luke: Scandal on the Storm set. Director
marries the star of her show. In secret

God, he's annoying. What am I doing?

> Amelia: Don't make me regret it before it's begun

> Luke: Alright baby mama, but in all seriousness... you're going to kill it today. Show that fucker why you're the man

Dammit, Luke. My chest tightens and I fight not to let my emotions move in. Now is not the time for him to be nice to me.

CHAPTER NINETEEN

LUKE

Amelia sends me a thank you text and I drop the phone like it's burning my fingers. If I don't keep things light and humorous, I'm going to fall apart at any second.

When I think back to our conversation yesterday, it mirrors an out-of-body experience. *Who was that guy?* I mean, sure, he was sensible and confident, and knew exactly what he wanted. But now, it's a new day and I don't know where the hell he went.

"Leave the arrangements to me?" What was I thinking? I don't know the first thing about organizing a wedding. My sister is halfway through planning one right now, and she's talked my ear off about it, yet I couldn't tell you a single thing she's arranged.

Where do I start? Apart from the divorce. *That* I can help with. You need me to *end* a marriage? Easy. I'm sure I can pay someone to do that. But entering into one? I'm at a loss.

Unless...I wonder if you can do it online these days?

Before the thought has fully formed, I type *"fastest way to get married in California"* and hit search... Bingo! Too easy. We just need Amelia's divorce to be finalized and we can be married in twenty-four to seventy-two hours. Gotta love technology.

I laugh to myself until reality sets in. I meant what I said—I will protect them both, no matter what it takes. But I have no idea what that's going to entail, and I've got to admit, I'm terrified.

Since I'm up early and don't have to be at the stadium for a couple of hours, I sneak in a workout to clear my head. But it doesn't help.

I try watching TV and listening to music, but that doesn't help either.

I'm just about to call Lainey to confess everything when I remember Amelia's car issues. When we arrived at the stadium yesterday, her car was in the parking lot, so it must have broken down there. I can't have her catching the bus all the time with the ridiculous hours she works. It's my duty to help out.

Even though I know she'll be pissed off about it.

It takes me all of ten minutes to arrange for a mechanic, and when it's done, I'm still no more settled. Though I will admit I do feel better knowing that Amelia will have her car fixed within the next couple of days. And I'm fully prepared for her wrath.

After cleaning the house, something I never do to distract myself, I leave early for practice and drive around for a while.

Luckily, when it comes to the game, I have a process, so once I'm in the parking lot, all it takes is a little pep talk in the form of telling myself it's *go time* and all of a sudden, I'm in the zone. Like magic.

Okay, not like magic at all... My pep talk included a lot more expletives and a slap in the face. But I got there in the end.

Pre-season is almost over. The final roster is set. It's our year.

Last year we were close. This year, we're a better team. There's no doubt in my mind that we are making it to the Super Bowl, and I am a huge part of that. Most tight ends peak before thirty years of age. But I'm not most tight ends. I've been playing the long game, improving every year and I've never been better. I know it. The coaches know it. Even the executives give me knowing smiles as they pass by. Nothing is going to stop me from having the year of my career.

Not a wife and baby... Or a TV show. If anything, they could be motivators. I'm yet to decide. But I'm about to find out.

I'm smiling when I arrive at the stadium, and that smile widens when I see Amelia's car.

I expect an onslaught of yelling when Amelia sees me since I gave the mechanic her number, but as I step inside there's a weird tension in the air, and it's got nothing to do with me. I only have to step foot through the entry to understand why.

From the moment the door clicks shut, a camera follows me as I walk down the hall—but that alone doesn't mean anything. We're used to people shoving cameras and microphones into our faces. It's the "*Cut! Can we try that again?*" that's throwing everyone off.

Everyone except Rookie, it seems.

Zane smiles as he nods, before turning around and rushing back to greet me near the door. "They want more swagger," he confirms when I raise an eyebrow. "Apparently my usual star power is lacking. But what can I say... I'm tired after celebrating my inclusion in the final roster. Not that I expected otherwise." *And they say I'm the cocky one.*

"If it's swagger they want, we all know you got this." I smile and of course he bounces his eyebrows. He can be an asshole sometimes, but I have no reason to piss him off. Easton, on the other hand, is already growly. *But when is he not?*

Keeley, Amelia, and the producers *all* warned us that it would be like this, but now that it's happening, it's bizarre. Yes, I joked about being the star of this show, but I'm a football player, not an actor. I don't think ahead when it comes to my moves. I memorized our playbook within a week of first seeing it, and now it all comes naturally to me. Funnily enough, even my own swagger comes naturally. I can't imagine trying to fake anything. Although, I suppose I need to get used to playing pretend.

I'm about to do six months of it.

For the sake of my baby. For *our* baby. For... God, the baby needs a name. Uhh... *Jelly Bean.* I'm going to call the baby Jelly Bean. That's much better than constantly referring to "it" in my mind.

Shaking off my thoughts, I smile to myself as I walk into the locker room, and when no one yells cut, a feeling a pride takes over me. Maybe acting comes naturally to me too.

The room is full of people I don't recognize, and the one person I expected to be here is strangely missing. I ignore my concern to get ready, and it's not until I'm half naked—my shorts around my ankles as I step out of them—that Amelia finally walks in like she owns the place, her presence drawing my attention as I pause to watch her.

She's laughing at something her assistant is saying, her face lit up in clear amusement, and as much as it pains me, I have to admit, it makes me smile. She's happy. It suits her.

If she'd been this happy during high school, my mind would have immediately conjured up ways to bring her down. I'm not proud of it, but she brought out that guy in me. Now, it's strangely different. And I don't know how I feel about that.

I continue to watch her as she flits around the room, smiling as she chats with my teammates, not even blushing when she finds them in a state of undress. But when she gets to me she pauses, unsure how to act, so I help her out a little. "I'm ready for my close-up, oh wise director. Where do you want me?"

The way I see it, I need to compartmentalize. I need to put Amelia in two different baskets. Amelia the mother of my child and future wife... and Amelia the director. *This* Amelia. The Amelia I've known since I was a kid. The Amelia that used to gloat when she got an award I thought I deserved. The Amelia that threw me under a bus with the fire. This is the Amelia I despise.

The other Amelia, the mother of my child, is different. She has to be. Otherwise it's going to get weird.

Director Amelia laughs as her eye line drops to my exposed briefs. "I hope you're talking about your face?" she sasses, and with her straight face, I have to wonder if she's taking the same approach I am, separating me into two Lukes. The cocky football player and the baby daddy. That, or she's really good at putting on a front. Either way, I'll take it.

"My face is best, because where you're gawking might be too much for the average viewer."

"You're right." She leans in close so no one else can hear. "That's best reserved for a different kind of show."

"Oh yeah?" I grin, betting she thinks about my cock on a regular basis.

"Yeah." She pulls back to meet my gaze. "When plastic surgery goes wrong."

I huff out a laugh and consider asking her why she kept that joke to herself—the guys would have loved it—but to everyone else, it could be considered a lawsuit waiting to happen and I'm not that mean.

Since we've caught the attention of a few of my teammates, I laugh again before turning to face them. "Amelia was just saying that she'd love a few close-ups of me, but didn't want to leave the rest of you out."

"Ha," Amelia fakes a laugh. "I was actually telling him that it's not that kind of show. I just didn't want to embarrass him in front of you all."

Reed snorts from beside us as he throws his clothes into his locker. "It would take a lot to embarrass Luke. We've all tried."

I shake my head as I finally continue dressing, pulling on my pants as Amelia's eyes stay firmly locked on Reed.

"Good to know, Reed. I'm always interested in new information about the team." Amelia grins before waving a hand around the room, her gaze briefly scanning my now-naked chest before she turns. "I better get moving. We'll be filming as soon as you're all ready."

She takes a few steps away before turning to face me, a wide sassy grin in place." Actually, you know what?" All eyes around me flash her way. "A close-up is a great idea."

I bounce my shoulders as I stand tall, hitting her with my cockiest smirk. "Anything for you," I say, reminding her that I promised to do as asked if she didn't mention the fire.

Amelia ignores me, and instead focuses on Reed where he's sitting in front of his things, his tattooed body on full display. "Reed, can I borrow you?"

I burst out laughing before giving her a nod and graciously accepting all the teasing from my teammates.

Amelia: one, Me: zero. Well played. I could wipe that smile off her face in a heartbeat by telling her about the car, but I'm not going to do that. It'll happen on its own soon enough.

Amelia holds back her smile until she turns away, but I don't miss the way it lights up her face, right before she steps out of view.

Reed stands up, eyebrows raised. "Should I follow her? This is my moment." He flexes his muscles as he bounces on his toes until I give him a friendly shove.

"Sit the fuck down. It's time to get serious."

"Says you."

"Yep. I'm always serious."

He rolls his eyes as Keeley calls attention to the room, giving us another speech about appropriate behavior on camera before it's time for practice.

Coach is wound up when we run onto the field, and I hold my breath, silently praying that Amelia doesn't ask us to try that again because I can't imagine that will go over well.

It's been a couple of weeks since the TV show was dumped on us, and while a lot of people aren't happy about it, they've at least made their opinions known. Coach Pierce, on the other hand, has never shared his feelings on the topic. But while he does everything they ask, he's clearly pissed about it all.

And it makes me think there has to be a reason behind that.

Pushing the conspiracy theories out of my head, I line up for our first play as the cameras turn my way. I throw them a wave, then it's on. I'm ready to show them exactly why I should be their star.

Throughout practice, my gaze naturally seeks out Amelia, finding her locked in various conversations with her crew members. Once again in her element. And a thought hits me. I may have joked about telling people our secret, but if it comes out, it's going to hurt her career, and I don't want that to happen.

I have to keep my distance when she's here. Yes, she can give as good as she gets, but now is not the time for joking around.

When practice is over, and our filming obligations are complete, I avoid Amelia as I make my way outside. The less interaction we have, the better, and I have a list of things to do if I want to keep things moving for us both.

First up, I need to tell Lainey. Not only because she'd kill me if I didn't but also because she can help.

When I arrive at her house, I knock twice before remembering she's forever waltzing into my place, so instead, I push open the door and announce my arrival before stepping inside, knowing that Thomas isn't home.

But because I'm a nicer person than she is, I wait for her reply.

"Coming," she calls out from down the hall seconds before stepping into view, a bath towel in her hands.

When our eyes lock, she raises her hands in the air. "I swear I didn't take her," she sasses about Shadow, waving the white towel as if it's her sign of surrender.

I huff out a laugh. "If I didn't have other things on my mind, you know I would have made you feel guilty for that comment."

"How?" She shakes her head as she folds the towel.

"By pretending she was missing."

"*Jesus.*" She pauses as her eyes flash to mine. "You're a dick sometimes. But you already know that. What things?"

Huh? "What things?" I repeat, confused.

Lainey pins me with her signature stare but there's a hint of concern in her expression. "You just said you had things on your mind."

"Oh, that." I clench the back of my neck as I walk toward her. "You tell Thomas everything, right?" I ask, knowing the answer but needing to gauge her reaction.

"I do." She hesitates, her task forgotten as she throws the towel back into the laundry basket. "What—"

"All good, just checking."

"Oh-kay." Lainey stares at me with a raised brow while I take a deep breath and attempt away around her little admission.

"I have this friend, and he's kind of got himself into a situation."

"Does Thomas know him?"

"He does, which is why we're going to call him Bob."

"Okay. And what situation is *Bob* in?" She leans against the wall pretending to be calm, but there's an obvious tension in her shoulders.

"He may or may not have gotten someone pregnant."

"What?" Lainey gasps as she stands tall. "For a second I thought we were playing pretend and that Bob was actually Thomas. But now... Oh. My. God. I'm going to be an aunt?" She squeals the last bit and I cringe.

What? "No, no one's going to be an aunt because *Bob* doesn't have any sisters."

"But—"

"At least he won't, if his sister tells her fiancé what I'm about to tell you."

Lainey stares at me for a second before her lips pull into the smallest grin, which she graciously hides.

"Okay. Spill." The words flow out of her mouth casually, but I know deep down she's dying to say more. And while I'm thankful she's holding back, I'm also not, because how do I begin? It would probably be easier if she was hitting me with rapid-fire questions.

But here goes. "Amelia's pregnant, and she doesn't have great insurance, so I... *Bob* thought it was a good idea to get married and now I... *he* has to organize a wedding. A quickie wedding away from prying eyes, but a legal wedding all the same."

"I'm sorry, what? Did I just black out?"

"This is a serious situation, Lainey. I—"

"You mean, Bob."

"Fuck, Lainey. I need your help but I'd rather not tell Thomas just yet. What can I do to ensure that?"

Lainey pauses, and I swear I can hear her mind ticking over until she smiles. "Anything?"

"Yes, anything."

"Okay. Hmm. I'm still stuck on the fact that my forever-a-bachelor brother is getting married and having a baby. I'm going to need some thinking time."

"Take whatever you need as long as you keep your mouth shut."

The smile drops from Lainey's face and she sighs. "I can do that for now. But not forever. How long do you plan on keeping this a secret?"

"As long as we can get away with it."

If I consider Lainey's reaction, I doubt anyone would believe me if I told them, but I still don't want to hurt Amelia's career. I've never hidden the fact that I have no intentions of getting married. But fake or not, it's happening. And she doesn't need that kind of attention right now.

Lainey sighs again. "Okay, but I need details. And don't worry about a payment. I won't say anything for now. But you should tell Thomas."

"I will. Soon. For now it's just you. Deal?"

"Deal. So..."

"Where the fuck do I start?"

"The beginning?" She lifts her shoulders in a half shrug.

"Definitely not." I laugh to myself. "That's a long story. Right now we just need to get to the juicy bits."

Lainey grabs my hand and drags me into the living room before pushing me onto the couch. "Luke, you are confusing the hell out of me. But I'm all ears."

CHAPTER TWENTY

AMELIA

Is it possible to have an easy life? Because mine is like an amusement park ride spinning out of control, and I don't know if I can hold on any longer. The whiplash is exhausting.

I fall into bed with that same giddy smile that's been plastered on my face since we called it a wrap for the day. I couldn't hide it if I tried.

Today was perfect. The crew worked seamlessly together, the players were receptive to our requests, and the small snippets I saw on the camera were beautiful. It was successful all around and as first days go, I couldn't fault it.

We have another couple of days of filming this week, then not much next week until the game on Sunday. All part of the deal to ensure we don't interrupt the team too much ahead of the season opener.

Not that I think that would be an issue. The guys were on fire today.

I've been to a handful of practice sessions since I started working on this project, and I have never seen the team gel like this. In fact, every session seems to bring them closer. I'd love to say it's because they were showing off for the cameras but it wasn't that. If anything, they forgot we were there, none of them paying us any mind.

The only minor blip on my happiness radar was Luke. After his marriage proposal, I expected things to be awkward between us, but he effortlessly reverted back to his usual cocky self and I went with it. It made life easier for me.

But something happened between our easy conversation in the locker room and when he ran off the field because he completely ignored me when I was waiting to congratulate the team. And it wasn't by accident. Some might assume I'd embarrassed him with my teasing, but it's Luke—he thrives on banter like that. No, it was definitely something else, and while it shouldn't bother me—when I first started this job I would have given *anything* for him to pretend I didn't exist—now, it's not sitting right.

Not that I've let him ruin my mood.

I spent too many years allowing that to happen, and nothing is going to affect me today.

Grabbing my phone, I hit call on Hayley's name and laugh when she immediately answers.

"Bitch, you have been killing me. I expected a call on your way home."

"Yeah well, that's hard to do on the bus."

"Bus? What happened to your car?"

I cringe. Due to everything that happened yesterday, I forgot about my lack of a car. I've had my Honda since I was sixteen and it was my grandmother's before that. I've been expecting something to happen for years, but of course, it chose the morning of my ultrasound appointment to stop working when I was already in a rush. That will teach me for trying to get in a few extra hours at work.

I called to arrange an emergency appointment to get it checked out, but when they told me the additional cost for urgency, I said I'd call back. And I never did.

"She died yesterday," I joke yet it's anything but funny.

"Did the mechanic say they can fix it?"

"I kind of haven't taken it in yet."

"What? Why? You shouldn't be catching the bus on your own, especially in the dark."

"That's not an issue, but it does add a lot of time to my trip. Time I don't have."

"So?"

"So, I can't afford it at the moment."

Hayley sighs. "I wish I could pay for you but I'm barely surviving. I've eaten Ramen noodles for dinner three nights in a row."

"You and me both."

"I hope you mean the money issue, *not* the noodles. You need more than that when you're feeding two people."

Two people? I can't help but laugh. *What is my life now?* "That's my problem. I'm spending all my money on good food and putting the rest into a baby fund. There's nothing left over for car issues."

"What about your rich baby daddy?"

"Hmmm," I stall as I sit up, trying to figure out how to tell her what went down yesterday. She's either going to laugh or yell at me for being so stupid, and neither is great for me.

"Don't play dumb," Hayley huffs, and I can picture her rolling her eyes. "You should ask him for money toward the baby stuff. You know, since you have to pay extra money for good food."

"Yeah, about that."

"Oh my God, you already did? You asked for money? You are my queen. We—"

"No, he offered it," I cut her off and she gasps.

"He what now?"

"I guess you could say, we're kind of engaged."

"What?" There's a loud bang before Hayley mutters "bloody hell" and a ruffling sound hurts my ear. "Sorry, I dropped the phone," she says as she comes back on the line. "Please explain how you're *kind of* engaged?"

"Luke wasn't happy about my lousy health insurance, and when I wouldn't let him pay for everything, he proposed marriage so I could use his insurance. And... I reluctantly agreed." I say the last part slowly and wait for her reaction.

Hayley goes silent but I know her well enough to guess what that means. "I can hear you smiling."

"I'm not smiling." She giggles softly before bursting out with the most obnoxious laughter. "Okay, I was smiling...and laughing. But my God, that man just gets better and better, doesn't he? You should ask him to fix your car too."

"No. Not happening. Have you forgotten everything I said about our past?"

"Nope, but that was in high school. People change."

"Okay, let's say we consider the present Luke instead of the past Luke. He's still a well-publicized playboy."

"I can't argue with that. But you said yes?"

I let out a long sigh. "I did. His arguments made sense and then he said he wanted to protect us both. Not just the baby."

"Wow."

"I know." I fall back onto my bed again and huff out a laugh. "But the car is my problem. That's not related to his baby."

"Seems related to me but I'll shut up. What happens now?" I'm about to argue when Hayley's tone turns serious. "I mean because you're still technically married and well, I didn't think you could stand each other. Although, that seems to be changing."

"We're keeping things quiet until my divorce is finalized and then I'm not so sure." I ignore her comment about us changing.

"Well, I'm here for you. You know that, right?"

"I do and it means the world to me, because, Hayley, I have no idea what the hell I'm doing." I run a hand down my face and squeeze my eyes shut, willing my heart to stop racing.

"We'll work it out. I'm happy to play mum with you. But I refuse to be a 'Mom'; I still can't wrap my head around that. Mom. Mom. Mom. Nope, it is and will always be Mum."

"What you're saying sounds exactly the same."

"No, it doesn't. Listen carefully. Mom. Mum. Mom. Mum."

"It's the same."

"Fine, you say them."

"Mom. Mum." It's weird to say Mum, but when it comes out of my mouth, I hear the difference. "Okay. You win. Guess that will make it easier for the baby. It can call me Mom and you Mum."

"Deal. But I hate saying 'it.' Can you and Luke come up with a nickname?"

"I'll add it to my list." I laugh.

"Good."

"Can we catch up this week? I could use a girls' night."

"Absolutely. I've got my callback audition on Thursday and—"

"What? Hayley, that's amazing. Why didn't you tell me?"

"Because I was worried I'd jinx it. But now I'm thinking I need to take the manifesting approach."

"Oh yeah?"

"Yeah."

"Congratulations! You got the role. I'm so proud of you."

Hayley laughs before cutting herself off. "Thank you. I'm going to be amazing in it. That Academy Award is mine."

"Damn straight."

"So, Thursday night then, to celebrate properly."

"Lock it in."

"Love you, Hayls. I couldn't do this without you."

"Love you too, Babe. I'll see you Thursday."

My smile returns, having lost it for a moment, and I'm about to hang up when Hayley rushes to stop me. "Shit. Wait."

"What's wrong?"

"We never spoke about your first day."

I bark out a laugh. So much for nothing affecting my first day buzz. "It was amazing, Hayley. Couldn't have been better."

My alarm goes off extra early the next day to give me the time to catch the bus, and while I'm on my way in the darkness, I curse myself for not paying the price to get my car fixed. Not that I'd ever admit that. A little public transport never hurt anyone. Still I stare longingly at my car as I walk across the parking lot, but as I'm stepping through the doors, my phone rings, cutting me from my thoughts.

"Amelia speaking."

"Hi Amelia, it's Nick, the mechanic. I'll be there at ten a.m. today. I just need your key."

"Excuse me? What? Who?"

"Nick. I spoke to Luke yesterday. He told me to confirm the time with you. So, I'll be there at ten. Is that good?"

Luke? *Goddammit.* Why does he have to be so annoying but also really hard to be mad at? I need my car. But... Ugh. I don't want to be indebted to him and—

"Miss? Does that work?"

"Oh. Yes. Thank you. I'll be standing by my car at ten."

"Thank you. See you then."

He hangs up and I'm left staring at my phone. I should have seen this coming, but since things got weird with Luke late yesterday, I never even thought about it.

Is this our life now—me falling apart and Luke riding in like a knight in shining armor, saving the day?

And if it is, is that really the life I want?

I try to focus on work, but by eleven a.m., my car's fixed and I'm feeling a mix of relief and guilt. I know Luke was trying to help, but I should be able to get things done on my own. I'm a grown-ass woman, for God's sake.

Despite knowing I have to talk to him, I put off the inevitable and don't seek him out until the end of the day, but when I find him in the halls, he completely ignores me. Again. He then continues to ignore me during the next two filming sessions and pretends not to notice me in the hall the following week.

He has me second-guessing everything and it's driving me crazy. He won't even let me say thanks. And while I didn't want to be friends, I'm now finding myself doing things to get closer to him, hoping he'll acknowledge my existence, and I hate that. Especially considering he's no longer pissed at me. He's just neutral. And I have no idea what that means.

When he blatantly walks away after I join a conversation he's in, it's the last straw, and I shoot off a text before bed that night. I'm not putting up with his shit. He wanted to be involved with the baby. He wanted to get married...and now this. *Who does he think he is?* I'll bet he's doing it on purpose, knowing it would be eating away at me.

When he still hasn't replied by morning, I'm pissed off and silently cursing his name as I arrive at work. I'm running through all the ways I can get back at him when I find him waiting in my new office, spinning around on my swivel chair, a pen in his right hand. With the light shining from above him, his black Storm cap casts a shadow across his face, but if I focus hard enough, I note that he's lost in thought.

It shouldn't surprise me that he hunted me down after my what-the-fuck text, but I am surprised that he knew where to find me, since I only moved into my private office yesterday.

"I'm sorry, do I know you?" I play dumb as my eyes bounce around the room.

Luke kicks his foot out to stop himself mid spin and smiles. "Funny." He points the pen toward me as he stands up and huffs out a fake laugh. "We need to talk."

"Uh-oh. Are you breaking up with me?" I huff out a laugh of my own until his expression turns serious. "What's going on?"

Luke takes a deep breath, and his pinched expression worries me. "First," he begins, standing taller, "I need the details for the lawyer, attorney, whoever you have handling your divorce." I nod as he speaks but, Jesus, this is getting real very quickly. "Second." He huffs out a breath as he removes his cap and runs a hand through his sexily mussed hair, drawing my attention until he speaks. "What the hell was that message?"

"What the hell is your attitude or lack of attitude? You get my car fixed but you won't even talk to me. It's weird. I don't like it."

"What?"

"You're pretending I don't exist. I couldn't even say thanks. What's with that? Did you change your mind about being a present father?"

"No. Fuck. I just don't think we should talk to each other in public."

"What?" His words catch me off guard, making me frown. He's the one that said telling people wasn't an issue. "What happened between 'where's my close-up'"—I put on my deepest and best Luke voice—"and now?"

Luke rolls his eyes at my impression but continues on. "I realized you'd be bad for my reputation. Once this is all over I'm going to have a baby. And babies get the ladies. I don't want them to assume I married you and then left after the baby was born. That would be the opposite of conducive to my goals."

"Your goals of what? Being the oldest playboy in California? I'm pretty sure Hugh Hefner will always hold that record. No matter how attractive or rich you are."

"Thanks for the compliment." He smirks as he raises an eyebrow, but something about it isn't Luke. I once thought his career and reputation were all he cared about, but that was before he found out about the baby. Now he's different.

"What's the real reason?"

"I told—"

"Bullshit."

"Bullshit? Don't act like you know me."

"I do. No matter how much that annoys you, I do." At least I used to, and I'm certain that boy is still in there somewhere.

Luke curses under his breath as he walks closer. "I don't want this"—he gestures between the two of us—"to ruin your career." He pauses and shakes his head before huffing out a laugh. "I'm not always an asshole. It's going to be hard enough with you being pregnant and... What? Why are you looking at me like that?"

What? I don't know how I'm looking at him but I'm speechless. I never expected this to be about me. That he was worried about me. Though considering he fixed my car without gloating, I probably should have considered it. "Thank you. I think."

"You think?" He barks out a laugh and shakes his head again. "Typical. I once again try to help and you don't trust me."

"No." I reach out and grab his arm when he brushes past me. "That's not what I meant. Are we really going to be able to do that? I mean, we're currently alone in my office and we have to work together and—"

"We can talk in a professional sense. If you need me to do something, I'll do it. Just like I fixed your car." *And here comes the gloating.*

"I didn't need you to—"

"Just accept it and move on. I'm here to help, but we shouldn't be friendly."

"Friendly?" It's been a while since we were truly friendly.

"You know what I mean. To anyone watching, our conversation last week came across as friendly banter. Flirty even. And that can't happen. Not if we want to keep this quiet."

"Okay. Thank you." *I don't know what else to say.*

"You're welcome. I meant what I said; I'm here to help. Send me the details of your lawyer and I'll keep you up-to-date. Until then, to professionalism." He lifts his fist for me to bump, and I can't help but laugh incredulously.

"To professionalism." I return his bump and he nods before walking away, completely stunning me. "And thank you," I call out. "For the car." As much as it pains me to accept his help, it was a nice thing to do.

Why don't people know this side of Luke? The caring, protective side. I've always known he existed somewhere deep down, but it's strange that he's never shown it to anyone else. He really should, because the protective side of him is *way* sexier than the playboy side he usually projects.

I don't move until he reaches my door, and I'm about to sit down when he calls out, "Oh, and Amelia, my sister knows."

His sister? *Shit.* Why is that worse than if it was a friend?

CHAPTER TWENTY-ONE

AMELIA

For the next three weeks, Luke does exactly what he said he was going to do and ignores me outside of professional conversations. Despite wishing I could pretend he didn't exist for most of my life, I struggle more than he does. Something about pretending we have a work relationship when he's the father of my unborn child doesn't sit well with me. But I'm trying.

"Morning, Amelia," Dylan says as he walks by, smiling with a new warmth as he begins to trust me. Most of the players are friendly with me now. You could say I've become a part of the furniture. While not all of them are completely comfortable with the cameras, they've separated me from that intrusion, and I'm grateful for that. Because this freaking team is growing on me.

"Dylan. Hi. How are you? How are the boys?" His wife, Summer, and their two boys came in to visit the other day—on a non-shoot day—and a new excitement welled inside me. When it comes to kids, I've never been that person. I wanted them, sure. I stopped taking the pill while I was married, but I wasn't one of those women that naturally gravitated toward kids. Now that I'm pregnant, it's a different story. Someone introduces me to a child and I immediately want to know everything about them. I'm a sponge. I've been reading up on all things relating to pregnancy and babies, but no matter how much I learn, it will never be enough. How can it be? There's no one-size-fits-all when it comes to kids. You just never know what they're going to be like.

Dylan stops walking and his smile widens. "Josh is a handful. We love him, but that's the best way to describe him, and Chris, my gentle soul, continues to blow my mind with how fast he's growing up. He wants to keep up with his big brother more than anything else."

"I can imagine."

"I never asked, do you have kids?"

"Not yet, no."

"I bet it would be hard with a job like this. You're always here. No matter what time of the day I'm here, you're here." I internally wince at his words, but he's not wrong. The long hours, the fast pace, the unpredictability of it all—it's not easy. But...

"I don't think it would be any harder than being a professional football player and having kids."

"True, and that's why I'm retiring." His eyes widen before he glances around. "That's off-the-record, right?"

I pretend to zip up my lips and nod. "Off-the-record."

"Thanks. I've told those that I have to tell, but haven't announced it to the team. It's hard keeping a secret, but I don't want them to start treating me differently yet."

Dylan just nailed my feelings completely. I've mentioned my pregnancy to Jim because he runs the business side of the company, and I assume he's mentioned it to Tom and HR, but I haven't announced it because I don't want to be treated differently. "Believe it or not, I understand. Your secret is safe with me."

A few of the other guys arrive for their weight sessions, and we chat briefly about what we're going to be filming. For some, the news pumps them up, while others visibly deflate, and I hate that. But it's the nature of the job.

Since the schedule for today doesn't require any specific action, I hand it over to my first assistant director Adrian to keep the team on track, then sneak into my office for some quiet time. I've had a headache for the past twenty-four hours and I need a slower day or it's likely to get worse. I promised myself I'd take care of my body, and now that it's not just me, I'm more determined.

When early afternoon hits, I'm scrolling through the footage they shot earlier in the day when I overhear Tom's voice in the hallway. "And here we are," he says, coming to a stop. "I'm sure Amelia can show you the dailies from last week," he continues, and I hold back a laugh. He's so old-school with the way he still refers to the footage as dailies. "She should be here. Last I heard she'd locked herself away to catch up on things."

"Amelia?" Luke's voice enters my mind and I freeze. "I thought George was going to show me the footage?" And I thought Tom was talking to a crew member. *Why would Luke need to see anything?*

"George is the one that mentioned it, but Amelia can show you. Hang on, I'll make sure she's inside."

I pause the playback and stare at the door just as Tom opens up, letting the bright fluorescent lights filter into the room, momentarily blinding me.

"Good, you're here," he says, barely glancing my way. "Can you show Luke the footage from last Thursday's practice? Our PR team wants to use some of it for a promo."

"Ah, sure." I'm confused by what that has to do with Luke because we had the players sign their lives away so we wouldn't need to seek extra permission, but Tom's the boss so I do as he asked. "Come in, Luke. Tom, do you know what I'm looking for?"

"Luke will know it. It's toward the end of the session. I'll leave you to it."

Luke steps inside just as Tom lets go of the door, shadowing us in the soft dim light of my lamp.

"Sorry. I've had a headache all day," I say when Luke looks around the dark room. "Feel free to turn on the overhead light."

"I'm good with this." He shakes his head as he moves toward me, and it snaps me into action, searching our files for last week's footage. "I won't be long," he adds as he reaches me. "But have you taken anything?"

"What?" I stare up at him confused until he points to his head.

"For your headache."

"Oh, right. Yes, I took some painkillers. Just waiting for them to kick in." I've been waiting around twelve hours, but I refuse to take anything stronger.

"Okay." Luke nods from the other side of my desk. "I'm sorry to interrupt you. I thought George was going to help me."

"It's fine. What do you need?" *And why is this so awkward?* We were more comfortable when we couldn't stand each other. This new normal is odd. It doesn't feel right and I don't like it.

It takes a few minutes, but we find the section of footage he needs, and as soon as I hit play, I get it. Luke is decked out in his perfectly fitted gray-and-black practice gear as he runs down the field and leaps into the air before catching the ball and rolling over the back of his opponent. The play is over in a matter of seconds, but it's everything we need to highlight the show. Especially since we have three different angles of the same shot. I click through the other files, and with each new angle, I grow prouder of my team. This footage is raw, fast-paced, full of action and suspense, and it's sexy as hell. The way they've captured Luke's muscles flexing as he reaches out and curls the ball into his arm, or the close-up of the sheer determination set in his features. It's something I could watch over and over. Hell, it's something I want to watch over and over.

My heart pounds as I swallow a lump in my throat before sucking my bottom lip between my teeth, trying not to voice my thoughts, while Luke stays silent.

I play the footage again, thinking that's all he needed, but when it ends, Luke leans over me to take control of my mouse, replaying the clips several times, his smile widening with each view. I hold my breath so I don't breathe him in and make sure to keep still with any movement likely to bring us closer.

"Fuck, I look good," he finally whispers after God knows how long, turning to face me, bringing his nose close to my cheek. My body warms and my legs clench, but I refuse to read anything into that. I'm blaming the pregnancy hormones because something like this wouldn't usually affect me.

He smiles and I let out a laugh. He's cocky but right now he can be, because he's right. It's great footage and it's going to make the perfect promo. Football fans will appreciate the play, and everyone else will appreciate Luke.

"For once, Luke, I'm going to give you this. Gloat away, because this clip is going to bring us viewers."

"Hell yeah." He laughs. "Don't worry, I won't bring this moment up too many times. But I'll always remember you saying it."

"Credit where credit's due."

"Thank you." He grins before nudging my shoulder with his, sending a tingle right through me.

"Look at us being civil while we're alone," I joke as I slide my chair back, trying to put some distance between us, needing to take my mind off his close proximity. "Maybe there's hope for us yet?"

I spin my chair away from him and stand up to turn on the light, hoping the brightness will snap me back to reality, but a sharp pain in my side cripples me and I grab the desk to stabilize myself. "Jesus Christ."

"What's wrong?" Luke rushes over, his hand settling on my lower back, his palm burning my skin. "What happened? Is it Bean?"

"Is it what?" I burst out laughing as I try to stand, but the pain takes a few more seconds to subside and when I flinch, Luke curls his arm farther around me, leaning closer to support my weight. I almost let him lift me until I remember I shouldn't and shake him off.

"Sorry, I'm okay. Just one of those joys of pregnancy."

"Are you sure?" He frowns, his hand still on me.

"Yep, it's caused by everything in here"—I wave my hands around my belly—"expanding. It's happened a few times."

Luke stares at me for a second, his eyes bouncing between mine as if trying to catch me on a lie, so I smile through the pain to put him at ease. "Oh-kay," he says slowly, still not a hundred percent convinced. "That's good. Sort of."

"I promise, the baby is fine. But...uh...what did you call it?"

Luke laughs before his usual playful demeanor returns and he takes a step back. "Jelly Bean. I couldn't keep saying 'baby.' It didn't feel right."

My heart skips but I ignore it and smile. *Hayley will be pleased.* "I like it. It is better than 'baby.' Do you mind if I steal it?"

"Of course not." He relaxes in front of me, putting me more at ease. "Your stealing has never bothered me. Remember you stole my answers to our math test in fifth grade?"

"Excuse me?" My jaw drops. "That never happened."

Luke folds his arms over his chest as he casually perches on the edge of my desk. "Then how do you explain *both* of us getting a perfect score?"

I half mimic his stance, crossing my arms and popping my hip. "We were *both* the smartest in our grade," I remind him.

Luke's cocky smirk lights up his face before he stands up and leans in, patting me on the back. "Thank you, Joy. I've waited years for you to admit that."

Dammit. I bark out a laugh as I once again shift away from his closeness.

"And on that win, I'm going to leave you to it." He points to the door and laughs until he glances back at me and his smile fades. "As long as you're okay?"

"Yes," I rush out as my chest tightens. "I promise. I'm fine."

"Good. You'd tell me if you weren't, right?" He frowns as though he's running scenarios through his head. "Or if anything else was worth telling me?"

"Definitely. I don't have anything to report at the moment. I promise."

"Okay. Great. Thank you. I guess I'll see you around."

"You will."

He walks away, only looking back when he reaches the door, hitting me with the most breathtaking yet somehow still cocky smile, and I can't help but stare at his mouth. He must use that as a secret weapon to get women, because holy shit, it's something else.

I think he says, "Take care, Joy," before he laughs to himself and disappears out of sight, but I couldn't be too sure. At least until I snap out of my daze and pray he wasn't laughing at me because I have no idea what expression I just gave him, though it can't have been good.

Fucking Luke.

I didn't want him to be the father of my child because I didn't think he cared about me. At all. And now it's almost worse that he does. Because what happens if he breaks my heart all over again? Or what happens if he breaks the heart of our child?

I shake off my thoughts and continue working, but an hour later, I'm still replaying our strange moments over and over when my phone rings.

I fumble around in my drawer until I find my cell, my eyes widening when I see who it is. *Stanton Lawyers.* The firm Luke paid to take over my divorce. A firm that was more expensive than my already expensive lawyer was.

I stare down at the screen, unable to answer because I'm terrified of what that will mean.

If they're calling to tell me it's done, then I'm all set to get married again.

And I am not ready for that.

"Amelia speaking," I answer at the very last second.

"Amelia, it's Richard," Luke's lawyer responds cheerfully. "I've got great news. Congratulations, you're officially divorced. I'm going to courier the decree to you tomorrow."

"Wow, thank you so much. I appreciate your help."

"Anytime." *Or anytime Luke pays you.* "How does it feel?"

"I'm not sure," I say honestly, and he laughs.

"Well, it's time to celebrate. If you need anything else, let me know."

"I will. Thank you."

I hang up but continue to stare at the phone for God knows how long, snapping out of it when a message comes through from Luke.

> Luke: I just got this text from my lawyer

He forwards me a message.

> Richard: It's done

Yep. It is. *So what now?*

Chapter Twenty-Two

LUKE

Our game is close coming into the final minutes. We may be sitting on twenty-five points against our opposition's twenty, but a stupid mistake means they have possession of the ball as the time ticks away. Miami needs a single touchdown to win the game, and they've been chasing our points every step of the way.

We're currently on four wins and zero losses as we hit the fifth week of the season, so you'd think we'd be favorites coming into this game, but Miami is also four and zero. Not to mention they made the Super Bowl last year. I may be cocky, but I can admit we need to push ourselves to the limits to hold this lead.

I'm on edge as their quarterback throws his pass. I hate watching from the sidelines when the scores are close. I'm not built that way. I much prefer to be in the action. Even if we lose.

Their offense makes it three yards and then four before the first whistle blows and I have to stop myself from screaming at our defense. It's too late in the game to be fucking around.

My heart pounds in my chest as play starts up again, and just when I think we've lost hope, our tackle, Levi, flattens their receiver to the ground, stopping him from making it another few yards.

"Yes. Go."

Thomas curses with relief but I don't dare look at him. We can't celebrate yet, and if he's smiling, I might get ahead of myself.

With less than a minute to go, I stop breathing, my eyes locked on the play. *Come on. Come on. Come on.*

Miami moves forward and either our home crowd goes quiet or I stop hearing them. This is it. They've done it, they're going to win and... *Holy shit!* Levi again! Out of nowhere.

We *won*. We fucking won.

The clock hits zero and the crowd goes wild. As they should. "Thomas!" I yell, joining in on the celebration.

"Fucking Levi," he cheers back at me before we both run onto the field.

You'd think it was the Super Bowl with the excitement coursing through me. But this win is more than just another point on the ladder. Miami is easily our biggest competition within this conference and they know it. But we won! We cemented what I've been saying since the pre-season began—this is our year.

When I reach the rest of our team, I dive into Levi's arms, as Zane slams into him from behind. "You're my hero," I yell above the noise. "What a hit."

Levi's cocky grin lights up his face as the others join in and the volume increases.

We celebrate on the field until the crowd starts to clear, and it's not until I stop cheering that I remember the cameras. And as I'm running toward the tunnel, shoulder to shoulder with Thomas, I spot Amelia and my smile widens on its own. *How was that for your show?*

I wait for her to turn away, like she's been doing since her divorce went through earlier this week, but she shocks me by flashing me a genuine smile in return, and while my cocky nature wants to say the smile's reserved for me, I know it's for the team. She may not have been a Storm fan before working on her show, but her excitement has been showing, and today, I'd say we turned her. Not that I blame her. I imagine it's hard not to get caught up in the hype when you work closely with the players. And considering it's likely to lead to higher ratings for her show, even better.

For the first few weeks after our agreement, we managed to keep things purely professional, just like we planned, but after our *moment* in her office and then when her divorce was finalized, the vibe between us changed. And I'm not sure what contributed more to that change—the fact that I panicked when I saw her hurting and couldn't keep my stupid hands to myself, or the fact that there's now nothing stopping us from getting married. Either way, we stopped talking altogether and it wasn't one-sided. It's easy to pretend things are fine until they become a reality. And now that

I've locked in our official nuptials for tomorrow, shit couldn't get any more real.

After showering and a talk from the coaches, we're called back onto the field for our postgame interviews, a change to our usual routine so that Amelia's team has more room to film. Or maybe it's for better aesthetics. I don't know; I didn't listen. I just did as I was told like the good professional guy that I am. But now that I'm here, it's absolute chaos. What the hell were they thinking? The guys have no idea what cameras they're supposed to be looking at and the media are not at all happy with the development. It would be comical if it wasn't a pain in the ass. Don't get me wrong, I've been loving the spotlight, but sometimes the extra theatrics or changes in our day can be off-putting.

As I wait for my turn to be interviewed, I see Amelia talking to our coach and his daughter across the field, and my eyes drift over Amelia's pregnant belly. She's been making an effort to hide the evidence—wearing oversized tees or extra layers, even though it's still warm outside, usually blaming the air conditioning—and it's working. My lips curl into a smile as our little secret comes to mind, but it fades the second I remember she can't hide it forever, and when the world finds out, things are going to get harder for her.

Because make no mistake, we have some very vocal players on this team.

"Don't tell me you slept with Coach's daughter?" Reed groans from beside me, and I internally jump since he came out of nowhere. I almost ask him "what the hell," until I get it. He must have caught me staring in their direction—in Amelia's direction—making me laugh.

"I'm not stupid." I shove at his shoulder. "I'm fully aware that's a one-way ticket out of here."

"So, you're what? Staring at her because you want to go there? Because she's off-limits? Because—"

"I slept with Amelia." My eyes widen and I curse under my breath. I didn't mean for those words to come out of my mouth, but now that they have, a weight lifts.

Reed spits out his drink as his eyes flash toward me, and I've got to admit, I'm a little proud of that reaction—I always thought nothing I did shocked anyone—but despite smiling about it before, keeping this secret from some of my teammates has been hell. Especially when I've caught a number of the guys drooling over her.

Since Reed's a rule follower, I wait a few seconds before saying something else and he panics right on cue. "Was it before or after we were told she's a no-go zone?"

"Before." I ease his mind, though it won't be eased for long when the news drops.

Reed breathes out a sigh in relief. "Thank fuck. I like having you on the team."

I laugh out loud, drawing the attention of the people around us before lowering my voice. The last thing I need is for Amelia to look my way. "You don't actually think they'd drop one of us for sleeping with a member of the film crew, do you?" I lean in closer, my tone slightly louder than a whisper. "They're more likely to fire the crew."

"Maybe." Reed shrugs, like he hasn't thought this through, but I'll bet all my money that he has...and I'm loaded. "I'd say we're going to find out one way or another," he adds with a frown, proving my thoughts. "Amelia aside, because you know, she's..." He trails off, waving his hand as though that finishes his sentence while my heart pounds in my chest. Maybe people *do* know.

"She's...what exactly?"

"She's married."

"She's *married*?" I fake ignorance while... *Shit*. I didn't consider the possibility of people knowing that information. So, why isn't he questioning *me* for sleeping with her? On that note, does Preston have social media? Someone needs to update his marital status to "divorced" before the baby news gets out. *Do people announce that?*

I mentally shake off my thoughts and smile. "Well, there you go," I say casually, sneaking a quick glance in Amelia's direction when Reed looks away. "How'd you find out?"

"By accident."

"By *accident*?"

"Yep. I was curious about what else she'd directed and...it doesn't matter. Point is, we are a football team, full of players, and I don't mean the football kind. Of course we're going to find out the consequences of breaking the off-limits rule. It's just a matter of when. I mean— Wait." He cuts himself off as his eyes widen, his gaze bouncing between me and Amelia. *Here it comes.* "She's *married*."

"Is she? Maybe she's recently divorced." I shrug, keeping my face straight.

"When exactly did you sleep with her?"

"About four months ago."

"Four months? But—"

"I will *not* calm down!" a voice yells from behind us, cutting off Reed as we both spin to find Amelia's douchebag colleague, Jake, storming toward where she's now talking with Tom. "I told you she wasn't the right person for the job," he snaps into his phone and my body tenses. "I need to end this now. She should be fired."

Reed's eyes bore a hole in the side of my face, but I ignore it, my gaze locked on Jake as I listen in on his not-so-private conversation. I'm about to follow him when he hisses his next words, making me pause.

"She's *pregnant*, Patrick. I'm not the one in the wrong."

Jesus Christ. How the hell does he know?

My eyes scan the field to check if anyone else was listening, but other than a few random people that wouldn't know who he was talking about, everyone else is distracted by the media. The *media. Fuck. Fuck. Fuck.* This is the worst possible time for him to be here.

My fists clench just as Reed grabs my arm, not that I acknowledge him, my eyes staying firmly locked on Jake as he moves toward Amelia.

"You slept with her four months ago?" he asks, putting two and two together.

"Yep."

"Shit. That doesn't mean anything. He might be wrong and—" I don't wait for him to finish his sentence before taking off after Jake, an irrational anger welling up inside me as I push through the crowd. I knew this guy was a dick, but if he thinks he's about to publicly humiliate Amelia, he's got another think coming.

I reach out to grab the back of his shirt when someone pulls me to a stop, making me turn in anger. "Don't," Reed whisper-yells, his voice curt.

"Let go of me, Reed," I grate, my teeth clenched as I try to subtly pull away from him.

"Wait," he says, his gaze shifting over my shoulder.

If he thinks I'm going to let this play out—

Reed lets go of me and pushes me behind him before rushing to Amelia's side. It takes me a second to register what he's doing, but when I reach them he's waving a hand in front of Tom's face, trying to get his attention. "I'm aware that you barely know me," he says, his voice low to avoid attention. "But I'm here to tell you that if you don't silence what this asshole is about to announce, we're all walking."

"Excuse me? Who the... Jake?" Tom's eyes find Jake's and his brows furrow. "I thought I said you weren't to come back here."

"You did. But Tom, you're going to want to hear this."

Tom's eyes flash to Reed as Jake opens his mouth. Reed stands tall with his arms folded over his chest, his bulging muscles clear through his shirt and his huge frame making him appear a lot more trouble than he is.

"Stop," Tom yells, his tone so final that I jump. "Whatever you have to say, Jake, you say it in private."

"But this affects everyone here and—" Reed spins around as I step in, pulling Jake back before getting in his face. I'm close enough to show him I mean business but not so close that I touch him. I wouldn't put it past him to pin me for assault. "Say another word," I grate, my anger rising now that I'm staring at his smug face. "I dare you."

Jake freezes, his gaze lifting to find Tom over my shoulder. "Are you going to let this happen?"

"You need to leave, Jake." Tom keeps his voice even but it's obvious there's no room for argument. "Meet me at the office. We'll talk there."

"Tom—"

"Go!"

Jake shakes his head before walking away with a huff, and it's then that I register how tight the tension is coiled through my body. My muscles relax the farther he gets from Amelia, but I don't unclench my fists until he's reached the edge of the field. My body heaves as I turn to check on her, but when he calls out again, I freeze.

"Do you really think you're going to finish this job with a—" My gaze snaps back, ready to chase after him when Easton beats me to it, shoving him through the gate and into the tunnel, cutting him off before he gets the last word out.

I stare shocked as Easton follows after Jake, and when they both disappear into the darkness, I snap out of it and shake off my disbelief.

As a team, we all have each other's backs, but Easton is not the guy that gets involved in other people's business. Especially if there are cameras around.

Jesus. The cameras.

I frantically search the media chaos to find most of them resuming their interviews, but God knows what footage they have. When I finally glance back to Amelia, I'm met with her panicked gaze before she turns away, beelining straight for her assistant. And I hate that I can't go to her. That doing so would make things worse.

My mind whirs as I contemplate what to do next, and I'm about to demand someone do something when I overhear Coach talking on his phone. "I need you to find Keeley. We need to make sure none of that gets seen."

I release a held breath as his words work to ease some of my anger, but as I walk away—hoping to lose myself in the crowd—I realize how much I'm still holding onto. I want to hurt that asshole. I want to chase after him and make him pay for what he tried to do. What he did. *Who the fuck does he think he—*

"Calm down," Reed cuts into my throughs before grabbing my elbow and subtly dragging me away.

"Don't tell me—"

"Play it cool then. Smile. I don't care. Just do something to avoid attention."

I pause and the second I do, I notice the eyes on us from around the space, including Thomas's questioning expression. *Jesus.* Reed's right. And here I was worried about Amelia.

"Thanks, man," I whisper back, shaking his hands off me but following without protest.

When we're once again out of earshot, Reed turns my way, his expression marred with concern. "So..." He hesitates before stepping closer. "It was never your brother, was it?"

"What?" I ask, taking a few seconds to catch up.

"The baby," he whispers and I almost laugh. *Oh right. I forgot I told him that little white lie.*

"Oooh. No. It was me," I confirm. "You're looking at a soon-to-be DILF, right here." I point to myself and huff out a laugh, bouncing my eyebrows as I throw out a joke like I'm expected to do, though my lackluster tone gives me away.

Reed's eyes widen. "*Jesus*. Aren't you freaking out?"

"I was. I'm past that now. I'm goooood." *I am so far from good I don't know what I am.* And maybe if I wasn't so distracted, I'd be able to have a proper conversation about it, but right now it's not going to happen. Especially when Easton returns, moving into my line of sight and I have to hold back from rushing over to him.

"You're acting weird," Reed cuts into my thoughts. "Are you sure you're not just telling yourself that you're fine?"

"That's exactly what I'm doing, Reed." My voice rises before I cut myself off. "Sorry," I say, softening my tone. "But I'm going to need you to work with me here."

Reed's demeanor reverts back to caring mode before patting my back. "This is going to be amazing. You've got this. I know you do."

My body deflates as I release a quick breath. "Thanks, man. I appreciate that." I had no idea how much I needed to hear that until this very second.

We keep up the 'everything's fine' charade for as long as possible, until Amelia passes by, refusing to meet my eyes while all I can think about is making sure she's okay.

Reed laughs from beside me, cupping my shoulder with his palm. "I'm sorry, I tried. But man, you are fucked."

I bark out a laugh, watching as Amelia walks away, my stomach twisted in knots. "Yep, I'm fucked," I agree without looking his way.

So fucked.

I've been trying hard to pretend I'm good with the way things are between Amelia and me, but the truth is that I'm in this *way* deeper than I realized.

And it's got nothing to do with our baby.

Chapter Twenty-Three

LUKE

I somehow smile through my media commitments and even project the fun and carefree Luke I usually am. But the second I get back to my locker, I have my phone in hand ready to text Amelia. The sad expression on her face when she walked away hasn't left my mind for the past forty minutes. I have no idea if Keeley put a ban on discussing the incident, but thankfully no one asked me about it because I'm not sure I could have kept my cool.

Who the fuck does that man think he is? And in what day and age is it okay to call a woman out for being pregnant? I can't fathom what he thought was going to happen. Did he think Tom was going to fire her on the spot and hand the reins over to him? And that we'd just accept that?

I squeeze my phone in my hand and will myself to calm down. He's gone and I need to focus on what's important. Amelia. Amelia is what's important. She never came back after walking off the field and I'm worried.

I'm worried.

It's like I've come full circle.

I went from wanting to protect her when we were kids, to being pissed off by the very sight of her, to caring about my unborn child, to caring about her, to suddenly wanting to protect her with all that I am. Whatever it takes. And as hard as I try to pretend that has everything to do with Jelly Bean, I know that's not true. Deep down I've always cared—there's no denying it—and I need to know she's alright.

Luke: Are you okay?

I stare down at the screen for a solid minute before accepting that she's probably not going to respond straight away, and instead, collect my things to leave. Reed nods when he catches my stare, but when I lock eyes with Easton, he turns away, just like he'd do in any other situation. As though nothing happened, and it pisses me off. I'd call him out on it, but I'm smart enough to know that now's not the time. I need everyone to move on from what happened with Amelia, not draw attention to it.

I'm on my way home when my phone finally buzzes, and I can't wait until I arrive to check it, pulling over to the side of the road the second I get a chance.

Only to be disappointed.

> Thomas: What the hell is going on?

Can't say I didn't know that was coming. I'm actually surprised it took this long; I expected him to chase me into the parking lot. It's the kind of shit that we do. And he'd have every right to question me. I should have told him sooner. It's been killing Lainey to keep it a secret, and I shouldn't have put her in that position to begin with.

Instead of texting him back, I drive straight to their house and prepare myself for the million questions. It's time I told them both everything that's going on. I could use my sister and my friend right now.

Lainey's eyes widen when she opens the door, but when Thomas sees me, he calls out from behind her.

"Well, this saves me a call. I appreciate that."

Lainey's brows furrow as she spins around. "What's going on?"

"Ask your brother."

I subtly shake my head when Lainey glances back before walking inside and closing the door behind me.

"There's something I need to tell you both."

Thomas raises an eyebrow as his lips pull into a suppressed smirk and he waves a hand in front of him. "Go on."

"I'm getting married," I blurt on purpose to wipe that smug expression off his face. "And she's having my baby." Thomas's jaw drops while Lainey bursts out laughing, and when he hears her, he smiles, assuming I'm joking.

"Hilarious. What's really—"

"He's not kidding. It's tomorrow. I'm the witness."

"What?" He spins Lainey's way and gapes. "I thought we weren't supposed to keep things from each other?"

"We're not. But this wasn't my secret to tell. Kind of like the secret you had that Luke kept quiet about?"

"Fuck, okay. I love you; you're forgiven. But you—" He turns and points at my chest. "You need to start talking."

"I will. Geez, can I at least sit down?"

Thomas shakes his head but follows me into the living room, and when I'm sitting, I tell him everything I told Lainey, letting him know we're keeping it quiet but that her dickwad of a colleague tried to announce it today.

"Thank God Reed and I overheard that asshole, because otherwise he would have announced it to the world."

"You don't think they'd actually fire her, do you?" Lainey asks, her voice full of concern.

"No," Thomas and I answer at the same time before I add, "We wouldn't let that happen."

"He's right." Thomas nods as he reaches for Lainey's hand. "The production company may have had some pushback when they first arrived, but we've all been pretty cooperative. We could easily refuse their future requests and make life hard for them."

"Or leak stories about the production."

"Point is, they won't risk it. Especially after you and Reed made a point of standing up for her. How is she feeling?"

My stomach twists, making me wince. *Isn't that the million-dollar question?*

"I wish I knew. She hasn't responded to my text, and I couldn't find her before I left."

"*Shit.*" Lainey worries her bottom lip. "Does she have anyone to talk to? About any of this? I should have asked you that when you first told me."

And cue the guilt. "She mentioned a friend, Hayley. But if I'm being honest, I never really asked. Things are complicated between us."

"I'll say." Thomas huffs out an incredulous laugh. "You two barely speak unless it's about the show."

"Maybe we meet up in secret. I would have thought you of all people would have considered that." I raise an eyebrow, referring to him dating my sister behind my back.

"Yeah, okay. You got me there. So is that what you're doing? Running around in secret?"

"Nope." I deadpan, making him laugh.

"The marriage is for insurance purposes," Lainey cuts in, rolling her eyes.

"No way."

"Way. And thanks for ruining my fun, Lainey."

"I was getting bored. Are you going to tell him or should I?"

"Go ahead."

"They're getting married so that Amelia and the baby can use his insurance. He wants to protect them."

Her eyes light up and Thomas smiles at her happiness. "How is it possible that you kept this a secret? The marriage I get, but the baby. You being an aunt. To Luke's child. I would have thought you'd be dying to tell me."

"I was. It's the one time he gets to invoke the brother-sister code."

"My mind is poouff." Thomas gestures as though his head is exploding and I laugh, despite feeling the same. "So it's all fake? And Amelia knows that too."

"Yes."

"And you're still fucking around? With others."

"What? No. I'm not an asshole."

"That's debatable but I wasn't accusing you. I was asking."

I fold my arms over my chest and glare at him. "It was your tone."

"Seriously." Lainey shakes her head. "You two are like children." She laughs until her face turns serious. "But I really hope you're not."

"I'm *not*." *Jesus, is my word worth nothing?*

"Good. Does this mean I get to meet her now? I've been waiting so long."

"No." *Hell no.*

"No? That's it? Well, since Thomas knows, I could go with him to the stadium for bring-your-fiancée-to-work day."

"That's not a thing," I scoff.

"Sure it is. It's this Friday."

Thomas subtly shakes his head and I bark out a laugh. We have an away game this weekend, so we'll be traveling Friday.

"I mean, Thursday. *Obviously.*"

"God, you're annoying. You're going to see her tomorrow at the wedding."

Lainey's jaw drops before she huffs like the child she was just accusing me of being. "I'll be on a screen with my mic muted."

"Close enough." I shrug, holding back my smile. I was grateful when I discovered some states including California had introduced legal online weddings because it would ensure our privacy. But now, I'm discovering there are more benefits.

"Ugh." Lainey pouts, making me laugh. "I'm getting a drink. Anyone else want some water?"

Thomas shakes his head. "I'm good."

"I'd love a coffee," I say as she gets up, ducking when she throws a cushion at my face.

"Two waters it is," she sasses before walking away, knowing full well I don't drink coffee at night.

When Lainey's gone, I turn back to Thomas just as my phone vibrates across the table. I rush to grab it, not bothering to hide my urgency, a tension easing when I see that it's Amelia.

Amelia: It's been a strange week

That's it? That's all she's giving me? It's not enough. I massage my temples as I figure out how to respond. When I lift my gaze after a beat, Thomas is staring at me, his expression pensive.

"How do you really feel about everything?" he asks.

"What?" I frown, trying to recall what happened to make him ask that.

"I remember something you said after Lainey and I broke up. God knows why it came to me, but it did."

Jesus, that was years ago and I was absolutely ragey. I can't imagine anything I said was making sense. Thomas continues to stare, his lips pursed as he thinks, until I laugh. "Don't leave me in suspense. What did I say?"

"It was something along the lines of 'You did the best thing for now. You have to play the long game. She'll be back when the time is right for both of you.'"

"Bullshit. That doesn't sound like me at all."

"You're right. But it was. At the time, I thought you were spinning some shit to make things better, but now... I'm not so sure."

"Of course that's what I was doing. You were spiraling. I had to do something."

"*Or*...maybe you've cared about Amelia for longer than you think? Why else would she drive you so crazy? Maybe you're playing the long game."

"Nope. I don't have that kind of patience," I joke. "This and that are completely unrelated."

I laugh off his comment, but it sits with me as we wait for Lainey to return, my face pinched as I struggle with the idea of his words. I know I've always cared about her, on some level, but what he's saying is so much more than that, and he's wrong. That applied to him and Lainey. This is an entirely different situation.

As soon as Lainey appears, I jump up and make an excuse to leave. I've said my truth, and I don't need to hang around while they pick it apart, which they'll undoubtedly do with or without me. Thomas already tried.

After saying goodbye, I pause in the driveway and send off a reply to Amelia, my body tense from her short response.

Luke: Can I see you? We should talk before tomorrow

My message turns to "read" almost immediately as though she was waiting by her phone, but I'm halfway home before she actually responds.

> Amelia: I'm just leaving my office. I can meet you somewhere

She's just leaving? Jesus.

> Luke: Does my place work?

> Amelia: Yep. See you in twenty minutes

I pull into my driveway, but don't bother going inside. Instead I sit on my front steps and wait. It's a nice night, and if I'm honest with myself, I'm too anxious to do anything else.

My phone buzzes in my pocket and my stomach sinks, expecting her to cancel, but when I check the screen, it's Reed.

> Reed: I'm here if you need me. Anytime

Some tension releases in my shoulders and I can't help but smile as I think about him defending Amelia today. I don't usually openly share any of my business, but who knows, one day I might take him up on that offer. For now, there's one person I need, and she's almost here. But am I really ready to talk?

CHAPTER TWENTY-FOUR

AMELIA

What the hell am I doing?

I subtly rub my belly as I wait for the light to turn green. I should have been at Luke's by now, but instead of taking the direct route, I took the scenic drive, delaying the inevitable. Trying hard to focus on the city lights and my relaxing playlist so I don't spend the time talking myself out of it.

Tomorrow I'm supposed to be getting married... and today was a mess of all messes to say the least. I narrowly avoided being outed on TV. Thank God, the live broadcasts were at the other side of the field. Not that anyone really knows who I am, but if one person did, the media would be all over it.

For some reason, Preston hasn't bothered to make our breakup public knowledge among his fans, so it would result in people either assuming he's the father, or dragging my name through the mud for cheating on him. Both shitty options.

God, for someone who prefers to live behind the scenes, I attract the wrong people into my life. First, Preston and now, Luke. *What am I doing?* Why couldn't I have accidentally gotten pregnant by a small-town accountant or mechanic? At least then I would have someone to do my taxes or fix my car rather than someone with the potential to propel my life into the spotlight. Although I suppose Luke got my car fixed, so maybe an accountant would be best.

My phone buzzes as I drive, and I don't need to see the screen to know it's Hayley checking in on me. I texted her after my chat with Tom and I wasn't in a great place. Sure, he was pleasant enough, just like Jim had been when I'd first told him about my pregnancy, but he wasn't subtle in alluding to this being my last big project for a while. With a baby in my world, it would be impossible to work the long hours needed in this job—not that I want to work that much when the baby comes along, or at all—but after a while, when I'm not breastfeeding and can look into daycare options...maybe, I'll go back. God, I haven't thought about what that would look like, but it's not going to be easy. It's hard enough finding work in this industry, let alone finding work that would allow me to have any kind of relationship with my child.

Maybe I should have been thinking about this before now.

When I finally arrive at Luke's, he's waiting out front, most likely convinced I wasn't going to show up, and he wouldn't be completely off base. We may not be making it official until tomorrow, but the fact that he wants to talk now suggests that our time is up and there's no going back. *Unless that's what this is? Is it him, taking it all back?*

And if it is...I'm not sure I'd be sad about it. I'm not sure about *any* of it.

All I know is that it's hard to remain the independent woman I promised myself I'd be after leaving Preston, when I'm about to marry a man for his money. It's been a month and I've yet to come to terms with it. Because do I really need it?

I've been to the emergency room once in my thirty-two years and that was after the fire incident with Luke. I mostly eat healthy. Mostly. At least I do now. And I keep fit when I have the time and the headspace. Have I let myself get run-down during times of stress? Yes. But would I ever do anything to jeopardize the health of my unborn baby? *Hell no.* Since finding out I was pregnant, my every decision has been about my baby. *About Jelly Bean.* Wow. Luke was right, it is better using that name. Because of Bean, I'm no longer the first in the office, letting myself sleep in when I need it. I eat when I'm supposed to, drink plenty of water, and take my prenatal vitamins. I'm listening to my body. If something ever felt off, I'd be the first to ask for help. But does that mean I need the best insurance? Plenty of women have babies without it. *Daily.* Just because I have a high-profile baby daddy doesn't mean I'm going to need it.

But what if I do?

How can I take that risk?

I put on a smile as I get out of my car and wave as Luke stands. "Are you okay?" he asks, his scrutinizing gaze locked on my face, pulling me out of my crazy thoughts.

"Of course." I laugh nervously. "Why wouldn't I be?" I wait until I reach him before adding, "I'm soon to marry San Francisco's most sought after bachelor and I'm pregnant with his baby."

Luke's face drops as he releases a breath. "Thanks for the sarcasm, *Joy*, but I was being serious. What happened after you left today? Why were you there so late? They didn't fire you, did they?"

His obvious concern gently tugs at my heart, but I try hard to ignore it. "I'm sorry," I say honestly, my shoulders relaxing as I glance up at the sky and blow out a breath of my own. "They didn't fire me. They were great about it, but things will be different after this project. And while I never expected otherwise and I wouldn't want them to be the same, I hadn't really thought it through."

"I understand that but it must still be upsetting."

"Honestly, I've been focusing my thoughts on life during pregnancy, and about marrying you, I haven't really thought much past Jelly Bean's birth, apart from writing a list of items I might need." Luke smiles at my use of his nickname and I huff out a laugh. "Sorry again. You don't need to worry about what happened today. I'm fine. And we have other things to discuss. Tomorrow's our wedding day. Right? So yay." I smile wide while Luke stares at me with a pissed-off expression.

"Okay." I laugh. "I'll drop the sarcasm. Thank you," I say seriously and I mean it. "I appreciate you stepping in when Jake turned up. And I appreciate your concern, and your text."

"Yeah, well, it seems I care. A little."

"Thanks." *Unfortunately, so do I.*

When I saw Jake storming toward me, I panicked. Without him saying a word, I knew that he'd somehow found out about my pregnancy and that meant my time was up. He was about to win. Yes, I'd already told Jim, but it would be harder for him to fight for me if I caused a scene on live TV. And make no mistake, I would have caused a scene.

But I didn't have to.

And I'm still a little shocked about that.

Reed coming to my rescue was confusing at first. Until I remembered he's a protective guy. He told me that himself.

But Luke.

Luke coming to my rescue had my heart racing for all the wrong reasons, and now I can't stop picturing him as a doting father to our child. A protector. And I hate how much more attractive that makes him.

I mentally shake off my thoughts as he laughs to himself before heading toward his front door. "Come in. It's getting cold out here."

"Thanks." I move to follow him inside but pause at the threshold. "Though I have to ask...why am I here?"

"Well, Amelia, it all comes back to me caring. I don't want you to be put in a situation like that again. It shouldn't have happened and because of that, we need some kind of plan."

Dammit, Luke. "Thank you." A plan is a good idea. *But why am I so nervous?*

I tuck my knees up to my chest as Luke passes me a glass of water before sitting on the couch opposite me. "So where do we begin?" he says with an awkward laugh, making me smile. It's good to know I'm not the only one feeling uncomfortable about everything between us.

"Since we're getting married tomorrow, maybe we should start there. Talk about how that's going to look, who we're going to tell."

"Sounds good and as I mentioned, Lainey knows and Thomas now too. Oh and Reed."

Reed? "Guess that explains why he came to my rescue."

"Actually, it doesn't. Believe it or not, like me, the guys care about you. Reed wasn't kidding. We would all walk away if they fired you. I mean we wouldn't walk away from football because that's insane. But I doubt any of the guys would continue with *Project Storm.*"

"And here I was thinking it was your dream to be an actor."

"Maybe it is. I'm about to play the part of a doting husband after all."

I try to laugh, but his words don't sit well with me and my face scrunches on its own. I wait for his laugh, but when I look his way, he's frowning. *Whatever that means.*

"Anyway, they're the people I've shared the news with, but I need to tell Coach."

My chest tightens despite knowing this was coming. "Okay, yes. That makes sense. Will you tell him the truth, or pretend we're really together?"

"The truth. It will be easier in the long run. What about you?"

I don't have to think about it before I answer, "Yes, you're right. I agree."

"No." Luke chuckles. "I mean, who else knows on your end? I remember you saying you wanted to tell your friend, Hayley."

"Oh, yes." My cheeks heat but I smile through it. "Hayley knows. But that's it."

"You're not going to tell your mom or Tom and Jim?"

"Nope. Tom and Jim know enough. They don't need to know about the marriage. And as for my mom, the less she knows the better."

Luke frowns. When we were kids, I had a good relationship with my mom, but a lot has changed since then. "Trust me," I add, hoping he'll move on. But he doesn't.

"Who does she think the father is?" he asks after a beat.

"She doesn't know."

"Obviously. But I'll bet she's asked."

"I'm sure she would if I answered her calls."

"What?" Luke's eyes widen before he schools his features. "But—"

"Do your parents know?"

"Not yet, but they will. Soon. I haven't spoken to them, but it's better to ask for forgiveness after I'm married than explain why they're not invited."

I nod as guilt threatens to darken my mind, but I refuse to let it. I know what will happen if I tell my mom. She was shocked about my pregnancy, and not happy that it wasn't Preston's. But discovering I'm also getting married, when she's still hoping I'll fix things with him...that's another story. True, she'll find out eventually, but as with Luke's family, it's better for that to happen after-the-fact. She'll just stress me out, and I don't need that while I'm pregnant. She already tried when I mentioned the baby.

"Next topic," I say with a grimace and pray that he lets me off the hook.

Luke shakes his head with a laugh but thankfully moves on, and I'm once again grateful for his kindness. "Let's talk about the actual ceremony. We have to make it real for the officiant."

"Of course. I don't have any plans to give the game away."

"I know, but what about vows, etc.?"

Vows? Jesus. *Why does that make me squirm?* "The standard ones are fine. I'm sure we can find something online." Luke's lips lift into a cocky smile and I cringe. "Don't tell me you wrote something?"

"I haven't." He shakes his head before looking away in thought. "But I bet I could think of something. What about—I promise to be open and honest. To never keep secrets. To protect you and any future children we might have. I promise to..." He continues on but I zone out. He's trying to be funny but his words bring up memories from the past, and I'm struggling to separate the man he is now from the boy he was then.

He promises to be *honest. No secrets.* To *protect me.* But it's all fake.

What am I doing? This is a mistake. God, what happens when I'm ready to find true love? I'm going to be doing it as a twice-divorced woman. Twice. In my thirties. Marriage is supposed to be about love, but instead I marry the guy who pretends to care. My body numbs as all the emotions from the past come rushing back.

"Amelia, what's going on?"

I curl my hands around my knees as Luke stands in my peripheral vision. I try to suck a deep breath to calm myself but struggle to take in air as the reality of it all sets in. *I know it's fake.* That's what it's supposed to be, but it's not that easy. Luke's not just some guy I'm having a baby with. We share a history. And the baggage between us is weighing me down.

"Amelia." Luke rushes to my side and drops to his knees in front of me before grabbing my legs, the warmth of his hands pulling me back to the present. "What happened?"

I suck in another deep breath before pinning him with my gaze, shaking my head. "It's not right."

"What's not right? The baby?" I shake my head again at the sheer panic in his eyes and he calms a little. "The wedding then? We're doing it for Jelly Bean. Think about—"

"Marriage means something to me, Luke. I know it means *nothing* to you, but it means...well, it used to mean *everything* to me."

Luke's gaze softens as though he gets it, but he doesn't. "Don't think of it as a marriage. I promise, you can still have the perfect marriage one day. This is just for now. Until the baby is born and—"

"Did you ever care about me?" I blurt out and instantly regret it. Talking about our past and our feelings makes it harder to pretend it's all meaningless between us.

Luke rears back as though I slapped him, his eyes wide as he responds, "What?"

"Sorry, don't worry. Forget—"

"No, I'm not going to forget it, but that's a complicated question."

"And it has no place in this discussion. We are talking about our present situation. Not the past."

"But you brought it up, so we need to talk about it."

"Nope." Now is not the time for us to be arguing, and I know how this ends.

"Amelia."

"Luke."

He shakes his head and stands before pacing in front of me. "What are we talking about here? Because you know I fucking cared. I—"

"You promised to be my *hero*, Luke. You said you'd always be there for me and you lied."

"Are you talking about the fire?"

"No. Yes. I'm talking about all of it."

"All of it? What else?" He stares at me with wide eyes, confusion marring his features. And I don't blame him. I'm still harping on about something that happened when we were kids. I should have moved on by now. I thought I had, but I guess I never expected to be so close to Luke again. It's bringing up bad memories.

"It doesn't matter. I shouldn't have mentioned it. It was so long ago and—"

"It does matter if you're still thinking about it. So let's get it all out in the open. Starting with the fire. It's about time we said our piece."

CHAPTER TWENTY-FIVE

LUKE

Amelia cringes but nods as she sits straighter in her chair. "The fire. Okay." She pulls a face and I internally wince, knowing what's coming. "I guess first up, I want to know why you ran."

I rub my hands down my face and curse under my breath. While so much has happened between us since our night together at the hotel, if we don't talk about this, we'll never move on. "You're not going to believe it," I say honestly, huffing out a laugh.

"Try me?"

"Okay." I release a slow breath and sit up looking at her when I speak, ready to start from the beginning. "I was the one that suggested the dare," I admit and then pause when her eyes widen. "The original plan was to lock you in the attic alone, but I thought that would be too easy. In hindsight, you probably would have given up sooner." Amelia nods without saying a word and it's worse than when she sasses me. I'd much prefer her snapping back at me than this new calm demeanor. "I didn't know being up there would make you panic. I—"

"I know what happened; I was there. But you never told me... Was it your idea to lie about the fire?" she cuts me off, her voice devoid of emotion.

"It was." I swallow a lump in my throat, holding on to one vital piece of information, still unable to say it out loud. "But it was a joke to scare you. I knew you wouldn't want to back out of the dare, and I was trying to push you as far as I could. At the time, I wanted to embarrass you."

"And then shit got real and you ran."

"I wasn't expecting the place to actually burn. But when it happened, I panicked. I ran to the police, hoping I could distract them long enough for you and David to escape without getting caught. But it didn't work."

Amelia bursts out laughing, but I can tell from her expression that this is anything but funny. "You expect me to believe that you left me to protect me?"

"I've done a lot of things to protect you. Is it really that crazy of an idea?" I think back on all the things I've done and shake my head. "It's like no matter what I feel, I can't fucking stop."

"So is that what this is? The marriage. It's you not being able to stop?"

My eyes widen before I shake my head and sit forward. *Fuck*. "No." I pause. "Not exactly."

"What does that mean?"

"It means that so much has happened since we were younger and what we're going through now is much more important. I'm not doing this out of some deep-seated need I have to protect you. I'm doing this because I want to. Because it's the right thing to do, for you and our baby."

"Just because you think you're doing something for the greater good, doesn't make it right. You know, we barely got out of the fire when you ran. David had to smash a glass door; I couldn't breathe. I still have breathing issues to this day. I get bronchitis now, because of that fire."

"*Jesus*. I'm sorry. I didn't know any of that. But I promise, my way wasn't any easier. I had to jump off the roof."

"So did I," she finally snaps. "The only way out was the second-story balcony. I was terrified."

"David helped—"

"I wanted *you*, Luke. Despite everything we'd been through, I trusted *you*. I let you kiss me and then you broke that trust again."

Fuck. My stomach knots as a wave of guilt takes over me. No, not guilt —regret. She was my childhood best friend and I treated her like shit over the years. All because of my stupid ego. Because I couldn't handle that she basically ghosted me and then took joy in competing over the years. "I fucked up. I know that. I knew that at the time, but I was so angry at you for getting me arrested that I never bothered explaining. But I've always cared. And that kiss was real. It may not have been real for you, but it was real for me."

Her face drops before she whispers. "It was real for me too. Doesn't mean it was right."

"No, it doesn't."

"This is so messed up, Luke. God, saying it all out loud. You set me up, you made me hate you, and now we're getting married."

"That was a different time. And you weren't exactly innocent. You hated me for years before that."

"Did you ever stop to question why?"

"Why, what?"

"Why I stopped talking to you when we were kids?"

"Of course I did. Because you never told me. You went away for the summer and came back as a different person."

"What?"

"You went to visit your cousin over the summer, and when you came back, you barely looked at me, except for that one conversation. And I'd barely started telling you about my summer when you walked away."

I thought I'd long moved past all of this—we were eleven—but as I think about it, my muscles tense and I remember how much it affected me at the time.

"Wow." Amelia looks at me like I'm crazy. "That's not at all how I remember it. But you go first."

My shoulders sag at her sudden attitude. This was supposed to be about healing. Why do I feel like things are about to get worse? "During that summer, I got mixed up in the wrong crowd. With my new teammate Trent and his brothers. We did some things I'm not proud of, and I got arrested trying to outrun the police."

I finally tell her the story I tried to tell her back then, and Amelia gasps, though her stiff stance tells me she's still waiting for something else.

"I was excited to see you when school started back. Hell, I was excited for you to scold me for being such an idiot over the break. But that's not what happened. At first I was confused, but then when I *really* paid attention, I noticed subtle differences from when I'd last seen you. Your hair was down and you always wore it up. Your shirt was untucked when you were usually a stickler for the dress code. And the kicker, you had a new attitude and a new friend—Melody—so I figured maybe you didn't need me anymore. Maybe you'd moved on without bothering to tell me or that I'd missed the memo."

Amelia stares at me in disbelief before she scoffs. "I'm sorry that happened to you. I'm sorry you got mixed up with Trent and his brother, and I'm happy you made it out the other side unscathed. But after saying *all* that, after admitting *you* were a different person, you think *I* changed? That *I* was too good for you?"

"Honestly, Amelia. It was a long time ago, but you never told me otherwise, so what was I supposed to think?"

She shakes her head before huffing out an incredulous laugh. "All this time. *God*. Of course it was me. Couldn't possibly have been something *you* did."

"What did I do?"

"You broke my *heart*. I trusted you and you broke me."

I rear back from the genuine shock as my mind reels. "I don't understand. I don't know what you think I did but—"

"Do you remember the conversation we had *before* I walked away?"

"I tried to tell you about my summer and—"

"No. First I asked if you had anything to tell me. If there was anything I should know. About *me*. Any secrets you wanted to share."

"Yeah, and I did. I was going to tell you about my arrest."

"Secrets about *me*, Luke. You were keeping a bigger secret than that."

"What?"

"Do you remember the last time we saw each other the night of graduation?"

My chest tightens as I think about that moment, recalling Trent teasing Amelia and me doing nothing to defend her. I know I was a dick, but that can't have been our issue because... "I apologized for not having your back that day. In the parking lot, remember? You said you understood. That you were okay. That you forgave me."

"That's right and I did. I forgave you for that. But I'm not talking about what that asshole said and your reaction. Or lack of reaction. Yes, that hurt, but it was nothing compared to what came next."

"What came next?" I search my mind for any other interactions we had after that but *fuck*, I was *eleven*. I can barely remember details from a conversation that happened last week, let alone twenty years ago. "I was a kid."

"I never faulted you for what happened at graduation."

"Then what?"

Amelia sucks her lips into her mouth before laying her head back on the couch and staring at the ceiling. "After you walked away," she begins, her eyes once again meeting mine. "After you left, I saw my mom and I couldn't face her. I didn't want her excuses for my dad's absence. So I followed you instead, hoping you'd walk me home. I called out but you didn't hear me."

"I don't remember that." I always walked her home. If I'd known she needed me, I would have waited. *Fuck.* Did something happen? I rack my brain to remember the events of that night but I can't... wait, she ran past me crying but her mom was calling out and... *I didn't go after her. Shit.* "Amelia, I—"

"I caught up to you that night," she cuts me off, her gaze now locked on her hands as though she can't even look at me. "You'd just reached Vicki's house and you were laughing about something with Trent." At the mention of Vicki, my face pales, and I realize what I did.

"I was about to call out again when I overheard my name." Amelia pauses but I don't need her to continue. Not now that I have that moment at the forefront of my mind. My stomach knots as my heart pounds in my chest. *How could I have forgotten that conversation?* It ate away at me for months after we stopped being friends, only I never knew that she'd heard me.

Fuck.

I run a hand through my hair as bile rises in my throat. There's no point pretending. *"Do you have any secrets I should know?"* she'd asked me, and I'd lied.

"I said something along the lines of... 'I can't believe Amelia's dad didn't show. I wish she knew where he disappeared to at night.'" The words sting like a knife in my throat as I speak them again now, cutting me from the inside. "I said that he cared more about Vicki than he did about you," I rasp, hating every second of this trip down memory lane. "I said that maybe if you knew the truth you wouldn't put him on that fucking pedestal. And then I said..." I trail off because I don't want to repeat the rest.

"You said?" Amelia pushes me to say it, even though she knows.

"I said I couldn't believe how upset you were, and that it was pathetic." Amelia briefly closes her eyes as my heart aches. "I didn't mean it, Amelia. At all. I was trying to be cool around Trent, and—"

"You knew," she cuts me off and I want to scream. *All this time it was me.*

"God, Amelia, I—"

"You *knew*," she repeats a little louder, cutting me off again. "You all knew my dad was fucking Vicki's mom... that he was playing happy families and *you never told me*. And what's worse is that Vicki ran out of our graduation because she didn't have a dad to dance with and I felt sorry for her. Her dad was gone. At least mine was still around. But that wasn't why she was upset, was it? No, she was upset because she wanted *my* dad to dance with her and that's why he didn't come."

She knew? Amelia knew. And we all acted like we didn't. Vicki told us all about it. She told everyone but Amelia. And I kept it from her. I lied to her face.

"I thought I was doing the right thing. I thought—"

"Did you know it was another year before anyone bothered to tell me the truth? I held onto that secret and pretended I didn't know because I couldn't bear to be the one breaking my mom's heart. But I soon discovered she knew too. And she kept him around. I didn't know what to do. Or what would happen to me if they split up. So I kept silent, allowing my heart to shatter while never saying a word." Amelia pauses again but this time I don't speak. I can't. Her broken expression has me in a choke hold.

She bites her bottom lip before shaking her head, as though trying to silence her pain, but it's written all over her face. And when I think she must be finished speaking, she finally glances up, pinning me with her broken stare...devastating me.

"I was a kid, Luke. They were supposed to protect me. And so were you. *You promised*."

Her voice cracks, hitting me deep in my chest.

She's right. I promised to be there for her. To protect her. But that's what I thought I was doing.

"I'm sorry, Amelia. I didn't know you were there. I kept it from you for the same reason you kept it from your mom. I couldn't be the one to break you."

Amelia nods before whispering to herself, "And yet, you did it anyway. You just didn't know it. You were a kid. I know. But even as a kid, your words can leave scars."

I want to argue... or beg her to let me take it all back, but I can't, it's too late.

"If I'd known you heard me, I would have come after you and explained. I could have been there for you. I could have helped."

"I was crying when I ran past you. If you'd have followed me, I would have told you everything. But for the first time ever, you didn't. And then school started back and you lied."

Jesus. She's right. Again. I didn't follow her because I felt guilty for not sticking up for her, even though she'd accepted my apology. And I felt guilty for talking about her behind her back and for the lies I said. Then at school I was thinking about me, not her.

It was all me. I turned on her. Me.

What do I say to that?

"I'm not making any excuses, but I was not in a great place when school started back, and when you wouldn't speak to me, I kind of lost my mind. After that, there was no going back. I was done."

I still remember the day Amelia's dad left her mom; it was the talk of the school. Vicki went from using it to get sympathy to announcing it to the world like she'd won. Amelia's dad had chosen her and her family. Now it was Amelia's turn to feel like the loser.

But in the end, he left Vicki and her mom too.

The disgust I have for that man is almost unrivaled. I may have been pissed off with Amelia, and God knows I threw the hate word around, but when it came to her dad, I discovered what hate really felt like.

And I should have been there for her.

"You didn't deserve any of that, Amelia, and I'm sorry that my stupid pride and the constant need I have to put myself first got in the way of me seeing that you needed me more. Regardless of whether you overheard what I said or not, regardless of whether or not we were friends, when it all came out, I should have been there for you."

"I'm sorry I held on to the hurt for so long, but I couldn't get past the fact that you knew and your harsh words when I thought we were friends. Then when you accepted my anger without calling me on it, I assumed you didn't care."

"You should have known me better than that." I force a smile. "You bruised my ego and there was no one there to snap me out of it. That was your job." Amelia grins at that and I relax a little. "I'm sure you'll be happy to know my sister has tried hard to take your place over the years. She's constantly reminding me that I'm not God's gift to the world. The two of you will get along nicely."

"Good." Amelia laughs. "You always needed someone to knock you down a peg. Though she didn't get through to you when it comes to women."

"No, she didn't." I chuckle. "She was too innocent when we were younger, and I was too far gone by the time she figured out the type of guy I was. But she'll be happy that you're doing a good job on that front. You and Jelly Bean."

"For now anyway. Once we're divorced, you can resume your playboy ways." Her hand falls to her stomach protectively, and I doubt she realizes she's doing it. As she fakes a smile, a thought hits me. *Does she imagine I'm going to be like her dad?* That I'm going to treat our child the way her father treated her?

"Amelia, I'm not him, you know?"

"What?" Her brows furrow as she frowns.

"Your dad. I'm not him. Jelly Bean will always be my number one priority. I can promise you that."

"Oh, I wasn't thinking that." She brushes away my concern like it's nothing, but I can tell she has more to add.

"But..."

She scrunches her nose, hesitation clear in her expression, making me internally grimace. "But?" I repeat.

"But...my dad said that too."

Of course he fucking did. That heartless piece of shit. "Amelia—"

"I don't think you're like him, Luke. I never have. You've always been up-front about the type of man you are."

"What's that supposed to mean?"

Amelia laughs, but it's not as light as it was before. "I mean that you're honest about what you want. Women know you're not the settle-down type. They know what they're in for ahead of time. My dad lied, he kept secrets, he was deceiving. There's a difference. And while you may have kept secrets at times, it's not the same. You're nothing like him."

"Okay. Good. I'm glad we established that."

"Me too. But with everything between us, do you honestly believe we can do this?"

"The marriage?" I question, a nervous energy filling my chest.

"Any of it."

"I do. For Bean. Especially now that everything's out in the open. It is, right? That's all of it?"

Amelia takes a deep breath and stares at the ceiling again as though it holds all the answers. And after the longest beat, she nods. "That's everything," she whispers, her voice breathy. "I'm sorry for getting you arrested," she adds with a smile, making me huff out a laugh. "If I'd have known you were arrested when you were eleven, I may have kept my mouth shut."

During my time being questioned by the police, I managed to keep myself out of the line of fire while never once mentioning Amelia's name. I thought I was clever until another officer arrived to let us all know that "Miss Amelia Rosenberg" had admitted she was with me at the time, and that she thought I had something to do with it all. She threw me under the bus while I tried to protect her. But it's all in the past. And it turns out, I'm the one more at fault here.

"I'm sure we both would have done things differently if we'd had more information. But I'm sorry for everything I've done. The list is too long for me to quote each thing individually."

Amelia's smile widens, but it still holds an uncertain edge.

"And now we're here, talking like adults," I joke because that's what I do. That's one of my default settings. That and making irrational decisions to protect the people I care about. "Who the hell are we?"

Amelia giggles but a yawn cuts her off, drawing my attention to the time.

"Jesus. It's after midnight."

"That explains why I'm being nice to you. My brain is obviously sleep-deprived."

"Obviously." I smirk.

"But I should go." She stretches her arms over her head before standing up. "What time should I be here tomorrow? Do we need to go over anything else before we dial in? Dial in." She laughs. "I can't believe I'm getting married via a webcam. In fact, I still can't believe it's possible to get married via a webcam."

"Anything is possible these days. And it's the best way to ensure no one finds out. But don't think of it like a wedding. Remember? You're taking the necessary steps to protect our child, via webcam."

"True. So... time?"

"You should stay." *What?*

"What?" Amelia voices my thought as I grimace before snapping out of it. It's not a bad idea. In fact, it's a good one.

"You should stay. We have to be online at nine a.m., and I don't want you driving home when you're tired. For Jelly Bean's sake."

"So what? You think I couldn't stay awake enough to protect my baby? That I'd risk that?"

"No, I wasn't—" Amelia's smile cuts me off. "Very funny. I'll show you to the spare room."

I turn to lead the way, but Amelia grabs my arm to stop me. "Jokes aside, I don't know if this is a good—"

"You're staying. Stop whining about it."

Her jaw drops, but I can tell by the heat in her eyes that she's impressed by my assertiveness. I told her I'd protect her and Jelly Bean and I meant it.

"Do you prefer hard or soft pillows?" I ask as I walk, not letting her hit me with another smart-ass response.

"Hard, please," she responds, making me smile.

"Done."

"And I need an extra one for in between my legs."

Huh? I come to a halt as I process that before lifting my shoulders in a shrug. If that's what she needs, that's what she'll get, but I need to learn more about pregnancy. "I'm on it." I wave my hands, motioning up the stairs. "It's the first door on the left."

Chapter Twenty-Six

AMELIA

So much to unpack that I don't know where to begin. But the kiss was real.

A dog's bark echoes through the air, waking me before my alarm the next morning, and I startle until I remember where I am.

My body sinks into the plush bedding as I stretch out my legs, making myself comfortable in the over-the-top king-size bed. I haven't slept that well in weeks. Months even. And considering how much is currently playing on my mind, that's saying something. I'm in heaven. And I bet the bed in Luke's bedroom is even more luxurious, knowing him. What I wouldn't give to sneak in and sl— *Woah, Amelia. Nope. Let's not go there.* Even if the thoughts are innocent.

Reaching for my phone, I grab it as it vibrates in my hands, alerting me to the time. Eight a.m. In an hour, I'll be marrying the man of my nightmares. I laugh at my own joke, but for the first time in as long as I can remember, my negative thoughts make me cringe. Especially after our talk yesterday.

And while there is so much to process, maybe Luke's right and we need to move on. We were both young. We both did and said things we shouldn't have. And while we'll never be as close as we once were, maybe we can be friends again. For Jelly Bean's sake.

I imagine co-parenting would be so much easier that way.

I'm about to get up when a soft knock on the door makes me pause. "Yeah?"

"It's me. Obviously. Do you want breakfast? I'm making eggs."

Ugh. The thought of eggs makes me nauseous, but he doesn't know that. "I'd love some toast if that's okay."

"Sure thing. Do you want it now or..."

"Now is good. I'll be right down."

My eyes drop to the tee I slept in last night and I cringe. Taking a deep breath, I channel the mind of a woman that doesn't overthink things and call out to Luke before he gets too far away.

"Luke?"

"Yeah?" The handle moves but he doesn't open the door.

"You can come in."

He smiles awkwardly as he enters, but I'm only able to focus on his face for the two seconds before I notice he's in a towel.

"Did you change your mind about eggs?" he asks, his arm locked on the door frame, drawing my eyes to his bulging bicep before my gaze drifts over his half-naked body.

"Huh?"

"Eggs?"

What? Ugh. That ruined the moment. "No." I scrunch my nose, forcing myself to shift focus. "I haven't been able to eat them lately."

"Damn. So what can I do for you? Besides let you ogle my body."

"Funny. You could have put on some clothes. Anyway, speaking of clothes. I... ah... I need something to wear."

Luke's eyes drop to the white tee I'm wearing—sans bra—and he visibly swallows before his eyes flash to mine and he hides his reaction with a lopsided smile. I internally cheer at eliciting the same lust-filled expression I felt for him before he speaks. "You mean you don't have a beautiful white dress purchased?"

"Sadly,"—I pout—"I left it at home."

"I should have let you leave." He grins, making me smile.

"Can I borrow something or not?"

"Will a white shirt do? Women wear men's shirts as fashion all the time. Right?" His justification almost makes me laugh but he's serious, making me melt a little. He's trying.

"A white shirt would be perfect."

"Coming right up."

He disappears for all of twenty seconds before coming back in with a shirt in hand and I freeze. If I'd known his room was so close last night, I never would have slept that well. Thank God, I had no idea.

"If you need anything else, let me know." Luke smiles again as he backs out of the room, but before he's completely out of sight, he pops his head in and laughs. "Oh, and there's toothpaste in the en suite but I don't have a spare toothbrush."

"What?" I'm taken aback by his thoughtfulness but joke to hide it. "You mean, you don't have care packages for your overnight guests?" I laugh until he pins me with his signature cocky grin and I melt.

"I don't have overnight guests. Most of them don't make it upstairs."

"Ew. I did not need to know that but at the same time...I feel special." And oddly turned on.

"Don't let your head grow too big," Luke says, his cocky self melting my lust.

"Oh Luke, it would never be as large as yours."

"Yeah, yeah. I'll be downstairs."

I laugh again as he closes the door, but when he's gone my brows furrow. *What was that?* I may have been joking, but my damn pulse picked up speed at the thought of it. And now I'm going to go downstairs wearing his shirt. To get married.

This is like a soap opera. Next thing you know, he'll be pinning me against a wall and begging me to touch him. He'll slip his hand under my shirt and— *What the actual fuck, Amelia?* Hormones. It's got to be hormones. Or maybe it's because he told me the kiss was real. And I felt things that I shouldn't be feeling.

What would have happened if the fire had never been real? Would we— *Nope. Stop right there.* We're moving on from the past.

I rush to the en suite and splash freezing cold water over my face in the hope that it will snap me out of this ludicrous notion, and open the drawer for some toothpaste. Despite what Luke said, I do actually find a brand-new sealed toothbrush, so I take that as a small win and brush my teeth before making a mental note to replace it for him.

After tying my hair in a loose topknot, I quickly get dressed, but pause as I'm buttoning his shirt. *This is weird.* No matter how I consider it or how many times I tell myself we're doing this for Bean, it's weird.

Blowing out a raspberry, I let the shirt hang over my black leggings—the only pants that fit since I haven't made the move to maternity wear—and straighten the collar. I'm tired, stressed, and a little bit pale, but it is what it is.

Welcome to my wedding day.

Maybe I should have called the hair and makeup artists from the show. But that would require me filling them in on what I'm doing, and I don't need anyone else telling me how crazy I am. Okay, no one is calling me crazy. If anything, Hayley thinks it's a smart move, but she also pronounces Z as Zed so what does she know?

I walk down the stairs hesitantly, but the second my bare foot hits the wooden flooring, I stop and take in a breath. Like my appearance, today *is what it is.* It's happening so I have to stop doubting my decision. This is a smart move. And it's temporary.

"Alright, Baby Daddy. I'm ready," I announce confidently when I find him in the kitchen. "Let's do this."

Luke chuckles as he turns around, but the second he sees me he pauses, his eyes full of fire. "Damn, you look good in my shirt, Ace. It's time to make you my wife."

Oh God. My heart skips but I ignore it. *I was not prepared for him to say that. And I was not prepared for him to use my old nickname.* But there's no way in hell I'm drawing attention to it.

"And are you both here of your own free will?" the officiant asks and I almost snap. *What kind of question is that?* No one asked me that at my wedding to Preston. My eyes flash to Lainey and Thomas—our witnesses—their eyes widening at the same time mine do.

"Yes, we are," I nervously answer for both of us before realizing my mistake when Thomas smiles.

"We?"

"Sorry." I grimace.

"I am too, your honor," Luke finally speaks, making us all laugh.

"I'm not a judge. But thank you for the promotion. Shall we begin?"

"Please." I hold back another nervous giggle as our officiant glances down at her paperwork.

"We're here today to witness the marriage of Luke Harrison Bennett and Amelia Jay Rosenberg."

I twist toward Luke when she says "Jay" instead of Joy, but I recover when he squeezes my leg off camera, my genuine smile shining through the shock. The officiant continues on, seemingly unaware of the silent conversation that transpired between us, and I make a mental note to double check the legal certificate has the correct name. Though, I know Luke better than that. He would have made sure everything was correct down to the very last period.

I'm lost in my thoughts, listening to the officiant give her spiel until it comes time to repeat after her and Luke squeezes my leg again before turning me around to face him. And thank God for that because I would have directed my words to the screen. "I, Amelia *Jay* Rosenberg, take you, Luke Harrison Bennett, to be my lawful wedded husband."

Luke winks as the officiant gives him the same line, and when he repeats it, the strangest warmth floods my chest. "I, Luke Harrison Bennett, take you, Amelia Jay Rosenberg, to be my lawful wedded wife."

And that's it. We're married. I'm married. Again. And it doesn't feel as wrong as I thought it would.

"Luke mentioned that you won't be exchanging rings, so by the power vested in me by the state of California, I now pronounce you husband and wife. You may share your first kiss."

Our what? Dammit, how did we forget that part?

Luke spins me again until we're face-to-face, but while I expect him to maul me with an over-the-top kiss, he surprises me by gently pressing his lips to mine, sending a spark through me as my heart fires. I'm struck still as emotions warm my chest until someone claps and Lainey cheers, breaking my trance. Then it's over. It's done. We say our goodbyes and the officiant drops off the video call, leaving the four of us alone, while my mind spins.

Lainey's the first to speak, or maybe it's more of a squeal. "You're married. My big brother is married."

"Lainey. You know—"

"Yes, yes. I know it's not *real*." She whispers "real" making the rest of us laugh. "What? Someone could be listening. Disconnect, I'm going to call you back."

Before any of us have the chance to respond, the video chat ends and then there were two.

"So, that happened?" I smile while my heart pounds in my chest, jumping when Luke's phone rings.

"One guess who that is?"

"You better answer. They were nice enough to be our witnesses."

"Nice enough? Lainey would have murdered me in my sleep if I chose someone else."

"It was still nice," I sass, making Luke roll his eyes.

He answers Lainey's call, and as they talk I stare down at my stomach, a peace settling over me. A peace I had no idea I needed until this very moment. We haven't added my name to Luke's insurance and yet, I'm already at ease. As though I just made the best decision of my life. For Jelly Bean.

I'm not sure how much time passes, but when I lift my gaze, Luke's staring at me as he speaks, a similar peace reflected in his eyes. All jokes aside, I may not be able to picture Luke as a husband, but he's going to be an amazing dad. And I have to admit, if I was destined to be pregnant, maybe I'm lucky that he was the guy.

Maybe this is all going to work out fine.

CHAPTER TWENTY-SEVEN

LUKE

In the month following our ceremony, Amelia and I settle into a new normal—living separate but married lives—and while Amelia still thinks we're crazy, it seems to be working. We're not the best friends we once were, but the animosity is gone and God, it makes things easier.

As soon as we were married, I added Amelia to my insurance as planned, but due to the time it took for us to actually tie the knot—waiting for her divorce—we'd passed the twenty-week scan before it was all finalized.

Still, the second we got the all clear, I booked one of the best OB-GYNs in San Francisco, and I'm already feeling better about the pregnancy. So is Amelia. She just refuses to admit it, preferring to pretend I'm being over-the-top because she loves to sass me.

Some things never change.

I'm feeling good the day after our appointment with Dr. Kelly, and as I get changed in the locker room, I'm revved up for another killer practice session, ready to show off more of my skills to the cameras.

Amelia smiles as she walks past but like always, she tries to hide it and the urge to call her out on it is strong. But at the same time, I kind of like having this little secret. Especially considering it's going to blow everyone's minds when they find out.

Luke Bennett a fucking dad. A fact no one saw coming.

I'm dragging my hoodie over my head when Keeley enters our locker room, her signature smile locked in place. And for the first time, a corny pickup line doesn't pop into my head. Maybe I'm maturing now that I'm going to be a dad.

I smile to myself as I get back to undressing, only to be interrupted again.

"Attention!" Keeley calls out from her usual spot on the bench seat, a folder in her hands. While her shouting draws my gaze, most of the guys carry on with their conversations until Wyatt whistles through his fingers, bringing the room to silence.

"Thanks, Wyatt." Keeley smiles. "I won't take up too much of your time but I have a quick request. We're now over halfway through filming, and I want to thank you all for your participation. I'm not sure I'm supposed to tell you this, but Amelia gave me a sneak peek at some of the edited clips this week, and it's stunning. Your heads are about to explode from how big they're going to grow. Especially you, Luke."

I bark out a laugh while some of the guys cheer, and when we get too loud, it's Thomas that gets our attention this time. "Anyway, with Thanksgiving coming up in a couple of weeks, the production company thought it would be good to get some footage in a more relaxed setting, and Coach Pierce has kindly offered to host an early Thanksgiving/Christmas BBQ after practice next Wednesday."

"He's what?" one of the guys calls out and Keeley rolls her eyes.

"You heard me. And it's a requirement that you all attend or I'm told you'll be on his shit list. His words, not mine."

"More like 'if I have to do this, you have to be there,'" I whisper to Dylan, making him smile.

"Got that right. There is no way he volunteered his home."

Keeley shushes us again before continuing on. "You're all welcome to bring your families. In fact, we encourage it. And we ask that you come with your smiles on and be ready to have fun. The filming will take place during the first few hours, for obvious reasons, and then you're free to relax."

She runs through some general house rules again, things we've heard a million times, but I tune her out, my attention locked on Amelia and Zane on the other side of the room. More specifically, the way he's whispering in her ear and making her hide her smile behind her hand. My eyes narrow as I try to read his lips, but it's useless from where I'm standing. I move to step closer when someone grabs my tee, holding me in place.

"Not a good idea if you don't want to draw attention," Dylan says, his voice low as his eyes remain on Keeley, confusing the hell out of me.

"The fuck, Dyl. What are you talking about?"

He stays silent until Keeley thanks us all for our time and steps down from the bench, and then he waits for everyone to start talking again before turning my way.

"You seem to forget I've known you for years. Longer than most, and the look you gave Amelia was not your usual 'I want to tap that' look."

"I don't have a look like that."

"You're right, you have many looks that suggest the same thing, but never usually a 'he better stay the fuck away from her or I'm going to go crazy' look."

"I don't have that look either."

"Okay, then I'll let you go."

He lets me go, but I don't move because he's right. I do want to go over there and tell Zane to leave her alone. But *dammit*. What is going on with me?

Dylan laughs from behind me, still watching. "Don't worry. We've all been there."

"Been where? I'm nowhere. You have it all wrong." I'm protesting a lot considering I don't know what he means.

"It means that you're jealous."

"Fuck off. What's to be jealous about? That he's over there signing a deal to give him more on-air time?"

"Yeah." Dylan rolls his eyes. "That's it." He finishes getting dressed before throwing his stuff in his locker and patting me on the shoulder as he walks past. "I'll see you out there. But Luke, he doesn't stand a chance, so don't waste too many brain cells worrying about that one."

As Dylan leaves, my gaze drifts back to Zane to find him alone and rushing to get changed, making me snap out of it because I should be doing the same thing.

I huff out a laugh and grab my gear.

I'm not jealous. I don't want Amelia getting fucked over by a guy like that. Right?

I'm looking out for her. That's all.

A week later, I'm in Coach's backyard with a beer in my hand and a smile plastered on my face—as per Keeley's prerequisite for entry.

Lainey and Thomas are talking to Dylan about something his son did while my eyes scan the crowd of players and their families, noting Amelia's absence despite the filming being well underway.

I arrived today thinking this was going to be an easy afternoon, but I didn't factor in her not being here when it's her job. How am I expected to keep a relaxed smile on my face if she's missing in action? I don't do well with stress. It's why I stay positive all the time.

The conversation moves onto pets—or more specifically, Lainey's desire to get her own dog when she's finished with her master's—and I'm finally distracted.

"Thomas, please buy her a damn puppy so she'll stop stealing mine."

"It's not stealing when she voluntarily comes to me. She loves me more."

"Oh, I'm willing to bet otherwise. Let's see who she runs..." The back gate opens and I lose my train of thought, watching as Amelia finally steps through the threshold, a blonde in tow. A blonde I'm going to guess is Hayley based on the description Amelia gave me.

Amelia laughs at something she says and it makes me smile. She's been struggling to hide her bump over the last week, and I know that made her nervous to come today. She's still not ready for everyone to know. But here she is, relaxed, like she should be.

I'm lost in thought until a presence settles beside me and Thomas's voice enters my mind. "Wifey's here," he announces with too much enthusiasm, and I have to hold back from punching him.

"Shut the fuck up," I snap, my gaze darting around to make sure no one heard him. "I'm allowed to say that, but you're not."

"Come on, you had to know I was going to joke about your nuptials. It's too good to pass up."

"I'm good with you joking about it. Just do it in private."

"Eh. You're no fun."

My eyes find Amelia again, and when I catch her gaze, my smile instantly returns. Although, because it's us, it's more like a smirk. She rolls her eyes just as Lainey steps into my line of sight, blocking my view. "I hope that smile's reserved for the mother of your child," she says, her voice a lot quieter than Thomas's was. "Not the gorgeous blonde standing next to her."

I shoot her an expression that says, "you're kidding me, right" and she laughs.

"What? I'm just reminding you to keep it in your pants."

"Thanks," I deadpan. "Whatever would I do without your guidance?"

"I often wonder the same. But you're smiling at Amelia, right?" she asks again, just to clarify, and I take the opportunity to piss her off.

"Nope," I lie, popping the *p*. "It's definitely the blonde."

I walk away and leave my words hanging in the air, picturing Lainey's shock, but when Thomas chuckles, I know he told her I was lying.

And of course I was lying.

I haven't so much as looked at another woman since I agreed not to. I haven't even had the urge. *Fuck, I really am changing.*

As I move around the many conversations, I catch Amelia introducing Hayley to her crew members before disappearing inside, and I can't help but follow her. I keep to myself as a few of my teammates grab drinks but as soon as we're alone, I approach her, watching as a sassy smile lights up her features.

"What can I do for you, Luke?" she asks as she searches through her bag, her smile peeking out through the hair that's falling in front of her face, making me want to lift her chin to look at me.

"The list is endless, Amelia. But for now, I'm checking up on you."

Her eyes flash to mine and her sass instantly fades. "Thank you. I'm good. Tired but good."

"Have—"

"Yes, I've been trying to get enough sleep. It just evades me."

"How did you know I was going to ask that?"

"Call it intuition." She bites back her smile. "But I appreciate that you asked."

"It's strange, you know?"

"What is?"

"Knowing—" I glance around the room to make sure we're alone. "Knowing that you're growing our baby and not being able to do a damn thing to help. Once Bean comes along things will be different, but right now, I can't do anything." My brows furrow and I blink a few times before huffing out a laugh. "Sorry, that's not your problem. I don't know why I said that. I didn't mean to make this about me."

Amelia's gaze softens before her face lights up with a warmth I haven't seen in a while. "I can't imagine how that feels, but you have every right to be feeling that way. And let me tell you, you're helping plenty. I—"

"Amelia," her first AD calls through the open doorway. "Sorry to interrupt, but can we borrow you for a minute?"

"Of course. I'll be out in a second." Her AD disappears and she turns my way. "I better go... but thank you."

"Anytime. And when you want me on camera, I'm ready for my moment," I joke, needing the energy between us to return to normal.

"Don't hold your breath." Amelia shakes her head with a laugh as she walks away, and I chuckle, grabbing another drink and making my way back outside.

Though, my thoughts don't leave her. It's not just the baby situation that's strange—it's everything. My life is completely different now than it was six months ago. But it's my life and I'm going to have to get used to it.

Time passes as I chat with the guys, and while the filming is obviously staged, they get what they need much faster than I would have thought, and before long the music is turned up and everyone starts to relax. If it was me, I'd be accidentally *on purpose* leaving the cameras running for the rest of the afternoon. I can guarantee the footage from this point on will be much more interesting. But I'm not a filmmaker. I just married one.

I smile to myself as Hayley wanders over, her perfectly manicured brows raised and her lips pulled into a wry smile. I don't know her at all, but I have a sister and I have Amelia, so I know enough to guess she's about to sass me.

"Luke Bennett. Number forty-two. The man of the hour. The baby daddy. The *husband*." *What is that accent?* Wait? She's Australian? And an actress. Oh, this is too good.

"Hayley Jackman. Actress. Not related to Hugh but still hoping she magically inherited his star power. The best friend."

Hayley's smile widens and if I'm not mistaken she's a little impressed. "Turns out Amelia was wrong—you *are* funny."

"Amelia knows I'm funny. If she says otherwise, it's because she's jealous."

"Okay, Mr. Comedian. It's time to get serious. What are your intentions with my girl?"

I shrug. "Same as you, I'd guess." *I want to be there for her.*

"You want to save up and move to LA?" She laughs. "Amazing. We could all move in together. You can pay for our rent."

"Amelia's moving?" My head snaps in the direction I last saw her as a pit forms in my stomach. LA may not be far but my life is here and... I'll barely see them.

"Not anymore, she's not," Hayley confirms, easing my mind. "She's setting up roots here. She's starting the nursery tonight. But thanks for answering my next question."

"What question?" My brows furrow. *Did I miss something?*

"I was going to ask how much you care about her. But I don't have to."

"I don't want to miss out on seeing my kid." I shrug as if that justifies my freak-out, but the truth is, I've kind of gotten used to having Amelia around.

"Of course." Hayley bites back a knowing grin and I roll my eyes. "Now that we've gotten that out of the way, don't fuck with her and we'll be great friends."

"What if I don't want to be friends?"

"You have no choice. I need you to introduce me to your teammates."

I bark out a laugh when she bounces her eyebrows, nodding her head in the direction of some of the players. I like her. I bet she's good for Amelia, not letting her take life too seriously despite her current situation warranting it. "Anyone in particular or should I choose?"

"You choose, but make sure they're single. I'm no home wrecker."

"You got it." I don't move right away, instead I stand still and tap my foot until she waves her hand in front of my face.

"Oh, you mean now?" I laugh.

"Obviously."

"Well, good timing. Here's Reed. Reed!" I wave to get his attention. "Get your ass over here." He's technically single.

Hayley laughs as Reed walks over. "Do all football players love each other's asses?"

"What?" I almost choke on my drink as Reed's eyes widen.

"What the hell did I walk into?"

"Never mind." Hayley giggles. "Maybe it's an Aussie Rules thing. They always celebrate by slapping each other's butts."

"Oh no. We do that too," Reed says with a grin. "I'm Reed. We haven't met."

"I'm Hayley. Amelia's friend." At the mention of her name, I seek her out again, finding her with Coach Pierce and her director of photography.

"Nice. Amelia's great. Is this one asking for advice on how to impress her?"

"What? No." I rejoin the conversation. "I don't need to impress Amelia."

"You don't?"

"Nope. I do it by breathing."

"Has he always been this cocky?" Hayley asks, a smile plastered on her face, and while I can obviously answer that question, I let Reed do it.

"He has. Ever since I've known him."

They start talking about themselves, so I leave them be and search for entertainment elsewhere. After grabbing another beer, I join a conversation about the Super Bowl and how pretty we're sitting leading into December, and it's much more my scene.

What an amazing story to tell my kid—"you were born after I won my first Super Bowl." God, if Amelia's up to it, Jelly Bean could be there, in her tummy. But if she is there, I'll have to make sure she's in a suite and not with the film crew. I'm not opposed to pregnant women working, but by then she should be staying off her feet. At least, that's what I've heard other people say.

I really should introduce her to Summer and officially to Lainey, so she knows some of the spouses of the team. It would be nice to—

"Luke, did you hear me?" Wyatt asks, drawing my attention.

With my mind on Amelia, I snap out of my daze, finding myself staring at her again. No matter where she is, I can't stop myself from seeking her out. And I can't put my finger on why that is. She's spent months around these guys. She may not know them as well as I do, but she knows them and they know her. Yet, I'm constantly checking up on her. Maybe it's because it's all I can do? Or I'm making up for lost time... I wasn't there for her back when she needed me the most, but I'll be there now. Even if it means I just ignored a question directed my way.

"What?" I ask, letting my eyes meet his at the last second.

"We're going to play ball. Are you in?"

"Ball? Yes. Of course. Who the fuck am I if not a ball player?" *Or a husband or soon-to-be dad.* I could absolutely use this distraction.

Wyatt raises a brow as he gives me some side-eye. "Oh-kay." He hesitates, clearly confused by my sudden enthusiasm. "Let's go."

CHAPTER TWENTY-EIGHT

AMELIA

There's a change in the air and I'm not sure I'm ready for it.

"Heads!" someone yells as I walk back into the yard, making me duck as I spin around and throw a hand up to protect myself. Nothing happens, but I don't move until a soft chuckle echoes beside me. "I traumatized you, didn't I?" Thomas says, drawing my gaze. "They're playing ball way over there. You're safe here." His line of sight drops to my stomach, and it's then that I notice I'm protectively holding my belly.

I smile and drop my hand before huffing out a laugh. "Well, that's embarrassing." I exaggeratedly wince.

"Nah, it's not. I'm the only one that saw, and I'm guessing I'm the reason you do it."

I wince again, this time for real. "Sorry, but yes, you are." Ever since Thomas hit me with the ball in high school, that's been my response whenever something's coming my way and sometimes when it's not even close. I can't help it. It's a reflex.

"God, I should be sorry, not you."

"Nah, you were just playing ball, like today. I got in the way."

"Who would have thought that we'd be here now, talking about it?"

"Not me, that's for sure. But there's a lot going on in my life that I never thought would happen."

I laugh but Thomas's expression turns serious, proving Luke's argument that they all care. "How are you feeling about everything?"

"You mean the show or..."

"Or...I mean the *or*."

"Honestly, I have no idea. My feelings change regularly."

Thomas smiles. "That's understandable. It's all new, and I imagine a bit strange considering what you're doing with Luke and—"

"He told you it was his idea, right?" I panic. The way he worded his response made it sound like I was the one that wanted this. Or pushed for it.

"He definitely did. He admitted he wasn't going to take no for an answer."

I visibly relax and Thomas laughs. "Were you worried?"

"A little. It's such a crazy idea that I don't want people assuming I agreed for the wrong reasons."

"Like what?"

"Money." *Oh God.* My mind flashes back to when I first told him I was pregnant and the way he freaked out. Maybe we should have done a prenup? I don't want his money when we divorce. I don't want that hanging over my head.

"Are you okay?" Thomas asks, concerned.

"Yeah, I just have a lot to process."

He nods, smiling sympathetically. "I'm here to talk if you need it and so is Lainey. She may be Luke's sister and he may be my friend and brother-in-law, but we've got your back. We're family. You're carrying around our future niece or nephew. And well, Luke is Luke." He grimaces comically and I burst out laughing.

"Thank you, Thomas. I really appreciate that."

"Anytime and..." he trails off a little distractedly before his gaze moves back to mine. "I'm in trouble. I promised Lainey I'd wait for her before talking to you and here she comes."

I turn to see Lainey walking our way with her lips pursed. "Thomas Kelly, I hope you didn't forget about me."

"Never." He grimaces. "Lainey, this is Amelia...in person."

"Hi Amelia. It's great to finally meet you. *In person.*"

"Likewise. Maybe we should have done it *before* the wedding." I smile shyly while they both laugh.

"Yeah, but that's Luke for you. He's the smartest guy I know, but sometimes he doesn't apply that to everyday life. You're a godsend for putting up with him."

"I don't really have much choice." I gesture to my growing stomach and laugh.

"I can't believe I'm going to be an auntie." She whispers the last part. "I hope you know that Thomas and I have your back. One hundred percent. I mean, I love Luke, but I'm willing to fight him if I need to."

My eyes flash to Thomas's as I laugh. "Thomas reflected the same sentiment." And while I know they're both joking—the warmth in their eyes when they speak about Luke gives them away—it's still nice to know they care.

We don't get to talk for much longer before Lainey has to take a call and Thomas gets called to join the guys. I try to find someone new to chat with, but the laughter coming from the game draws my attention so I make my way over—cautiously scanning for flying footballs as I go.

When I'm close enough that I can see, but far enough away for safety, I search for Luke among the players, and find him at the same moment he lifts his tee to wipe sweat from his brow, revealing his toned stomach and that V that makes me want to reach out and touch him. He laughs at something one of the guys says before spinning his cap backward and throwing his hands in the air, showing the guys he's ready. My heart pounds, my eyes glued to his every move, and I swear it all happens in slow motion. The way his eyes light up with his smile, and the sliver of skin that stays visible as his muscles flex. I—

"Nope," Hayley says as she spins me around, breaking whatever spell I was under. "I'm all for you fantasizing about that gorgeous man, but let's keep it to a private setting."

"Jesus." I glance around to see who else saw me, but everyone's in their own world.

"No one saw, except maybe that girl over there talking on her phone."

"Goddammit. That's Luke's sister. I was just talking to her."

"Ohhh. That's less than ideal."

"You think? She knows it's fake. I can't have her thinking I'm crushing on Luke."

Hayley's eyes widen before she smiles. "Is that what this is? I thought it was the pregnancy hormones."

"I'm not crushing on Luke, but I don't want his sister to think I am."

"Best you don't look at him now then, because *damn*." She bounces her eyebrows as she stares over my shoulder, and it takes everything in my power not to turn around. "Actually, scrap that. Luke is good-looking and all—I don't need to tell you that—but Mr. Reed Coombs just took off his hoodie, and I don't think I've spent enough time studying that man's body. Or any of these guys. Can I be your assistant at the next game?"

"After that comment? No."

"Even though I just saved you from—"

"Even so."

"Some friend you are," she jokes with a wink.

"Hey, I brought you here."

"Very true and I love you for it."

She squeezes my hand before making her way through the crowd and stepping onto the makeshift field. "Is this a boys' game or can anyone join?"

I laugh as she grabs the ball from Wyatt, before I subtly search for Luke again, my lips pulling into a frown when I don't find him. God, *why am I so drawn to him*?

"Are you looking for me?"

"Jesus Christ." I jump as I spin around, clutching my chest. "Where did you come from?"

"Behind you." Luke raises an eyebrow as he points over his shoulder. "I was getting a drink." He holds up a bottle of water and smiles.

"Thirsty work?" I ask and internally scold myself. *Thirsty work?* Come on, Amelia.

Luke raises a brow as though he knows exactly what I'm thinking before he laughs. "I've definitely worked harder, but since I needed a drink, I guess it is."

I smile to hide my embarrassment and turn back to the game.

"Did I hear you're working on the nursery tonight?" Luke asks, leaning in close.

"Seriously?" I spin to face him again. "Is nothing private around here?"

"I don't know, you tell me, Ms. All-Access Pass." He flicks my top where my "crew" pass would usually sit as he steps in front of me, blocking my view.

"Touché." I laugh. "And yes, I bought a few things for the nursery. They arrived yesterday."

"Does that mean you checked the envelope?" Luke's eyes widen and I can't help but laugh. Our new OB-GYN asked if we wanted to know the sex of the baby. Luke was all for it, but I wanted a surprise. So instead, she gave me an envelope with the answer, in case I changed my mind. But I haven't. "Nope. I'm seeing this through. We'll find out when Jelly Bean's born."

"Damn. It was worth a shot. So, can I help?" he asks, his tone completely neutral, like it's no big deal.

"Why?"

"Because as I told you, I want to help with things." He leans in closer until he's barely a breath away and whispers in my ear. "Jelly Bean is half mine, remember?" His warm breath sends a chill down my spine, but I manage to holdback from shivering.

"I know that, and I know you offered to help. But this is different. The idea is that I'll have a nursery at my house." I tap my chest in case he needs a visual explanation. "And you'll have one at your house." I poke him in the shoulder just to drive my point home and smile. "You get to set up your own nursery."

Luke stares into space like he hasn't heard a word I'm saying before finally focusing again. "Should we be living together?"

"What?" I almost choke on nothing.

"I hadn't thought about having two homes until you mentioned it. Would it be easier to co-parent if we were living together?"

I burst out laughing before covering my mouth with my hand. "Definitely not. Are you—" He bites back a smirk, the movement cutting me off mid-rant. "Ha ha. You're funny."

"I try," he says with a laugh. "And believe it or not, I bet I could work on both nurseries. I'm clever like that. Let me help."

"I—"

"Before you say no, I should tell you that I'm going to keep asking and annoying you until you change your mind. I don't have much going on at night these days."

"Why not?" Luke stares at me pointedly and I don't need him to explain it. I've taken away his hobby...women. *Goddammit*. I should *not* feel guilty about that. Or uncomfortable. I shouldn't be feeling anything.

"I wasn't going to say no," I say honestly, trying harder to let him in. I could definitely use the help. "I'll text you my address."

"Thank you. I'll come around as soon as they release us from this hell."

"Shut up. It's not hell. You're having a great time."

"Been keeping track of me?"

"No more than you've been keeping track of me. You haven't exactly been subtle."

"Touché." He nods before giving me a shrug.

"Why is that?"

"Just making sure you're okay." He shrugs again and the sincerity in his tone throws me off guard. Though it shouldn't. He's shown me time and time again that he cares about Jelly Bean and me.

"Thank you," I rush out as a new warmth settles in my chest.

"Anytime. But I better get back to the game. Tonight?" he confirms as he walks backward through the crowd, his eyes on mine as he hits me with a killer smile, sending my heart into a spin.

"Yes, tonight," I mouth, shaking my head as I bite back a smile, trying not to draw too much attention to the fact that he's coming over to my place.

When he's gone, I make my way over to Keeley, joining her as she chats with a woman I haven't met before. The woman's eyes meet mine when there's a pause in conversation, and as she brushes her long, caramel hair away from her face, I smile in return. I'm about to introduce myself, assuming she's one of the partners, when Keeley grabs my arm.

"Just the person I wanted. This is Emery. She's going to be taking over my role while I'm away next week."

"Hi, Emery. I'm—"

"Amelia. Yes, I know. Keeley told me all about you and the project."

"Oh, great." That saves me time. "When do you start?"

"I'm officially starting tomorrow. Keeley thought it would be good for me to meet everyone here. Speaking of, I'm being summoned." We all turn to find Zane waving her down. "He's one I have to watch, right?"

"Yep," Keeley and I answer in unison.

"He's nice enough. But a little full of himself."

"And he will absolutely try to get in your pants."

"Noted. Thank you."

As soon as Emery's gone, I turn back to Keeley. "You're going away?" I ask because this is news to me.

"I am. My sister's getting married in Cabo. It's a last-minute thing—which is typical of her—but I finally get my vacation, so I'm not complaining."

"That's amazing, Keeley. I'm jealous. I would love a few days on the beach and..." I trail off as a thought hits me, making me smile. "Does that mean your brother is going with you?" I grin comically. "Because if that's a yes, I really should know who will be missing from filming."

"Yes, he'll be there." Keeley grins, seeing through my ploy to figure out who her brother is. "But he's flying himself and his family in on the morning of the wedding and flying out the next day. Thankfully, she's getting married midweek."

"His family, huh?" My eyes narrow.

Keeley laughs again as I search the yard. There are quite a few guys that have families, but none that are from around here.

"And you said you were local?"

"Nope. You assumed."

"*Dammit.* Where are you from?"

"I'm originally from North Carolina. My sister still lives there. She's marrying one of the guys from the Carolina Bulls baseball team."

"Bullshit." I bark out a laugh, drawing attention. "Sorry, I mean... *bullshit*," I whisper. "Guess you and your sister are alike then."

"Yep. But she found a decent athlete. I've yet to believe they exist, my sister's fiancé aside."

"What about your brother?"

"He's okay, but he can be a grumpy asshole at times and—"

"Easton," I whisper-yell a little too excitedly. The grumpy asshole gave it away. "Your brother is Easton."

"Shhh." Keeley laughs. "And yes, you caught me. As I'm sure you can guess, the decision to keep it a secret was all him."

"I'll bet." I subtly glance at Easton to find him talking to Dylan and his wife, Summer, with their kids playing on the grass by their feet. "Did Easton come alone?"

"Yep." She frowns. "His girlfriend doesn't like coming to these things, and she doesn't let him bring their son."

"That's hard." I'd love to ask if they get along because I can sense some tension, but I leave it alone. I don't want her to think I'm trying to seek out information for the show.

"It is hard. She's nice and all, but they've been drifting since their son, Isaac, was born."

"Oh, that's sad." A pit forms in my stomach, and I have to fight myself not to focus on my situation with Luke.

"I'm sure they'll work it out; it's all new to them. They're still navigating what it's like. Isaac's two and a half and he wasn't—" She cuts herself off but I can guess what she was going to say.

"He wasn't planned?"

"No. He wasn't. I shouldn't have said anything."

"Why? I won't tell anyone. This is all off-the-record."

"No, I mean..." She glances down at my stomach, and I laugh nervously.

"You noticed."

"I did, and I wasn't going to say anything, but I didn't want you to think I was suggesting unplanned pregnancies cause issues."

"How do you know mine was unplanned?"

"Because you told me you were getting divorced."

Oh, right. I did tell her that. "What gave me away?"

"Nothing major. A few subtle hand touches to your stomach. Baggier clothing."

"Oh. Shit."

"And Coach Pierce accidentally mentioned it." My eyes widen before she quickly clarifies. "He thought I knew and he hasn't told anyone else. But you know you don't need to hide it?"

"I know. I'm just not ready yet. I'd like to get through a few more weeks of filming before people start treating me differently. And since it's winter, I figure I can wear big coats. Sort of." I laugh, opening my coat to show her. It's technically not needed, but I'm happy to pretend I'm one of those people that feel the cold.

"Do you really think you'll be treated differently?" Keeley asks with genuine intrigue.

"I know I will." It might be coming from a good place—asking me if I need a break or checking if I'm okay. But it's still different.

I just have to hope that when it all comes out, I'm strong enough to handle whatever's thrown my way.

When the sun fades, and the moon joins the party, the crowd gets a little rowdier. I consider sticking around, but I'm ready to go. In fact, I've been ready to go for a while. I turn to search for Hayley when I lock eyes with Luke across the yard. He's deep in conversation, but when he sees me, the most beautiful smile graces his lips, making my traitorous heart skip a beat. *What is going on here?*

I keep watching as he says something to his teammate before jogging over to me, his smile never wavering.

"Are you ready to leave?"

"I am. I've had enough socializing for one day."

"Sounds good. I'll grab my—"

"You don't have to leave," I cut him off. "I can get started and you're welcome anytime."

Luke chuckles, but I don't see what's funny. "I'm coming now. I'll meet you at your place. Don't forget to text me the address."

"Okay. I won't."

He turns to walk away but I grab his arm, an anxious knot settling in my stomach. "Luke." He turns my way with a grin. "My place isn't like your place. It's...uh...Remember how I couldn't get insurance?" My way of saying I get by but I am not at all wealthy.

"You worry too much." He bops me on the nose. "I'm sure I'll love it." He winks before turning and jogging away again, while I'm left confused as I try to process my feelings.

Why does he have to be so good to me? It would be infinitely easier if he wasn't.

CHAPTER TWENTY-NINE

AMELIA

L uke arrives within ten minutes of me getting home, making me rush.
I assumed I'd have at least half an hour to tidy up before he arrived.
But nope, he's here.

"Did you actually say goodbye to anyone, or just walk away?"

"Did you?" he counters with a raised brow.

"I spoke to Hayley but she decided to stay, and I waved to Keeley. I
wanted to say goodbye to your sister and Thomas, but I couldn't find
them."

Luke chuckles. "Don't worry about them. Soon you'll be seeing them
so much you'll be begging me to get you away."

"Why?"

"Lainey loves kids. And she loves being an auntie to Dylan and
Summer's kids. If you're not careful, she'll move in here."

"They don't have kids of their own, right? I think that's what Thomas
said."

"They don't. But you never know with those two. They follow their
own rules. So they tell me."

"Kind of like us? We're in a very nontraditional relationship."

"We're in a relationship now? Good to know."

"Shut up." My heart pounds when he winks at me. "The nursery is this
way." I change the subject. "The sooner we start, the sooner you can leave."

Luke chuckles again before following me into the nursery—which is
actually my bedroom—and I hold my breath, waiting for whatever remark
he's going to throw my way.

He takes a moment as he frowns before turning to face me. "Do you like it here?" he asks, perhaps holding his judgment until I answer.

"It's close to everything and comes with a parking space. That's not easy to find."

"No, it's not. But you didn't answer my question."

"It's not how I pictured raising my child, but it's mine and it's home."

"Does that mean you'd be opposed to me buying you a bigger house?" Luke invades my personal space as he bounces his eyebrows. "With a separate bedroom for Bean."

"Yes, definitely." I push him away. "As '*opposed*' as one could be. You're already doing enough. Which reminds me. We didn't do a prenup. Is there any way around that? Something you can do after-the-fact?"

"What?" Luke huffs out a laugh. "Are you scared I'm going to take your framed movie posters in the divorce?" He tilts his head toward the two frames I have hanging in my room. One for *Labyrinth*—my favorite movie—and one for *The Shawshank Redemption*—the movie that made me want to be a film director.

"Are you mocking me?" I frown. I love those pictures.

"What? No, I actually want them. I remember watching *Labyrinth* with you as a kid."

"You remember that?" I'd somehow forgotten.

"Yep. It traumatized me when those fiery things pulled out their eyes." He shivers, making me laugh. "But David Bowie was cool."

"He was. Though I wasn't worried about you taking any of my possessions. It was more about me—"

"What do you want, Joy? Whatever it is, it's yours. We don't need a prenup."

"What? No. That's not what I'm saying." Luke laughs again and I have to shake my head. "You drive me crazy; you know that?"

"Yeah, I do. It's why we work." He walks over to the boxes of furniture I have laid out on the floor after once again catching me off guard. "Where should we start?" he asks, snapping me back into the present as I hide my frown, my pulse spiking.

It's why we work. Something about that warms my heart and yet it's confusing as hell.

W e stand back to study the crib and I burst out laughing. "What did you do?" I can't put my finger on it but something is definitely wrong. I tilt my head to the side, just as Luke does the same, and when I glance his way, he's frowning with the most puzzled expression in place.

"What did I do?" he questions, his frown deepening. "I followed the instructions but... Ah shit."

"What?" I bite back a smile. "What happened?"

"I put the left side on the right side."

"That shouldn't matter, should it?"

"It matters if you want to see the cutesy pattern rather than the unpolished ridges."

"Oooh. Whoops. I forgot about the 'cutesy' pattern." I bite back a smile at his description. "Yes, I want to see that."

"I'm going to have to take it apart."

"It's almost midnight. I'm pretty sure there's a law about noise at this time of night."

"Damn." Luke scratches his head. "You're right. I'll come back and fix it tomorrow so you can have it all set up. But tonight I can help with the wall stickers. That's pretty quiet."

I smile as a tightness works its way into my chest. "I appreciate it, but you don't have to help with that."

"Will you need to reach up high?"

"Yes."

"I'm helping."

"I have a stepladder, or I can stand on the bed. I'm good. I don't—"

"Where's the box, Amelia?"

"Luke."

"I saw it around here somewhere."

"Tha—"

"Let me do this," he pleads and I freeze, even though I was going to say thank you. "Please, Amelia. I feel useless. It's the least I can do." The sincerity in his eyes almost breaks me, and my heart once again slams in my chest.

"I was trying to say thank you. I'd love your help with the stickers up high. I'll do the ones I can reach. But your skills better be perfect."

"Thank you. And don't worry. These hands were made for precision."

He laughs but my mind goes where it shouldn't, imagining the way his fingers worked my core. The way it felt to have him buried deep inside me and—*God, not again.* "I'll grab the box."

"Thanks," Luke calls out, thankfully oblivious as I walk away.

We're halfway through the wall design when I give up. Luke wasn't kidding. Every one of his stickers is beautifully aligned, not an air bubble in sight. Meanwhile, I've done two and had to carefully peel one of them off when it got a crease. "I'm done. How the hell are you doing that so easily?"

"I told you, these hands—"

"Yep, I don't need a reminder. But can we finish this tomorrow, with the crib?" I fake a yawn, but it instantly brings on a real one, making Luke laugh.

"Tomorrow is good. I've got the morning off but I have to be at practice by eleven. Can I come by early?"

"Yeah, of course. I'll be up. What time is it now?" I reach for my phone but he beats me to it.

"It's two."

"*Two.* We've been working at this for two hours."

"Yep."

"Jesus." I fall back on the bed and cover my face with my pillow before blowing out a breath. That explains why I'm tired.

The pillow disappears and I find Luke leaning over me, staring as he bites back a smirk. "I'm going to go. Get some rest. I'll let you sleep in and come in the afternoon instead. Deal?"

I stare up at him, my gaze locked on his mesmerizing eyes that even as a child I could get lost in. And my heart stops as a flutter takes over my chest.

When I don't respond, Luke reaches out and jokingly pats my cheek, the warmth of his hand making my skin tingle and my heart race. "Are you okay there?" he asks, snapping me out of my daze as my head spins.

"You should stay." I blow out a breath, unsure if I'm making the right decision, but unequivocally knowing that I don't want him to go. "Let me return the favor."

"Really?" His brows lift.

"Yes, really. But you're sleeping on the couch," I rush to clarify when he eyeballs my bed. Baby steps. I'm not sure I can trust my emotions. It all scares the hell out of me.

"Of course." He smiles. "Thanks, Wifey. I'll take it."

I smile to myself as I curl my arm farther around his waist, shuffling closer until the heat from his bare skin radiates through my body, warming me from the inside. A soft contented mewl escapes my lips as he rolls over to be closer to me, the movement making my hand brush against his hard—

My eyes shoot open, and I spring away from Luke so fast that I almost fall off the bed. Luckily, or not so luckily, Luke's sharp reflexes kick into action and he reaches out to grab me before pulling me into his arms.

"Easy there," he says, his voice all gravelly and hot. "Why the freak-out?"

"Because of this. You." I wave my hand back and forth between us as I move out of his hold. "In my bed. I was cuddling you."

"I know. Did you happen to note it was one-sided? I was sleeping."

"What?" *Ugh.* "Please explain how this could possibly be my fault?"

"I don't know." He bounces his shoulders. "You must have sought me out in your sleep."

"Sought you out? As in I got out of bed, walked into the living room, dragged you in here, lifted you onto the bed and positioned you comfortably so that I could wrap my arms around you?"

"What?" He stares at me like I'm the crazy one, yet he's the one that ended up in my bed. "That didn't happen." He shakes his head. "Your couch is really uncomfortable, so I got into bed next to you but stayed close to the edge. And at some point you must have rolled over to cuddle me."

"Well, obviously I thought you were—"

"If you say your ex-husband, so help me God..."

Okay. That's a touchy subject. "I wasn't going to say that," I snap, and it's not a lie. I must have been dreaming. But who was I dreaming about? *God, why the hell did I snuggle against him?*

Luke shakes off his annoyance before huffing out a laugh and jumping out of bed, making my traitorous gaze lock on his naked chest as I miss his presence. *Why does he have to be so beautiful?* Why does his body have to be so—

"You're drooling," he announces, cutting into my thoughts.

"Go home." I turn away, making him laugh again, and God, if it isn't just as sexy as his body.

Everything about him is sexy, and right now I'd like to climb him like a tree and— *Goddammit.* What am I doing? *I'm broken.* That must be it. It's the only explanation that's not completely insane.

How did I go from not really caring about my sex life to wanting someone to touch me so badly that I'm seriously considering Luke as a viable option? He's not. Last time we had sex I wound up pregnant and... Well, I guess the worst-case scenario has already happened so... *No. Jesus.*

Luke laughs at my spiral until I meet his gaze and his expression turns serious. His eyes blaze with a fire I haven't seen on him since the night we conceived Jelly Bean, and it hits me in the chest. This isn't just an attraction. But it's dangerous either way.

My mind reels as Luke huffs out another laugh and turns away.

"Do you need anything before I go?" he asks, glancing around the room. With his focus elsewhere, I find my eyes dropping to his half-naked body, drinking him in again while my mind fogs, all rational sense making way for thoughts of the man standing in front of me.

"Amelia?"

"Nope." I force a smile as I avert my gaze. "I'm good."

"Okay. I just need my...there it is." He moves closer to grab his phone from the bedside table, and his proximity makes me freeze. He's so close I could reach out and touch him. He could touch me... *Nope. I can't.*

Luke groans, drawing my attention, and when I glance up he's staring at me with his teeth clenched in frustration. "I told you not to look at me like that," he grates, but I can't remember him saying that at all.

"Like what? When did you say that?"

"Last time we fucked. You were staring at me like you are now. Like you want me."

Jesus. My legs clench as desire pools at my center, his words taking me back there, and I internally curse myself but thank my lucky stars he can't see under the sheet. Only when he groans again, I'm certain he can read my thoughts.

"Fuck, Amelia. Tell me what you want?"

You. I've never wanted anyone more in my life, but I'm goddamn terrified of getting hurt again and it's not just me I have to worry about now. "Nothing," I rush out instead of sharing my thoughts. "I don't want anything."

"So if I was to check your panties right now, I wouldn't find them wet? I wouldn't find you dripping for me?"

Holy shit. I am now.

My breath quickens but I fight to keep my cool. "It doesn't matter what you find, Luke. We can't."

"We can't, what?"

"Luke, please."

"That's not helping, Amelia. I love hearing you beg, and it's obvious how much you want me in your expression. Tell me I'm wrong and I'll walk away." He subtly adjusts his cock in his pants, and like the desperate woman I am, I can't stop myself from watching.

"You're wrong," I lie when what I really want is for him to rip my clothes off and devour me, but I can't say that. Things are finally good between us, and I refuse to do something that ruins that.

"I'm wrong?" Luke's brows rise as his gaze drops to my legs beneath the sheet, and sure enough, I'm squirming. "You don't want me to ease your suffering?"

"No," I whisper. "I promised myself I'd never let you touch me again." My words come out weak and he knows it. I wait for the smirk. The teasing. But it doesn't come. Instead, he steps forward, his dark eyes penetrating my soul, making me want things I have no business wanting.

I want him.

"Can I try something?" he rasps as my heart pounds in my chest.

"No, I said—"

"I promise," he cuts me off. "I won't touch you." He holds my stare, but his nostrils flare ever so slightly. He wants this, wants me, and God, I feel the same.

"No pressure." He holds up his hands while my pulse spikes and I struggle to take in air. "But I want to make you feel good."

Jesus. My breath hitches while a spark rushes to my core, making me more desperate. I don't want to do this, but I also do. So badly. And I can't say no with him staring at me like that.

"Okay," I give in, my voice breathy. "Tell me what you want to try. But no touching."

"I promise, no touching," he confirms. "But I can't tell you what I want to try. I have to show you. And you're going to be my hands."

CHAPTER THIRTY

LUKE

I raise an eyebrow in challenge, acting as though I could take it or leave it while I'd do anything for her to trust me with this. I've seen her watching me. Her desire. And while I know it's possible she feels that way because of her pregnancy hormones, I can't deny the way I want her all the same.

Before she has the chance to talk herself out of it, I step closer, leaning in until my lips are a breath away from her ear. "Lie back and close your eyes," I whisper, pausing when she gasps ever so slightly. "For whatever my word is worth, my hands won't touch any part of your body. I promise."

"And after?"

"What do you mean after?"

"Will you go before I open my eyes?" What? *Jesus Christ.* Is she about to pretend I'm someone else? Or pretend it never happened? I'll take the latter if I have to choose.

As much as it pains me, I know I'm not in any position to question her, so I give in, meeting her gaze as I do. "Deal," I agree, and while she visibly relaxes, her eyes never leave mine as her breathing increases. I was wrong. She's not picturing someone else. She wants me. She just doesn't *want* to want me. And the feeling is mutual. It would be so much easier if the desire wasn't there. But I can't fucking shake it.

Amelia squirms again, and when I catch the rise and fall of her chest, it breaks the spell she has me under, snapping me into action.

"Lie back," I demand. "Eyes closed. And before you argue—"

She does as asked without further comment, and my heart races. I'm aware that no touching means I won't be getting any action, and yet, I have never wanted to please someone more than I do right now.

I want her writhing under my gaze. I want her puffing and panting from my words. I want her screaming my name as she comes apart.

And I know exactly how to do it.

She lies awkwardly across the bed and I can't help but smile. She may have been married before, but she has this innocence about her that makes me want to corrupt her, but at the same time, it's her innocence that sets her apart. I'm used to confident women throwing themselves at me. Thinking I want them to show me every skill they've got to offer. And I'm not going to lie—that works for a good fuck. But this, having Amelia on the bed—vulnerable and trusting me with her pleasure—hits differently, and I can only imagine it's that.

I grab a pillow and walk to the other side of the bed, positioning it behind her. "Lift your head. This will make you more comfortable."

Her eyes flash open as she stares up at me before lifting herself and lying back down. "Thank you. That's better."

She closes her eyes again and I take my time, slowly removing the sheet from her body until she's no longer able to hide. She clenches her legs, briefly drawing my gaze to the top of her thighs, but it's the little sliver of her stomach that really catches my attention, my eyes widening as I take in her bump. My heart jumps and I suck in a breath. *Fuck,* I knew women felt random emotions during pregnancy, but no one talks about the men. Amelia's beautiful. Always has been, but now... God, she is breathtaking.

She shifts uncomfortably and opens her eyes again, raising an eyebrow. The movement snaps me out of my daze and I huff out a laugh. "Sorry, but I'm not going to lie. You are fucking glorious right now. I want to savor this."

"Luke," she scolds, squeezing her eyes shut as I continue to get my fill, but when she groans, I shake myself out of it again, my attention returning to her face.

"Okay. I'm focused. Back on task. Ready."

"Luke."

"*Okay.*" *God, this is harder than I thought it would be.* "I'm going to grab a pair of your panties, and what you feel next will be them, not my hands."

"What?" There's a panic in her voice as her legs clench once more, but her eyes remain shut, telling me she's still with me.

"Trust me," I say, but while it's not a question, of course she sasses me.

"I want to. I just—" Her words stop when I open her top drawer, instantly finding a pair of pink lace panties among a sea of black. A pair that looks like they've never been worn before, making me smile—I have no qualms pretending she bought these for me.

She opens her mouth to speak again, but I cut her off when I repeat my words. "Trust me," I say, knowing that she already does. I just haven't made things easy on her when it comes to that.

Amelia takes a deep breath before nodding and relaxing into the bed.

"Thank you. Now I need you to remove your panties for me."

Her lips thin but she does as asked, lifting her ass off the bed before sliding her panties down and holding them in the air. "Do you want them or—"

"Nope, I've found another pair."

With her eyes still closed, Amelia nods and releases the pair from her hands as she waits for me to continue. Her breath quickens, and I watch her chest rise and fall. While I've wanted more than anything for her to blindly trust me, it blows my mind to know that she is.

Sliding the panties onto her right ankle, I pull her leg to the side, before doing the same with her other leg, repositioning her so that she's spread for me. And *fuuuck*... a vision of me licking her beautiful pussy flashes across my mind, and I have to stop myself from reaching for my cock. What I wouldn't give to taste her again. *Just a little—*

Amelia kicks her foot out of my hold, and the movement cuts into my thoughts. I'm about to argue until she repositions herself with her feet flat on the bed and drops her knees toward the mattress, opening herself up for me, putting her pussy on full display for what I wish was my own pleasure.

But other than the view, this is all for her.

With her bunched satin thong in my hand, I take a moment to enjoy her beauty as I move slowly onto the bed, positioning my face as close as I can without touching her. She's dripping in anticipation, and it takes everything in my power not to give in and break her rules.

I bite back a groan before pulling myself together. This was my idea. I can do this. I want to do this. For her.

"Whatever you do," I say, my eyes glued to her reaction, "do not touch yourself until I tell you to."

"What? Um. Shit. Okay." Her words are frantic but she nods and sucks in a breath, her fingers curling into the sheet beside her as she tries to relax, handing over complete power.

As I study her, I lightly blow on her clit and smile when her hips buck and her mouth drops open. She clenches again but instantly relaxes as if anticipating my desire to scold her.

"Good girl. I need your legs open if I'm going to make you come."

"Oh God, Luke."

"I know. It's coming."

I blow again and she squirms, but this time she stays open for me, letting me slowly brush the satin across her center, moving it up and down, back and forth, around, teasing, but never giving her enough until she's a writhing mess in front of me.

After a minute of torment, she moves her hand to her stomach before pulling it away again and shaking her head. "Luke, I can't. I need—"

"Don't touch," I scold, causing her to whimper as her head falls back and her ass lifts off the bed.

"God, Luke. This is..."

"What. What is it?"

"It's too much but it's not enough and I don't know. God, I don't know."

"Is it good?"

"So good." She moans before lifting her arm and biting down on the flesh of her shoulder, silencing her cries.

I remove the panties, but keep blowing on her clit until she's frantically shaking. "I need to touch. Luke, please. I need..."

"Okay."

"What?" She pants, pausing as her breath stops.

"Okay. You can touch yourself now."

"Oh, thank God—"

"But I want you to listen to my directions. Can you do that?"

"Yes. Please. Tell me."

I don't make her wait, needing to see her come apart just as much as she needs it. "Okay, Amelia, slowly run a finger through your pussy. Imagine it's mine. Teasing you, making your body come alive." She does exactly as I say, while I swallow back a lump in my throat, working hard not to let her hear how affected I am.

"Good girl. Now roll *my* finger over your clit. Once. Twice."

She lets out a mewl as her ass lifts off the bed again and she wriggles under her touch. Under *my* touch. While I lose my mind watching her.

My hands clench at my side to stop myself from touching her or myself. I'm desperate to palm my cock, but more than that, I'm desperate to run my tongue through her wet pussy. I want to be the one eliciting her moans —not just my words, but me.

"Do it again," I whisper as I stare at her center, my own breath picking up speed. "Again, Amelia."

"Oh God. Yes."

Fuck. "That's it. Now a little faster, harder. If I could touch you right now I'd be lining my cock up to that beautiful entrance. Would you be ready for me? Ready for me to sink inside you? Imagine it. Can you feel me there? Can you—"

Her body spasms, cutting me off as she cries out, spreading her legs wider to give herself better access and me a better view.

Witnessing Amelia come apart like this is a new kind of torture I never knew existed, but at the same time there's something so fucking beautiful about it. Because it's her. By now I'd usually be thinking about what comes next, but I'd do anything for her to keep going, to see more.

Her movements pick up, and her whole body quivers as she rides her hand, pleasuring herself. No, as *I* pleasure her. And my cock hardens to an unbearable level. But I hold strong. That wasn't the deal.

I keep my focus on Amelia, my gaze locked on her every move, and when she's teetering on the edge of her release, I help her fall. "You are a goddess, Amelia. Fuck, it feels incredible inside you. So tight. So warm. Now come."

"*Jesus*, Luke. Holy shit."

She screams out my name over and over as her body thrashes around, and all I can think about is the sound of my name on her lips. The pure ecstasy in her voice. And I want more.

She slows her movements as her ragged breaths deepen, and I stay still until her body stops pulsing and she closes her legs, a tightness building in my chest. This is it. It's over and now I have a decision to make. I can walk away before she opens her eyes. Just like she asked. Or I can beg her to let me stay, but I'd risk breaking her trust.

Without a word, I collect my clothes and get dressed before slowly walking to the door, my balls so fucking blue there's a chance they'll fall off, but I did this. It was all me, and as much as I'd love to turn around and ask her to return the favor, I promised her I'd go as soon as she came, and that's what I'm going to do.

I hold my breath until I reach the elevator, and it's not until I'm inside that I let out a loud sigh. "Fuuuck. That was intense," I whisper to myself, laughing like I'm crazy.

My phone buzzes when I reach my truck, and when I see Amelia's text, my laughter intensifies.

> Amelia: Thank you

> Luke: Anytime. And I mean that. It was my pleasure

But now I need to fix the little problem I have. And the way I see it, just like when I was back up in Amelia's room, I have two options—find some way to relieve this tension, fast, *or* work it off at the gym. I start the ignition in my truck and stare straight ahead, unsure which way to go. But I have my answer within seconds. If it wasn't broad daylight right now and I wasn't parked in the busy street, I'd be tempted to help myself, but that's not an option, and since I don't want anyone else to help, it's gym time.

Wait. What?

I don't want anyone else? Since fucking when? Until now, my thoughts have been that I *can't* have someone else. Because of the deal I made with Amelia. But suddenly I'm thinking I don't want anyone? *What the hell is going on?*

Amelia. Amelia. Fucking Amelia.

I let her get under my skin. Again. I could have anyone I want. I could be an asshole right now and break our deal. But I no longer want to.

What I want to do is sink inside Amelia, just like I described to her. I want to—

Jesus, I want *her*.

My mind whirs as I drive, and before I know it, I'm pulling into the stadium parking lot, desperate to work out this messed-up tension consuming me.

I don't bother warming up since Amelia did that for me, and instead, jump straight onto the treadmill with my earphones in, hitting go on my playlist as I move, increasing the speed until I'm forced to run.

I stare at the windows in front of me, but rather than see through them, it's like they're projecting images back to me. Amelia telling me she's pregnant, Amelia and me getting married, Amelia screaming my name. The events of the past few months keep rotating through my mind until I'm completely spiraling.

I increase the speed again and turn up my music, hoping to distract myself, but it doesn't work. I can still visualize her. Still feel her and it's driving me crazy.

I run faster, pushing myself to the limits as a song I don't recognize blasts my eardrums, finally drowning out the nerves.

My legs shake, but I keep going until Easton appears in my line of sight, making me jump as he holds his hands up in front of me.

He mouths something, but I don't hear him until I slow my machine and hit stop on the music.

"Jesus, Luke," he barks when I reach a comfortable jog. "You're going to hurt yourself."

A sharp pain radiates through my calf, but I shake my head, pretending I'm fine.

"What do you think you're doing? Are you okay?"

"I'm fine," I lie, slowing the machine again until I'm at a fast walk, easing the cramp in my leg.

Easton scoffs. "My bad. Great. I'll be on my way then." He turns around, and I huff out a laugh. Easton usually keeps to himself, but I've seen his protective side a couple of times now, more so since he became a dad. But something he never does is fuck around and joke. The sarcasm is dripping from his words. But I pretend not to notice.

"Good. And *I'll* get back to it."

Easton's nose flares as he spins back around, his fists clenched at his sides. "Do you think I'm stupid? You are not fine. Do a proper cooldown, get showered, then meet me at the door. We're going out."

"I'm fine." *That's the last thing I need right now.*

"We're *going*. Pretend you're doing it for me if it helps. I've had a bad couple of days and I need a friend."

"Shit. You do?"

"No, fucker. Just hurry up." He folds his arms over his chest and waits for me to respond. I want to tell him no, because I can't imagine anything worse than spending time with a guy that's always grumpy, when I'm already in a mood, but I could use his help. Since he knows a little about what I'm going through.

"Fine," I toss out like a child, while Easton doesn't bat an eyelid. "Give me fifteen minutes.'

It pains me to do as he asked, but I take my time to cool down properly, stopping when my leg is back to normal. And when it comes time to shower, I slow my pace further, something I'm sure he didn't want, because I'm petty like that.

But when I finally walk out, a smirk on my face, I get no reaction.

Easton's waiting exactly where he said he'd be, talking on his phone, not at all put out by my tardiness.

"You ready?" he says when I reach him, his gaze averted as he pockets his phone.

"As I'll ever be. Where are we going?"

"That new bar at the Westerly Hotel?" Great, the same place I shared my night with Amelia.

"So, East wants to go West." I laugh, instead of letting myself spiral again.

Easton finally meets my stare, making sure I note the lack of amusement in his eyes. "Are you going to be a fucker all your life?"

"Probably," I say honestly, because this version of me comes out when I don't want to be myself. And right now, I don't know who the fuck I am.

CHAPTER THIRTY-ONE

LUKE

It's only midday and I've already downed three shots aptly named "Panty Droppers" plus two whiskeys and... I've got to admit, I feel better.

"I can't believe I skipped practice." I fake a gasp or maybe it's real; I can't tell. Either way... "I can't believe you skipped practice. For me."

"We didn't skip practice; it was a voluntary team workout. We both worked out before anyone else arrived."

I ponder that but he's right. We have a bye this weekend. Well, ain't that lucky.

"You're a good guy, East. Have I ever told you that?"

Easton huffs out a laugh before shaking his head. "And we've made it."

"Made it to what?" I stare at him confused until he laughs again.

"What's going on in your life, Luke? Anything you want to get off your chest?"

"Ahhh. I see what this is. You're trying to get me drunk so I'll spill all my secrets."

He raises his hands in the air. "You caught me. So spill."

I stare at him deadpan, but when he stares right back, I can't stop myself from laughing. "Okay, you win. But first, I don't think I've ever heard you laugh before. It's nice; you've got a good laugh. I feel special having heard it. And second,"—I wave my hand in the air before flashing him a smirk—"you've been played." I point at his chest. "I don't have any problems."

"You don't?"

"Nope. I'm fine. So what if I'm falling for the mother of my child?

What does it matter if barely two months ago I thought I hated her? Life is still good."

Easton's lips almost form a smile until his eyes widen. "Your child?"

"What child?"

"I don't know, man. You mentioned the mother of your child."

"Oh. Yep." I chuckle. "I'm going to be a dad." His jaw drops a little, making me laugh. "Come on. You all knew this was going to happen one day. You had bets going."

"I didn't. Having kids is nothing to joke about."

My face drops. "I know. Sorry."

"Don't apologize. Do you want to talk about it?"

"I wouldn't know where to begin." I grab his shoulder but he shakes me off. "I've known Amelia forever." I pick up my drink and raise it to my lips before putting it back down. "It's not like I had a random hookup and the condom broke. Although, that's exactly what happened but it's different. Because it's *her*."

"Okay. If I'm understanding correctly... Amelia's the mother of your *unborn* child?" He says unborn slowly, almost like it's a question.

"Yes. And before you ask, it's the same Amelia."

"I wasn't going to ask."

"You know, Director Amelia."

"Yep, I got that. I even knew she was pregnant, but I didn't know it was yours. I should have guessed though with the way you defended her."

"You defended her too, and you don't like the crew."

Easton's nose flares and he sits tall. "That guy was a fucking asshole and needed to be put in his place."

I'm not going to argue there. "I'm curious, what did you do?"

"Nothing." He shakes his head. "I just stood my ground and followed him out of the building."

"Well, thanks."

"I didn't do it for you." Easton takes a sip of his drink, rolling his eyes as I smile.

"No, but you did it for my wife and kid. Same, same."

"Wife?" He half chokes on his drink before coughing to recover. "She's your wife now?"

"Yep." I nod with a force that makes my head spin. "You're probably wondering why I'm here, instead of with her, right?" *Hell, I'm wondering the same.*

"Nope. That thought never crossed my mind."

"Shouldn't you be at home spending time with your wife and kid too?"

"She's not my wife."

"She's not?" My brows furrow as I tilt my head to the side, studying him. Is he bullshitting me right now? "Don't you have the same last name?"

"We do. For Isaac's sake. But she checked out... Goddammit, this isn't about *me*. When did you get married? Last I heard you were bragging about being single for life."

"Things change, people change, and now I think I'm falling for her."

"Your wife?"

"Yep."

"Fuck, I'm confused."

"You and me both." I'm so fucking confused. Easton's right; I had plans to be a bachelor for life. I never wanted to settle down, yet I'm pretending to play happy family with Amelia and it actually feels right. Only we can't tell anyone about it because it's fake and—

"Oh shit."

"What?"

"You're not supposed to know about our marriage. Did you drug me?"

"What the hell, Luke?"

"I don't know. I just thought I was better at keeping secrets." I kept Amelia's dad's secret for years. God, I'm an asshole.

"Luke, you knocked back five shots within the first twenty minutes of our arrival."

"Five shots? I could have sworn... Okay, then. Maybe I did it to myself. Come to think of it, I haven't had much to drink lately. Maybe I've gotten weak. Should we dance?"

Easton laughs out loud, and while it's definitely one of those sarcastic laughs, like he can't believe what he's hearing, I still take it as a win. "It's the middle of the day."

That's right. Huh. I guess I'll have to get the party started. But that's not important. "I've made you laugh twice now." I hold up two fingers. "Does this mean we're friends?"

Easton shakes his head, but there's something in his expression that tells me he doesn't hate me like I thought he did. "Don't push your luck," he says, and I may be drunk but I swear I can see his suppressed grin. "Go and dance. I'll be here."

I don't drink anymore while I'm dancing, and it doesn't take long to sober up as I sweat the alcohol out of my system.

I try to keep to myself, but since there aren't many people on the dance floor during the afternoon, and almost everyone knows who I am, I don't have much luck. I'd normally be in my element in a situation like this. Laughing, flirting, taking my pick of the women throwing themselves at me, but right now I don't want that.

And if I'm being honest with myself... I'm actually a little uncomfortable. Especially when the third woman tries to subtly rub her hand over my junk...I'm out.

"I think I'm broken," I whine when I get back to the table, falling into the seat beside Easton. "I am in desperate need of a good fuck and I could have half of those women." I gesture around the entire bar before laughing. "Who am I kidding, I could have *any* of those women. But I don't want them. And the one woman I do want, I can't fucking have."

"Why? Because she's off-limits?"

"What?" I stare at him confused. "No. I don't care about that. But it's complicated."

"Because..."

"Well, for one, up until recently, she hated me."

"Mmm, yep. That would make things difficult. What did you do?"

"Why does it have to be *me* that did something?"

"Because you're you."

"Asshole. The feeling was actually mutual between us."

"Was?"

"God, you ask a lot of questions."

"I wouldn't have to if you just told me the full fucking story."

"Jesus. Okay. We used to be close but I messed up. Only I didn't know I messed up, so instead, I made the assumption that she thought she was too good for me and hated her for it. Years passed. We started to talk at a party at an old, abandoned mansion. There was a fire. I tried to help her. She got pissed off because I ran the other way. And in the end we were both questioned by police. She was released, while I was arrested based on her statement. Cut to fifteen years later, we had sex, she got pregnant, we got married so I could add her and Jelly Bean to my insurance, and now she's in my head. I don't hate her anymore. I want her. *Only* her. And it's driving me fucking crazy."

Easton stares at me like I *am* crazy then laughs. Loudly. "Anything else or did you just give me your entire life story in less than a minute."

"That's pretty much it. Oh, and I obviously became a phenomenal football player along the way."

"Of course. Sometimes I wonder why we never became friends, but then there are moments like these where it all makes sense."

"Hilarious. Feel free to give me some fatherly wisdom whenever you're ready."

"Fatherly wisdom?"

"Yep. I'm ready when you are."

Easton pauses as a server places another whiskey in front of him and a water in front of me, and when she's gone, he sighs.

"You admitted yourself that you're falling in love with Amelia and—"

"Woah. What? Who said love?"

"And," he continues, ignoring me, "judging by your reaction to her being too cool for you in high school, I'd say you liked her back then too."

What? I burst out laughing, grabbing his whiskey and knocking it back before he has a chance to take a sip.

"Okay, oh wise one." *Since none of that's true, I know it's got to be something else.* "Tell me, East, when your wi–girlfriend was pregnant, did you ever feel different toward her?"

"Different how?"

"I don't know. More attracted to her. Because she was carrying your child. But only then."

Easton stares at me in confusion. "Is that the excuse you're trying to tell yourself? Do you want me to say yes?"

"Please. Yes, that would be great."

"Then yes," he deadpans. "I was extra attracted to my girlfriend when she was pregnant, but it went away as soon as my son was born. Happy?"

"Yes. Perfect. That must be what's happening. It has to be. Because I can't fuck things up for us. We need to make this co-parenting thing work."

"A little part of me wants to ask more... but a big part of me does not want to get involved in this mindfuck. I do have one thing to say though..." He trails off and I stare at him in anticipation, like his words are going to make everything right in the world. "Maybe you should try talking to her and telling her how you feel. And...maybe you should try actually being married."

"What?"

"Which part was confusing?"

I'm looking his way but I'm not seeing him as my mind replays his words. *Fuck.* He's right. What the hell am I doing here? I may not know what I feel, but I'm not going to figure it out drinking with Easton.

"You've been awesome, man, but I've gotta go," I announce, standing up with a new confidence coursing through me. "I need to talk to Amelia."

CHAPTER THIRTY-TWO

AMELIA

He did what I asked, and it made me realize I want something else entirely.

No matter how hard I stare at the plain bowl of ice cream in front of me, I can't figure out what's missing. Does it need chocolate topping, or nuts, or...pickles?

I laugh to myself. Nope, I have not had that craving yet. But I'm definitely craving something more than plain vanilla. What kind of person only has vanilla in their freezer? Sure, I did it because I thought it would deter me from eating it, but now I'm desperate for something sweet and it's not doing it for me.

I contemplate going out, but when I peek down at my red bathrobe and pink fluffy slippers, I decide against it. Going out would involve me getting changed out of my comfortable attire, and since I called work this morning and told them I wasn't coming in for the day, getting dressed is counterproductive to my lazy day goals.

So instead, I need ideas and I need them fast.

Amelia: What's a good topping for vanilla ice cream?

Hayley: Coffee liqueur

Amelia: 😶

Hayley: Oh... for you? Peanut butter. Nutella

Peanut Butter or Nutella. Hmmm. Both good options but—

Hayley: Popcorn or M&M's

My mouth waters the second I read her message, and I'm walking toward the pantry before the idea has fully formed. What about popcorn *and* M&M's. That's a thing, right? Or is it a weird pregnancy thing? What am I saying... Do I care? Nope. I *need* it.

Hayley: Jelly

Hayley: Maple syrup

Hayley: Pickles

Hayley continues to message me as I thankfully find a bag of microwave popcorn and a bite-size packet of M&M's. I can't remember where the latter came from, but who am I to question it. I glance down at the screen, smiling at her options while I get the popcorn ready for heating.

Hayley: Vegemite

What? I gag and quickly type out a response as I set the timer.

Amelia: We can't be friends anymore

Hayley: 🫠 I haven't actually tried it on ice cream but I was going for salty and sweet. Never say never, right? And you need me

Amelia: You're right, I do. And you gave me Popcorn and M&M's so I guess there's that

Hayley: Good. Is this a pregnancy craving or an emotional binge?

Amelia: Can it be both?

Hayley: Definitely. Want me to come over?

Amelia: Thanks, but I'm good. I just need to think

The popcorn starts popping at an alarming rate so I turn off the microwave before I burn it, and the second I open the door, I moan as the smell of the hot, buttery goodness permeates the air.

This is exactly what I needed, and I can't wait to dive in. My phone buzzes again as I'm mixing my concoction, and I smile at Hayley's response.

Hayley: Here if you need me. 🩶

Amelia: I know. Thank you. 😘

I don't know what I'd do without Hayley, but then I remember there's more than one person by my side. I've got Luke and I practically pushed him out the door.

He gave me another mind-blowing orgasm, and instead of returning the favor, I let him leave.

And on that note, I still can't believe he did that without touching me. No wonder he's cocky. If he'd have asked me how I felt before walking away, I probably would have confirmed that he was God's gift to women, because that man... God, just thinking about him makes heat pool between my legs. I can't get his words out of my head, or his voice, the way he was assertive yet restrained—and his need—the fact that he *wanted me* made the moment so much hotter.

I wanted to give in. I almost did. But he left. He proved to me that he was listening, that he cared, and he walked away.

And now, as I glance down at my messed-up but delicious bowl of emotions, a little part of me feels guilty. A tiny part. Maybe the size of my big toe. Because Luke is used to no-strings so he's probably thinking nothing of it.

After making myself comfortable on the couch, I turn on the TV and hit play on the first movie that pops up on the screen—a psychological thriller about a missing child. I'm fifteen minutes in with my heart lodged in my throat when the tears coat my eyes. I can't watch this anymore, and I'm one of those people that can watch everything. The good, the bad, the sappy, the unhinged. I've never had an issue with any movie or series for as long as I can remember, but I can't do this. Just a glimpse of the mother's grief has a crippling pain taking over me. How could anyone go through that?

I turn off the TV and let the tears fall just as someone knocks on my door, making me jump. Since I'm not expecting anyone, I stare at the entry, questioning if I imagined it, until it happens again, louder this time.

"It's me," Luke calls out, making me panic.

Shit. I regard my pajamas as I frantically wipe my face before pausing when he knocks again.

"I know you're in there. I've already checked your office and they said you were home sick."

I stand slowly and wrap the robe farther around myself before walking to the door. I've just grabbed the handle when he knocks again. "Don't make me have to sign shit for your super, because I will if it will get me inside."

"What?" I throw open the door before folding my arms across my chest and gesturing for him to come in. "You've used your fame to break in to someone's apartment before?"

"Nope." Luke shakes his head as he closes the door behind him. "I took the chance that it would piss you off enough to open up. And here we are."

"Ugh."

"You love it. But now that I'm here... Are you okay?"

"Other than having your annoying ass bothering me, I'm fine. Why?"

"My annoying but hot ass aside... Your assistant told me you were sick and you're standing in front of me with a tear-soaked face. So excuse me for wanting to know."

"Shit," I mumble under my breath as I wipe my face again. "I needed a day off. I'm not sick. We weren't filming today so I'm not messing anything up. I just needed—"

"Woah." Luke raises his hands in the air. "You don't have to justify it to me."

"Okay. Good."

"But you do have to tell me about the tears because honestly, it's freaking me out a little bit."

I huff out a laugh as I smile. "It's so silly."

"I can't promise I won't think that, but I'm going to need you to tell me anyway."

My shoulders drop, and while I could throw out another smart-ass comment, I don't want to. I want to share this with him. And more. "I was watching a movie about a missing baby and I couldn't handle it."

Luke's eyes widen before he squeezes them shut and shakes his head.

"Go on. Tease away." I preemptively roll my eyes.

"Fuck no." He shivers. "Why would you watch that? But also, what happened? Did they find it? Was the baby okay? I kind of have to know now."

"I couldn't finish it." I scrunch my nose when his jaw drops.

"What was it called? I'll search for it."

"Stop." I gently shove his shoulder and laugh. "I don't need to know."

"Well, I do. And thank you for unlocking a new fear I never knew existed." He stalks over to the couch and makes himself comfortable while huffing like a child, and my heart warms because of it.

I'm not in this alone. I have a partner in crime. Someone as terrified as I am. And I'm not letting him in. But why?

"I'm sorry," I say with a soft smile, my gaze locked on his confused expression as I slowly walk over. "Sometimes I forget that I'm not the only one going through this. I heard what you said at the football gathering, and

I wasn't lying when I said you are helping, but I never really processed what you meant."

"What did I mean?" He shrugs with a grimace, making me laugh.

"Stop. We both know you're a smart guy. You know what I'm getting at."

"I do." He stands and takes a step closer, invading my personal space. "And you're right, I feel alone in this too. But we shouldn't be. Because we're in it together."

He brushes the messy hair away from my face before gently running his thumb across my cheek under my eye. "I'm here for you. I'm not sure how much clearer I can be about that."

"I know."

"So why do you keep fighting it?"

"I don't..." A tightness fills my chest as I trail off. No matter how hard I try to let him in, or talk about it, I can't. And I hate that I don't know why.

"Is it because you don't trust me? Still?"

"No," I rush out. "That was a long time ago and we talked about it. This is different. I get this sinking feeling whenever I try letting you in. Like a huge wave is pushing me under the surface and I can't fight my way out, yet I'm an amazing swimmer."

"Jesus." He cringes. "That doesn't bode well for me."

"No, sorry." I laugh softly. "I don't mean that you make me feel that way. It's something else. Something bigger."

Luke nods in understanding as his hand drops to my waist, giving me a squeeze, heating my skin through my clothes. My eyes drop to the connection, studying the way he holds me.

"I'm not going anywhere, Amelia," he rasps, breaking into my thoughts. "And I won't let you drown. I won't let you lose yourself."

"What?" My eyes flash to his, and the intensity of his gaze has my heart pounding in my chest, but it's his words that steal my breath. "Why?" I manage to whisper as everything from the past few years floods my mind. "What...what made you say that?"

"Which part?"

"That I was losing myself."

"Because that's what you're feeling, isn't it?" He shrugs like it's no big deal but he's wrong. It's a huge deal because he just saw me better than I've ever seen myself.

"That's it." I shake my head incredulously. "That's why I keep pushing you away. It's why I'm always reluctant to accept your help. I don't want to lose myself. I can't." *Not again.*

Luke's gaze turns sympathetic before I break out of his hold, suddenly uncomfortable.

"Sorry, I..." I shake my head and turn away, needing to move on from the talk of our emotions. But Luke doesn't let me get too far before grabbing my wrist and pulling me to a stop, spinning me around.

"Don't pull away from me. You're not giving me a chance, Amelia. I can promise you I won't let that happen."

He locks me with his arresting gaze, and the emotion staring back at me is like a heaviness weighing me down. "Thank you. For everything," I whisper. "But I need you to stop looking at me like that." *I'm not ready for it.*

"Like what?"

"Like you're in love with me."

Luke frowns and his brows crease almost comically. It would be cute if my heart wasn't threatening to beat out of my chest. He doesn't say anything for the longest moment and then... "Maybe I am?" he rasps, his voice cracking. "Or at least, maybe I'm on my way there."

"What?" I shake my head as I step back. "Don't be ridiculous. Is this about the sex?"

"What sex?"

"This morning."

"Amelia," he chuckles as he speaks, "that wasn't sex. If we had sex, you wouldn't be questioning my feelings right now."

"What does that mean? Luke, do you realize how crazy that sounds? You don't love me. You can't and— Oh." I let out a gasp and freeze, my eyes flashing to my stomach as a strange sensation takes over me.

"Amelia—"

"Wait." I grab Luke's arm as if holding him in place is going to silence him. "Please."

He does as I ask, and we both stand quietly while I pray to get the sensation again. I'm just about to give up and continue with our conversation when it happens.

"Luke," I whisper, a fresh layer of tears pricking the back of my eyes as I glance up at him. "I felt Jelly Bean kick." I've felt movement before like a swish through my middle, but this was definitely a karate move.

"What?" he asks in awe, his voice so soft I wouldn't have heard it if I wasn't paying attention. If I thought his eyes reflected love before, it's nothing compared to the intense stare he's pinning me with now.

"Bean's kicking," I confirm, trying to ignore the butterflies threatening to take over me. "Do you... ah... do you want to feel?"

I don't know if he'll be able to feel anything, but at this moment, now, I want him to know that he can. To extend a small branch to show him that I know he's here. That it's not just me.

His eyes drop to my stomach before moving back to my face. "Are you sure?"

"Yes."

The word has barely left my lips when Luke's huge hand slides through the gap in my robe, before he tentatively palms my stomach, making me giggle.

"You won't feel it like that. Here." I place my hand over his and push down, adding a little pressure. And then we wait.

Seconds tick by with neither of us moving a muscle until it happens again, softer this time, but still, my eyes light up as a giddy excitement runs through me. "Did you feel that?" I ask.

Luke frowns, his silence breaking my heart.

"I'm sorry." I frown along with him. "Maybe it's too early to feel it from the outside?"

"Don't be sorry." He waves off my concern. "Your euphoric expression is more than enough. For now. I can't remember the last time I saw you that happy, that *excited* about something."

My nose scrunches at his compliment and I shy away. "It's surreal but also wonderful and I'm sorry."

"Don't. Be. Sorry," Luke repeats pointedly before laughing. "I'm happy that I was here for it." He reaches up and cups my face again, his gaze rendering me speechless until I remember that it shouldn't.

Our eyes bounce back and forth until I can't take it anymore, the tension overwhelming me.

"Luke," I whisper, shaking my head.

"I can't stop thinking about you, Amelia. I've never let another woman consume me like you do. And it's not because you're carrying my child. It's been like that since we were kids. I may have thought I hated you, but I couldn't get you out of my mind."

I suck in a breath, trying not to gasp while his words take over me, working hard to fill my self-doubt. But it's still there.

"What if it's fleeting? What if I allow myself to want you and you change your mind?"

"Jesus. What the fuck did he do?"

"Who?"

"Your ex. Your dad. Pick someone."

"You."

"Fuuck. Amelia, I will never be able to make up for that, but I'm not the same guy. At least, I'm trying hard to be different. For you."

For me. The regret in his eyes and his broken expression make me want to believe him and I know he's trying.

"Everything about this is different, Luke. The feelings, the intimacy. All of it. And it's scaring the hell out of me."

"The intimacy."

"God, I don't know why I just said that. But Preston and I... It was different. The urge. The tension. It's bigger now. But... Shit. No. This isn't about us. We have to think about Jelly Bean." I pause, staring through to his soul, begging him to listen. "What if we mess this up? Whatever it is?"

"And what if we don't?" He moves closer and my breath hitches as he steals the air from my lungs. My heart screams at me to say yes, to pull him into my arms and kiss him, to let myself fall along with him, but then my brain takes over and I find myself shaking my head. Because there's a burning question that we can't answer right now. A question we have to consider.

What if we do?

CHAPTER THIRTY-THREE

AMELIA

Luke squeezes his eyes shut as his nose brushes against my cheek, and I'm about to speak when he lets out a strangled groan and drops to his knees, resting his head against my stomach. His arms curl around my legs, and he bunches the material of my satin shorts before staring up at me, his teeth clenched as though it pains him.

"We can't," I rush out, but my voice holds no conviction as his pleading eyes meet mine.

"There's something here, Amelia. I don't know what it is but it's something. Can't you feel it?"

My heart skips as if reminding me that I do. I feel all of it, but it's not that simple. "Yes," I whisper, "but it doesn't change a thing."

Luke suppresses a groan as his hands lower, causing his fingers to brush against my skin. The sensation sends a spark through me and my legs quiver, giving my true feelings away.

"Please, Amelia. I need you to focus on the here and now. To trust that this is real. Even if it's just for today. Just. This. Once."

The raw desperation in his tone has me melting against him. I want this as much as he does, but we'd be blurring the lines of our arrangement, more than we already have. If it ends badly, the person who loses the most can't defend itself.

"Luke."

"I know. Fuck, I know."

He groans again, louder this time, before his lips touch the sliver of bare skin between my shorts and my top. It's so faint that I can't tell if I imagined it, but a warmth lingers either way.

For a torturous few seconds, I hover on the edge as a need pools between my legs. I fight an internal battle, trying not to react as I decide between what's right and what I need.

When he finally moves again, he kisses a path across my stomach, and my heart pounds so hard he couldn't possibly miss it. But I don't speak. I don't tell him to stop. Even though everything is screaming at me to pull away.

"Fuck, Amelia." His fingers bite into my skin, his touch frantic... kissing, nibbling. "*Jesus.*" He curses himself before releasing his hold and staring up at me once more. "Tell me to stop," he begs. "But also, don't. Please don't." His breath is so rushed and needy that it silences me. I have never felt this wanted in my life. I have never had someone so desperate to have me that he's on his knees begging. And it's hard to say no when I need him all the same.

"I can't," I whisper and his head drops back as he bites his lip without waiting for me to finish. "I can't tell you to stop because I want you, Luke. I'm just so scared."

"I've got you, Amelia. I won't let you drown."

His words penetrate my heart, and for the first time I don't see the guy he projects to the world. I see the boy I remember, the teen I found again that night in the attic, the guy I once thought was put on this earth to protect me.

"I trust you, Luke. Here and now, I trust you completely."

Luke's eyes flash to mine as he curls his fingers beneath the band of my shorts and panties, holding them like a lifeline, a guttural groan ripping from the back of his throat. He kisses my stomach again, before standing up and walking me backward toward the wall.

And when my body hits the plaster, something snaps between us and there's no going back.

I'm not sure who's the first to move, but within seconds, I'm clawing at his shirt, as his hands sink into my hair. We pause for the briefest of seconds, our eyes locked as a moment passes between us. This is a big deal. No matter what we tell ourselves, this is bigger than tonight. I just pray we're not making a mistake.

As soon as the moment passes, Luke presses his mouth to mine, consuming me in a possessive kiss, his hold on me tightening. I let out a soft moan and he takes advantage, slipping his tongue inside my mouth as he tilts my head, positioning me so he can deepen the kiss.

My heart races as our tongues dance, and while I struggle to take in air, I want more. I don't ever want to stop. My grip on his shirt tightens as I drag him closer and he groans, breaking our connection to kiss a path down my neck, his hands gliding to the top of my robe so he can push the material from my shoulders.

He moves me away from the wall, and I let the robe drop to the floor before lifting my arms and allowing him to glide the silky camisole over my head, leaving me half naked in front of him.

"This body. Fuck... I can't get enough of it." He kisses his way toward my breasts, wrapping his lips around one of my nipples, his tongue lavishing the bud.

I cry out as my body bucks against his, and the sensation of him finally touching me again is almost too much to bear. This morning was amazing. A moment I'll never forget. But this is so much more than that.

I run my hand through his hair, gently tugging on the strands as he moves to my other nipple, before making his way across my ever expanding belly, staring up at me with his signature smirk.

But when my legs shake under his intense gaze, his brows furrow before he stands up, pushing my shorts down in the same movement, not bothering to wait until I've stepped out of them before spinning me toward the couch and perching me on the arm, facing him.

"I've got you," he repeats before pressing a chaste kiss to my lips and dropping to his knees, spreading me wide, his eyes locked on my core as he clenches his teeth. "God, Amelia," he groans. "You're always wet for me. Always ready." I try to close my legs but he stops me, his voice as much as his touch halting my moves. "Such a beautiful sight. And while I can't wait to sink my cock inside you again, I need to taste you first. I need *all* of you. Not being able to touch you this morning almost killed me."

He slides my panties to the side and runs his tongue through my heat, making me cry out as my body shakes. "God, Luke."

"I know. But I promise, no teasing this time. I need it too much."

As he licks me again, he presses a finger to my entrance and ever so slowly pushes inside me, as if knowing I'm going to need a moment to get used to it again. After giving me a second, he curls the tip and rubs against my wall until I cry out, my body grinding against his face, seeking my pleasure, just like he once asked me to do.

"Yes. Good girl. Fuck, you're gorgeous when you take what you need."

Jesus. That mouth.

He makes me want to please him. To do more to elicit the sexy raspiness of his voice.

Because with that and the control in his tone—the praise—I am butter in his hands.

"Make me come, Luke. I need to come."

"With pleasure."

He sucks my clit into his mouth and pumps a finger inside me before adding a second and twisting them around. I thrash against his face as the pressure builds inside me, the sensation of my impending orgasm sitting just out of reach.

As if sensing I'm close, Luke removes his fingers and penetrates me with his tongue before slowly licking toward my clit as his finger hovers closer to my back entrance, the tip resting against my hole. I have never done anything like that before, but just the thought of it, the fact that he's pushing me out of my comfort zone while his tongue curls against my clit and his thumb rubs against my core, has me flying over the edge until I'm cursing the heavens for relief.

"Oh Godddd," I moan as my body jolts and my release coats Luke's face. My eyes find his as he smiles up at me, his tongue teasing me until my body spasms and I have to beg him to stop.

When he finally slows his movements, my breath calms, and after giving me one last lick, he stands up, the warmth of his body surrounding me before his touch caresses my skin.

"You're perfect, always, but when you come apart like that..." He groans. "The way you trusted me. You're incredible. Are we still okay?"

"Yes," I rush out. "More than okay."

"Good." He leans closer until his breath warms my neck. "Do you want more?"

God. My legs clench again as a shiver runs through me. "Yes," I whisper breathlessly. I hate that I can't see his expression right now, but it's better that I don't. I'm already hovering dangerously close to falling for him, and it's too fast. We need to slow down. Everything is backward. Though I can't deny the way he makes me feel wanted. The way everything he does makes me feel wanted and safe. "Take me, Luke. For tonight, whatever you want. I'm yours." *We can work the rest out later.*

"Amelia, fuck." His voice wavers and the warmth of him disappears as he stands up and moves away. I'm just about to panic, thinking that I've said the wrong thing when the sound of a condom packet permeates the air and I actually laugh.

"Little late for that, don't you think?" I sass before covering my mouth, terrified that I ruined the moment. But Luke chuckles.

"I didn't want to assume, you know, because..."

He trails off as my smile fades until I get it. He's protecting me again. "Have you ever gone without?"

"Never. But I had a condom break once." He winks and I burst out laughing. This shouldn't be funny. We're talking about him sleeping around, but for some reason, and God knows why, this is different. And I could be deluding myself into thinking he's changed, but deep in my gut I feel it.

"Do you...ah...want to go bare?"

"You have no fucking idea how much I want that. But only with you."

My heart jolts as I take the condom from his hand and toss it near the discarded packet. While that's not the most romantic notion, it means something because I want that connection too. I want him everywhere. I want him to own me.

A fire sparks in Luke's eyes before he grabs my hand and pulls me to my feet, walking me to the front of the couch.

"Wait. You don't want to use the bed?"

"You don't have a headboard."

"So?" I swallow a lump in my throat as he spins us around and drops his pants to the carpet, letting his cock spring free between us.

"So..." He sits down, and slides to the back of the couch before reaching out and taking my hand again, gliding me forward until I'm positioned between his legs. "I want to see you when I slide into you." He curls his fingers through the top of my panties. "I want to see your face when you moan my name and come on my cock."

It takes everything in my power not to moan for him now as he slowly drags my panties down my legs, but I hold strong. "We couldn't do that in bed, lying down?"

I'm not sure why I'm questioning him, but since missionary is a coupley position, my head runs rampant, questioning if he's avoiding it.

Luke bites back a smile as he grabs me behind the knees and pulls me on top of him until I'm straddling his lap. "Believe it or not, Amelia, this muscle ain't fake. If we're in the bed, lying down and I lose control... I don't want to accidentally hurt you. Or Jelly Bean. And trust me when I say, I have never lost control before but something tells me I could easily lose it with you."

Oh.

"Okay," I say as I gasp, ignoring the tension in my chest, writing it off to lust.

"Okay?"

"Yes." I bite my lip and nod before releasing it. "Please."

"Fuck, Amelia. You're killing me."

With his eyes locked on my center, Luke grabs his cock, pumping it a few times, and my need builds, my core pulsing as I wait for his touch.

I lift to my knees and he lines himself up with my entrance, groaning as I slide down his shaft, painstakingly slowly, a little to tease him and a lot to readjust myself to his size.

Luke watches as his cock disappears inside me, and the second he's buried to the hilt, he lets out a pained groan. "Jesus, Amelia, this is incredible. *You* feel incredible. I need to move."

"Move. Please."

He responds with his actions, his palms curling around my waist, and he lifts me up and slams me down onto him, pumping into me as our bodies crash together. It's fast and messy, but when I open my eyes and find him staring up at me with the same loving gaze he had earlier, the world stills.

A silent conversation passes between us, and we both slow to a gentle rhythm, rocking back and forth, as my heart beats out of my chest. This isn't sex; we've moved way beyond that and it scares the hell out of me.

"Luke," I whisper, as emotion overwhelms me.

"I know, Amelia," he whispers. "I know."

We naturally pick up speed again, and it's not long before the pressure swirls around my body, my release imminent.

"I need more. I'm close."

Breaking our stare, Luke bites down on my nipple and I cry out, increasing my speed until I'm pounding against him, desperate for him to join me. I lean back, giving him better access as I move to grab his hair, but he stops me when he presses down on my clit, the pressure sending my body soaring.

I scream out his name, and he pumps a few more times before he grunts out mine and follows me over the edge, his cock pulsing inside me. "Yes, Amelia. God."

We continue to rock slowly as our ragged breaths calm, and when our movements naturally come to an end, Luke pulls me closer until my forehead rests against his.

"So tonight you're mine," he whispers as I close my eyes and breathe him in, the idea of that settling inside me. I hum in response, my way of saying yes, until he palms my face, making me open my eyes to stare at him. "But tomorrow we're going to talk. I want more, Amelia. And I think you do too."

My jaw drops as the air rushes from my lungs, and I'm just about to speak when Luke presses his mouth to mine. "Tomorrow," he whispers against my lips. "Don't think until tomorrow."

CHAPTER THIRTY-FOUR

LUKE

After cleaning ourselves up, Amelia yawns, so I jokingly carry her to bed, tucking her in like a child. She tries to resist, but to no one's surprise, the second her head hits the pillow, her eyes drift shut.

"I just need a minute," she whispers groggily, and I bite back a grin, waiting until her breathing slows before I sneak away, pausing at the door to glance back at her. She rolls to get comfortable, and I finally smile until her hand wraps protectively around her stomach and my body tenses.

While I could never regret what just happened, a heaviness settles in my chest, the truth of her reasoning weighing me down. Jelly Bean is my number one priority, but I can't hide away from the fact that I'm falling for Amelia. Being with her again, having that connection, that pull, made my feelings stronger, and it's too late to go back.

But where do we go from here?

I walk quietly into the living room and fall onto the couch, covering my face with my hands. This is more emotion than I've ever allowed myself to feel and there's a reason for that. I'm not sure I'm equipped to handle it. For years I've played the role of the easy going playboy, the comedian, the guy without a care in the world. And I played it well because I truly believed I was him.

It was easier to be that guy.

It *is* easier to be that guy.

But I was kidding myself to think I could stay that way forever.

Now I'm a husband and soon to be a dad. And as terrifying as that is, it's the most real version of me that's ever existed.

How do I stop myself from fucking it up?

I'm saying all the right things, but what if I'm wrong? What if I hurt her again?

I'm mid-spiral when the sound of my name cuts into my thoughts.

"Luke?" Amelia's soft voice echoes through the silence, and at first I wonder if she's talking to herself until she calls out again, her tone a little more frantic. "Luke?"

"I'm here. I'm here." I jump up from the couch and jog into her room, pausing at the threshold. Amelia's gaze drops to my naked chest before meeting my eyes, but there's no lust in her expression. Instead she seems confused.

"I thought you'd gone."

I smile at her sleepy state and shake my head. "Not yet." I laugh until her face drops. "Wait. I didn't mean that. I wasn't planning on leaving."

"Good." She nods, a smile finally gracing her lips before she stretches through a yawn. "Is it tomorrow yet?"

"It's not." I smile. "You've barely been asleep." Amelia pouts and it's so goddamn beautiful it takes me a second to continue. "And you *need* to sleep. You've got filming tomorrow and I have practice. We may not be playing this week, but I still need to keep up my A game."

"I know. I know. But...if we're not talking until tomorrow, will you stay?"

My eyes flash to the couch, thinking about how much I hated it last night, and despite loving it a little more now, I'm still not sure I can sleep there. "Ah..."

"With me." Amelia giggles. "Here." She pulls the sheet away from her body and pats the bed beside her. And this is it. Other than when I snuck into her bed at five a.m. this morning, I have never slept with another woman. Ever. And yet, with Amelia, it's not as big a deal.

"That sounds a lot more appealing." I slide in beside her and she curls into me but moves her hand awkwardly across my abs as though she doesn't know what to do with it. I grab her palm and settle it over my heart before pressing a kiss to her hair.

She moans happily, and that little sound breaks my resolve and I can't wait anymore.

"I changed my mind. I want to talk now." Amelia raises her brows as she glances up at me but doesn't argue. "I may not know what the fuck I'm doing, but I want us to spend a day together. On a date. I want to go back to the beginning. To do all the things we skipped. What do you say?"

Amelia stares at me with wide eyes before blinking a few times, and just when I think I've broken her, the most breathtaking smile lights up her face. "For the infamous Luke Bennett, that means more than a proposal, so... yes, I'd love to."

Thank fuck.

When I wake up the next morning, I'm snuggled against Amelia, my hand curled around her, secured under her belly, as if I instinctively knew not to hold any higher, in case my arm was a dead weight.

As my senses come back to life, Amelia's soft breaths filter through the air while the heat of her body radiates against me. And I like it.

It doesn't freak me out like I always thought it would.

As gently as possible, to not disturb her, I slide away and sit up, checking the time on my phone, disappointment filling me when I have three minutes before my alarm is set to go off. Barely enough time to kiss her good morning.

I stretch my arms as I glance back over my shoulder, smiling as she sleeps peacefully. Seeing her like this, so innocent and quiet, you'd never know she had so much sass, but I wouldn't change it for anything. I like that she challenges me and stands her ground. I just wish I wasn't part of the reason she's closed herself off, or that she hadn't been hurt in the first place.

Visions of a young Amelia play in my mind, and the more I picture it, the more I understand. She's never had a man in her life that treated her properly. Never had an equal. Someone she could blindly trust without thought. And I can't imagine what that's like.

Despite my faults, and I have many, I've always had support if I needed it, always had someone I could turn to. I may not have wanted someone in my life, but no one's ever made me hurt like that. Except maybe Amelia. I'm starting to think Easton was right. I hated her *so* much because I cared *too* much.

I stand up to get ready just as Amelia's alarm goes off at the same time mine does. She groans before blindly reaching out and grabbing her phone, silencing the noise as she rolls over.

"Hi." She smiles when she catches me watching her. "Are you going to turn that off?"

I snap out of my daze and silence my alarm before diving back onto the bed and wrapping myself around her.

"What are you doing?" She giggles as she tries to wriggle free.

"I'm embracing this life. Doing what couples do. Right?"

"Some do, sure. But we are not a couple."

"Not yet." I bite my lip as I bounce my eyebrows before smothering her again.

"Okay, okay. I have to get up. I can't be late today."

"Want me to drive you?" A thought hits me as I sit up and I frown. "Actually, can you drive me? I caught an Uber here."

"What? You're supposed to be off-limits to me. I can't drive you to the stadium. I may as well have a sign on my head that says, "I slept with number 42."

"I know where you can get that sign," I joke and cringe until Amelia bursts out laughing.

"Believe it or not, I know your reputation. I'm aware this isn't a first."

"Actually it is."

"What is?"

"You. You were my first."

Amelia's expression morphs into one of skepticism before she rolls her eyes. "Are we playing pretend or do you think I'm stupid?"

"Neither. You are the first person I've ever spent the night with." Amelia's jaw pops open, making me chuckle as I lift a finger to close it for her. "Is that so hard to believe?"

"It's not, but it is...if that makes sense."

"Nope. But you're tired, and pregnant, so I forgive you."

Amelia smacks me in the face with her pillow and I catch it before bursting out laughing. "Was it the pregnancy reference?" I ask, settling the pillow protectively against my chest.

"It was both. You don't tell a woman she's tired either."

"Noted. I have a lot to learn."

"You're off to a good start. I wouldn't be too worried."

"Thank you. So, how about you get ready and drop me off at my place on your way? I start later than you. I'll make breakfast while I wait."

"Um..." She hesitates, making me roll my eyes.

"It's just breakfast, Amelia. I'm not moving in."

"Okay. Thank you."

I press a kiss to her brow before jumping up in search of my clothes, and I've just found my sweater when I come across a bowl of melted ice cream mixed with popcorn. What in the—

"Ah, Amelia. What did you eat for dinner last night?"

She groans, and I can't stop the smile on my face as she asks, "Any chance we can pretend you never saw that?"

"Yep." I chuckle. "That works for me."

After spending the night at Amelia's, I somehow manage to get my ass to practice on time only to find the parking lot empty. I rack my brain trying to remember if I missed something, and Easton's parting words come to mind. "Don't forget practice is an hour later tomorrow."

Dammit. I was so caught up in getting to Amelia that I did exactly what he told me not to do. I forgot. But thank God it was an hour later and not earlier, so that's a win.

After dumping my bag into my locker, I consider a quick workout until Amelia's beautiful face enters my mind. If our practice is an hour later then maybe she has some free time.

Decision made, I make my way through the halls until I find Amelia's office, and I'm just about to knock when someone calls out my name, making me cringe like I'm in trouble.

"Luke Bennett?"

"Yep." I turn slowly to find Keeley's replacement, and I have to hold back from raising my hands in the air like I've done something wrong. Yes, I was about to sneak into Amelia's office, but since I haven't yet, I'm innocent.

"Hi..." *Dammit.* What was her name?

"Emery." *Yes, Emery.*

"Hi Emery. How are you?"

"Good. Are you looking for someone?"

"The director asked if I could pop my head in before practice. She had some notes for me."

"Oh." Emery's face lights up. "I can't wait to view some of the footage. I was actually on my way to visit Amelia now."

"Huh. Well, there you go. I can come back."

"No, that's okay. I won't be long. We can go together."

"Perfect." I smile on the outside but internally grimace. *Amelia is going to kill me. But also... this could be fun.*

I wait for Emery to catch up and knock on the door as she reaches me, smiling once more.

"Come in," Amelia calls out and I take a breath, praying she goes along with my ruse.

Emery opens the door and signals for me to go in ahead of her, but I shake my head and insist she goes first. You know, because I'm a gentleman and not because I want Amelia to see her first.

She thanks me before Amelia glances up from her desk.

"Emery?"

"Hi, Amelia. I know you asked Luke to see you, but I hope you don't mind, I just had a quick question."

Amelia's eyes briefly widen when she spots me, but she recovers quickly. "Yes, of course. But if you need me for longer, I can chat with Luke later. It's not time critical."

Emery's gaze flits toward the images on the office wall, giving Amelia the chance to shoot me a what-the-fuck look, which I of course smile at. "Actually, I don't have time later," I lie because I'm here now. "This works better for me. If that's okay with you both."

Am I being an ass? Yes. But now that I'm here, I need to kiss her so fucking badly that I can't leave without it.

Emery nods as she walks closer, handing Amelia a document while I pretend to be distracted. She mentions something about Coach Pierce not being available for their meeting today before setting up another time and heading on her way. My brows furrow after she smiles, but I school my features before turning to face Amelia.

"Is your coach usually so elusive?" she asks when Emery's gone, her puzzled expression similar to mine.

"No. He's not. But he's not a fan of the filming when it's such a big year for us. So maybe it's that?"

"Most likely. I've seen something similar with a few of the players. Anyway, apparently I wanted to see you?"

"You did," I deadpan. "But God knows why when you're not supposed to be spending time with the players. Must be important."

She bites back her smirk, but when I tug my lip into my mouth and shrug, she bursts out laughing. "What do you want, Luke?"

"Just this." I stalk toward her, spinning her chair to face me before sinking my hands into her hair. She releases a soft gasp, but I don't let her argue before pressing my lips to hers, molding our mouths in a bruising kiss. She doesn't move at first, but when I suck her bottom lip into my mouth, she lets out a moan before kissing me back, her hands wrapping around my neck to pull me closer.

A fire ignites inside me, and it takes everything in my power not to lift her into my arms and take her on her desk. I want to devour her. And only her. Always. But it's more than that. I want it all.

We continue to consume each other until voices filter in from the hallway and Amelia pushes me away. I move in for one last kiss, but she turns her head, just as Tom enters her office.

"Amelia. Luke. Hi."

"Tom. Good to see you. I'll leave you two alone. Thank you for showing me that footage again, Amelia. It will really help my game."

I nod to Tom as I walk past and he holds the door open for me, smiling at my perfectly appropriate explanation for being here. At the last second, I glance back to see Amelia fix her hair, while Tom is none the wiser.

That was fun. I get why Thomas and Lainey snuck around for so long.

As soon as I'm back in the locker room, I shoot Amelia a text, just to be on the safe side. The last thing I want is for her to be pissed off at me again.

> Luke: I couldn't help myself. You're in my head.
> Forgive me? 😄

Amelia: You could have gotten me fired! But that
kiss... you're forgiven. Just don't make a habit
of it. 😏

I don't respond because I can't agree to those terms. Now that I know
what I want, it's hard to stay away. But more to the point—I don't want to.

She has me hooked. I'm hers. I just need to convince her that she's
mine.

CHAPTER THIRTY-FIVE

LUKE

I only catch Amelia's eyes once during our practice, when they pause in filming. But just seeing her annoyed blush when I wink is enough to get me through.

And tomorrow, I get to spend the day with her.

"I heard you went out with Easton yesterday," Reed says when we're back in the locker room. "How'd that go?"

I huff out a laugh and peer over at Easton, finding him with his usual gruff persona. "You make it sound like that's a big deal. We just had a few drinks."

Reed raises an eyebrow as he stares at me, waiting for me to change my response.

"Okay." I laugh. "It's a big deal. And it wasn't my doing. He kind of forced me when he found me mid-breakdown."

Reed frowns until my smile widens, and he laughs. "I always knew there was a nice guy buried deep within that muscle. Deep, deep within."

"Reed, you see the good in everyone."

"Not everyone. The jury is still out on Zane."

We both glance at Zane as he talks to Emery. "He's a dick and thinks with one, but so was I in my first season. Remember?"

"Luke, you were still a dick last season. And this season..."

"Alright, I get it and I guess I can't argue."

"Nope. How are things with—"

"I'm not talking about that here, Reed." I throw my bag over my shoulder when I'm done and smile his way. "I'm off; enjoy your Saturday. I'll see you Sunday to watch the games."

Reed does nothing to hide his confusion as I slap him on the back. "You're not coming out?"

"Nope, I've got plans."

"Plans, hey?" He smirks, his eyes flashing toward the film crew as if that will clue me in on what he's alluding to, and turns out, it does. But it's annoying.

"Why the fuck are you looking at me like that?"

"Because you never miss a night out yet you've missed a few."

I lift a shoulder as I walk away, but not before calling out. "People change."

Amelia arrives a few minutes early for our date, and I tell Shadow to sit before opening the door. After a quick hello, she steps inside, and it's nice having her in my space again. This time, under very different circumstances.

"Sorry, I'm a bit early. All the lights were gre— Hello." She spots Shadow and her voice trails off. "My God, she's even more beautiful up close."

"This is Shadow, my firstborn." I bite back my smile until she laughs.

"Hi, Shadow." She takes a tentative step closer. "Can I pet her?"

"She'd be pissed if you didn't. She loves people. Especially those that exude warmth."

"I do that?" She stares at me confused until I laugh.

"You don't normally, but you are right now. It's obvious you're a dog person."

"I am. But you already knew that. Remember we found that lost puppy when we were...seven, I think?"

"I do. You begged your parents to let you keep it, and they finally relented an hour before the owner came forward." She bends down to pet Shadow, and I keep my fingers crossed that she doesn't get too excited. I don't usually have her inside when people are over.

Amelia sighs longingly as Shadow licks her cheek. "It broke my heart."

"So much so that you made me sneak into their yard to check up on it and make sure it was being treated properly."

"Oh my God. That's right. And there were two of them, so I gave in knowing it was better to keep them together."

"Yep. Maybe Shadow can sense your love of dogs."

"Maybe." She smiles up at me. "She's amazing, Luke. I can tell she's loved."

"Yeah, well, I had love to give and needed it to go somewhere. But don't worry, I have plenty to share."

"What?" She panics like I'm moving too quickly, and I hold back my smile at how adorable she is.

"For Jelly Bean. It's our first date, Amelia. Don't get ahead of yourself."

"Of course. How silly of me."

Amelia pets Shadow for a little while longer until I drag her away, leading her through the house until we get to my theater room. "Since I can't take you out to a movie without being seen, I thought we could try this." I guide her into the room to show her the mini movie theater I'd set up, complete with popcorn machine and snack bar. Amelia gasps before covering her mouth with her hand and turning my way.

"This...I...I'm speechless. I want to say something about how I didn't think you had it in you, but I'd be lying. Because I've come to realize you can be a sweet guy when you want to be."

"I know when to pull him out of hiding. I'm clever like that," I joke so things don't get too mushy.

"Thank you. I love it. What movie are we watching?"

"I have options. From old favorites to new releases, the choice is yours."

Without picking a movie, Amelia beelines for the snack bar and starts filling a bowl while I get set up with *Labyrinth*, almost certain it will be her choice. Especially after I admitted to being freaked-out by the red fiery things.

"Would it be okay if we watch *Lab*—" She cuts herself off when I press play and an image of David Bowie takes over the big screen.

"What were you saying?" I tease, getting a light slap on my arm in return.

"I wanted to see your reaction with the fire things."

"Really?" I say, holding back my sarcasm. "That thought never crossed my mind."

After grabbing a small bag of popcorn, I make myself comfortable on the couch but groan when Amelia sits down on the opposite end. "This is a date, Amelia. Do you know what people do on movie dates?"

"Watch a movie?"

"They snuggle and make out."

"Are we fifteen?"

"Nope. But I'm still going to need you over here."

She doesn't budge, but when she senses me glaring her way, she lets out the cutest little laugh. "Okay, fine. I'm coming."

"Good girl. That can be your first for the day."

"My wh—" She rolls her eyes when my meaning hits, and then sits beside me. "Very funny."

"I thought so. Now come here." I slide her closer and wrap my arm around her shoulders, pulling her into me until she wriggles around to get comfortable.

"Happy?" she asks as the opening title music begins.

"Very. Thank you. Are you?"

She glances up at me, her body snuggled into mine, her eyes full of the warmth I mentioned earlier. "I am. Thank you."

We talk and laugh throughout the entire movie, with Amelia reciting random lines and trying to scare me in the moments she thinks might make me jump. To no one's surprise, I'm no longer freaked-out when we get to the fiery part. In fact, I actually find it comical. And when the movie ends, I've got to admit, after all these years, I still enjoyed it. But maybe I enjoyed the live commentary more than anything.

"Good choice for your all-time favorite. And even better that it's one you can show your kids."

"Exactly." Amelia sits up excitedly. "What's your favorite? You used to love *Remember the Titans* when we were young."

"Still do. That will always be one of my favorites. But I also really love biopics like *A Beautiful Mind*. Oh, and *Moneyball* was great too."

"I love both of those movies. Do you ever go to the movies or do you tend to stay away?"

"I avoid them. I could go, but it's easier to watch in the comfort of my own home or with friends at their places."

"That's sad." She frowns. "We'll have to organize a private screening of the first episode of your series. Maybe we can hire out one of the smaller theaters."

"You mean we don't get a big fancy premiere?"

"Do you want one?"

"Fuck, yeah. But I might be the only one. And Zane."

"I guess we can ask."

Our conversation moves away from movies, and I suddenly remember what I should have shown her when she first arrived.

"I forgot to tell you, I started clearing out one of my spare rooms for the nursery," I say proudly as her eyes light up. It's been two days since she mentioned it, but I couldn't help myself last night. I wanted to show her I was taking this all seriously. That I was moving forward and helping.

"Can I see it?" She stands as if not taking no for an answer.

"Of course." I take her hand and walk toward the front of the house, past the staircase leading her away from the bedrooms she knows about. When I glance back at her, her brows are furrowed, making me hold back my laugh.

"Where are we going?"

I don't answer until we're standing in front of what used to be the home office, but it's now almost bare, ready for a crib. "I wanted the nursery to be on the ground floor so I was never too far away."

"But isn't your bedroom upstairs?"

"It was. But there's a spare room with an en suite next to this room, so I figured I'd swap to sleep there."

I wave my hand around the space, and when I glance back at her, there's awe in her expression. "Who the hell are you?"

I bark out a laugh as she turns to face the nursery again, and I wrap my arms around her from behind, pressing a kiss to her head. The situation doesn't necessarily warrant it considering it's a first date, but I can't stop myself. "I've been asking myself that question a lot lately, and I'm yet to figure it out."

"Well, I like you. This version of you. Much nicer than the asshole playboy."

"Hey, I take offense to that. I was never an asshole to anyone else. I reserved that all for you."

"I'm honored." She grins before shaking her head and weaving herself out of my hold. "It's a good idea. To have everything down here. You'll have your own space, but Bean won't be too far away. It's going to be great." I sense a sadness to her tone, but by the time I check, she has a smile in place.

"It would be even better if I knew what colors to make it." I lighten the mood.

"And you will. When the baby's born." Amelia smiles while I roll my eyes. In truth, I'm happy either way. It would be nice to know, but I can see the appeal of a surprise too.

"So what's next?" she asks, her brows raised. "There was a mention of dinner?"

"Yeah." I chuckle. "I made dinner. Hope you still like chicken tacos. I remember a time when they were your favorite meal."

"When I was ten," she exclaims, but before I can respond she adds, "but yes, I still love them."

I knew it. I smirk, but hold back my gloating.

After taking her back to the kitchen, I offer for her to wait at the table while I finish preparing dinner, but she insists on hovering around me and I don't mind the company at all. We talk about life, football, her music videos—even though that brings the conversation dangerously close to the topic of her ex-husband—and our friends. Amelia tells me about the film role Hayley's waiting to hear about, and I tell her about my sister's upcoming wedding to Thomas, joking about how they went behind my back when they first got together.

Our conversation is effortless...easy.

It's perfect, and I hope like hell Amelia feels the way I do.

CHAPTER THIRTY-SIX

AMELIA

I never would have guessed I'd be dating Luke Bennett, but here we are. And I don't hate it. At all. In fact, I like it. I want more.

L uke steals chaste kisses throughout dinner, but it's not until the dishes are in the sink that I sense a shift in the air.

"Have you had a nice day?" he asks as he walks toward me, before grabbing the elastic of my waistband and pulling me closer.

I ignore the goose bumps that coat my skin and smile. "I have. You did good."

"Thank you. Does that mean I've earned a proper goodnight kiss?"

"That depends? Are you kicking me out?"

"Nope. Just taking it early."

"I'll allow it."

He tugs me closer until our bodies crash, and before a breath has left my lips, his hands are cupping my face as he presses his mouth to mine.

My fingers glide under the cotton of his tee, skimming over the ridges of his abs, and he groans at my touch, deepening the kiss as his hold turns possessive. And for the first time, I want to give back. I want him to burn for me like I burn for him. I want to please him.

Pulling my lips from his, I push him back and unbuckle his belt. Without breaking his stare, I flick open the button on his pants and slide the zipper down, a new confidence taking over me.

His muscles tense under my fervent gaze, but when I slowly crouch down, dragging his jeans along with me, he lets out a tortured groan.

My lips pull into a victorious smile until he catches me by the arm and lifts me to standing.

"You are a fucking goddess, Amelia. But you are not getting on your knees for me."

The sternness of his tone catches me off guard, but I stand firm. "What if I want to?" *What if I need to?*

"If you want it that badly, you can wait until after our baby is born. I'll be more than happy to accept your offer then."

My heart jolts but I roll my eyes and open my mouth to complain. Only to stop myself. I can't pretend his argument doesn't make him sexier, and there are other ways I can please him; I just have to get creative. "Okay." I give in. "Do you want to watch a movie or something?" I sass, knowing very well that's not what he wants to do.

"No, Amelia. I do not want to watch a movie. I want to lay you back on the counter and spread your legs until your pussy is on display for me. Then I want to take my time eating my dessert, and when I'm done and you're screaming my name, I'm going to drop your feet to the floor and fuck you from behind while you watch us in the mirror."

Oh God. My knees go weak as my arousal pools between my legs and my center throbs. I have never wanted sex this much in my life, and I really hope it's not just the hormones taking over.

"That works," I squeak out, making Luke chuckle.

"Is now good?"

"Yep. Ready when you are."

Luke smirks at my quick response as he steps out of his jeans. "I bet you are."

The two sides of Luke can be a mind spin, but God, do I appreciate them both.

Without waiting another second, he pulls my leggings down before my panties follow, and when he removes my shirt and bra, leaving me completely naked in front of him, my stomach knots while his eyes drink me in. The heat in his gaze as he slowly rakes over me makes me want to shy away, but I don't. I never have with him, and while it's new, I like that he brings out a confidence in me.

But I need him.

"Didn't I mention I was ready? Now," I pant, not bothering to hide my desperation, and I wait for him to laugh. But the heat in his eyes turns to fire, and before I know it I'm in the air as he carries me over to the counter, spreading me out exactly as planned.

He slows then, his eyes on my center as he pumps his cock and his tongue sneaks out to coat his lips. I wriggle under his stare but keep my legs locked open, loving the way he's watching me.

An idea comes to mind, and I skate my hand down my body, waiting for him to notice. His gaze snaps to my fingers as I glide them through my heat, and a guttural groan rips from within him.

"God, Amelia." His eyes linger as I massage my clit. "Fuck, I'd love to keep watching." He pumps his cock in rhythm until he stops suddenly. "But I can't hold back. Not again. I need you."

He groans again before his mouth is at my core, replacing my fingers with his tongue. He laps at my center, his fingers spreading me apart, and within seconds I'm writhing beneath him.

He's barely had time to lavish my clit when I'm squeezing my legs shut and begging him to stop.

"Wait. I know you want this, but I want to watch and I need you inside me."

Without a response, Luke slides me to the edge of the counter and lowers me to my feet, spinning me around. But instead of standing behind me like he said he would, he bends me over and turns my face toward the mirror before dropping to his knees.

"I wasn't finished eating."

Jesus Christ. A rush of heat floods to my middle as his tongue flattens against my most sensitive areas. He licks slowly, working his way to my back entrance, making me squirm when he stops just before he gets there and makes his way back. He repeats his actions torturously slowly until I'm bucking against his face, then he pulls back and smirks at me in the mirror. "This is the part I love. When you fuck me with abandon."

"God, Luke," I cry out as my middle pulses with need, waiting for him to give me more of his tongue, but he stands and lines himself up with my entrance, sinking into me in one go.

I scream out his name as he rolls his hips into me, and when I stare at our reflection, he groans, his expression highlighting his restraint. "Don't hold back. I need more, Luke. Don't hold back."

His eyes widen before he grabs my hips and slams into me. With one hand wrapped securely around my stomach, I use the other to push against the counter, meeting his intensity, thrust for thrust, as my orgasm builds.

Luke grunts as I cry out, and when I'm hovering on the edge of ecstasy, he glides his hand around to my heat and circles my clit, sending me flying.

"Yes, oh God, Luke. That's..."

"I know. Fuck, I know."

He continues to pound into me, and when he finds his own release, he groans out my name before folding his body over me, grabbing the counter to support his weight. My eyes lock on his in the mirror and a moment passes between us. A perfect moment, like two souls finally connecting.

My breathing slows, and just like last time, when we both come down to earth, Luke carries me to his bed, but this time, he slips in beside me, engulfing me in his warmth before falling asleep. And I was right; his bed is phenomenal. I take a moment to just be and then drift off to the soft sound of his breathing, thinking about how easy it is with Luke, not just the sleep, but everything.

And it terrifies me because I could get used to this. Only there's one question standing in my way... Am I ready to risk my heart again?

Work is crazy over the next month, so we only manage to sneak in a few moments together. And other than taking Shadow for a quick walk, it's never in public. And it's never enough.

I miss him. And I wish there was some normalcy between us, but that's not in the cards just yet.

I ache for him. For more. But that's the nature of both our jobs, and I'm used to it from my time with Preston. Not that I want to compare any part of my current relationship with my past, but it's impossible not to find similarities. They're both in the public eye—Luke more so than Preston—and they both have jobs that take them away for extended periods. And while that was never my issue with Preston, suddenly with Luke at an away game, I'm lonely.

When the game's set to begin, Hayley comes over for a viewing date, armed with some fancy ice cream flavors and a smile. I can't help but laugh as I dig in to my mix of chocolate, caramel, and cookies and cream.

"This is much better than my own concoction. Though I did love the popcorn and ice cream."

"You did? I was just throwing out random fun stuff."

"I figured that out when you said Vegemite."

"I will get you to try it one day."

"We'll see." I laugh to hide the fact that the thought makes me nauseous.

"So... I—"

"Shhh." Hayley shushes me as she rushes over to her phone and turns up her music. I start to giggle but when I hear a familiar voice, I gasp. "Is this..." She trails off as her eyes flash to mine.

"It is." It's Preston's song. The one he wanted my ideas for.

"I like it." Hayley smiles. "It's more emotional, more angsty. It's—"

"About me."

"What?" Her eyes widen as she clicks through her phone and starts the song again. "Dammit, it doesn't have the lyrics. Do you know them?"

"By heart." I nod.

"It sounds like unrequited love. I thought you were married when you were kids."

"We weren't kids." I roll my eyes. "I was in my twenties when we married, and we didn't actually get together until after our junior prom."

"Okay, so why the song?"

"He wanted me and didn't think I wanted him. Only I did."

"But...I sense a but."

"But I'd recently kissed Luke and I was all messed up over it and because Preston and I were close friends, I'd told him about it."

"He wrote this when he was sixteen? Damn."

"I told you. He's talented, he just got stuck on the wrong path for a while. Maybe things are turning around for him."

"Thanks to you."

"The song was him. My ideas just gave his record label the push they needed to release it."

"You don't seem as bummed about Preston and the divorce anymore."

"Bummed?"

"Yeah." She laughs.

"I'm not as bummed. I'm in a good place. I might even be happy."

Hayley bites back her smile. "This wouldn't have anything to do with a certain football player you're dating."

"How did you know we were dating?"

"I didn't. I was joking because the two of you keep spending time together. Not to mention, you're carrying his child and you're married. But you just confirmed the dating part."

Dammit. I bury my face in my hands. "God, this is so messed up. Falling for Luke is a bad idea. No, having any kind of feelings for Luke is a bad idea."

"Why?"

"Because I've been there before."

"After you kissed?"

"Yes, no, I don't know. It wasn't exactly like that. Yes, I got butterflies when he kissed me, but that wasn't what broke us. It's the lack of trust that almost destroyed me. Despite the fact that you and I became friends almost instantly, I don't trust easily. Luke was a big reason for that when I was a kid. And then I stupidly put my trust in him again. He had it for no more than an hour and he shattered it. I don't know if I can do that again."

A flash of pity crosses Hayley's face before she schools her features. "You were both sixteen. A lot has changed since then."

"Has it though?"

"I hope so. At least I hope it has for me because I was an awkward sixteen-year-old and I just got the role of a badass heroine."

"You got it?" I squeal and throw myself awkwardly into her arms. "I didn't want to ask because it's been weeks and they were supposed to tell you already."

"They were delayed when the director got sick. But I got it. You are looking at the next queen of the big screen."

"Yeah, I am." I can't stop my widening smile. "I'm so happy for you. And you're right, people can change. You certainly have. But I refuse to let anyone blindside me again."

"Good. You shouldn't. But you can't close yourself off. He's trying. And the way he stares at you—"

"Nope," I cut her off but smile. "I'm not ready for that yet."

"Okay." Hayley bites back her smile before giving me a nod. "But for the record, if anyone looked at me like he looks at you, I would be dropping my panties like nobody's business."

I laugh until my smile fades. "I really like him, Hayley."

"Well, duh."

I roll my eyes and laugh just as my phone rings on the counter in front of Hayley. She glances down at the screen before her eyes flash to mine.

"It's your mom." Her nose scrunches for good reason. I still haven't told my mom about Luke because I'm not ready for her to tell the world. Like she always does. And even though it doesn't seem like she's mentioned the baby to anyone, it's more crucial to keep this a secret.

"Leave it. I'll call her back later. You don't need to be witness to that conversation; she's still annoyed that I had to work over Thanksgiving." I'm not avoiding her calls. I just like to be prepared when we speak.

"You didn't have to work, we—"

"I know. Not the point."

"Right."

Hayley pushes the phone away and it cuts off a few seconds later. But we barely get time to resume our conversation when her phone rings and she gasps.

"I don't think it's about Thanksgiving."

"What do you mean?"

"She's calling me." Hayley holds up her phone to show my mom's name on the screen. They met one time and Mom got her phone number to what? Put Hayley on her gossip call list?

"I think she's calling about something else." She frowns as I groan. "It doesn't mean—"

My phone rings again, cutting Hayley off as her phone continues to blare and panic takes over me.

It's my dad.

"No, no, no, no, no. This is bad. They know about Luke." I'm only guessing, but I have the strongest feeling that's what it is.

And if I'm right, it means Mom told him about the baby too.

Fuck my life.

Chapter Thirty-Seven

LUKE

We're six points ahead coming into the last few minutes of the game, and while it's not inconceivable they could still win, I'm already celebrating. We're currently on top of our division with the most wins in our conference, and with a few weeks to go, my confidence is growing.

Thomas throws his next pass and it sinks perfectly into Reed's hands, hitting its mark like magnets drawn to each other. We're all in sync, there's no doubt about it.

New York's tackle cuts through the pack, making his dash toward Reed. With my eyes on the play, I run ahead, my focus exactly where it needs to be until someone crashes into me from the side, knocking the air out of my lungs as I'm flattened to the ground.

And fuck it hurts.

But it doesn't matter. Because in the few seconds that it takes for me to open my eyes again, the whistle blows and my teammates cheer as they race across the field.

We did it again. We fucking did it.

This is our year, and no one is going to stop us from going all the way.

I'm about to jump up when a hand appears in front of my face, and I lift my eyes to find Dylan staring down at me, his eyes full of emotion.

He hasn't announced it yet, but I've caught him holding back his tears a few times and I'm almost certain it means he's retiring this year.

He pulls me to my feet and slaps my back before we both jog over to the celebrations, the spirits high after yet another glorious win.

My eyes scan the edge of the field, but the disappointment settles the second my mind catches up. I knew she wasn't here. None of the crew traveled with us and yet it's strange not having her at my game.

In a few short months, Amelia's clawed her way under my skin and buried herself deep, but I wouldn't want to do a damn thing to change it.

I'm getting used to having her around. No, I want her around. All the time.

Our celebrations continue as we head back to the locker rooms, and as we run through the motions of our postgame commitments, my high never wavers.

"We are killing it." Reed slaps my back as he walks past, dropping down on the bench beside me. "I know they say not to celebrate early, but fuck that. We are going all the way, my man, no doubt about it."

"Hell yeah, we are."

I throw my gear into a heap just as Dylan interrupts, his somber expression instantly dampening my mood. "Luke man, have you got a sec?" His eyes flash to Reed's before settling back on me, and I find myself on edge.

"Yeah, sure." I turn to Reed. "I'll be back in a minute." Reed nods as I follow Dylan to a private corner. "What's going on?"

"I've got alerts set for articles that mention my name." I raise a brow and open my mouth to tease him but he cuts me off. "Don't say anything dickish. This isn't about me."

"Okay." I nod. "Go on."

"On top of that, Summer insisted I set alerts for Thomas's name too, and I just received this article. It names Amelia and mentions that sources say she attended the same high school as you and Thomas. That's why I got the alert."

Fuck. "Is it bad?"

He turns his phone around to show me a clear image of Amelia and me walking with Shadow. It would be completely innocent if I wasn't staring into her eyes like she hung the moon while touching her now-obvious pregnant belly.

While she's not necessarily hiding her pregnancy around work anymore, this isn't what she meant when she said she felt better about people knowing.

"It also speculates that you're the father."

"Understandably." I laugh because I don't know how else to react. "I mean, look at the photo."

"Yep."

"I am, by the way."

"I assumed that too—not because of the image, but because of the way you act around each other."

"*Shit.* Guess there's no point getting my agent to deny it."

"I doubt it."

Jesus. "I wish I knew who the goddamn source was and what else they know."

"Can't help you there. This is all I have."

"Thanks for showing me. I'll handle it." How? I have no fucking idea.

I have a missed call from my agent when I check my phone and then ten calls from my mom and three from Lainey. Since the article was dated today, I'm going to go out on a limb and say it's either very public, or Mom has alerts set for my name too. And I really hope it's the latter.

I huff out a long sigh and bury my face in my hands. We knew this was a possibility, but I have never been photographed that close to home, so I never considered it. *God, I'm a fucking idiot.*

"Are you okay?" Reed asks, his bag over his shoulder, ready to go.

"Nope."

"Is Amelia okay? The baby?" Worry is evident in his tone and I must admit, it hits me in the chest.

"They're okay." I hope. "Dylan just showed me an article and we've been outed. The world officially knows, or at least assumes, that Amelia's having my baby. But I appreciate your concern."

"*Damn.* What are you going to do?"

"I'm going to talk to her. And then I'm going to count down the minutes until I'm with her again."

"Sounds like a solid plan. Does that mean you're not coming out?"

"Nah, I need to talk to Amelia."

"Fair enough. Well, we're here for you if you need us."

"We?"

"Yep." He nods without giving me any further information and walks away while I take my time packing my things, waiting for the locker room to clear out.

As soon as I'm alone, I call Amelia. Three times. But she doesn't answer.

I'm about to call our travel agent to change my flight when she texts me.

> Amelia: I'm heading to bed. Long day. Can I call you tomorrow?

Dammit.

> Luke: Of course. Get some rest. Jelly Bean needs your energy. 😊

> Amelia: Thank you. And good game today, but can you try not to get yourself flattened next time?

I bark out a laugh as some of the tension leaves my body. She's joking. She's okay. And that means she hasn't seen the article yet. I've got time to figure this out.

> Luke: Anything for you, Ace

I smile as I pocket my phone, but I've barely had time to grab my bag when it goes off again, signaling another text, then another, then another until I'm almost too afraid to look. My mom is not a texter, but I wouldn't put it past her to ask Ryan to text on her behalf, and I can't ignore her for too long since we're getting close to Christmas. Taking a deep breath, I reluctantly check the screen and frown.

REED ADDED YOU TO A GROUP

REED ADDED UNKNOWN

REED ADDED DYLAN

Unknown: What is this?

Reed: Luke's secret is out so I thought he might need this. You two became fathers in the public eye. I figured you could help

REED CHANGED THE GROUP NAME TO "LUKE'S SUPPORT GROUP."

Dylan: I'm here for it. Whatever I can do. Sorry I had to be the bearer of bad news

Unknown: No thanks. If he needs me he knows where to find me

I huff out a laugh. I don't need any more information to guess who unknown is, and I think he gave me all the advice I'm going to get when he took me out.

Reed: Come on, Easton. Luke needs us

Yep, called it.

Unknown: Oh and what fatherly advice do you bring to the table?

Reed: How about... Not to be a jerk all your life. It fits other situations too

A small smile pulls at my lips. I was going to shut this chat down but maybe...

Dylan: Mom... Dad... please don't fight. Luke's watching

Well, that's a little bit funny and I can see what they're trying to do. Reed and Dylan anyway. And since they know I'm reading the messages...

Luke: Did Summer write that text, Dylan? You're not that funny

Reed: What a way to join the party! Welcome to your support group

I update Easton's number in my phone just as he responds.

Easton: I'm out

Luke: No you're not or you'd have left the group

EASTON LEFT THE GROUP

LUKE ADDED EASTON

Luke: Stop being a dick, East. You heard them, I
need your support. I'm better already

Not a lie. I'm definitely better. But the guys can't really help me with the current situation. Unless one of them knows how to make things go away.

Luke: Anyone know how to make people forget
articles they've already seen? Specifically
people related to me

The second I press send, a sinking feeling hits me in the gut. I shouldn't be worried about my parents; I should be worried about Amelia's mom. She can't find out like this.

I itch to call Amelia again, but don't want her to panic unnecessarily. I need to stay calm. I need to think things through; I need a plan. And I need some air.

The guys keep firing messages with Dylan and Reed trying to brainstorm ideas while Easton stays mostly quiet, occasionally popping in to tell them their ideas suck. And when I step out of the locker room, I stop reading, calling my agent back instead.

But as I suspected, there's not much I can do. I can either ignore it, or make a statement, and either way, I'm not making that decision alone.

As I walk through the halls on my way outside, Lainey calls again, and I suck in a breath before answering.

"Is Amelia okay?" she asks the second I say hello, and the love in her tone makes me smile.

"I think so. She texted me to say she was going to bed, but she joked around, so I'm hoping that's a yes."

"You didn't call her?"

"I tried." *Should I have tried again?*

"You really like her, don't you?"

"She's alright." I smile as I picture her rolling her eyes when the reality is that I don't think I like her; I think I'm in love with her.

"You don't have to explicitly say it for me to know, Luke."

"Good. Can we move on to the bigger question here?"

"What's that?"

"How much trouble I'm in with Mom."

"Oh, she'd disown you except that she wants a grandchild and she thought she'd have to wait for Ryan."

"Did you confirm it?"

"God, no. I am staying the hell away from that. But you should call her."

I let out a long sigh and sink against the wall. "I will. I promise."

"Thanks. And thank you for ensuring you're the hot topic of conversation at Christmas. Ooh and you can bring Amelia now." She lets out an excited little squeal. "You know, since it's no longer a secret."

A knot forms in my stomach but she's right. The secret's out.

Things are about to change. Let's hope it's for the better.

CHAPTER THIRTY-EIGHT

AMELIA

My mom has her faults but I always thought she'd have my back when it really mattered. Until now.

I'm pacing my tiny apartment, staring at the baby furniture when my phone rings. I rush over, expecting it to be Luke but it's my mom. Again.

I don't know what to say to her. I must have asked her a million times not to share my private life with the world, but she continues to— *Nooo.* She wouldn't have leaked it. *Right?*

"Did you speak with someone in the media?" I answer her call before it goes to voicemail.

"Excuse me? Is that how—"

"Just answer the question."

"That wasn't me."

I let out a long sigh of relief until she continues speaking. "I think it was your father."

Jesus. As if he hasn't hurt me enough.

"The original photo didn't name you—it only named Luke—but the second I saw it, I called your dad. I was excited, and I wanted someone to share that excitement with me. But when I saw the article again a few hours later, it had been updated."

"Why him? Why not call one of your friends?"

"He's your dad."

"No, he's not. He hasn't been my dad for a long time. Not since he walked out of my life. And I know we're different, that you were never able to cut him off, like I was, and I get it... you never stopped loving him. But didn't you love me too? *Don't* you love me too? Because my child hasn't even been born yet and I know with absolute certainty that I would never treat them the way you've treated me. No matter what happens with Luke, my child will always be my number one priority."

"I'm sharing good news. Why would you assume that means I love you less?"

"Because I explicitly told you not to. Many times. And after I separated from Preston, I *begged* you not to talk to anyone about me, and yet I still got calls from both Preston and Dad when I got my new job."

"They care about you."

"I want it to stop," I snap and then pause, shaking my head as a dizziness rolls through me. "I wish I'd never told you I was pregnant," I add, softer this time. "But I wanted to trust you and I can't do it anymore. Dad walked away when I was thirteen, and I left Preston over a year ago. It's time you moved on or..." I trail off. I'm not someone that dishes out threats. That's not me. But I can't let her continue to bring me down. There's too much at stake now.

"Or what?"

"Or you won't see your grandchild at all."

"Amelia, you're being—"

"I can't, Mom. Please, just give me some space."

I hang up without saying goodbye and drop to the couch as my head throbs. It's been a long time since I ended a conversation with my mom in a good mood, but she's never made me physically hurt.

Taking a deep breath, I massage my temples to try and alleviate the stress, but it doesn't work, so instead I lie down and close my eyes, hoping I just need to rest.

I'm not sure how much time passes, but I'm startled awake with a knock at my door. My first thought is Hayley, but I know she has a meeting about her new film today, which means unless someone's found my address, it's Luke.

I get up slowly and walk over to the door, but I don't make it before he knocks again, and when I open up, his hand is raised, ready to go for a third time.

"Hi, I—"

He doesn't say a word before pulling me into his arms and wrapping me in his hold, allowing me to breathe him in. And God, is he the air that I didn't know I needed.

"Are you okay?" he asks, holding me at arm's length so he can look me in the eyes. "I didn't see anyone taking a photo of us or I would have paid them off, and I would have been here sooner but I wanted to wait until morning. You said you were tired. But God, it's a mess. I was walking through the airport today and the whispers were everywhere. Please tell me you're alright."

"I'm fine." I smile to reassure him before adding, "Unless you count the fact that I was recognized at the local store this morning and told I was a lying whore. Okay, she didn't actually say that, but the look she gave me screamed it in my face and it's only a matter of time. Oh, and my mom called. It turns out she told my dad about our baby and you, and he thought it would be a great idea to speak to the media and tell them who I was. Have you actually seen the article? The photo is so clear and—"

"I'm sorry."

"What?" I may have been staring at him since he walked through the door, but for the first time, I stop and really focus on him. And the regret in his expression guts me. "Oh, Luke. You have nothing to be sorry about. You didn't do this."

"I know, but it's because of me that they made a big deal out of it. If you were walking down the street, pregnant with some other man's baby, no one would have batted an eyelash."

"Depends. If it was Preston's they might have."

"Amelia," Luke growls, making me smile for the first time since my mom called. "Can we please not mention—"

"No, hear me out. This was always going to be my life. If I'd stayed with Preston, I would have been photographed. It's something that's always lingered in the back of my mind. But that's not what bothers me in all this."

"Okay?" His expression turns puzzled. "What is?"

"That we lost our bubble. It was nice knowing that we had this huge secret only a few people knew."

The corners of Luke's lips pull into a small grin before he reaches for my hand and tugs me toward him. "Yeah, it was. But we can keep that up."

"How? The world will know soon enough."

"True, but we can still keep secrets. Like the secret of me sneaking into your office to pleasure you while you're editing the show."

"What?" I bite back a laugh while that pleasure pools between my legs.

"Or the secret of what we're going to name our kids or their due dates."

"Kids?" I raise an eyebrow. "Plural?"

Luke laughs out loud as he tugs me again until I'm engulfed in his arms. "The point is that they don't know everything. We've got some secrets left."

"Thank you."

"For what?"

"For being you."

A spark flickers across his eyes but before I can process it, it's gone. "You're always welcome." He smiles instead, but it barely lasts more than a second before it's replaced by a scowl. "Now, who the fuck looked at you like you were a whore?"

His serious expression has my insides melting as I stare at the man that's worked his way back into my heart, or maybe he's the man that never truly left it.

"It was harmless, but thank you."

"It's not harmless if it hurts you."

"I'm sure it's not the worst that will happen."

"Fuck, I hate that but you're right. I want you to stay at my place."

"Luke."

"No, wait. Now it's your turn to hear me out. You can come and go as you please, parking in my garage without anyone ever knowing. You'll have more space. We can set up an office for you on the days you don't feel up to going to the stadium. And..." He pauses, leaving me in suspense.

"And?"

"Lainey lives around the corner. You'd have someone nearby if you needed them."

"Hayley's close by."

"Yes, but she's about to be a movie star."

"And what? You don't think she'll have time for me anymore?"

"No. Not in the way you're saying it. She'll always be your friend, but you know she'll have less time. If you're worried, this arrangement can be until Jelly Bean is born. We can have separate rooms and—"

"You'd let me have a separate room?"

Luke's face scrunches as he shakes his head. "Hell no. What was I thinking? Can you pretend I never said that?"

"Consider it erased."

"Thank you."

I smile before shifting my gaze to the ceiling and blowing out a raspberry. "What happened to us taking it slow? To dating?"

"Life happened and I promised you I'd do whatever it took to be there for you. This is me doing that."

"It's not just you wanting sex every night?"

"Nooo. Wait. I mean, I obviously won't say no to that because I'd be crazy, but it's not the main reason."

"Okay."

"I'm serious, Amelia. I—"

"I said okay."

His head flicks back as his eyes widen, clearly expecting more pushback, and I don't blame him. I haven't exactly made things easy on him. "You'll move in?"

"I will. But for the record, I think we're both crazy for this."

"There's nothing wrong with crazy. Should we pack now?"

I huff out a laugh and bury myself in the comfort of his arms, my heart racing when he presses a kiss to my head. I have no idea what the future will bring, but right now, his warmth is keeping me grounded. And I never saw it coming. So while my head tells me to say no, to delay this move as long as possible, my heart is screaming at me to say yes. And for the first time, I'm going to listen.

"Let's do it." I rest my chin on his chest and smile up at him.

"Yeah?" he asks, surprise lighting up his face.

"Yeah. I'd love to move in with you." I smile before adding, "For now," making Luke burst out laughing.

I wake up in Luke's arms, his heavy limb *under* my belly, just like the last time we woke up together, as if even in his sleep he's protecting our child. After wriggling out of his hold, I stretch my body, feeling better after a proper night's sleep in his ridiculously comfortable bed.

Only my headache still lingers.

After pressing a kiss to Luke's shoulder, I get up and leave him sleeping as I get ready for work. But when I'm packing my bag, I sense his presence behind me before he wraps his arms around my waist. "Who knew that sharing my bed would help me sleep better."

"Probably a large majority of people who partake in that thing called monogamy."

"Ah, those people. Smart."

I laugh as he spins me around, but the second his mouth meets mine, my laughter turns to longing as his lips gently caress mine. This is what I always wanted. Someone who wants me as much as I want them. "I wish I could have stayed in bed all day," I whisper when he pulls away, my head a little dazed.

"Now there's an idea." He grabs my hand and pulls me toward the door but I hold strong.

"I have to go."

"I know." He sighs, his shoulders dropping in defeat. "But one day we are making that happen. You deserve a day to rest."

"Deal." I smile.

"In the meantime, I'll be there at some point today, so I might pop in."

"I thought you were off."

"We are, but I'm meeting a few of the guys for a workout. A stipulation of a new group chat we've got."

"What does that mean?"

"It means that a few of the guys started a group chat to offer me some dad advice. But Easton only agreed to be a part of it if we also made it about football. So...Reed texted to say we should all work out today and Easton was happy about that."

I fall silent and bite back a smile. God, I wish I'd heard about that in one of their interviews. Audiences would eat that up.

"What's so funny?"

"I'm not laughing."

"Your veins are practically popping with how hard you're trying to hold back."

"Okay." I giggle. "It's not funny so much as freaking adorable, and I wish I could show that side of you all on the show."

Luke bites his lip before gracing me with a mischievous grin. "Want me to mention it on the record? It might help my image. I want to be adored."

I work hard to keep my straight face, but when he bounces his eyebrows, I burst out laughing. "You don't have to worry about that. Wait until they see Luke the soon-to-be dad. Because I can guarantee, Tom will be begging us to talk about that before the end of the day."

"Do you want that?" His face softens as the smallest crease forms between his eyes.

"I don't think we'll be able to avoid it. But I'm telling you now, I won't be making an appearance and neither will our child."

"Good, I'd rather keep you both to myself." He tries to secure me in his hold again but I wriggle free.

"I have to go."

"Fine. I'll see you later."

"You will."

No one says anything when I arrive in the edit suites a short time later, but it's obvious that everyone knows. There's a strange energy in the air that's following me around, and I notice people stop talking when I pass by, or watching me out of the corner of their eyes, like I'm about to do something newsworthy.

I keep to myself, focusing on what needs to be done, but when my headache gets progressively worse over the course of the day, I can't do it anymore.

"I'm going to work from home for the afternoon," I announce to the crew in the production office, and I swear everyone collectively relaxes. Which means, I have to address the elephant in the room. "Tomorrow, we're going to chat about the article I assume you all saw, and then by Wednesday everything will be back to normal. Deal?"

"What article?" our runner asks while others chuckle and nod.

"Someone fill him in while I'm gone. And be here tomorrow, eight a.m., for a chat."

A weight lifts as I make my way out to the parking lot, but it's short-lived when I find what's waiting for me. Or more specifically, who.

I freeze, as I stare into eyes the same olive-green color as my own, my pulse racing as a shiver runs through me. It's been years. Probably close to fifteen, but other than his gray hair and wrinkles, he's barely changed. "What are you doing here?" I ask, though I already know the answer.

"Nice to see you too, Amelia. I came because I wanted to talk."

"Now?"

"You've been avoiding my calls, why else—"

"I don't want to talk to you," I cut him off loudly, before scanning the lot. The private lot for players and staff. "How did you get in here?"

"A friend. It doesn't matter. The point is that I needed to see you in person. To talk."

"We have nothing to talk about."

"Oh, we have plenty, but first, you're pregnant with my grandchild. Surely that warrants a conversation."

"Okay. Yes, I'm pregnant. But you knew that a month ago, didn't you? You're here because of Luke."

"That's ridiculous. Your mom called and I have a right, Am—"

"Excuse me? You lost all your rights the moment you left. Actually, you lost your rights long before that."

"You've labeled me as the bad guy and yet you're with someone exactly like me. What kind of guy do you think I was when I met your mom? Hasn't she ever told you? Warned you away from guys like me? I was on the college basketball team, I slept around, and I never wanted to settle down. But then guess what? I thought I'd try something different. That I'd sleep with one girl for a while. And within a month your mom got pregnant with you..." He trails off as my eyes widen and a pit forms in my stomach. *Why hasn't anyone told me this story?*

"I'm going to guess by the shock on your face that you've realized it's history repeating itself."

"You're not half the man Luke is. You have no idea—"

"Everyone knows his reputation, and if they didn't, the current articles circulating are filling them in. I'm not saying this to hurt you. I'm trying to prove a point. If you don't think I can change, what makes you so sure that he can? You were always so naive, Amelia. So—

"Stop." Luke's booming voice echoes from behind me before he rushes forward and stands between us, his hand resting against my hip as he moves me behind him. "Say what you want about me, but stay the fuck away from Amelia."

"Or what?"

"I'll make you." Luke gets up in his face, but I grab the back of his shirt to pull him away. Not that it works. He barely budges.

"Yeah, right." My dad—*Damien*—sniggers. "You'd fuck up your entire career if you did."

"Try me." Luke stands his ground, his fists now clenched by his sides. "Amelia means more to me than any of this." He waves back toward the stadium. "I don't give a fuck what happens to me. So I suggest you leave before I ask my friends to help remove you."

I turn slightly to find Reed and Thomas hovering near the door, and I have to bite back a groan. Now they're all risking their careers for me.

"Go, Damien. Please," I beg, my eyes boring into his, hoping that if he actually cares about me like he says he does, that he'll give in and walk away. He stares back at me, anger in his eyes until a moment passes and they finally soften.

"I want you in my life, Amelia. That's all."

"Just go."

My body deflates as he turns and walks away, but I wait until he's gone before allowing myself to crumble.

CHAPTER THIRTY-NINE

LUKE

I. Am. Raging. It takes everything in my power not to go after Amelia's deadbeat dad until she grabs my arm and almost falls to the ground, struggling to suck in air. The anger drains from my body along with my blood as panic takes over me, a memory of her panic attack in the attic flashing through my mind. "Amelia, what's going on?"

She shakes her head as tears prick her eyes and my heart seizes. "Amelia, please." Dropping to my knees, I pull her into my lap and wrap my arms around her, locking her into my protective hold. "What happened? What did he do before I got here? Are you hurt?"

Out of the corner of my eye, I see Thomas and Reed take a step forward, but I subtly shake my head, silently telling them to go back inside.

Amelia shifts in my arms before pulling back to look at me. "I'm not hurt," she whispers. "Not in the physical sense."

"Fuck, Amelia. You should have let me go. I wanted to hurt him. I held back because you tugged on my shirt."

"It wouldn't have helped. The damage was already done."

"Damage?" A tightness wells in my chest. I only heard a bit of what he was saying about me, but I know enough. He was comparing us. And if Amelia hates anyone more than me, it's him. Pointing out our similarities doesn't bode well for me. "What damage?"

"For years after he walked away, he kept his distance. I never got a card on my birthday. There was no contact. But when I graduated from high school, he called. I refused to speak to him at the time and have refused again every other time since. Right up until today. Because while a tiny part of me always wondered if I was missing something, I never allowed myself to find out. Instead, I chose to pretend I never heard from him to stop myself from spiraling. Because if he hadn't changed, and he hurt me again, then I'd be forced to admit that maybe I'm not lovable. That I'm not..." She trails off as she wipes frantically at a rogue tear as it falls down her cheek, her gaze staring through me. "Mom distanced herself when Dad left, Preston chose music over me, time and time again, and..." She shakes her head, but I don't need her to fill in the blanks.

"And I broke your trust, making you believe I never cared."

"I'm sorry." She sniffs before letting more tears fall. "I don't want to feel that way and I don't blame you anymore, it's just..."

"It still happened and it was another knife to the chest."

"Yes."

"Amelia, I need you to look at me." She lifts her eyes, but once again, her gaze is vacant, until I grab her face in my hands, silently begging her to break out of her daze. A beat lingers between us before her eyes soften and she subtly nods.

"Thank you. Now I need you to listen. Can you do that?" She nods again but it's not enough. "I mean, really listen."

"Okay," she says before squeezing my hand.

"I know this is hard to believe considering the way he acted, but I'm sure your dad loves you. My guess is that he flipped to defense mode. Hurting you before you hurt him again."

"I hurt him?"

"He probably thinks so, though he absolutely deserves it. But maybe he's hurt by the fact that you refuse to talk to him."

"Right. And good. He should be." She pouts and it's so adorable that a small huff of a laugh chuffs out of me.

"I'm not going to disagree there. My point is that you are lovable. You are loved."

I love you.

Woah. The thought hits me as emotions swirl through my chest making my heart swell. I knew I was falling, but am I there? *Jesus.* Yes, I love her.

"I promise you're loved. Sometimes people just have a strange way of showing it."

My confession sits on the tip of my tongue but I hold it back. It's not the right time. Amelia's trust issues aside, if I tell her now, she's forever going to link my profession to this moment, and she deserves better.

She stares up at me with narrow eyes, confusion marring her features. "Do you want to know something funny?"

"Sure." My confusion mirrors hers. I thought we were having a deep conversation but who am I to judge?

She smiles as if reading my thoughts. "I believe you," she whispers with an awe to her tone. "I don't know why, but I do."

"Good, I'll take that as progress."

Her smile widens before she glances around the parking lot and gasps, jumping up. "I'm good now. I promise."

"What are you doing? There's no one out here."

"I know but we're still on the ground in a parking lot. I'd rather not be here when anyone comes out."

"Fair enough. Shall we get you home?"

"Don't you have your team workout? I don't want to poke the bear."

"What?" My brows furrow in confusion until Amelia bites back a grin. "Oh, you mean Easton. Don't worry about him. His bark is way worse than his bite. Come on, let's go."

After walking Amelia to her car, I jump in my truck and follow her home. *Home.* Amelia didn't question me when I used that term earlier. She went along with it and now she's on her way to my place, without a second thought.

And there's another small step for progress.

Breaking down Amelia's walls was never going to be easy—especially when I'm the one that forced her to erect them in the first place—but I'm not giving up until she knows her worth and I've convinced her that I know it too. She needs to understand that I'm here for her and for Jelly Bean and that I'll do whatever it takes to show her how much they mean to me.

And when the time is right... I'll *tell* her too.

She pulls into my garage a few seconds before I do, but takes her time getting out of her car and then hovers near the door waiting for me, reminding me about my little present.

"I got something for you. So you don't have to be awkward anymore," I say as I reach her.

"Who says I'm awkward?"

"No one. Would you believe I figured it out all by myself?"

"What?" She fakes a gasp. "Shocker. So what did you get me?"

"This." I hold up the key chain I had made by a friend's wife who has one of those online craft shops. I actually got it done before asking her to live with me but I was hopeful. On one side it has the Storm logo to make it appear generic but on the other side is a message just for her.

"Keys? To your place?" she asks without noticing the keychain.

"Yes, keys. To *our* place. So you can come and go as you please."

"Okay. Thank you."

She smiles shyly but continues to stand awkwardly by the door until I burst out laughing. "Are you going to test them out?"

"Why? You've got keys."

"God, you are lucky I l—like you because you are a royal pain in my ass, minus the royalness."

"Okay, jeez. I'll try it."

When she lifts the keys, her eyes catch on the key chain and she laughs. "Aww you stole me a Storm keyring. I love it."

I keep quiet while she unlocks the door and remain that way as she walks in, making her way to the cabinet where I always throw my keys.

"They work," she whispers. "Thank you. I appreciate this."

My shoulder lifts in a small shrug before I walk away and wait for her gasp of realization, counting down the seconds until she sees the other side. I'm about to say something—thinking she hasn't noticed it—when she bursts out laughing.

"Luke."

"What?" I ask, all innocently.

"Are these keys you had lying around or..."

"Or what? What's the issue?"

"*I'm obsessed with number 42?*"

"You are? That's nice to know."

She rolls her eyes as she catches up to me, but it's impossible to miss the smile she's hiding beneath her fake annoyance.

"Admit it. It's cute." I bounce my eyebrows until she bursts out laughing again.

"I'm beginning to wonder if you proclaimed yourself an eternal bachelor because deep down you knew no one would put up with you."

"Or maybe I was waiting for the right person to come back into my life." The words are out before I can stop them, but since it's not a lie, I own it and wait for Amelia's freak-out. But it doesn't happen. Instead her lips pull into the most beautiful smile and her eyes soften.

"Who knew there was a sweet man under all that playful hotness."

I burst out laughing as her smile turns into a sassy grin. "No one knew. Because this is yet another version of me reserved only *for you*."

And I can't imagine ever wanting to be this way with anyone else.

Amelia works for the rest of the afternoon, while I mentally plan her new home office. She tried to tell me it wasn't necessary since she'd only be working for another month or so, but all I heard was "I'll be working for another month or so," which means she needs an office.

When dinner comes around, we work together, creating a meal out of the food I have in my fridge and then we talk as we eat, catching up on the part of our days that we missed, discussing our plans for tomorrow.

Like a married couple. A real one.

And it feels right.

I almost consider texting Easton to give him kudos for his advice, but I don't because his grumpy mood might dampen mine.

We sit down to watch a movie after dinner, but we're barely a third through when Amelia gets up and walks toward the kitchen, rubbing her forehead. "I'm not feeling so good."

"What do you mean?"

"I'm nauseous and my headache has moved to my eyes. I think I'm getting a migraine."

"Shit." My pulse spikes as my chest burns. "Is that normal? Do you get migraines?"

Without answering, she closes her eyes and buries her face in her hands. "God, I can barely see."

"What?" I rush to her side and gently touch her hips, guiding her back toward the couch but pause when she groans. "What can I do? Tell me how to help." If I was worried before in the parking lot, it's nothing compared to now.

"I don't... I'm really dizzy." She blinks rapidly as she speaks and when she's finished, she sways slightly, almost falling away from me until I clutch her in my arms, my panic rising. *"Amelia."*

CHAPTER FORTY

AMELIA

L uke lifts me into his arms and carries me back to the couch, lying me down on a soft pillow as his frantic voice echoes in my ear. I blink a few times, trying to clear my eyes, but it takes a couple of seconds for me to remember I've had migraines before and my vision isn't getting better unless I sleep for a while.

"I'm okay," I finally manage to whisper when he says my name again.

"What happened?"

I shield my eyes from the light and try to focus on his expression but it hurts. "I've had a bad headache on and off for days now, maybe weeks, but that's the first time it's turned into a migraine. I haven't had them for years. I used to get the same dizziness and blurred vision. I need to sleep it off."

"I'm calling someone."

"What? Who?"

"Your OB-GYN. She has an emergency line."

"This is hardly an emergency, Luke. It's a migraine." I try to sit up, but a pain radiates through my head, sending me back down to the pillow.

"Humor me then," Luke says, and I don't have to look at him to know that while he's giving me attitude, he's panicked. "You don't even have to be the one to call. I'll call. I'll play the part of the freaked-out soon-to-be dad and you can remain cool, calm, and collected."

I bite back a smile at his over-the-top concern but stop arguing. He's allowed to care. "Okay. I'm sorry. I'm just not—"

"Used to someone putting you first? I know. But I'm going to need you to get over that. Fast."

"Noted." I smile, before closing my eyes and blindly reaching for his hand, only for him to grab mine and intertwine our fingers.

Luke makes the call, and as he talks, he lets go of my hand and runs his fingers through my hair, the soft movement lulling me into a relaxed state. I drift in and out of sleep, hearing bits and pieces of his conversation, but have no idea what's actually being said until he rouses me.

"Sorry, what?" He speaks into the phone. "Yes, I'll check."

"Have you had any pain, nausea, or vomiting?"

"Nausea, yes, but that's been constant. As long as I eat, I'm better."

"Okay. And what about swelling?"

"Swelling?"

"Yeah, your legs or face, etc."

"I don't think so." I frown but keep my eyes closed.

"Weight? I mean she's having a baby so yes, she's putting on weight." He pauses. "I don't think I can answer that without getting punched."

What? My eyes flash open until it pains me and I close them again.

"Okay, doesn't her doctor have a record of this?" He pauses again. "Oh, right. Okay. It's possible she's putting on more weight than just the baby, but I haven't noticed."

Oh God. I bury my head under the pillow and shrink away. Am I putting on more weight than I should? It's possible it happened gradually, but I'm avoiding old photos of myself, so I have nothing to compare.

"Yep. Now? Okay. Tomorrow. Thank you."

I pull the pillow tighter around my face, barely hearing his rushed goodbye, and then wait for him to fill me in.

Seconds pass by before the pillow disappears and something warm covers my eyes. "I wasn't sure if warm or cold works better for you as the Internet mentions both, but I didn't want to shock you with cold. Let me know if you'd prefer it."

My heart pounds in my chest as the warmth soothes me. *God, this man.* "Warm is better. It's what I used to do."

"Perfect."

"What did the doctor say?"

"We have an appointment tomorrow."

"What?" I sit up quickly, making myself dizzy as the cloth drops into my lap. "Why? It's a migraine." I subtly grab Luke's hand to steady myself, and when I open my eyes he's dimmed the lights.

Luke raises an eyebrow as his face scrunches, and while I know he wants to snap at me, he's doing so out of love.

"Okay. You don't have to say anything. Tomorrow is good. We need to make sure Jelly Bean is okay."

"And you," he practically growls. "How is it possible you and Preston lasted so long when you're so goddamn stubborn?"

"I wasn't like this with him. It's something I reserve for you."

Luke's frustration makes way for his smile and he huffs out a disbelieving laugh. Though I have no doubt he believes me.

"What time tomorrow? I have to let work know." I close my eyes again and lie back down, reaching for the cloth but not finding it. I'm just about to open my eyes when it covers me again, a little cooler this time.

"Nine a.m."

"Thanks. Does that affect your practice?"

"Don't worry about me. Come on, I'll take you upstairs so you can sleep. Hopefully you're better in the morning and we can stop panicking."

I want to argue but now's not the time. If it puts Luke's mind at ease, I'll go to the doctor. "Thank you. I appreciate your help."

"Good."

My OB-GYN, Kelly, asks me to do a few tests before checking my blood pressure and performing a mini ultrasound to check on Jelly Bean, and when she's done we're asked to wait.

We're alone for barely a few minutes, but it feels like hours as Luke paces the room, his muscled arms momentarily distracting me as he continues to rake his hands through his already mussed hair.

When Kelly returns with a neutral expression, Luke drops to the chair beside me as if he'll be scolded for standing, and leans forward with interest, making me smile through my nerves.

I reach for his hand and curl my fingers through his, watching as his body instantly relaxes into the chair. He throws a quick smile my way, but when Kelly clears her throat, his focus shifts.

"You're in the early stages of preeclampsia."

"What?" I ask as Luke huffs out a breath.

"I was worried about that," Luke says, drawing my gaze.

"You were?" *What in the world?*

"You did the right thing by calling our emergency line last night and coming in today. Most symptoms present like general issues, for you a migraine. Others present with indigestion type pain, while some show nothing at all. Because we've caught it early, we don't have to do anything rash. Amelia, I'll start you on some medication for your blood pressure, and we'll monitor the baby regularly."

"We can come in weekly," Luke advises, making me snort laugh.

"That's going to cost you and at this stage—"

"It's not an issue. Please."

"Okay." Kelly smiles. "You've got yourself a good man here, Amelia. Hold on to him. I'll have our receptionist schedule a weekly appointment, but I need you both to promise to remain calm. Stressing will make this worse."

"Of course," I answer before Luke can argue again. "I'll make sure I take it a bit easier. I have a job that can be considered stressful at times, but I have a lot of people who can help me." A thought hits me and my stomach churns. "Am I still okay to work?"

"For now, yes. But if your condition worsens, you may need to finish up earlier than expected."

"Okay." I let out a sigh of relief. "I'm happy to do that if I need to." But for now, I need to make sure everything is in order before I go.

"Great." Kelly stands and we both mimic her movement. "Here's your prescription for the blood pressure medication, and I'll see you next week. But if anything happens in the meantime, please don't hesitate to call. You caught this early, but it's a serious issue."

"We know. Thank you."

Luke's quiet as we leave, but the second we're in his truck, he spins my way. "Are you okay? How are you feeling? Are you sure you should be working? What can we do?"

"Woah. First, thank you. Kelly's right; I'm lucky to have you in my life and on this journey with me. I don't say it enough, but Luke, you've been my rock through all of this and I don't know what I'd do without you."

He stares at me for a moment before he does a double take. "Did you really just say that?"

"Yes." I shove at his shoulder and laugh, but of course, his muscled body doesn't budge. "That was me. I said that. I'm sorry I haven't said it enough so you actually believe me."

"I believe you. And thank you."

"You're welcome." He opens his mouth to speak again but I cut him off, preempting his concern. "Second, I promise to take it easy at work. I'll speak with our first assistant director and get him to take on a bit more responsibility. He's more than proven himself and has been an AD for years. I'm actually going to mention him for my role while I'm taking time off."

"Okay, but I'm going to talk to everyone there and make sure they keep an eye on you."

"You don't have to—"

"Please, Amelia. I'll feel better about everything. You're not the only one stressing."

"Oh, I know. And thank you. We can talk to the crew together."

"Good. Let's grab your medication and head to the stadium then. If we're quick enough, I should be able to make it onto the field before practice begins."

"What happens if you don't?"

"I get a fine." He shrugs.

"What?"

Luke grins as he bops my nose. "No stress, remember? You worry about you and Jelly Bean and I'll worry about me, you, and Jelly Bean."

"You, Luke Bennett, are lucky I love you." I laugh at my joke until my heart flutters and a rush of emotion takes over me. *Do I love him?* I can't. Can I? It took me years to feel it with Preston, but we were young and I didn't really know what love was. But now, I can recognize it and it's impossible to deny that it's there. "I—"

"Yeah, yeah." Luke laughs. "You're not exactly easy to live with yourself," he jokes back, pulling me out of my daze, though the feeling still lingers. "Let's go, so I don't get that fine." He starts the engine while I silently nod, my gaze locked on the side of his face. And a thought hits me. I may have tried hard to deny it, but I've felt this way for a while.

CHAPTER FORTY-ONE

LUKE

I'm anxious every time I'm away from Amelia, but when I'm with her, I'm the picture of calm. I've done my research, so I know how serious preeclampsia can be, but I'm trying to stay positive. We caught it early. And Amelia's been working hard to lower her blood pressure. She's even had Adrian, her First AD, stepping up, just like she promised, putting me slightly at ease.

A couple of weeks pass and suddenly we're a few days from Christmas and it's been the last thing on my mind. But I have to buy presents or I'm going to have a lot of pissed-off people in my family. We may not spend much time together anymore, Lainey and me aside, but that's always been our thing...presents. Only this year, I have no idea what to buy. My head's been elsewhere.

So I enlist some help.

"Thank you, Lainey. It's been a crazy few months, and I've only had enough head space to focus on Jelly Bean, Amelia, and football."

"Jelly Bean, eh?" She bites back a smile as she bumps her shoulder into mine.

"Yes, Jelly Bean. Since we don't know if it's a boy or a girl, it was easier to give it a name."

"Oh, so it has nothing to do with the fact that you give the people you love nicknames."

"I told you, I don't do that. You and Amelia have them because you're annoying."

"Amelia has a nickname? Since when?" I sense her eyes burning a hole in the side of my head but I choose to ignore her, answering with a shrug.

"When, Luke? If you don't answer me, I'll ask her, which will make it a big deal and—"

"Alright, Jesus. Do sisters ever stop being annoying?"

"Nope. Why would we? It's why you have siblings."

I huff out a laugh as we enter a jewelry store, momentarily distracting Lainey as she gasps. "Are you buying Amelia a ring? Please tell me you are. Please, please."

"No." I roll my eyes. "I'm not giving her a ring for Christmas. Plus, we're already married."

"But you don't have rings."

"I'm not getting her a ring. We are here for that necklace Mom is always talking about."

"The diamond one? The one she says is too expensive?"

"Yes."

"I thought you said you didn't have any ideas."

"Well, I wasn't going to get this, but it will take longer to come up with another idea, and there's only so much Lainey time I can handle."

Lainey bursts out laughing, seeing right through my bullshit. "It's guilt, isn't it? For not telling her about Amelia and the baby."

"Fine, yes. I'm full of guilt. Happy now?"

"Immensely. So when did you give Amelia the nickname?"

"Jesus. It was when we started middle school, but I've stopped using it because it wasn't exactly a nice nickname. I used it when we weren't friends." *We don't need to get into Amelia's other nickname right now. I've already said enough.*

"Okay."

"Okay? That's all you have to say?"

"No, I have plenty to say on the matter, but I don't want you to walk off and leave me stranded here. I'll dissect it with you on the way home."

"You're a dance therapist, Lainey, not a real one."

"I know enough." She shrugs, ending the conversation. *Until later, apparently.*

We spend the next hour bouncing from shop to shop, with Lainey providing me with so many ideas that I'm almost done before we've stopped for lunch. But when it's time to get Amelia something, I stall.

"What about some piece of film memorabilia? Or you could do what

Zac Efron did in that movie and pay to close out Universal Studios so you can take her to the backlot. I bet she'd love that. Hell, I'd love that and I'm not obsessed with movies. You need to suggest to Thomas that he should be *that level* romantic."

"Isn't he always?"

"Yeah." She smiles lovingly and I almost joke about regretting my comment, but for the first time, I get it. I understand her loved-up persona. Because I feel it.

Lainey starts talking about Thomas's dislike of the holidays as if he wasn't my best friend growing up, and while I'd usually call her out on it, something she says resonates with me and I get an idea.

"I know what to get Amelia."

Lainey pauses for a second as I catch her off guard and then she smiles. "Yes. Where are we going?"

"I'm dropping you at home. I've got some planning to do. Alone."

"Booo. You're no fun. Can you at least tell me what it is?"

"Nope. But I will tell you that yes, I gave Amelia a nickname because she was under my skin." Lainey opens her mouth to argue so I quickly add, "But I must have cared about her more than I realized to have let her get to me. So maybe you're right."

"I knew it. What was the nickname?"

"Ding. Sorry, my therapy session is over."

"Very funny," she deadpans.

When Amelia declines my invitation for her to come to Christmas lunch for the third time, I finally accept it. She told me her mom stopped making an effort around the holidays after her dad left, so I wasn't really expecting her to say yes. But while I was happy to respect her wishes when it came to my family, I wasn't going to let her get away with not celebrating at all. It was going to be my present to her. She just didn't know it.

"Are you staying at your parents' place tonight?" she asks on Christmas Eve as she pulls the blanket up under her chin like a shield, comforting herself. "Or do you drive back in the morning?"

"Actually, I'm not going tonight. Christmas Eve got canceled." I canceled it. Or, at least, I told them I wasn't coming. That I was starting my own traditions. With *my* family.

"What do you mean it got canceled? When?"

"A couple of days ago. It doesn't matter. But I'm going to need you to get dressed. We're going out."

Her eyes widen and she glances down at her protective shield. "What?"

"You heard me."

"Luke, it's Christmas Eve."

"Is it?" I gasp, before hiding my face with my hands. "How did I not know that?"

"You're hilarious."

"Get up. I promise this won't be stressful, but if you don't oblige, I'm going to have to force you."

"Okay, Jesus." She frowns as she flicks back the blanket to reveal she's wearing a pair of plaid pajamas despite it being midafternoon. "I might be a little while." She runs her hand through her messy hair and I can't help but laugh.

"Take all the time you need."

I make myself a sandwich while I wait, but it's only about thirty minutes before Amelia speaks from behind me.

"I'm ready, sir."

I turn loaded with a smirk, but she knocks me off my feet. Not literally but enough that I have to grab the stool beside me. Amelia is always beautiful—even in her plaid pajamas and messy hair, she was absolutely stunning. This isn't about her physical beauty. At least, it's not *only* about that. Rather she has a glow about her and a sparkle in her eyes that I haven't seen before. She's breathtaking in every sense of the word, and I find myself at a loss for what to say.

"You...I... Wow."

"Thank you." She giggles, and then because she can't help herself, she adds, "Nice to see you got changed for the occasion."

I bark out a laugh as I glance down at my ripped jeans and old sweater. But in my defense, I planned to get changed; I just thought she'd be longer. "I'm on it. You were faster than I thought you'd be."

"I didn't do much, and I wasn't sure what we were doing. Should I—"

"You're perfect. Everything about you is perfect."

Amelia smiles before turning away, and I swear the hint of a blush coats her cheeks. But that can't be right? Surely I haven't gotten under her skin like she has mine.

"I'll be right back," I say as I walk past, running my hand gently across her stomach in her fitted dress, loving the way she shivers when I release her.

After quickly throwing on a new pair of jeans and a fitted long-sleeve tee, I'm back down the stairs before Amelia has her shoes on.

"Let's do this," I say, making her laugh.

"Do what exactly?" Her eyes narrow but I don't miss the way they momentarily drop to my chest. I'm not stupid—I know this shirt shows off my muscles.

"We're going to create our own Christmas traditions. I have a few options, or we can make up something completely different."

Amelia bites back her smile. "Be careful or I'm going to get used to the romantic side of you."

"Good, because he's here to stay. So what do you think? Should we visit the Christmas displays? Find some carolers? Eat pudding? Can you eat that? I'm sure you can. Or we could-"

"Oh, I know." Her eyes widen excitedly as she reaches out to grab my arm, sending a spark to my heart. This is what I wanted. This is what she deserves. To finally know she has a family that loves her. "Let's try to find as many decorated trees as possible."

I consider that for a beat before the idea excites me too. "I like it. Am I allowed to commission a private plane?"

"What?" Amelia laughs.

"I figured we could find more that way."

"No." She laughs louder. "We're staying in San Francisco."

"You're no fun. But okay. I guess we can do that."

She jokingly smacks my arm until I laugh again and then we're on our way, in search of a great Christmas tradition. One I hope to do for years to come.

Whatever it takes.

CHAPTER FORTY-TWO

LUKE

"Slowdown," I call out, but Amelia doesn't listen until I catch up and clasp her hand, slowing her to a brisk walk.

"I'm pregnant, not sick. I'm allowed to walk fast. We've got less than an hour left."

"I didn't know we had a rule to get home by midnight," I say, raising an eyebrow even though she can't see it, as she's too busy focusing on the GPS on her phone.

"Yeah, well, I'm worried you're going to turn back into a rat."

"Excuse me? They. Were. Mice."

Amelia struggles to stifle her laugh as she shakes her head. "Not the point. But I'd like to find as many trees as we can before midnight. Set ourselves a challenge to beat."

"Next year might be more difficult with a little one in tow, but I like the idea."

"Oh, don't worry, you can wear Jelly Bean strapped to your chest. It will be easy."

The way she speaks so nonchalantly about our future has my heart picking up speed. Barely a month ago, I was fighting her to let me in, and now I'm firmly planted there. In her head, in her decisions. In her future.

"Do you think—"

"There it is!" she exclaims as we turn the corner, finding Christmas tree number seven. At least, oversized Christmas tree number seven. There've been at least twenty smaller ones along the way. I'm sure Amelia knows the exact number.

"Wow. This one's gorgeous," she gushes as I step by her side, my eyes locked on her face, taking in her awed expression.

"As is my date," I whisper before wrapping my arms around her and swaying to the music, watching the lights sparkle.

"Jelly Bean is going to love this tradition. Or any tradition," Amelia says, turning her head to face me. "Thank you for planning this. I've had fun."

"The night isn't over yet." I kiss her cheek and then spin her around to face me. "We have thirty minutes left of Christmas Eve, which is just enough time to get a hot chocolate and finish at the skating rink when the clock ticks over to Christmas Day."

"Another great idea. We might pass some more trees on the way. We're currently sitting at twenty-nine." *I knew she was keeping track of them all.* "But as much as I like the idea of an ice skate, I should leave the skating until next year."

"I wouldn't let you on the ice if you tried," I scold until she pouts, making me laugh.

"Come on—we better be quick before they close."

It's well after midnight when we get home, having walked slowly back to the skating rink and spent some time enjoying our hot chocolates before leaving. But despite walking several miles in search of the trees, neither of us mentions going to bed. Instead we both gravitate toward the living room, getting comfortable on the couch.

"Because it's already Christmas Day, we should exchange presents," I say with an excitement building in my chest. "Unless you've changed your mind about spending it with my family?"

"I haven't." Her nose crinkles. "But maybe next year? With Bean." I'll take it. I'll take any plans she has for me in the future because God knows I have a lot of plans for her. Some next year, some right now.

"Next year works for me. So presents?" I ask, hoping she'll agree.

Amelia giggles when she registers my anticipation. "Sounds good. I'll go and get yours."

I follow her quietly as she disappears into Jelly Bean's nursery—where she thought she'd secretly hidden my present—and listen as she gasps right on cue before rushing back out of the room, where I'm waiting.

"Luke. It's... It's perfect."

While she was sleeping last night and late this morning, I filled the room with things for Bean. Before then, we had a crib and rocking chair. But now, there's jungle-themed wallpaper, which took way longer than Amelia's wall originally did—most likely due to my cockiness before I'd begun. I also bought us a stroller, a changing table, and more soft toys than you could ever need, including a small plush football with my number on it. There's a bookshelf with hundreds of books for different ages and a *Boss Baby* film poster mounted on the wall.

"How...When... I... I don't know what to say."

"You said it all when you said it was perfect."

"When did you do this?"

"Last night. With some help."

"While I was upstairs?"

"Yep."

"Is that why you had the music going all night?"

"Yep."

"I assumed you'd fallen asleep on the couch like you did the other night."

"I know."

She glances into the room again before her gaze shifts back at me, her eyes welling with tears. "I haven't bought you enough now." Her tears fall as her face drops into her hands, making me feel guilty.

"Amelia. You didn't have to get me anything. And if it makes you feel better, I didn't get you anything either. This is your present, and technically it's for Bean."

"It's better than anything you could have given me."

That's what I was hoping for. "And you've already given me plenty tonight. You just haven't realized it."

Amelia's expression turns puzzled before she hands me a small box. "Well, I want you to have this anyway. We think alike." She shrugs.

"Oh, yeah?" I rip into the wrapping paper, making her laugh when I don't bother to keep a single piece reusable, and when I find her gift, a tightness fills my chest. I'm about to have a baby. I've obviously known this for months but her present makes it so much more real.

"You made Jelly Bean a number 42 jersey."

"I did." She nods as fresh tears prick the back of her eyes and I fight to hold back my own.

"And a pink plush football?" I say in confusion, until a tear falls from Amelia's eye as she nods. "Pink." My eyes flash to her stomach. "Jelly Bean's a girl?" *I'm having a daughter.* I stare at her in awe.

"Yes." She nods again, more forcefully as more tears fall. "I finally opened the envelope. We're having a girl. You're going to have a daughter."

I quickly step into the room and drop the jersey and football onto the rocking chair before turning and stalking toward Amelia, grabbing her face in my hands. Emotion threatens to clog my throat, but I swallow it down as I stare into her soul. "Thank you. This present is everything. You are everything. This family is more than I ever thought I wanted. And God, I love you."

Amelia's eyes widen as her breath hitches. "You love me?"

"More than words can describe." I smile at her shocked expression. *How did she not know?*

She pauses for a beat, staring at me with more emotion than she's ever shown, and then whispers the most beautiful words. "I love you too, Luke. So much."

Now it's my turn to be shocked as my jaw drops. "You do?" I ask stupidly, though she wouldn't have said it if she didn't.

"Yeah, I do. More than words can describe."

Without waiting another beat, I glide my hands into her hair and tilt her head, our lips barely a breath apart. Locking her gaze in mine, I find the words in her eyes, her expression reflecting her love, and my heart pounds.

"Thank you," I whisper before pressing my mouth to hers and caressing her lips as I pour everything I can into the kiss, showing her what she means to me.

Our mouths mold together, moving in sync as all the emotions take over me.

Amelia's the first to break away as she sucks in a breath, and when a yawn escapes her, I remember how late it is. Despite her argument, I press another chaste kiss to her lips before carrying her to bed and holding her in my arms, wanting nothing more than to grasp onto this moment for as long as I can.

I never thought I'd fall in love. It wasn't something I ever wanted. And it took me by surprise. But now that I've said it out loud, it's the most natural thing in the world, and I know with absolute certainty that I wasn't closed off to love. I was waiting for Amelia. Waiting for her to come back so that all could be right in the world.

"I love you," I whisper again as she's falling asleep, sensing her sleepy smile in the dark. And when I hear her soft snores, I sit up and gently place my hand on her belly, feeling for Jelly Bean's movements. "I love you too, Jelly Bean. My baby girl. My angel. Thank you for bringing your mom and me together. We owe it all to you and we're going to have an amazing life together. I can't wait to meet you."

New Year's Eve comes and goes, with most of us taking it easy, having a quiet one as we prepare for the final game before we have to get our minds set on the playoffs. Amelia and I spent New Year's Eve together, but by ten p.m. she was asleep on my lap, having been so busy trying to make sure Adrian's ready to take over her role.

Amelia's at work when I arrive home from practice the following Thursday, and I've barely stepped through the door when my phone alerts me to a text and then another. I panic, knowing she can't always call if they're filming, and rush to check my phone, finding it's the Luke support group chat.

> Dylan: I hate to once again be the bearer of bad news but have you seen the latest article, Luke?

> Reed: I just grabbed my phone to text you. Bria showed me when she arrived for lunch

I start typing a response, having no idea what they're talking about when Easton enters with his thoughts.

Easton: Did you know that the more people read and share gossip articles from piece of shit online magazines the more they produce them? So here's an idea... ignore it

That's probably the most Easton has ever written in our message chain, so I give him a thumbs-up. But unfortunately, I have to know. Especially if it involves Amelia.

Luke: Send it to me

Easton: It's better if you don't know

Reed: So, you've seen it. You read that piece of shit online gossip magazine?

Easton: 👍

While Easton and Reed are arguing over text messages, Dylan sends me the link, and the second I open it, I groan.

Is San Francisco Storm's star tight end cheating on the mother of his child? We speak to three women who say that he is.

"*Motherfucker.*" I bite my tongue and shake my head as that term takes on a new meaning. "*God-fucking-dammit,*" I say instead and instantly feel better. *About that anyway.*

How are we supposed to stay stress-free with shit like that going on?

Dylan: I'm sorry, man

Luke: Not your fault. Thank you for letting
me know

Dylan: At least you didn't do anything wrong.
You and Amelia weren't together

Fuck. They believe I did it? I shouldn't have to justify myself, and Easton knows how I feel, but for some fucked-up reason, I don't want him to think badly of me, more than he already does.

Luke: They're lying. I don't have to read the
article to tell you that

Reed: Good to know

It is good to know. The problem is, who outside of my friends is ever going to believe me?

CHAPTER FORTY-THREE

AMELIA

I love him. I really freaking love him. And while it snuck up on me, I've never been happier.

"That's it. That shot is perfect. Who knew I'd be saying that about a football series? But God, this is all stunning photography. I can't wait for the world to see it."

Adrian smiles proudly, making me turn to compliment him directly. "I can't thank you enough for all that you've done to help me these last couple of weeks."

"You make it easy." He laughs before his face drops. "I mean, this job is not at all easy. But I find it easy working with you. Sorry, for you."

"With me," I confirm. "You're going to have to own this role when you take over while I'm on leave."

"What?"

"I've spoken to Tom and Jim, and I mentioned that you could cover my workload. It would be short-term at this stage but the business is growing, so who knows what the future will bring."

"Wait. They actually said yes? They're promoting me rather than finding someone on their own?"

"Yep. Apparently, they trust me. A woman. Who would have thought it?"

Adrian laughs. "You know it's only Jake that thinks that way, right? We all respect you."

"I know, and I appreciate it. I wouldn't have stayed if I hadn't felt welcome. Although I have been told that I'm stubborn as hell, so who knows, maybe I would have stayed to spite you all."

Adrian's smile widens. "Something tells me that's exactly what you would do. You're a strong woman. We've all seen your strength and I admire the hell out of you. Thank you."

"You're welcome. You don't need to suck up anymore though. You've earned it. The job is already yours."

"You know Jake's going to be pissed off that he's not getting this role."

"Yep. I sure do. But do you want to know how much I care?" I curl my fingers into a zero and purse my lips. I know he's going to have something to say about it, but I also know this team has my back. They won't cooperate if he's at the helm.

"And that's why you're the boss." Adrian grins but it's somewhat nervously.

"I wouldn't worry about him coming after you. He thought this position belonged to a man. And now it does. How can he argue with that?"

"This position will always be yours. I'm just filling in."

"Nope, what did I say before? You need to own it. You're going to be amazing."

Adrian's all smiles as he heads back to his office, and when I'm alone an hour later, Luke pops in to say hi.

"What are you doing back? Didn't you go home?"

"I did, but... ah... how are the stress levels?"

"They're good, why? Did you come back to lower them? To run around in secret?"

He laughs but there's an edge to it that's not usually there.

"What's going on?"

He walks inside and closes the door behind him before standing tall. And when I note that he didn't lock it this time, I almost thank him until he speaks. "There's something I have to tell you but I want you to know—"

My phone rings, cutting Luke off, but I don't pick it up, my eyes firmly locked on his. "You were saying?"

The call stops, but within seconds my office phone rings and I get a text, making me finally sneak a glance.

Hayley: Call me back ASAP!!!!

My brows furrow as I check the number on my work phone, vaguely recognizing it. I have no idea if it's Hayley, but I take a chance knowing she's got the number.

"Sorry, Luke, Hayley says it's urgent and this might be her."

"Amelia, wait—"

I press the answer button before he speaks and grimace in apology. He visibly deflates but nods before dropping into the chair opposite me and running a hand through his hair.

"Hello?" I ask, hearing a rushed sigh before Hayley responds.

"Thank God. Preston's been trying to call you."

Ugh. I've been ignoring his calls. "I have nothing to say to him."

"You should call him back."

"What? Why?"

"He said something about a fire from when you were kids and said it was urgent and that he promised not to hurt you."

"He called you?"

"Yeah, your mom gave him my number."

Jesus. That's a lot of effort to speak to me. "Okay, I'll call him back after I've had a chat with Luke—"

"Please call him now. You know I'd never take his side over yours, and I know you're supposed to be keeping your stress levels low, but he was worried. And he mentioned his news would affect Luke too. He said he could help."

"Okay." A panic works its way into my chest but I try to shut it down. Panic leads to stress, stress leads to... nope. I can't think about that. "I'll call him now."

Luke is going to hate this.

I hang up from Hayley and turn to find Luke staring at me in question.

"We—" he begins as I say, "I—"

"Sorry." Luke smiles. "You go first."

"Thanks. I have to call Preston. He's been trying to call me and Hayley said—"

"Don't. He probably just found out about the baby and—"

"It's about the fire."

"What? Why?" I'd laugh at the fact we had the exact same response if I wasn't so worried.

"I don't know. That's why I have to call him."

"Okay, do you want me to leave?" His eyes flash to the door but thankfully he doesn't move, because...

"God, no. I want you to stay so you can take the phone away from me if it sounds like I need it."

"You want me to help you?" His lips pull into a smirk as he raises one eyebrow. Gloating.

"Yes, Luke. I need it."

"You know I'll always say yes. I've been here doing anything I can since the beginning."

"I know. I'm sorry."

"It's okay. Call him. I'll be here."

He sits back in his chair and lifts his ankle to his knee to get comfortable before crossing his arms over his chest. I'd take it as pissed-off body language if I didn't know him as well as I do, and the reality is, it's more of a shield.

Preston answers before I've registered the phone ringing, and the urgency in his voice has my pulse racing. "Amelia, thank God. You're a difficult person to get a hold of. Thank you for calling me back."

"What's going on, Preston? Why did you have Hayley call me?"

"Because you wouldn't answer me and I needed to speak to you."

Déjavu hits me along with a wave of nausea. This reminds me of the beginning of my talk with my dad, and I can't handle that much emotional stress right now.

"Get to the point, Preston. Please."

"Okay. Sorry."

Luke's eyes flash to mine and he sits up, getting ready to take the phone away, but I shake my head. Preston hasn't done anything wrong; I just want him to tell me what's going on.

"My agent got a call from some guy named Jake who wanted to meet me. He said his company was interested in doing a short series about the band. I was dubious at first but agreed to a meeting."

Jesus. What the hell could Jake want? If they were doing a show, surely they'd talk to me about it. A thought hits me and I gasp. "You never announced that we were divorced."

"What?" His voice waivers as though my question threw him off his thought process.

"You never announced it."

"Yes, I did." He scoffs. "But believe it or not, no one cared so it didn't make the headlines."

"Okay."

"That's not the issue, Amelia."

"Then what is?"

"I met with him yesterday."

My eyes widen. "You met with him?"

"Yes, and he's going to release news of the mansion fire and pin it on Luke. He's been talking to a lot of people and claims to know things. Only he doesn't know everything. He was hoping I'd throw you under the bus because he assumed we ended badly."

We did end badly, but that's not important.

"What does he know and what did you tell him?"

"Jesus, Ames. I told him nothing. If anything I threw myself under the bus. I said everyone was there, including me, and that it was a house party that got out of control. There was no one to blame. But he knows Luke was arrested as a kid, so I don't know if he's going to try and spin it somehow."

Tension rises in my chest and Luke must read it in my expression because he stands up this time, walking over to grab my hand. "Fucking Jake," I say, locking eyes with Luke, so he knows it's not Preston I'm worried about.

"If he comes to you," Preston continues, "you need to plead ignorance. I wouldn't put it past him to pretend he knows more than he does. He was hinting at that with me."

"I didn't do anything wrong. So why would you help Luke?"

"I was kind of hoping it might make up for me being an asshole."

"Wow, okay. I'm... I don't know what to say."

"Say you forgive me. I was a dick and I didn't appreciate what I had. But maybe that was for the best. There was always something between you and Luke. I knew it. Hell, everyone knew it. I think you were the only two who never saw it. And maybe this is how it was always meant to be."

I pull the phone away from my ear to check that it's really Preston on the call before responding. "Thank you, Preston. I appreciate that."

"You're welcome. Take care." I move to hang up but he calls out, "Congratulations, by the way. You're going to be an amazing mom. And I know that for sure because you always took care of me."

"Bye, Preston."

I blink a few times before turning back to Luke, a mixture of shock and anger coursing through me. "Is this going to be our life? People always trying to get in the way? Always creating problems?"

"Not if we don't let them."

"Jake's trying to cause issues with you and the fire. He told Preston he's going to leak the story to the media, but my guess is—"

Someone knocks and the door opens without me inviting them to come in.

"Amelia." Tom enters the room with purpose before coming to a halt when he finds Luke. "And Luke. Hi."

"Hello, Tom. Nice to see you again." Luke smiles.

"You too. I've been hearing your name a lot lately." Tom's lips purse but to his credit, Luke's smile remains.

"All good things I'm sure," he responds, forcing me to bite back a grin. *Only Luke.*

"Of course. Do you mind if I have a word with Amelia?"

"Nope. Go for it." He stays standing by my side, and I swear it makes me love him a little more, but I know what's coming.

"Alone," Tom adds, exactly as I expected. "It's a private matter."

Luke doesn't answer. Instead he turns my way, his gaze full of concern. "Want me to stay?"

Always. "No, I'm okay."

He gives me a pointed look, not believing me, but I reassure him with a smile. I am okay. Or at least, I can handle this. Thanks to Preston, I know exactly what's going on. Jake was never going to leak the fire to the media. He pitched the idea for the show. And Tom's here to tell me all about it.

CHAPTER FORTY-FOUR

LUKE

I hover outside Amelia's office trying to get a hint of what's going on, but I can't hear a damn thing. *What a fucking mess. A stressful mess.*

At first I thought Hayley was calling to tell Amelia I was cheating, and maybe that would have been better because at least I could have explained that I'm not. Whatever's going on with Preston and Jake seems so much worse, and the concern etched into Amelia's features is freaking me the fuck out.

I should be in there, telling her it's all okay, but instead I'm stuck out here, helpless. Again.

I'm not sure how much time passes as I pace the halls, but when I'm almost at my breaking point, my agent calls.

"Brett, any news?"

"They're not going to take the article down, but they won't print anything else unless they get new information."

"Are you kidding me?"

"Unfortunately not. It's how the world works. Rumors make the news every day."

"Yes, but that wasn't a rumor. That was three women saying they had proof."

"But they don't, right? And thankfully the reporter they spoke to works for a college buddy of mine. So we're good. Unless..."

"We're good. They don't have any proof."

"Then sit tight, and hopefully after your Super Bowl win, it will all blow over."

"Yeah. Hopefully." I fall back against the wall opposite Amelia's door and stare, unmoving, somewhat dejected until Brett sighs. "You're really worried about this, aren't you?"

"I can't hurt her again."

"Maybe you won't."

"Thanks, man."

As I hang up, I hear voices and freeze. Tom walks out first, his face red, anger marring his features. He glares my way and huffs before shaking his head and continuing on his path.

The second he rounds the corner, I rush to Amelia's door as she's stepping out, her expression drained.

"What happened? Are you okay?" My hands settle on her waist as I study her, making sure her breathing is calm.

"Jake pitched the fire to Tom and Jim," she says as she pulls me back into the room. "They want to feature it in the show."

My heart seizes but I can't think about me right now. I promised I'd protect Amelia and Jelly Bean with whatever it takes, and I'm not backing down now.

"Let them," I say firmly while my stomach knots. "They don't have permission to feature you, and if they find out about me, so be it."

"What if the team drops you?"

"They won't," I lie. The team might be forced to drop me if the truth comes out.

"Tom says that Jake has statements from our old classmates and they're willing to be interviewed on camera." *Fuck. All for goddamn ratings.*

"Okay." I don't know what else to say.

"You're not worried?" The calmness in her tone suggests that she's not, and since I need it to stay that way, I lie again.

"No, because one...we're not supposed to let anything stress us out. And two...I don't believe anyone came forward." They would have done it by now if that was the case.

Amelia's shoulders drop and she huffs out a sigh. "I didn't want to believe that either. Preston said something similar. But Tom was pretty convincing and I don't know."

"Amelia, no matter what happens—if this comes out or doesn't, or hell, even if I'm dropped from the team—you are not allowed to worry about it. As hard as that is, I need you to promise me that. Okay?"

"Luke, you're being ridiculous. That's not just something I can switch off."

"I'm not worried." I put on a smile for the sake of her health. "And if I'm not worried, neither should you be."

"It's not that easy."

"What did you say to Tom?"

"What?"

"He was pissed off when he left. What did you say?"

"Exactly what Preston told me to say. That it was a party that got out of hand and a fire started accidentally. No one was to blame."

"And?"

"And I quit."

"What? Amelia!"

"I told him that Jake was lying and that the fire wasn't a newsworthy story, but he mentioned articles from back in the day. I refused to give him anything. Even when he said it would help my career significantly, and that I needed to consider myself and my baby's future. No one else. Basically he was saying that I shouldn't be lying for you. Oh, and it turns out, they knew I'd gone to school with you and Thomas. And they knew of some controversy surrounding Thomas that he hoped I'd explore. That's why they gave me this specific project. They thought I'd be able to get extra information out of you. That's why I quit."

"Amelia, I mean this in the nicest of ways but... Are you *crazy*? This job was your dream."

"Exactly. It was. And I still have grand plans to be a director one day, but I refuse to play their games. I really thought they were decent people but—"

"This is my fault."

"What? No, it isn't."

"How can you say that? They're right. You had no loyalties to me or Thomas. Maybe if things were different, you could have used that connection to get ahead. But then—"

"Are you hearing yourself?" Her hands fly to her hips. "And do you really think I'm that type of person?"

"No. I don't." I inch closer and grab her hands, easing them off her. "But I—"

"Wanted to share in my burden."

"I want you to be happy." I press a kiss to her fingers. "To be a mom and live your dream, and I don't want to get in the way of that." *I don't want to hurt you more than I already have.*

Amelia's gaze softens, though I wish it wouldn't. When she finds out that I'm holding back, it's going to break her. But I need to wait until she's better.

"I am happy, Luke. You and Jelly Bean make me happy. And I will still be getting a director credit on the show. They can't take that away from me. I have no doubt I'll be able to find another job when the time is right. For now, it's a blessing. I can focus on Jelly Bean and my health."

"That is a positive, but you were sad when I first came back in. No, not sad, defeated."

"I was. I am. But only because I'm going to miss this. Either way, I'd be finishing up soon, right?"

"Right," I confirm but her sadness seeps into my chest.

"Cheer up." She laughs. "This is a good thing. Now, help me pack up my stuff."

Things are calmer for the next few days. Amelia doesn't hear anything more about the fire, telling me that Adrian's keeping her in the loop. And I have to believe he'd tell her if he knew something. He seems like a good guy.

As for my little issue, it went away. People stopped commenting on the article and there hasn't been another one since. I know this because I followed Dylan's lead, putting an alert on mine and Amelia's names, and so far, I haven't come across anything that's not football related.

When Saturday comes around, I try to get myself in the right headspace for tomorrow's final game before the playoffs. But it's a struggle. While Amelia's stress has thankfully lessened, mine has increased and I'm at a loss for what to do.

Amelia's already up when I get out of the shower that morning, and when I get downstairs, she's got a huge smile on her face, the sight of it easing my tension until she speaks.

"I want to come to the game," she announces, and I freeze as a million thoughts run through my head.

"Amelia, I don't—"

"Lainey called and invited me to go with her. And before you say no, I'll be in the box, not down among the chaos."

My eyes drop to Amelia's hand gently cradling her stomach and I shake my head. "It's still a no. We were told not to stress. Watching football is stressful."

"Only if you care," she sasses.

I stare at her deadpan until I picture her in my jersey—the material pulling over her beautiful tummy as she cheers—and emotion wells in my chest. I never really stopped to think about what it would be like to have someone there for me. Yes, my parents often come to my big games, and Lainey's usually there now for Thomas. But this is different. And I really fucking like it.

But I have to say no.

"What's that look for?"

"Just thinking about how amazing it would be to have you there."

She hits me with a beaming smile until she registers my expression. "But it's still a no?" She frowns, her eyes full of so much sadness it burns in my chest.

"Fuck, Amelia. You're killing me."

Her expression shifts before her eyes well with tears and she steps forward, and just when I think I'm going to have to give in, she wraps her arms around my waist and smiles. "Thank you."

"For what?"

"Everything. I wasn't thinking. But I've been feeling better and I just wanted to be there for you."

"I know." I press a kiss to her brow and rock her slightly. "And it would mean the world to me, but I can wait. Your health means more to me than having you at my game."

She nods with a smile, before burrowing farther into the protection of my hold.

"Thank you," I say, a wave of relief running through me before the longing hits.

I'd love to have her there, to be able to play for someone I care about, but I wouldn't be able to keep my head in the game.

Amelia rests her chin on my chest and stares up at me. "For what?"

"Everything," I repeat her words back to her.

"What about the bad?"

"*Everything*. Because it all led to this. I've got you. We're about to have a little girl. The playoffs are coming up. Life is good." And I'm praying it fucking stays that way.

Amelia blushes and it makes my heart happy. She never blushes, but I've managed to elicit that reaction a few times now.

"I agree." She smiles brightly. "Life is good and oh... Jelly Bean agrees because she's kicking with force this time."

Amelia grabs my hand and places it over her stomach in time for me to feel Jelly Bean kick again. "There you are, Angel." I smile as my heart races. "Not long now."

"You know what else isn't far away?"

"What?"

"Your practice. You have to go."

Shit! "I do. I'll be home later. I love you both." I kiss her softly on the cheek and stomach before taking off toward the hallway, grabbing my keys, pausing momentarily when Amelia calls out, "We love you too," making my chest swell, giving me the extra strength I need to focus.

Our practice goes well but I'm mentally exhausted by the time it's finished with everything catching up with me. We've been pushing ourselves to the limits, but God do we mesh. I don't know what's different about this year, but we are working in sync like I've never experienced before. And it's addictive. The better we play, the better we want to be. We're unstoppable.

I'm feeling good when I get home, but when I walk in, it's silent, sending a small spark of disappointment through me. I spent most of my adult life coming home to no one, but now that I've had a taste of it, I like having Amelia around.

After dumping my bag, I tiptoe up to the bedroom, expecting Amelia to be napping. But when I find the room empty, I panic until I hear movement from the en suite, spinning around as Amelia steps into view, wearing my jersey. *Nothing but my jersey.*

"I didn't think you'd want this to go to waste." She waves her hands in front of her body as I swallow a lump in my throat, my eyes drawn to the apex of her bare legs.

And God, is she beautiful.

"Amelia. Fuck. Get over here."

She giggles as she sashays my way, swaying her hips as she moves, her playful gaze locked on mine. And the second she's within reach, I pull her into me, one hand slipping under the jersey while I grab her chin with the other, tilting her face to mine.

"I have to admit. I pictured this. But seeing it? Fuck, you're a vision. Don't ever take it off."

"Ever?"

"Ever. Ever."

"Noted." She laughs and the sound runs through me before I lean down and press my lips to hers, exploring her mouth in a slow kiss. Without parting, I walk her back to the bed and spin around until her legs hit the mattress, but before I can lift her, she breaks away and sits down, reaching for the band of my sweatpants.

"Amelia."

"I'm not on my knees so you can't say no." She pulls my pants and briefs down in one go, watching as my cock springs to attention, already hard from me picturing sliding into her with my name branded on her back.

She licks her lips and I stifle a groan as my cock twitches.

"Am—"

She cuts me off when she circles her hands around my legs and pulls me forward before gently wrapping her fingers around the base of my shaft and pressing her lips to my tip. I bite back another groan as she licks away the pre cum and sucks my length into her mouth.

"Jesus Christ."

She works in a perfect rhythm, her hand pumping me as she alternates between sucking and licking, all while staring up at me, her wanton gaze boring into mine as I fight to stave off my release.

"God, Amelia. This is heaven, but I want to come inside you. No, I need to."

She gasps against my cock, and the vibrations make me jolt until I pull out of her mouth and lift her to standing. "Onto the bed," I demand, watching her eyes widen before she does as she's told, turning around and crawling on, the jersey lifting to reveal she's completely naked underneath.

She pauses with her ass in the air and glances over her shoulder, a coy expression in place. "Like this?"

"Hell no." As much as I would love to take her from behind, she's seven and a half months pregnant, so that can wait. "You need to lie down and get comfortable. I want to make you feel good. What's best for you?"

"Oh. Um...lying on my left side?"

"Done."

She lies down as I crawl in behind her, positioning myself with my cock resting against her ass. She jumps at the sudden intrusion before wriggling her ass to burrow into me while I picture negative thoughts to stop myself from coming.

Wrapping my hand around her, I cup her pussy from behind and find her already wet, my fingers easily slipping between her folds. She cries out as she bucks her hips, and I've barely had time to rub her clit when she stills my hand.

"I've been thinking about this since I put on your jersey an hour ago. I don't need teasing. I'm ready. Fuck me, please."

Jesus fucking Christ. "Okay."

I angle her hips until my cock sits at her entrance and then slowly glide myself inside, clenching my teeth as inch by inch she takes me. The second I'm buried, she uses my finger to pleasure herself, and my cock pumps on its own.

"Jesus. You are ready."

"I told you. Now move."

"With pleasure."

As we both rub her clit, I rock into her from behind, my speed increasing as she pushes against me, meeting my fervor. My balls twitch and I almost come without her until her walls tighten and she cries out my name, her hips bucking uncontrollably.

"Yes, Amelia. Come for me."

"Oh God, Luke."

I release into her as she screams for me, her body convulsing as she shakes her head. "Slow, slow," she rushes out and I do as asked, slowing my movements while our bodies jolt against each other.

This is fucking heaven.

I smile while my body relaxes, but the second I'm able to think straight, I panic.

CHAPTER FORTY-FIVE

AMELIA

My breathing slows as Luke pulls out of me, and I'm just about to roll over to face him when he sits up suddenly. "Was that bad?"

"What?" I giggle. Is he insane? Since when was he insecure? "I would have thought my screams in the throes of passion answered that question. Was it bad for you?"

"No, Amelia." He huffs out a laugh. "I meant for your stress levels."

"Oooh." *That makes more sense.* "No. That was the opposite of bad. I'm quite relaxed right now. But I appreciate the concern."

"Good. On both counts."

He nods but doesn't move until I start laughing again. "Luke Harrison Bennett, you better get down here and cuddle me or I am going to riot."

He finally chuckles. "Okay, I'm coming."

I fight not to say "that's what she said" as he drops down with a thud, making me bounce, before wrapping me in his arms. His hand sneaks under my jersey again, but this time to cradle my belly, and my heart races.

Then it hits me. I don't just love Luke. I'm in love with him. And it's scary as hell because there's something about this love that's different from my love for Preston. Deeper somehow.

I don't only feel loved, I feel protected. And for me... that's *everything*.

It's nice to finally have someone on my side. Someone more than a friend. An equal. Someone I know is going to consider my feelings when they consider their own.

We rest together for a few minutes until I'm desperate for the bathroom, and when I'm back, I strip off the jersey to change into my comfy pj's, ready for some much-needed sleep. But as I'm reaching for my top, my phone vibrates across the nightstand and I groan before blindly reaching out to grab it, checking the screen at the last second to find that it's Luke's.

Laughing to myself, I move to put it back until an alert pops up on his screen.

Luke Bennett scandal.

Oh God. *The fire.*

My heart pounds in my chest as I put his phone down and grab my own, ignoring the messages from Hayley. I quickly bring up a browser before searching his name as I struggle to take in air. This can't be happening. This is the last thing Luke needs.

His name brings up lots of hits, but it's the first one that draws my attention, making me pause. And when I click on the link to open the photo, the blood drains from my body.

Luke in a nightclub with a beautiful blonde perched on his lap, her expression anything but innocent with his lips parted and her hooded eyes. He's staring up at her with a gaze full of lust and his hand under her dress. No, not just his hand, his *arm*. Suggesting his hand is most likely making its way where it really *fucking shouldn't be*, if it's not already there.

My stomach churns as bile rises in my throat, but I can't look away. No matter how hard I try, my eyes stay glued to the screen, making me nauseous.

"Oh Jesus, Amelia," Luke curses as he rushes onto the bed. "Don't look at that." He grabs my phone before rolling me over to face him, his expression falling when he meets mine. "It's not what you think."

"What do I think?" I say in a daze, struggling to focus with the image burned into my brain.

"That I cheated on you. That I've continued to fuck around. But I haven't." He studies the photo and shakes his head. "This was taken over a year ago, *before* we first slept together. Why the fuck would they release it now?"

"You don't know?"

"What? No."

"Couldn't possibly be because Storm's favorite bachelor is having a baby and was just seen in another photo looking very loved up. This makes me look stupid and naive."

"No." Luke shakes his head as my heart pounds in my chest. "It doesn't. And that's why I didn't want you to know about them. Because I knew your mind would go there. But it's not true. You're not stupid. Or naive. I haven't been fucking anyone. It's just gossip. I know who that is. She'll raise hell to get this removed, and she'll tell the world it was last year."

I stare up at him while he panics, but while he said so much, my thoughts are stuck on one thing. He didn't want me to know about "them."

"How many are there?"

"What?"

"How many articles like this are out in the world?"

Luke's shoulders drop and I see the moment he knows he fucked up. "There's one more," he whispers, making me slide away from him.

"So you hid it from me?" I reach for the sheet, tugging at it frantically until he lifts up and lets me drag it away to wrap protectively around myself, suddenly conscious of the fact that I'm practically naked. "Amelia."

"Just answer the question."

"Yes," he whispers before straightening his shoulders. "But I did it for you. I was going to tell you. I came to your office to tell you. Then Preston called and you quit your job. You're not supposed to be stressed."

"And you think it's less stressful for me to find out like this? Don't you think it would have been better coming from you?"

"*I don't know,*" he yells but it's not directed at me. I can tell he's annoyed at himself. "I don't know any of this. But I'm trying. It's all new and I'm—"

"I should go." I get off the bed but keep the sheet in place. "I just need some time and—"

"Wait. Please." Luke rushes to my side and grabs my hand to still me, but I snap it back so fast you'd think it burned me. "Fuuuck! Amelia, please. Please. Don't do this. I just wanted to protect you. All I've ever wanted to do was protect you. Stay. We need to talk about this. I can't let you go. I didn't do this."

"I'm not ending things, Luke. I just need a moment. Please."

"I can't." His voice breaks. "I can't let you walk away when you're hurting. It kills me to see you like this. And it's not good for you or Jelly Bean."

"How does it feel to know you're the one hurting me?"

Luke's eyes close but it does nothing to hide the pain in his expression. "I didn't do what they're saying. You have to believe me."

"That's the thing, Luke. I do believe you. Considering your reputation, I never *once* thought you were still out there fucking around. I stared at that image and never for a second believed it. You told me you wouldn't and I trusted you completely. I was embarrassed more than anything. But what's *hurting* me is that you once again kept something from me."

"But—"

"It doesn't matter that you thought you were doing the right thing. Look where that got us last time."

He drops to his knees and stares up at me. "I'm so fucking sorry, Amelia."

"I know. I—"

"No, wait. Let me speak. I fucked up. I know I fucked up. And I know you don't want my excuses, but I couldn't be the one adding to your stress. I couldn't do it. I *can't* do it. I'm supposed to be helping you. I'm still following our pact."

"What?" My eyes widen as a new image enters my mind, one of a ten-year-old Luke, carrying me off the road as blood seeps from a cut in my leg.

"I promise, I'll protect you more from now on. I'm never going to let anything or anyone hurt you again. You can count on me, Ace."

God, I'd almost forgotten about that.

"Oh, Luke." His broken expression shatters my heart, and when he lifts his gaze, my stomach knots, hitting me with the sudden urge to protect him. "I'll stay."

His eyes widen as his body physically deflates. "You'll stay."

"Yes," I whisper as he stands up, before I reach out and pull him into my arms. "I'm sorry, Luke. It's just—"

"I know, believe me. I know. And you have nothing to be sorry about." He presses his hand to my heart and shakes his head. "We have to calm you down. Fuck, I'm so sorry."

"I'm okay. I promise I'm okay."

"I love you so fucking much." He presses a kiss to my forehead before holding me in his protective arms.

"I love you too. More than I ever thought I'd love anyone."

I'm standing on the field as Luke accepts his championship ring, my proud gaze locked on his smile as everyone around me stares, their whispers flowing through my mind.

"Why would she stay with him?"

"It has to be money."

"I heard they have an agreement and it's all fake."

All fake.

Then the laughing begins. So much laughing.

I spin around to say something but come face-to-face with two young girls from sixth grade in an otherwise empty school yard. One of them whispers to the other as they look my way, snickering behind their hands.

"I can't believe she doesn't know about her dad."

I wake with a start and frantically search my surroundings until Luke's peaceful snores fill the air from beside me.

It was a dream. Just a dream.

And I've forgiven Luke.

But why can't I get over it? He was protecting me. I understand that. I would have done the same. But I can't shake this feeling.

I shift uncomfortably for God knows how long until at some point I must fall back asleep, and when I'm roused again, Luke's pressing a kiss to my forehead. "I have to go, but you should sleep. You were pretty restless last night."

Shit. I sit up. "I'm sorry, did I keep you awake?"

"No. I'm fine. I promise. Are you okay?"

"Yes, I'm good. I promise," I repeat his words back to him and smile.

"Are we?" he asks, his expression anxious.

"Yes, I promise that too." I widen my smile to reassure him and I'm not lying. We *are* okay. I just need to overcome these feelings that I have. It's a me problem. "Have a great game today. I'll be watching."

"No you won't," Luke growls, making me laugh.

"Okay, I won't be watching. I'll be waiting."

"Good." He grins and I shake my head. "I'll see you tonight."

"You will."

He throws me another uncertain look, but I blow him a kiss and call out as he steps into the hall. "We love you, Luke. Go and show them how it's done."

His smile returns as he shakes his head, chuckling, telling me he loves me before disappearing down the stairs. And I sink back onto the bed, covering my face in my hands, trying to control my thoughts to ease my rapid heart rate.

But it doesn't work. And when Hayley calls a few hours later, I'm a mess.

"Hayley. Oh God, Hayley. There are photos of Luke with some girl and another article about him sleeping around and I—"

"Shit. I know," she cuts me off. "But I didn't know you did. Where's Luke?"

"What?"

"I've seen them. Are you okay?"

"*Jesus.* When? Here I was thinking it was only Luke hiding things from me."

"If he hid it, he was doing the right thing. It would have been better if you never saw them. Everyone knows they're lying. He didn't want to stress you, and neither did I. Please tell me you didn't do anything rash."

"Like what?"

"Like break up with him."

"I didn't. We're good. It's me that has issues."

"No sweetie, it's not. You need to work this out together. You need to talk."

"We did. We were. And I realized he was just protecting me, so I stopped fighting him. I didn't want him stressed before his game. But then I had a dream, and I can't get rid of this tension in my chest."

"Did you tell him about that?"

"No."

"So you held something back to protect him?"

Goddammit. "Yes," I whisper as tears prick my eyes. "What am I doing, Hayley? Why do I make things so hard for myself? And Luke."

"Because of your dad, and I use that term lightly because he's not your dad, not anymore. But that man did a number on you, and then Preston was a dick, and Luke even... You haven't had a lot of opportunities to trust men. But Luke's trying. And the two of you are as cute as hell together."

"Is hell cute?" I giggle as I sniff back the tears.

"It is in my head."

"Okay, good." I stare at the mirror in front of me and my entire body calms. "Thank you."

"Anytime. They've just called me for my script read-through so I have to go, but I can come over later if you want?"

"That's okay. I'm feeling better."

"Yeah?"

"I promise. And when Luke gets home, I have grand plans to offload all of my worries onto him until he's drowning in them."

Hayley bursts out laughing while I smile. "That's what we like to hear. And you know he'll take it all on and he'll love it. All he wants to do is make you happy."

"I know. I'm lucky to have him."

"You're both lucky. As am I."

"Thanks, Hayley."

"Bye, Ames."

I do feel better as I hang up, except for the guilt that now lingers. I need to make it up to Luke. I haven't made this easy on him and he's trying. He's always been trying.

And he loves me. More than anyone has ever loved me before. Including my family. It's time I showed him I feel the same.

An idea comes to mind and I grab my phone to call Lainey. Luke said I couldn't *watch* his game, but he never said anything about being there at the end to help celebrate the win. As long as I avoid the stress, I'm good.

I want to be there, and I know how much it will mean to him.

I'll stay in the background until Lainey tells me it's done.

It's perfect. And I can't wait.

CHAPTER FORTY-SIX

LUKE

When I arrive at the stadium, I'm still a little on edge. Amelia may have said all the right things, but I fucked up and I need to make it up to her. *Why the hell didn't I tell her everything when I first found out?* She was already stressed about the fire, so we could have gotten it all out of the way and been done with it. But no, I had to go and mess things up again. And I'm still holding something back.

My mind whirs as I get ready, but when I see a message from Amelia, it all clicks into place and I'm finally able to focus on the game.

> Amelia: We are rock solid, Luke. I'm going to stop thinking about the past and focus on the now. I love you. Go and kick some Vegas ass

I send off a quick reply as a huge smile lights up my face, and of course Reed notices.

"Someone's in a good mood," he teases, his brows raised.

"What's not to be happy about?" *Now anyway.* "We're playing our last regular-season game. If we lose, we'll still be at the top of our conference. We're heading into the playoffs stronger than ever. I'm going to have a daughter. Things with Amelia are good and—"

"Hold up. You're having a girl?"

"I am." I grin wide and Reed laughs out loud.

"Something about that is poetic justice."

"Fuck—"

"Get out of my way, Wyatt! I'm going to kill him." Easton's deep voice echoes through the room, drawing everyone's attention as Reed and I spin to find Wyatt holding him back from charging toward Zane.

"What the hell?" Reed questions under his breath. "What happened?"

"I have no idea."

Zane throws his hands in the air and steps back, but his signature cocky grin remains tattooed on his face. "Fuck off, East. I've done nothing wrong."

"You expect me to believe that? You've been a cocky little shit since you started here, and I'm the only one that puts you in your place. Was it payback?"

"You may be a grumpy asshole, East, but I don't care enough about you to intentionally piss you off."

"Stop calling me East."

"Think about it, *East*," he begins, ignoring Easton's request as he steps forward. "When would I have seen her? How the fuck was I to know she was your woman?"

Oh, shit.

My eyes flash to Reed and we both take off toward Easton and Zane, sensing that Wyatt's going to need backup.

I step between them, waving to get Easton's attention and hoping like hell that I don't live to regret it. "He might be right, Easton," I say, putting myself in the line of fire. None of us have seen Macy since Isaac was born. Zane only started with us this year, so he may be telling the truth.

Easton stills his movements as his eyes flash to mine, but before I can speak, Reed cuts in.

"He's a rookie, East. I doubt he's taken the time to learn all of his teammates' names, and it's been a long time since any of us saw Macy," he says, repeating my thoughts.

"Then how the fuck does he know why I'm angry?"

Jesus. The room falls silent and all eyes flash to Zane's as he rolls his eyes. "She told me." He shrugs, making me step closer to Easton, anticipating his next move as he tries to break through Wyatt's block.

Until Zane adds, "After the fact."

"Fuuuckk," Easton yells as his fists clench into tight balls, but he stops charging forward. And all I can think is *holy shit*. East mentioned she'd checked out, but to purposely fuck with him like that...

When Reed moves to talk to Easton, I spin around and shake my head at Zane before he continues to stir the pot. "You may not have done anything wrong because of a technicality, but you better wipe that grin off your fucking face before we let Easton come at you."

Zane's eyes widen so slightly that I would have missed it if I wasn't staring at him, and I'm just about to say more when the door slams open and Adrian rushes into the room. "Luke, I—"

"Not the best time," Thomas says, stepping closer to cut him off.

"It's—"

"It's the perfect time," Zane calls out and I almost punch him myself. "Maybe he could film this?" This kid has a lot to learn about the bond of teammates.

As expected, Easton rushes forward again, but while he manages to shake off Wyatt, he hits a brick wall when it comes to Reed. "You little motherfucker," Easton yells, not at all worried about the consequences of fighting with a teammate. "You have no fucking respect and—"

"Don't you mean *wife* fucker?"

Easton dives past Reed, but I catch him seconds before his fist connects with Zane's face. But only because I don't want Easton to regret it. If it was me, Zane would be a dead man. He deserves it. "Stop. You—"

"Would you all shut the hell up?" Adrian's demanding voice takes over the room, making us freeze. I honestly didn't think he had that in him.

He runs toward me as someone starts to apologize, but his words cut them off.

"It's Amelia."

His panicked expression has the blood draining from my body as my heart clenches. "What's happened?"

"She's here. But I don't know what's going on. Jake dragged her into one of the edit suites and locked the door. He's—"

Fuck. "Where are they?"

"I'll take you." I release Easton and rush after Adrian, ignoring the stares of my teammates.

"Luke, you can't leave," one of the coaches yells, but it doesn't stop me.

"I'm leaving."

"*Luke.*"

I continue to ignore them as I get to the door, but when Thomas steps forward as if to come with me, I finally pay attention, shaking my head almost violently.

"I love you, man. But no. You're needed here," I tell him.

With that, I take off after Adrian, running through the halls as a sharp pain rips through my chest like a stab to the heart.

Amelia has to be okay.

She has to be. The alternative isn't an option.

Amelia calls out as we reach the door, her voice shaky before she sucks in a frantic breath. My panic turns to sheer terror as I yank on the door handle, desperately trying to get inside.

"Open the fucking door, Jake. Security is on their way."

Adrian stiffens beside me as he grabs his phone, and two seconds later, he says, "I need you to call security to meet us at the edit suite."

"Thanks. God, I—"

The door flies open, stealing my focus, and I rush into the room, my eyes struggling to adjust to the low light as I search for Amelia.

"I'm here," she calls out. "I'm okay."

I race toward her voice just as my vision improves to find her huddled on the floor, her arms wrapped protectively around her knees, her body trembling. "I'm okay," she repeats but there's a waver in her tone.

Dropping to the floor in front of her, I cup her cheeks and search her face, looking for signs of pain as the room is bathed in light.

Amelia blinks a few times before grabbing my hands and nodding, her eyes boring into mine, her expression neutral in an attempt to reassure me. But it doesn't.

Lifting her to her feet, I make sure she's stable, before pressing a kiss to her head and spinning around to face Jake, reaching back to clasp Amelia's hand.

"Tell me why I shouldn't hurt you?" I seethe.

"You're overreacting. We were just looking at some footage. Though it was rather interesting. Did you know Amelia's afraid of fire? And not even real fire. All I did was show her a clip of a house burning to the ground and she freaked out, began hyperventilating. I think she was having a panic attack, and it made me question if someone's been lying. You said the fire wasn't a big deal. That you all got out easily. And yet..."

"It means nothing," Amelia snaps, her voice still hushed as she works to calm her breath.

"It means *everything*," Jake retorts. "Admit that you lit the fire, Luke, and I'll leave Amelia's name out of the show."

"You're delusional. You'll never get the sign-off for that. Management will shut you down before the first episode has aired."

Jake laughs and the vile sound echoes through my head. "We've already got the sign-off from your owner. We can air whatever we want as long as it gets ratings. He's selling the team. This show is his final send-off, ensuring he continues to make money after he's gone."

What the fuck?

"You're lying." I step forward and push up my sleeves, threatening him with my stance.

But he doesn't flinch. "I'm not. All he asked was that I provide proof."

"You don't have it," I say confidently but *fuck*, he better not have it.

Jake shrugs and his careless attitude has my muscles tensing. *Who the fuck does he think he is?* I clench my fist, but I don't get a chance to move before Amelia's fingers curl into my tee. "Luke," she whispers under her breath as though attempting to stop me, but we both know she's barely making an effort. She'd let me go if I asked.

And I really want to ask.

"If it's not the fire," Jake continues, "I'll just go with my next story about how the show's former director slept with one of the players while she was still married in an effort to extort information for the show. That one might be juicier."

And I'm done.

"Or,"—I race forward as I speak—"I could break your jaw." I grab him by the shirt, my fingers curling into the fabric as I force him back against the wall. "How's that for a fucking story?"

"It's perfect. Because now I have witnesses," Jake calls out over my shoulder, his words pulling me to a stop. I drop my hold on him and spin to face the door, the blood draining from my head when I come face-to-face with our GM and one of the guys from security.

Jake shakes his head as he steps around me, his expression manic.

"He came at me. He attacked a crew member of the show when all I did was ask him a few questions." He leans in close to me and adds, "This is the stuff awards are made of." He chuckles quietly until my GM speaks up.

"I'm here to protect my player. And you should be made aware that these rooms have security cameras."

"What the hell does that mean?" Jake asks, his voice strained all of a sudden.

"It means the security team was already on their way here. They saw you threatening Amelia."

Jake's deep growl bellows in the air, drawing my attention as he steps toward Amelia, his shoulders stiff as he stares her down, threatening her with his stance. "You," he shouts, sending me into a rage.

"Eyes on me, asshole. Stay the fuck away from her."

Jake glares my way for the briefest of seconds, and his smirk sends me over the edge.

"You're a dead man." I launch toward him but he backs away just as Amelia calls out, stepping into his path with her hands raised in the air.

The world stills and everything moves in slow motion. I watch helplessly as Jake hits the edge of the desk, stumbling toward Amelia and sending her crashing toward the ground. I take off in a run as she grabs her stomach and spins to change the direction of her fall, slamming her head into the metal cabinet.

The room falls silent while I cry out, "Amelia," catching her seconds before she hits the concrete floor.

But it's too late.

CHAPTER FORTY-SEVEN

LUKE

My ears ring as I pace the halls of the ER, waiting for someone to come and talk to me. All I know is that Amelia is conscious and breathing on her own, but I've never been more grateful for that little certificate that says I'm her husband. I don't know what I'd do if they refused to give me any information. Actually, I do...and it would involve some not so nice language and threats.

Being kept in the dark and these moments of unknown are killing me.

The minutes pass as I try to distract myself, imagining Coach's face when Thomas told him I wasn't going to play. The disappointment in his eyes. I should have spoken to him, but since I'd already forgone traveling with Amelia in the ambulance to talk to Thomas, I'd done enough. I've always thought my greatest achievement in life would be winning the Super Bowl, but that's not true. I have two great achievements. One is finally getting the girl I didn't know I needed and the second will be my daughter.

I'm exactly where I need to be.

Lainey rounds the corner when I'm almost at my breaking point and throws herself into my arms, squeezing me so tightly I can't breathe.

"Where is she?" she asks frantically.

"They've taken her for some tests but I don't know anything else."

"Okay, that's good. How are you holding up?"

"I'm fine. I'm not the one—"

"No, but—"

"I'm fine, Lainey. Shouldn't you be at the game? Thomas would be expecting you—"

"Thomas would expect me to be here. Since he can't be."

The tightness in my chest intensifies and tears prick my eyes. It's one thing to panic on my own, but to see the fear reflected back at me from someone else makes it all the more terrifying, and I hadn't realized how much I needed Lainey here. "Thank you."

Lainey nods before her eyes bounce around the room, her gaze full of concern until she notices me staring and replaces the concern with a smile. I'm about to tell her I'm fine, again, when Amelia's mother arrives and I have to bite back a groan.

As though she dressed up for the occasion, Alice is wearing a satin blouse and a pearl necklace, while her expression screams "I need attention; my daughter is sick."

The second we lock eyes, hers widen before she schools her features and walks over, her shocked expression making way for a fake sympathetic grin.

"I can take it from here," she says, placing her hand on my arm as though she's comforting me. "I'll call you once I know anything. You should go home."

"That's okay. I'm good here."

"I'm not asking. You should leave."

The fuck? "Like hell." I shake her off. "I'm staying. There is nothing you can say that will make me walk away. Nothing."

Alice clenches her fists, steam practically rolling out of her ears. She was always a good mom to Amelia when we were kids. She always showed up until Amelia's dad left. Amelia told me herself that they're barely speaking now.

"You've done enough," she says, lowering her voice. "We've all seen the news. I wouldn't be surprised if you're the reason she's here."

"Excuse me." I step into her personal space as her words seep into my thoughts, and I hate that she's fucking right. I am the reason she's here. If I'd just kept my cool. Fuck, I need her. "Why are you here?" I snap. "How did you know to come?"

"It doesn't matter," Lainey cuts in before Alice can answer. "Anyone who cares about Amelia has the right to stay. Come on, Luke. Let's stand over here. Give her some space." Lainey tries to drag me away, but Alice calls out to get in the last word.

"She's my daughter. I know what's best for her and—"

"She's my *wife.*" I shake Lainey off as I growl, making Alice gasp, reminding me that's probably news to her. But I don't care. "She's my wife and she's carrying my child," I continue, enjoying the shock on her face. "I am *not* leaving."

"Mrs. Rosenberg," Lainey begins, "it's—"

"Creed," Amelia's mom cuts in. "It's Ms. Creed."

I knew that was her last name. She'd gone back to her maiden name after her divorce. I hated that Amelia kept that jerk's name, but I never questioned it. Until today. She knew what he'd done and she kept his name? Why?

Lainey continues pleading with Alice, but I tune them both out. No matter the outcome, I'm not moving. Not unless it's in the direction of Amelia's room.

An alarm goes off somewhere in the hospital, and my anger makes way for panic as I drop into a chair, sinking my head in my hands. *What's happening, Amelia? Please be okay. I need you both to be okay.*

"Excuse me." An unfamiliar voice enters my mind as someone touches my shoulder, making me jump as I glance up. "Are you Amelia's husband?"

"Yes." I stand up and nod. "Yes. Is she okay?"

The nurse gently clasps my elbow as she guides me away from the chaos, away from Alice, thankfully before she sees us.

"Amelia suffered a head trauma during her fall, increasing her blood pressure and putting the baby at risk," she fills me in as we walk.

"Jesus. What does that mean?"

"Doctors had to perform an emergency C-section and—"

"No. *No.*" My heart races as I struggle to get air into my lungs. "They can't. She's thirty-five weeks. It's too early. And I should have been there. I *should be there.*"

"Your baby was distressed from the fall, and no one notified us that you were here. With your wife's preeclampsia, this was the best course of action. You can see her now. I'm one of the nurses from the Special Care Nursery, I can take you."

"See who?"

"Your baby."

My baby? A wave of emotion takes over me and I suck in a breath. "Is she okay?" Yes, I'm repeating the same question over and over but I need answers. "Will there be any complications?"

"She's good. She—"

"Wait. What about Amelia?"

The nurse's eyes soften before she stops walking and turns to face me. "Your wife lost consciousness during the procedure. She woke up shortly after, but doctors are concerned she might have swelling on the brain. They've taken her in for a CT scan."

Fuck. Tension coils around my heart, but I try to stay calm.

"And if she does? Have swelling, I mean?"

"They may need to operate."

CHAPTER FORTY-EIGHT

LUKE

The nurse falls silent as we approach the nursery, and I follow along, my mind stuck in some kind of limbo as I fight myself to remain calm. I can't panic. I have to be there for Jelly Bean because right now, Amelia can't be.

But fuck, I'm scared.

She walks me into an empty room before disappearing, and when she returns, my world and everything I thought I knew changes in an instant as the most perfect little girl is placed in my arms.

"Congratulations, Dad. She's perfect."

Fuck yeah, she is. I'm a fucking dad.

My eyes fill with tears, and for the first time in forever, I let them fall. I'm holding my daughter—this tiny human is part me and part Amelia. And she's everything.

"Is she okay?" I ask again, my voice choked with emotion.

"She is. You've got yourself a fighter. The doctors will give you more information, but she's breathing on her own, she's taken to the bottle like a champion, and despite her small size, she's a healthy weight. We'll need to monitor her for a little while and she may need some help with her development as she grows, but yes... she's going to be okay."

Bean shifts in my arms and the nurse smiles. "If you want, you can give her skin-to-skin contact. It's very beneficial for newborns."

"Yes, I read about that. Can you hold her?"

I pass Jelly Bean over before rushing to remove my tee, then reaching for her again the second I'm done. It's already strange not having her in my arms.

When she's snuggled into my chest, I sit down and take a deep breath, trying to control my pounding heart. I read so much about the joys of having a baby, but no one ever described this. At least not in great detail. Though I'm not sure this feeling could be explained.

It's like my life's purpose has shifted and while I always thought I was born to be a football player, I was wrong. I was born to be Jelly Bean's dad. My job is to love and protect her with all that I have, and fuck, that's a huge responsibility to take on.

But I want to take it on. No matter how scary it is.

The nurse leaves us alone to get a bassinet, and I stare down at Bean, my heart growing to make sure it's big enough for all the love she'll need, and when the door clicks shut, I can't help but smile.

"It's just you and me now, Bean. We have to help each other out while we wait for your mom. But you don't need to worry. She's just getting some much-needed rest so she has lots of energy when she meets you." God, I hope that's all it is. She just needs rest. "You're going to love your mom," I continue as Bean's tiny fingers wrap around my pinky. "She's the coolest. Much cooler than me. She's smart, and beautiful, and funny. And she loves you with everything she has. You should see her eyes light up when she talks about you."

The more I speak, the more the tension grows inside me. Jelly Bean needs Amelia to hurry up and get better. Hell, I need her to hurry up and get better. I can't do this alone.

When the nurse returns, Jelly Bean is fast asleep, so I gently transfer her into the bassinet, holding my breath until I'm sure she stayed asleep.

"Are we allowed any other visitors?" I ask before the nurse disappears again, thinking of Lainey waiting patiently. "Can I ask my sister to come in?"

"Of course, but only one at a time."

My mind drifts to Amelia's mom, and for the briefest of moments, guilt takes over me. But that's not my decision to make. When Amelia's back and thinking clearly, she can decide if she's ready to see her. Though I can at least update her on what's going on.

I send off a quick text to Lainey, letting her know where I am and telling her the news, and before I've put my phone away, she responds.

Lainey: I'm on my way. I'll let Alice know

I pace the room as I wait, but the second Lainey arrives—her concerned expression boring into mine—I shatter.

"Fuck, Lainey. I can't do this alone. I can't..." I trail off as I sit down, my head sinking into my hands. "I thought I was okay. That I had my shit together, but I'm drowning."

"Oh, Luke." I suck in a breath as Lainey rushes over and squats down in front of me. She opens her mouth to say more, but I shake my head.

"I threw myself into this relationship like I've thrown myself into everything, but I'm worried I can't handle it. *What if I can't handle it?* I have no clue what I'm doing and I'm terrified I'm going to fail her. No, I'm terrified I'm going to fail her again. Like I have so many times over the years. *Like I'm still doing.* I made a pact when we were kids that I'd make her life easier, that I'd help fight all her battles, but I keep fucking it up. My latest mistake ended with swelling on her fucking brain. And even if I wanted to help now, I can't. I can't do a damn thing and it's killing me to sit around and wait."

"All she needs is for you to be here for her. And none of this was your fault."

"I was too focused on hurting Jake when I should have removed her from the situation. Jelly Bean needs both her parents, and instead of protecting Amelia, I let my rage take over me. And now I can't be there for her. I can't do anything to help."

"No, you can't. But you can be here for your daughter. Just like you are now." She stands up and takes a step closer to the bassinet, her eyes lighting up. "She's beautiful, Luke. Look at her."

"She is. She's perfect and I'm so scared I'm going to fuck this up too."

"You won't. The fact that you're this worried is proof of that. You won't let yourself mess up."

"Maybe so, but I fucked up with Ace when I was worried, so what makes this any different?"

"Why does that name sound familiar?"

"What name?"

"You just called Amelia Ace."

I did? "Right. Sorry. I used to call her that when we were kids." When I admired her for something or needed her to be strong. Like now.

"Of course you did." Lainey rolls her eyes until something clicks in her expression. "So, Ace is Amelia."

"Yep."

"Well, there you go." She grins, making me snap out of my grief for a second.

"What does that mean?"

"Nothing. I just remember thinking you were in love with that girl. But I didn't know Ace and Amelia were one and the same."

"I wasn't in love with her. I was a kid."

"A crush then. Either way, you love her now, right?"

"More than anything, except maybe..." I trail off as my gaze finds Jelly Bean, and Lainey sighs beside me.

"God, even I love her more than anything. But don't tell Thomas that. She really is perfect."

"Well, she's half me." I shrug with a straight face.

Lainey laughs before her expression turns serious again. "You don't have to do that, you know."

"Do what?"

"Always hide your feelings. You know how that turned out for Thomas."

"He has a great life." I jokingly scoff. "I'd say it turned out pretty well."

"Now. But for a long time—"

"I know, Lainey." My face softens. "But I promise I'm good. Having you here has helped."

"Good, I'm glad. Do you want me to stay while you wait? Or... is there anything you need?"

"No, that's okay. If you leave now you can probably catch the end of the game and—"

"The game is not important. You are."

A thought hits me and I cut her off. "Actually, yes. Can you go to my place? There's a baby bag already packed in the nursery, but could you grab a few things for Amelia? And feed Shadow. I won't be going home tonight. Amelia should be getting a private suite. But either way, I'm staying."

"Of course. I'm happy to help."

"Thank you."

"Anytime." She stares at me for a moment, her expression apprehensive. "I'll head off now in case you need something soon."

"One more thing," I rush out and then cringe when her eyes widen.

"Yes."

"I need you to stop looking at me like that. I need you to remember I'm your annoying older brother. Deal?"

Lainey shakes her head as she grins. "I can handle that. But—"

"*Lainey...*" I groan.

"Oh, stop. I'm happy to let things go back to normal. But I'm here if you need to talk."

"I know."

She squeezes my shoulder before smiling at Jelly Bean one last time and waving goodbye. And the second she's gone, all of the darkness returns until I'm on the brink of spiraling. How long am I going to have to wait? Surely they know something by now.

"Sir?" I start and spin around, finding a new nurse by the door. "They're moving your wife into her private suite now, if you want to go and see her?"

My eyes widen as my heart finally starts beating properly. "God, yes. How is she?"

"The doctor should be there soon to talk to you both, but she won't need surgery at this stage."

Oh, thank God. My entire body sags as the tension leaves my body. She's going to be okay. She has to be.

"What about J...what about our baby?" My eyes flash to Jelly Bean sleeping peacefully in her crib.

"How about I bring her in after five minutes?"

"Yes!" I exclaim before cringing. "Sorry, I mean, yes, that would be great. Thank you."

The nurse laughs as she gestures for me to follow her but I struggle to move, my eyes locked on Jelly Bean. She's so small. So fragile. I never want her to be alone.

"Would you prefer she came with us now?"

"Yes. But I need to chat with Amelia first. Five minutes is okay." *I hope.* "Just point me in the right direction so you can stay here."

I stare at Bean for another few seconds before leaving a piece of my heart by her bedside and moving to the door, a lump firmly lodged in my chest.

What a fucking day.

"Third door on the left." She points down the hall. "But she might be asleep so—"

"Got it. I'll be quiet."

I do the right thing and quietly approach Amelia's door when I desperately want to burst in there, but as I reach for the curtain, Amelia's voice cuts into my thoughts and her curt tone makes me smile. "How long?" she demands. *There's my girl.*

I pull back the curtains to step through as she continues her argument.

"I want my... Luke?" Her eyes widen as they lock on mine, and she tries to sit up before groaning in pain and lying down again.

A sharp pain stabs me in the chest as I rush to her side and clutch her hand, careful not to hurt her any more than she already is. "I'm here, Ace. I'm here. Fuck, it's so good to see you."

Amelia stares at me with a blank expression, and a wave of nerves flows through me. Until she speaks. "It's game day?" she says slowly, in question, her brows furrowing in confusion, and I can't help but laugh.

"Yeah. It's game day. But I'm *exactly* where I want to be."

"But—"

"No buts." I bop her nose before pressing a kiss to her forehead. "How many times do I have to tell you that you and Jelly Bean are my priority?"

At the mention of our daughter, Amelia's eyes well with tears. "I've barely seen her, Luke. They let me hold her for a second but then my head hurt and I blacked out. By the time I woke up, she was gone from the room."

As if sensing her mother's pain, a soft wail draws our attention to the doorway as the nurse brings Jelly Bean inside. Amelia squeezes my hand before releasing her grip and reaching out, the tears now streaming down her face.

"Oh my goodness. Come here, Baby."

My heart swells as my girls are finally reunited, and before I know it, I'm crying too. *Again.* And I *never* cry.

"She's here, Luke." Amelia giggles through her tears, her eyes never once leaving Jelly Bean as her wails fade away. "She's here and she's okay. Right?"

"She's better than okay. She's perfect. You both are. I'm one lucky asshole."

"Some would argue you've dropped the asshole recently. But some might not." She shrugs and I burst out laughing.

"I hope you never change, Amelia. Even when we're old and gray, I still hope you're giving me grief."

"It's why I was put on this earth." She grins before her gaze returns to Bean. To Bean. Shit. She needs a name.

"What should we—"

"Any ideas on—"

We both speak at the same time before laughing. "You go first."

"Not that I don't *love* 'Jelly Bean,'" Amelia begins and I smile, knowing we were thinking the same thing. "But she needs a name."

"She does. And I can't believe we waited until now to discuss it. Do you have any thoughts?"

"I started a list a while ago, but when things got busy, I stopped adding to it."

"Where is it?"

"On the back page of my journal." She cringes.

"You still keep a journal?"

"Almost every day."

"So the list is at home." That makes life difficult. I don't want to wait to name Bean.

"No, it's at your place actually. In the—"

"Like I said, *home*."

"Okay. Okay. Well, it's there."

I grab my phone to text Lainey and ask her to grab it. "Bedside table?" I guess.

"Yes, it's under my book."

"What book?"

"*Romeo and Juliet*." She cringes as alight blush coats her cheeks.

"Okay...I sense a story." I laugh, living to tease her.

"I love the Baz Luhrmann movie, but I always wanted to do a modern take on the ideas and themes of the story. It's been done so many times now, but I still keep it close by to remind me of my passion. It gets lost sometimes. Especially when I'm making a docudrama about a football team." She laughs to herself before continuing on. "I was going to make Juliet a fighter. She was going to stand up to her family and fight for her love. She was going to be bold and brave and... They both were." She shakes her head. "Romeo would have been a protector and—"

"What about Juliet?" I smile, cutting her off, something about the passion shining out of her giving me an idea.

"Did you tune out? I said I would have—"

"No." I chuckle. "What about the name Juliet? For Jelly Bean. J for J."

"Juliet?"

"Yes. You were born to create big things, and the Juliet you just described is the type of person I'd love our daughter to be. Brave, bold, passionate like her mom. Your version of Juliet."

"You mean, *our* version of Juliet."

"Yes, I mean our Juliet. What do you think?"

"I love it." We both stare down at Juliet once again sleeping peacefully, like all she needed was a cuddle from her mom. "Juliet. Our beautiful Juliet."

"My beautiful family." *Thank fuck they're both okay.*

Amelia smiles as the nurse pops her head in to talk us through breastfeeding and other options for Juliet, before advising us that the doctor will be in soon.

When she's gone again, I stare down at our tiny girl tucked securely in Amelia's arms as she attempts her first breastfeed and a rush of awe washes over me, until Amelia glances up in a panic. "I'm so scared, Luke. What if something happens? What if—"

"The doctors are monitoring you. We're going to do everything they tell us to do and we're going to keep you safe. You're going to make a full recovery." *I refuse to believe anything else. I can't. I'll break again.*

"Not me." Amelia shakes almost violently. "Juliet."

"Amelia J—Jay Rosenberg, you need to get that thinking out of your head right now. Because I am here to tell you that I am taking both my girls home from the hospital, and we are going to have a long, incredible life together. Forever. With no ongoing complications. Got it?"

"Forever?" She quirks her brow, the tension in her shoulders shifting.

"Yes, *forever*," I repeat, my gaze boring into hers. "Whether you like it or not, you are stuck with me. You both are. Because I think I've loved you all my life, and I plan to love you for the rest of it." Amelia opens her mouth to speak but I cut her off. "Don't even think about arguing with me."

"I wouldn't dream of it." She shoots me a sassy grin. "Believe it or not, that's exactly what I want. I can't imagine my future without you, and I'm trying really hard not to regret the past."

"Don't regret it. Ever. Let's just focus on building a beautiful life from here on out."

"Deal. I love you." She yawns through her declaration, though she tries to hide it.

"I love you too. And after we've spoken to the doctor, it's time for you to sleep."

"I can't, I—"

"You can and you will. I'll stay awake for Juliet, and I'll wake you if she needs you. First step to recovery is rest. I'm not taking no for an answer."

"Remember how you asked me never to change?"

"Yep."

"I don't feel the same about you. I wouldn't mind it if—"

"Don't bother finishing that lie." I bop her nose and she laughs before yawning again. "You just told me you loved me, and we both know you love me exactly as I am."

"Ugh, fine. I'll sleep."

"Good."

CHAPTER FORTY-NINE

AMELIA

I wake up worse than before my nap, my head aching and my body stiff, but when I find Luke half-naked, sitting on the chair across from my bed, a sleeping Juliet snuggled against his chest, I fight to push through it.

Because my God, is it a sight to behold.

A warmth spreads through my body, at least the parts of my body I can feel, and I smile longingly. If I hadn't just had a baby with this man, I'd be begging him to impregnate me. This is the type of photo I was telling him would get ratings for the show. Women would die for this. But they're not getting it. I'm keeping it to myself.

A sinking feeling takes over the warmth as my mind goes to the production, but I ignore it. I need to know what happened after Jake knocked into me, but I'd rather wait until I'm out of the hospital. I don't want to cause myself any more stress.

I continue to study Luke and Juliet silently as he scrolls through his phone but when his stomach rumbles and he panics that he woke her, I finally speak.

"She's good," I say with a quiet laugh. "But you need some food."

"Hey." His gaze shifts to me and he smiles. "You're awake. How are you feeling?"

"Like death warmed over. The nap made it worse."

"Shit." His smile drops and I instantly regret being honest until I remember I promised myself I'd be more open from now on. Luke deserves that. "Should we mention that to your doctor?" he asks, as he scans my face. "They said you needed rest and—"

"I'm okay, Luke. I promise." *I am.* A little tiredness is nothing compared to what I could have been feeling. The doctor said I had a minor head trauma that led to my increased blood pressure. During my C-section, I lost blood and my blood pressure dropped suddenly. When I momentarily blacked out, they worried it was caused by the head trauma, but found a combination of the stress, blood loss, and nausea to be the factors.

As good as that news was, my head still pounds, which I'm told may take a little time.

"Okay." Luke's a little pouty at my request, but he accepts it and moves his attention back to our latest obsession—Juliet.

"You look good with a baby." I bite my lip as I let out a soft sigh, wishing I could be over there snuggling with them.

Luke cocks his eyebrow and smirks. "I look good with anything."

A laugh bursts out of me before I cover my mouth and clutch at my stomach and head, making a note that laughing hurts.

"Shhh," Luke scolds me. "You'll wake her."

Of course. Silly me. "God knows how she could possibly be sleeping on your rock-hard abs."

Luke's smirk turns mischievous and I preemptively roll my eyes. Whatever he remarks, I walked right into it. "Why, thank you, Amelia. Yes, I do spend a lot of time working on my body."

"Shut up." I laugh again, but softer this time to avoid injury. "You know what I mean."

"I do. I'm just testing you to make sure your spark's still there. Just like the doctor ordered."

"The doctor said we had to keep an eye on random personality changes, Luke, not—"

"That's what I'm doing. If you hadn't told me to shut up, I would have been worried."

I huff out another laugh before stretching my body, the sensation in my legs still not quite back to normal. Not that I need my legs right now. I was lucky. With rest and medication, the swelling on my brain should reduce within a few days, and since I'm also recovering from a C-section, I'll be in the hospital for monitoring just in case.

God, it was scary for a while. Not that I was all that scared for myself. The only one I was worried about was Juliet. But the midwife assured me she's as happy and healthy as can be expected. I need to let myself believe it.

Luke's stomach rumbles again, and he curses under his breath.

"Go and get food," I snap, jokingly. "You're keeping me awake."

He bites back another smirk, but instead of arguing, he stands up and brings Juliet over. "Do you want to hold her or—"

"I do," I say quickly, desperate for more time with her. I've already missed out.

"Thought you might." His lips pull into a smile before he gently places her in my arms. "I won't be long, but if you need something please buzz the nurses."

"I will." He gives me a pointed look and I add, "I promise."

"Good. Oh, and while you were asleep, Lainey brought in some of your things. They're in that bag over there. And... *Dammit.* Speaking of visitors. I completely forgot that your mom was here. Lainey filled her in on what was going on earlier, but you should call her. Or I could talk to her if she's still there. Either way, she needs to know you're okay."

Guilt eats away at me again. "You're right. I'll call her. They said my stuff was in that top drawer. Can you check for me?"

Luke opens the drawer and pulls out my phone before handing it over, but when I try to bring it to life, it's dead. "Dammit."

"Want to use mine?"

"I don't know her number." I wince. *Why would I? It was always on my phone.*

"How about I check if she's still in the waiting room. In the meantime, I'll ask if any of the nurses have a charger. Do you need anything else before I go? Anything from your bag?"

I glance down at my hospital gown and laugh. "No, thanks. I can't use any of it. I'm stuck in this gown until I can walk. But thank you. I'll be fine until you get back."

"Okay. I love you both." He presses a kiss to my head before ever so softly kissing Juliet's cheek and then he's gone, leaving me alone with her for the first time.

And I don't panic like I thought I would. In fact, it's the opposite. A new confidence takes over me as my heart grows beyond belief, my gaze roaming over her tiny body, still shocked that she's lying in my arms.

I have a daughter. No, I don't just have a daughter, I have a family. And while I'd never want to lessen what Preston and I once had, this is more real than anything I've ever felt. Like everything I've done in my life has led me to this moment. To Luke and Juliet.

To think, I almost pushed him away. Hell, I did push him away. But thankfully, Luke being Luke, he wouldn't let me. He was always around, showing me that despite our pasts, he was going to be there for me and Juliet, that he was willing to do whatever it takes.

And he was.

He left his team for me. He was prepared to fight Jake. He's here when he should be playing in his final game before the playoffs. I never asked for any of that. But he did it because he cares.

Guilt swirls through my middle but I try to ignore it. He knows the consequences of missing a game and doesn't regret it, so neither should I. Plus, I get it. It may have taken me a lot longer than it did for him, but this is it. Luke is my person. And I'd do whatever it takes to protect him too.

A nurse comes in with a phone charger, and my mind drifts back to my mom. Luke's right, I need to call her. We need to work out how to make our relationship better because I couldn't imagine not talking to Juliet one day, and while she's not making it easy by continuously going against what I've asked, I could cut her some slack. A little anyway. A tiny bit. I can throw her a bone. If she takes it, great, but if she doesn't, I tried.

Juliet startles in her sleep and her little hand pulls at a knot in my hair, making me groan as my eyes flash to the bag Lainey packed for me. Maybe I should have asked for a brush. Knowing Luke, he was probably hinting at that. I can't imagine what I look like right now.

I laugh to myself just as I spot my journal hanging out of the end pocket and I smile. That man knows me better than I know myself. It's not often I miss a day of writing. If only there was someone to get it for me.

As if I conjured her to appear, a different nurse comes in to check on us, and I ask her to pass me the journal before she leaves.

With Juliet in my left arm, I manage to angle the journal just enough to open it to my last entry, frowning when I find the wrong handwriting. At first I panic, automatically thinking I have an issue with my memory until my gaze locks on the details at the top and bottom of the page. *Dear Amelia* and *Love, Luke.*

My heart flutters with a mix of nervousness and giddiness. These journals contain my deepest thoughts and feelings, and while I don't plan on keeping things from Luke moving forward, I'm not sure I'm ready for him to read all the raw details of the past.

On the flip side, I need to know what he wrote. Even if he read every page, or skim read to the good bits and this is his response, I need to know.

So with my heart lodged in my throat, I read it.

Dear Amelia,

I opened your journal with the grand plan of pouring my heart out onto the page but now that I'm staring down the barrel of the pen, it's incredibly nerve-racking. And you do this every day. I guess that highlights your superiority over me, and... WOW! Jesus. These things are like magic. They make you say stuff you'd never admit to out loud.

Please pretend you never read that.

And now to the serious stuff. Here goes.

I don't know what the fuck I'm doing. I don't know the first or last thing about being in a relationship, and I'm finally going to admit that I'm scared. This isn't something I ever wanted for myself and it's definitely not something I planned for.

But with you, my love is the most natural thing in the world. As though I was made for you. And maybe that's true.

I can still remember the first day I saw you. You were being chased by your older neighbors and hating every second of it. Even then you knew how to pout to get attention and you sure got mine.

Then two days later, we started at the same kindergarten in the same class. You were nervous, struggling to let go of your ~~dad's~~ Damien's arms, and I vowed then that I would always look out for you. But I didn't openly make that pact until years later. And for a while, I kept that promise.

Until I didn't.

All I've ever wanted was for you to be happy and safe. Even when I thought I hated you, deep down I knew I'd protect you with all that I had. But I fucked up. Over and over again. And this last time, you could have died. Hell, you could have died in the fire all those years ago if it wasn't for David.

I've made so many bad decisions in the name of "protecting" you that maybe you'd be better off without me. Maybe it would be easier on you if I stayed on the sidelines and let you live your life with Juliet and someone else that made you happy, while I protected you both from afar.

Only however noble that might be, I can't bring myself to do it.

I'm not an insecure guy, in fact some would say that I'm cocky as hell but I'm terrified *that I'm not built for this. That I've messed up too much to deserve this life.*

Despite that, I can't do this life without you. No, it's more than that... I don't want *to. And I swear I will fight for you and fight against you if you try to tell me we're not meant to be.*

Because for me, it's always been you. And for you, deep down, it's always been me (sorry, Preston, but also not sorry).

In short, I'm probably going to fuck up again. And there will be times when you want to scream at me or throw something. But I can guarantee that I'm going to love you with all of my heart for as long as you'll have me. No, wait... fuck that, I'm going to love you for as long as I want to, even if you don't want me back.

You and Juliet are the world I didn't know I was missing. And I thank the stars, every day that I somehow found you both.

I'm sorry and I love you.

Love, Luke

PS Don't worry, I didn't read anything.

P.P.S I know traditionally I'm supposed to write "Dear Diary" but that felt weird. Actually, do you still write "Dear Diary"? You call it a journal now, right?

P.P.PS In case it wasn't clear... I love you.

Trust Luke to make me laugh as tears stream down my face like a waterfall and my heart breaks for him and all that I've put him through. "What did I do?" I never once stopped to think about his reasons for doing things. I knew him. I *knew* how much he cared for me but I never let myself trust him. "Oh, Luke."

"I'm here," he says, stepping into view, his face paling at my tears. "What's wrong?"

He rushes forward as I hold up my journal before dropping it back on the bed and wiping my face. "You wrote in here?"

Luke scratches his head and the palest of pink coats his cheeks. "Ahh yep. Did you read it?"

"I did." His nose scrunches, embarrassed, but before I can say anything, he continues on. "That was me finally opening up to someone. To you. I tend to hold things back and suffer in silence, but I made a promise not to do that anymore. I want you to know everything."

"There was a moment there when I thought it was going to be a breakup note."

"Yeah, well, if I was a decent man, I might have walked away and let you find someone better. But I'm too selfish for that. I need you too much."

I force myself to bite back my smile and reach for his hand. "You are the least selfish person I know, Luke. Even now, I bet you made the decision to fight *because of me*. Because as you said... deep down I knew it was always meant to be you. Sorry, Preston, not sorry."

Luke laughs as he squeezes my hand and then it's my turn to pour my heart out.

"I'm sorry. So, so sorry. I should have trusted you all those years ago, or at the very least, I should have confronted you on it. And more than that, I shouldn't have given you such a hard time when you were trying. I wish I wasn't like this. I wish I could trust more easily, but I want you to know that of all the people in this world, I trust you the most. And I promise to do all that I can to show you that you mean everything to me. That I was made for you, as you were for me. That it's always been us. Even when it wasn't. I love you."

Luke stares at me, his eyes full of emotion as he lightly grips my chin, lifting my face until I'm looking him in the eyes. He brushes his thumb across my check, collecting my tears as his own eyes water. "We're going to be okay. This is going to work out, isn't it?"

I smile as my heart soars. For the first time since I was eleven, I have a home. "Yeah. I think it is. Things may be uncertain, and fast, and chaotic but they'll be wonderful. How can they not be when we have Juliet?"

"She turned our world upside down and threw us into situations we were not prepared for. Situations I never thought I'd want to be in. But I've loved every second of it." My chest tightens as all of Luke's love reflects in his expression while he stares down at Juliet, and when his gaze meets mine again, my heart hammers in my chest, threatening to break out. "She's our beautiful storm," he adds with an adoring smile. "And I wouldn't want it any other way.

CHAPTER FIFTY

LUKE

I'm bouncing Juliet in my arms the next day, trying to get her to sleep when Thomas and Lainey arrive for a visit, and the second my eyes lock with Thomas, I know I'm in trouble.

"I'm guessing you didn't come just to meet your niece?" I whisper so I don't wake Amelia, my eyes flashing to Lainey for her reaction. To which she cringes.

"Of course I came to meet my niece," he says until I raise an eyebrow and he chuckles. "*And* to talk about practice tomorrow."

"What about it?"

"Nope." He holds up his hand. "More important things first. She's beautiful, Luke. All her genes must come from her mother or her aunt." He winks at Lainey as I roll my eyes.

"You're funny. No cuddles for you then."

"Ooh. Can I have one?" Lainey whispers excitedly. "I've been so patient."

I'll give her that. She's seen Juliet three times without a cuddle. "Yes, you can hold her, but if you wake her, you die."

"Brutal but fair."

I gently pass Juliet into Lainey's arms and smile as both her and Thomas's eyes light up with him settling in behind her. Giving them a second to themselves, I make myself busy getting a drink, before Lainey walks over. "How's Amelia doing?"

"She's good. Great. The doctors are happy. The swelling hasn't reduced today, but it's no worse and other than a shocking headache, she hasn't had any other symptoms."

"That's a relief. Except the headache." A tension leaves Lainey's shoulders, and I realize she's been carrying around my worry, just like I used to do for her when we were younger.

"Thank you for being here yesterday. I don't know what I would have done without you."

"You would have been fine. You know how to step up when you're needed. But I'm always here. You know that."

"I do. And likewise."

"Is it my turn now?" Thomas asks, almost bouncing on his toes, making me suspicious.

"Are you two..." I trail off when Lainey's eyes widen as she reads my thoughts.

"No. At this stage, we're just happy to be proud aunt and uncle."

"Okay."

Thomas takes over from Lainey and bounces her like I was as the conversation drifts back to football.

"I wish I didn't have to bring this up now," Thomas says with an apologetic expression. "But I strongly advise that you talk to Coach before practice tomorrow. If you show up as though nothing happened, he's not going to be happy."

"Oooh, and do you think Coach expects me to give him an apology gift basket too?"

"Don't be a dick. I get why you left, and I would have done that same thing in your position, but you missed a game. You disappeared minutes before we ran out onto the field without telling him yourself. Or anyone. I'm just saying that if you want to guarantee your position for the first game of the playoffs, you need to talk to Coach."

"He already fined me. I've been punished."

"Luke." His voice raises before he softens it again. "What is going on with you? We're so close to the end. To what we've been working for. We have a shot of making it to the Super Bowl. A shot to win."

"I know." Jake's words play through my mind again, and while I hate that he got to me, which was most likely his plan, I still can't stop thinking about it. "Jefferson is selling the team," I admit, refusing to carry this burden alone. Thomas laughs, thinking I'm joking, and I wish I was. "I'm not kidding and Coach knows. It's why he's been so stressed out this season."

"Fu—" His eyes flash to Juliet's before he continues. "I mean *Jesus*."

"I can't talk to Coach without asking him about it. That's why I'm hesitant."

"Just pretend you don't know. That's what I'm going to have to do now that you've told me. How do you know, by the way?"

"Jake."

"Jake?"

"The guy that knocked Amelia over."

"Shit." He covers his mouth with his hand, making me chuckle. "And you believe him?"

"Unfortunately, yes. It makes sense. Jefferson wants to cash in on the show before he departs."

"Goddammit. Did Amelia know?"

All our eyes flash to Amelia and my chest tightens. I hate that I gave so much to the show and they were ultimately playing her. Hoping she'd get information. Assholes. "She didn't know, but she's going to talk to Adrian about it. Once she's sure she can still trust him."

"Jesus Christ. If it's true and we win, he makes more money."

"Yep, because the ratings will skyrocket and more people will watch."

"It's actually very clever."

"I know." I nod. "I'm impressed. But for us, who knows what it means."

"If you need me there when you talk to Coach, I guess I can come." He visibly grimaces, making both Lainey and me laugh.

"Gee, thanks for the enthusiasm."

"You know what I mean."

"I do. But I'll be fine. I'm a big boy. Hell, I'm a dad. I can take on anything."

Lainey giggles as her eyes bounce between Juliet's and mine. "It suits you. Who would have thought?"

"Definitely not me. But I wouldn't change it."

I 'm anxious as I walk through the stadium halls the next day, and it has nothing to do with the fact that I missed a game. I'm anxious about being away from my girls. Amelia may have been up and walking today, but she still has a long road to recovery and I want to be there to help.

Not that she'll let me. She practically pushed me out the door with her words. "I am not married to a nobody," she joked. "I married a football star, so I expect you to get off your ass and go back to work." I was standing at the time, but the sentiment was there.

And she's right. I do need to go back to work, especially if I want to play in the Super Bowl, and God, do I want that. My life goals may have shifted lately but it's still high on my list of things I want to do before I die, and I'm not getting any younger.

Since I'm early to talk to Coach, I wander past the production office out of habit, and it's not until Adrian calls out that I remember I shouldn't be there anymore. I have no reason to be.

"How's Amelia?" he asks, his gaze full of concern. "No one knows anything."

"She's better than expected after what she went through, but not quite out of the woods."

"That's good. Good. And I hear you have a daughter?"

"We do." I smile as images of Juliet flit through my mind. "She's perfect. We were really lucky."

Adrian smiles before shaking his head. "Really lucky. Fucking Jake. I never liked that guy, but I didn't think he was capable of that."

"People do lots of things when they're threatened, and he was definitely threatened by Amelia."

"Rightly so—she was going places."

"She still is." I smile again. "I have no doubt in my mind."

"I don't doubt that either."

"Do you know what happened to Jake?"

"As you know, the police were called when Amelia was rushed to the hospital, but since it was an accident, they couldn't do anything. I told them he locked Amelia in the edit suite but they'll need Amelia to file a report. I was going to try and call her today, but I don't think she needs that on top of everything else."

"Thank you. Maybe hold off for a day. Her recovery is the most important thing right now. But I'll talk to her about it. Do Jim and Tom know?"

"Yes. They fired him. But I'm not sure if they just did that to avoid a mass exodus, because we all would have walked if he wasn't sent packing."

"I guess it's still a good outcome. Whatever their motives. Especially considering Amelia doesn't work there anymore."

"True. God, what a mess. Please send her my well wishes."

"I will. Thanks, Adrian."

I turn to leave, but Adrian calls out, stopping me in place.

"Oh, and Luke. I hate to have to say this, but I overheard Jake telling Tom about his source. He said it was Amelia's dad. I'm sorry."

Jesus. Fucking. Christ. That's going to kill her. And when I find him, I might have to inflict the same pain.

I thank Adrian for letting me know, and as I walk away, tension weaves its way through my body. I hadn't thought about Amelia reporting Jake. I knew him knocking her down was an accident, and since I was basically ready to beat the shit out of him, I didn't think there was anything she could do. But Adrian's right. She needs to report him. And put that fucker of a father in his place. Then maybe after that, she can move on.

When I round the corner toward the Coach's office, my phone buzzes, making me pause to check it before I go in.

Amelia's name flashes across my screen and I smile before releasing a slow sigh.

Amelia: I hope it went well with Pierce

God, I miss them already. I'm a completely different person. I type out a quick reply as the man of the hour pops his head out and notices me, a scowl forming as he waves me in.

Luke: Thanks. I'm about to see him. How are my girls?

Amelia sends a selfie of her and Juliet, and my heart bursts as I move to follow Coach inside. My girls. *Fuck, I'm lucky.* I pause again as a smile lights up my face. No matter what happens today, I have them both waiting for me. I can handle whatever life throws my way.

As long as Coach doesn't bench me for our first playoff game. *Which I guess I'm about to find out.*

"Coach." I nod as I sink down into the chair opposite him, pocketing my phone.

"Bennett." He nods back before huffing out a long breath. "How's your family?"

Huh? I was not expecting that. "They're good. They're both as healthy as can be expected considering what happened."

"Good. I knew this production was a bad idea. I tried to stop it."

"I know. But some good things came out of it. I have a wife and a little girl now."

"A wife? Did I miss... actually, you know what, never mind. I don't care. I'm happy they're okay, but if you ever fuck me over like that again, you're out."

"I know. But I make no promises."

"That's fair. I'd do the same for my wife and kid. And I hate admitting this, but we needed you out there. We still won but it was a tougher fight." I bite back a smile and nod until he laughs. "You're not going to say anything?"

"I wasn't sure if you wanted me to acknowledge the compliment."

"Good point. Moving on. In short, the fine is enough. You can play next week as long as you attend all practice sessions leading up to the game."

I knew that was a given, but a knot forms in my stomach, already missing Amelia and Juliet. "Deal."

"Good. Now fuck off so I can make a call."

I jump up to leave, but before I get to the door, I cringe and spin around. *Dammit.* Why can't I walk away?

"Ah, Coach?"

"What?" he growls, his scowl re-forming as he glances up at me.

"Jake said something when we were fighting the other day."

"Who the fuck is Jake?"

"The other director—it's not important. What is important is that he said Jefferson was selling the—"

"Don't finish that sentence. You're not supposed to know about that, and it will be better if you just push that information from your mind. We have playoffs to win. We need to focus on that."

"But—"

"But nothing, Luke. I can't deal with it right now. It's best to leave it alone until it's official."

"Okay."

"Good. I'll see you on the field."

He picks up his phone, ending our conversation, so I do what he asks and leave it alone. It's in Jefferson's best interest that we win the Super Bowl, so as long as he doesn't mess with that, I can wait for it to come out.

And for all I know, it could be a good thing for the team. It's best to just sit tight and wait.

It's time to focus on the game.

I'm away from the hospital for no more than five hours, but when I finally get back, a weight is lifted. Amelia's better than when I left, and Juliet's sleeping peacefully in her bassinet. All safe and well.

"Hey, you," Amelia says as I walk in. "How was practice and your chat with your coach?"

"No issues. Coach said he missed having me on the team but that I couldn't gloat about it."

"Did you gloat?"

"A little." I shrug, making Amelia laugh. "To my teammates."

"I'll bet."

"How are things here? Did you speak to your mom?"

"I was going to. Until I saw a message from my dad asking to meet his grandchild. The grandchild he knew had been born. She told him. *Again.*"

I cringe at the mention of her dad as an internal battle rages inside me. That fucking man. All my instincts tell me to keep the information to myself. She's been through too much and I can't hurt her anymore. But I also made a promise to change, and keeping her in the dark breaks that promise. Which means I need to get everything off my chest. *Everything.*

"I'm sorry, Amelia. You deserve better than your parents. And—"

"It's okay. Maybe it's for the best. It will help me move on. I felt guilty, but now I don't. I have my own family and that's more important."

"It's still hard and—"

"At least they taught me what not to do as parents."

"You're right. We will never be like that. Actually, let's promise we'll never be like either of our parents."

"Why? Your parents are great. They're coming in tomorrow, right? After Hayley?"

"They are and they weren't bad parents. But they made a few bad decisions. Yes, most hurt Lainey more than me, but still... Let's not do that. Anymore."

"Agreed. And—"

"I need to tell you something. Well, two things." I grimace as my stomach knots.

Amelia frowns but she nods before trying to sit up a bit straighter. "Whatever it is, you know I'd prefer to hear it than never know."

"I do. But I'm still sorry."

"What is it?" She sounds panicky, making me rush.

"Your dad was Jake's source for the fire. I don't have the details, but Adrian overheard Jake telling Tom."

"Jesus Christ." Amelia's face scrunches before she huffs out a laugh. "I guess that makes cutting him out of my life a hell of a lot easier. But why would he do that? To hurt me, to..." She trails off, her eyes watering before a lone tear falls down her cheek.

"Money?" I guess, though I have no idea. "Maybe it's always been about money. Vicki's mom was wealthy and—"

"You might be right. Maybe that's why I've never really cared about money. Maybe deep down, I knew not to make it a motivator for me."

"Could be." I'd prefer it was money. I'd hate to find out he hurt his daughter to get back at her or something. If he's been trying to talk to her all these years, it must have been hard when she never got in touch. "Question. Why'd you keep his last name if you never planned to reconnect with him?"

Amelia's body sags as she blows out a breath. "At first, Mom wouldn't change it. Dad told her she had to change hers, so she kept mine as Rosenberg as a connection to him. But then when I got older, I didn't want to change it. It was my name as much as it was his. I felt like he'd stolen my childhood, and I didn't want him to steal my identity too. It's silly. I know. But—"

"It's not silly at all. It's who you are."

"It was, but now I feel different. Anyway, what's the second thing?" Amelia nervously nibbles at her bottom lip, cutting into my thoughts while my heart races. I want to ask more, but I can tell she's not ready to talk about it. And I have a confession to make.

"I...I lit the fire," I blurt, admitting it out loud for the first time since it happened. "Well, a group of us did."

Amelia's jaw drops before she shakes her head. "What?"

"We were messing around, and I guess over the years people had filled the bath with trash, and we lit a fire as a joke." I step closer, needing to see her reaction. But instead of the anger I expect, she reaches for my hand and nods for me to continue. "While we were watching it burn, I overheard the girls talking about your dare and I got the idea to go up to the attic with you. And to fake the fire. The real fire was contained when I left. The guys were supposed to put it out. But I should have put it out."

"Why didn't you tell the police that? You didn't mean for it to burn—"

"Because we still lit it. Accident or not, we were stupid kids playing with matches. And if I told the police, I wouldn't only be ruining my future and my career but the future of my teammates too. I know it was a shitty thing to do, and I've regretted a lot about that day over the years, but I'd never do that to my friends. They got out of there. The police never knew they'd been inside that house. We fucked up. We made a mistake, but they didn't deserve to suffer because of it. It's why I was so desperate to keep it out of the show. I didn't care about me, but I couldn't exactly tell you that."

"The show. God. Do you think Jake knows?"

"He seems to think it was only me, and because of that, I stopped caring if he knew or not. My consequences ceased to matter the second I saw you trembling on the floor of the edit suite. If I knew my confession could take your pain away, I'd do it in a heartbeat and keep my friends out of it. But it's too late for that. I've lied to you, kept things from you, and hurt you so much that I'm just as bad as your dad was. Worse even. But I promise I'll never be that man again. I'm trying and I'm sorry for everything I've put you through."

Amelia squeezes my hand as she smiles. "I know and I've forgiven you. We've got a new start to life. An amazing future with our daughter. You need to stop apologizing for the past. Having said that, any other secrets you want to share before we begin?"

"Not so much a secret." I smile. "But Jake was fired. And Adrian said you should press charges against him for locking you in the edit suite."

"Wow. Okay. That's a lot to process. Do I have to do it now?"

"I don't know. I'll find out. But your recovery is what's most important."

"Thank you. Anything else?"

"Nope." I shake my head. "I'm an open book from now on."

"Good. Except let's keep the fire a secret between us. I'd rather the police never found out how stupid you are. *You lit the fire?* What the hell were you thinking?"

"I wasn't. Turns out, I'm not as smart as people think."

"I always knew it." She winks, making me finally laugh.

"Smart or not, it's time for us to move on from the past and be better. For Juliet."

Our gazes flash to Juliet's bassinet and I smile at her cute little expression, getting lost in the rise and fall of her chest, watching as she wriggles.

"That works for me," Amelia says after a moment, drawing my attention. "And it's not going to be a problem." She laughs, shaking her head.

"What's not?" I ask, confused.

"Us being better for Juliet. She already has you wrapped around her finger."

"She does. No doubt about that. As does her mother." I wink just like she did, making her laugh again as I press a kiss to her hand. "There are worse things in the world than being under your spell. And not having you both tops that list. I'm going to work hard not to fuck...I mean, mess it all up."

"Good. Because I kind of like having you around."

Chapter Fifty-One

LUKE

I arrive home after a run with Thomas and strip off my sweaty tee before making my way into the living room, finding Amelia breastfeeding on the couch.

The past three weeks were a whirlwind while I balanced my time between the hospital and practice, my games and other football commitments, and then settling Juliet in at home.

But I couldn't be happier.

As I walk past, Amelia glances up from her book, smiling before her gaze drops to my chest, and she practically drools over my abs. Her lust-filled eyes rake over me as she sucks her bottom lip into her mouth and nibbles on the flesh.

"Fuck, Amelia. Don't look at me like that," I groan. "Especially while feeding our daughter."

"Like what?" The desire in her eyes makes way for confusion before she pouts, making her even more beautiful, if that's possible. But I hold strong. She's only been home for a week and she still has weeks left of recovery. I refuse to be the one that delays it.

"You look like you want me to eat you."

"Oh God, can you?"

"What?" My balls tighten and my cock twitches beneath my shorts. "Amelia," I warn.

"Oh, don't get shitty with me," she huffs, trying to hide her smile. "You're not Mr. Innocent here, walking around looking like a hot and sweaty tall glass of water. When I'm really, *really* thirsty."

I bite back another groan and shake my head, until a thought hits me and I smirk. "I'm guessing that means your passion for me didn't weaken with Juliet's birth."

"No, it didn't." Her eyes drop to my chest again and she stares at me longingly. "But right now I'm wishing it did, because—"

"God, okay. Jesus. I'm putting clothes on before I break my own no touching rule."

"Thank you." She sighs in relief. "Preferably layers. All the layers."

"As you wish."

I jokingly roll my eyes when she smiles her thanks, but as I walk away, I can't help but laugh. This woman is my everything. My girls are my everything. I don't know what I'd do without them. And I never want to have to find out.

Abandoning my need for food, I detour to the shower and wash myself with a clenched fist, practicing restraint so I don't pump my cock to relieve the tension, because Amelia can't. *Not yet.* And it will be all the more sweeter when we can come together. *At least that's what I'm telling myself.*

After drying off, I get dressed in *all the layers* and head back into the living room, dropping onto the couch next to her. I'm just about to ask if Juliet's asleep when she cries out, her tiny wail answering my question.

"Want me to take her?"

"Yes, please. I enjoy the sight."

"The sight?" I raise an eyebrow, as I huff out a laugh.

"As if you don't know what I mean. I wasn't kidding when I said people would go crazy for a picture of you with a baby. Hell, I'm going crazy over it."

I laugh as I reach out, letting Amelia shift Juliet gently into my arms. And my heart jolts just like it always does. I'll never get used to this father and husband business—caring for someone or two someones more than I care for anything else in the world, including myself and football. And that's saying something because I have always highly regarded both of those things.

"If I'd known how many women I could get by having a baby, I would have done it years ago. Judging by your expression, I'll bet Juliet gets me ten times more attention than Shadow does." I maintain my straight face as a thought hits me. "Holy hell. Imagine if I went for a walk with Juliet *and* Shadow."

"Ovaries exploding everywhere."

"Hell yeah. But it's too bad for them." I shift Juliet into one arm and reach out to clasp Amelia's hand. "I'm already spoken for. And I have no plans of that changing anytime soon."

"Good." Amelia lifts her lips in a half smile. "Because I have no plans to let you go." She makes a show of letting go of my hand, laughing at how funny she is as she grabs the book she was reading. Some romance novel that she tells me will emotionally destroy her before she gets to the end. God knows why she finds that entertaining, but it is what it is. She offers me the book and smiles. "If you could just hold this in your free hand while I grab my phone, that would be greatly appreciated. I'm currently jobless, and I could make a killing selling that photo to the media. It's the trifecta. A tough football player, with a baby, reading a romance novel. It's the stuff dreams are made of. Or fantasies."

"Still as annoying as ever, I see."

"It's why you love me." She laughs.

"I'd love you no matter what," I say and I mean it. "But like I said in the hospital, I also never want you to change."

Amelia smiles before stepping forward to hug me, but I push her back. "Uh-uh. You have a photo to take. You never know when we might need the extra cash."

She rolls her eyes before she bursts out laughing like it's some big joke. But of course she takes the photo. And then her face drops and I know what's coming.

"Any news?"

Thomas and I have been waiting on edge for Jefferson to announce he's selling the team, but he's still keeping quiet about it. My guess is he'll wait until our season's over, but it's goddamn annoying to keep this secret from my teammates. With a new owner comes a level of uncertainty, and despite us being favorites to win the Super Bowl, who knows what's going to happen. Coach is amazing, but he's burned a lot of bridges to get here. And I know our GM has a few enemies of his own. The last thing I want is for us to be the top team this year and then become the talk of the town for all the wrong reasons.

"Nothing yet," I tell Amelia. "And I can't ask because I'm still keeping my mouth shut until it's all officially announced, and at this stage that's likely to be after the Super Bowl." *Which we fucking made.*

"Which you are going to win."

"Yeah we are." I laugh. "And it's going to be that much sweeter knowing that you're there. In my jersey."

Amelia was reluctant to come at first, and I've got to admit I felt the same. But when Thomas, Dylan and I were able to secure a private suite for our families, she jumped at the chance to come, knowing that Juliet would be kept away from the masses.

"Ugh." Amelia blows out a breath and I wait for her to sass me. "I wasn't going to wear your jersey but I guess I can. If it's that important to you."

She bites back a grin as she walks past, swaying her hips, and I drop the book to the table, reaching for her hand before pulling her into me. "I cannot wait for the day I can fuck you again. That jersey is going to see every surface of this house."

She visibly swallows before licking her lips, her eyes hooded until she snaps out of it and pouts as she walks away. "You're a tease. I hate you."

"No, you don't," I call out after her. "You love me."

She flips me her middle finger before disappearing, and I chuckle as my heart races. God, I love her.

Later that night, I'm making myself comfortable in bed when Amelia shushes me, having finally gotten Juliet to settle. After checking on her again, Amelia tiptoes over and lies down, a soft sigh leaving her lips as she rests her head on my lap.

"You're not sleepy?" she asks, gazing up at me with a pinched brow, concern marring her features.

"Not yet. I'm just going to read for a bit." I show her my book—*So You're A Girl Dad?*—and she bursts out laughing before covering her face with her hands. "What's so funny? I need to get ahead of this. Before long she's going to be bringing her male best friend home, and we're going to think it's cute but find out years later that they've been in love the whole time and now she's pregnant with his baby."

"Wow."

"Yep."

"And when exactly did you fall in love with me? Because I only fell for you a few months ago," she sasses, making me stare at her deadpan.

"Keep telling yourself that."

"You broke my heart."

"Couldn't have done that if you hadn't cared to begin with."

"I hated you."

"There's a fine line between love and hate."

"You are annoying."

"That's hardly fair because I can't argue with that one."

Amelia bounces her eyebrows before wriggling her head in my lap and making herself comfortable. "Can you read with me like this?"

"Yeah. I'm good."

"Good." I huff out a laugh as the corners of her lips pull into a smile and she adds, "I love you, Babe."

"Babe?"

"What?" She mocks confusion. "You didn't think you'd escape your own nickname, did you?"

"One can hope."

"You love it."

"Maybe," I scoff, until the edge of her smile widens.

"Lainey once told me you claimed to reserve nicknames for people that annoy you."

"She's right."

"So, Juliet annoys you?" *Dammit. Busted.*

"You know she doesn't. I guess I can't get anything past you, can I?"

"Never. After all, I am the smartest in the room."

"Not a chance. I won that title when I asked you to marry me. Smartest idea any of us has ever had."

Her eyes flash to mine, and the love reflected back at me is blinding. "It's almost like you wanted it to work out this way. With us as a real family."

"Hmmm." I shrug, my gaze back on my book, giving her a noncommittal answer. But she knows that truth. I may not have planned this, but deep down, on a subconscious level, I knew there was no way I was ever going to let them go.

Like a storm, Amelia blew back into my life, but fuck, was it glorious.

Wait. Another storm? God, I'm fucked. My two girls are going to be chaos.

We're both quiet for a few minutes, and the dead silence makes me stretch up to check the crib, finding Juliet sleeping peacefully. I smile before running my fingers through Amelia's hair.

"I may not have been thinking long-term when I proposed our fake marriage, but the second you said 'I do,' I had the strongest feeling that there was no going back. At the time, I thought that was a negative, but it wasn't. It was the start of something perfect." Chaotic but perfect.

My smile widens until Amelia doesn't respond, and when I glance down, her eyes are closed.

"Amelia?" *Still no answer.*

I bark out a quiet laugh. It figures. Of course she'd fall asleep when I try to be romantic. Even when she's dead to the world she can sass me.

"It's scary how much I love you. Both of you. But I do. And you're stuck with me. Now please, for the love of God, will both of you have a long sleep."

I smile to myself as I grab my book, and I'm just about to start reading when Amelia takes a deep breath. "We love you too," she whispers sleepily, making me smiles. "But it's hard to sleep when you keep talking."

"Noted." Her eyes remain closed but I catch the subtle nibble of her lip as she bites back her smile. "Night, Ace."

"Night, Babe."

Babe. I guess I'll take it. She can call me whatever the hell she wants as long as she's safe, happy, and in my arms. *Forever.*

A little while later, I'm on my third chapter when my eyes get heavy. I'm just about to move Amelia off my lap when my phone vibrates on the bedside table.

> Reed: Now that Luke's found his end game, we need a new group name. What do you guys think?

I chuckle quietly and start typing but Easton beats me to it.

Easton: My vote is to delete the group

Luke: OR…

LUKE CHANGED THE GROUP NAME TO "EASTON'S SUPPORT GROUP."

Reed: Yes! Nailed it

Reed: This is going to be so much fun

Dylan: I'm staying for this, even though I won't be on the team anymore

EASTON LEFT THE GROUP

LUKE ADDED EASTON

Luke: You love us, there's no use denying it. We're here for you, man

EPILOGUE ONE

AMELIA – THE BIG DAY

Today's the day and no matter what happens, it's going to be life-changing.

With my heart lodged in my throat, I bounce Juliet softly in my arms as we enter the last few minutes of the game. The score is tied, but even with his helmet on and the distance between us, I can tell Luke's confidence hasn't wavered. Not making the Super Bowl was never an option in his mind, and now that they're here, they're out to win. It's their year and they know it.

I watch as Luke lines up for the next play and smile through my nerves. The love I have for this man is beyond anything I've ever felt before, and while it's still scary as hell, there's a giddiness running through my veins at the thought of finally finding my person. I have no doubt in my mind that I'm exactly where I'm meant to be in life. Everything that came before this moment happened to bring us together. I may never understand it, but I know it's the truth. It has to be, because I've never felt more alive and I've never felt so centered before. Like I've truly found my purpose. I wasn't born to be a muse. I wasn't meant to be a shadow of my former self. I was meant to shine, and even when I'm at home in my pajamas, nursing Juliet, Luke makes me feel like I do. He makes me feel like I'm the star of our show, like I'm the most important person in the room—Juliet aside. He lifts me up.

Through all our faults, and we have many, the one thing that makes us perfect for each other is that we're equals. No matter what happens in life, I know he's got my back, and I have his. If I wanted to go back to work tomorrow, he'd support me. If I wanted to stay home and raise babies for the rest of my life, he'd support that too. And if I wanted to walk away from our relationship—not that I could ever fathom that—he'd support my decision. He'd fight like hell, but in the end, he wants what's best for me.

I've never had that. Not with my parents, not with Preston. I've never felt that sure, that protected, that safe. And I've definitely never felt that loved.

Lainey bounces on her toes beside me before grabbing my free hand. San Francisco has the ball as the clock ticks down, but I still hold my breath. Cincinnati has played a hell of a game, and it could still go into overtime and go either way.

Thomas launches the ball, and my breath hitches loudly, or maybe it was a collective hitch from everyone in the room. Either way, there's a breath of silence, then chaos ensues in the suite as the ball hits its mark, landing in Easton's outstretched hands before he runs ahead with Luke protecting him from the side.

Barely a few seconds tick by, but I'm so tense that when my phone vibrates in my pocket, I jump, startling Juliet. She settles quickly, but when I glance up, I see Easton slam the ball to the field as the whistle blows. *Touchdown.*

The crowd erupts in cheers as tears coat my eyes. Summer and Lainey jump up and down screaming, but when they see me, they stop, opening their arms wide for a hug. We sway to the fanfare, my chest full of awe as we watch the guys fall all over each other in celebration.

They did it. They won.

Luke said they would, and they did. He was confident from the beginning. He knew what he wanted, and he went after it. Exactly like he did with me.

"You girls should go," I tell Summer and Lainey when it's obvious they're lingering for my benefit. "The guys will be expecting you on the field."

Lainey hesitates until I shove her toward the door, but not before giving me one more sad pout as she glances toward the field.

Luke and I agreed that Juliet and I would stay up here until the crowds had gone. We agreed to meet once his media commitments were over. After the formalities. But that doesn't mean they have to stay with me.

My pulse races as I wait, but it's only a few minutes before the door slams open and I startle to find Luke racing through the opening, his expression a mix of love and relief, his smile wide.

"What are you—"

"We fucking did it," he cuts me off as he wraps Juliet and me in his arms, careful not to hurt her. "And you're here. My girls are here."

He pulls out of the hug and stares into my eyes with so much emotion that my heart seizes momentarily.

"Fuck, I love you." He grabs my chin and turns my head to the side, locking our lips in an all-consuming kiss. A kiss that only lasts a few seconds but fills me with more love than I've ever felt before.

When he releases me from his grasp, he winks before taking Juliet from my arms, cradling her against him. And like always, I marvel at how tiny she is against his huge body.

"Did you see Daddy?" he coos, like the smitten man that he is. "I did that for you, Angel. For you and Mom."

She doesn't even wake but still curls her body into his warmth, making my heart melt. Luke just played the biggest game of his career and won, but instead of soaking up the moment and the praise, he's here, with us.

"You did it, Babe." I glance up at him in awe, beyond proud of my man for more than just the Super Bowl.

"Hell yeah, I did." He laughs like he's joking, but the emotion in his expression gives him away.

"But you should be down there celebrating," I begin but he cuts in before I can say more.

"I'm exactly where I want to be, Ace. They know what this means to me. I needed to see you both and nothing was going to stop me."

Butterflies wreak havoc in my chest but I ignore them. "Will you get in trouble?"

"Oh definitely." He chuckles. "So, I can't stay long. But while I always thought a Super Bowl win would be my everything, it means more to me than I thought it would because I have you here supporting me. I love you, Amelia. Thank you."

"I lo—"

"Luke," a security guard interrupts us, "I gotta get you back down there, man."

"Okay. Okay. I better..." He trails off, pointing to the door.

"Yes. Go. I love you. And congratulations."

He reluctantly passes Juliet back to me before pressing a kiss to both our foreheads and hesitating again.

"Go." I laugh, pushing him toward the door, just like I had to do with his sister. "We'll be here when you're done. I promise."

As per the original plan, Luke came back to see us after the on-field celebrations and interviews were over and escorted us to our hotel before heading off to the official after-party.

Considering I didn't have a late night, I'm still exhausted by the time I fall into bed after feeding Juliet, and it doesn't take long before I'm drifting off to sleep.

As expected, I'm still alone when Juliet wakes me at three, but Luke creeps in while I'm feeding her, a giddy smile still locked on his face.

"How is she?" he whispers as he strips quietly, his eyes on Juliet.

"She's great. Just hungry. How were the celebrations? I thought you'd be out all night."

"Me too, but I kind of missed my girls."

"You see us plenty. This is your big day."

"It is, but just because I'm home, doesn't mean the celebrations are over." He raises a brow, as a cocky smirk settles into place.

"Is that so?"

"Yep. I'm sure we could think of something to do after Juliet's back asleep."

"Definitely. I could use a massage. It's stressful watching the Super Bowl."

"I thought that only happened if you cared."

"Well, it turns out that I do. Very much so."

Luke chuckles before flopping onto the bed, his eyes drifting closed.

"How do you plan on celebrating when you're ready to pass out?"

"I'm fine." He bolts upright, almost startling me. "I just needed those few seconds of shut-eye."

"Okay. You're acting weird. And why aren't you drunk? I thought for sure you'd be drinking yourself stupid."

"Nope. I had two very important things to come home to."

"Things?" I raise an eyebrow.

"People."

I almost feel bad that he's here for us, but when he takes Juliet from my arms and sings her to sleep, I snap out of it. Luke is not one to do something he doesn't want to. If he wanted to celebrate with his team, he'd be there. This is where he wants to be. With us.

A warmth spreads through my chest, and the second Juliet's back in her portable crib, I jump up and wrap my arms around him from behind. "You were amazing today, Luke. I'm so goddamn proud of you. You manifested the shit out of that win, never once doubting yourself or the team."

Luke unclasps my hands and steps out of my hold before spinning to face me, cupping my cheeks. "That's not the only thing I manifested this past year."

"Oh yeah?"

"I manifested you."

"You hated me."

"Nah. I wanted to hate you, but I never really did. Not completely. You, on the other hand, can hold a grudge."

"And you'd be wise to remember that." I bite back my smile and he huffs before walking me over to the bed and perching me on the edge.

"It's all up here." He points to his head as he sits beside me. "I remember everything." He puts on a creepy voice as his eyes widen, making me laugh.

"Stop, you sound like a stalker."

"If you leave me, you bet your ass I'll be stalking you."

"I don't doubt that." A yawn escapes me but I try to hide it. "Sorry, the excitement of today really got to me. I'm not usually this tired. I thought Juliet's random sleep patterns were making me accustomed to little to no sleep, but today feels different."

A flash of a frown mars Luke's features before he hides it. "I'll let you sleep then. Juliet will be up again before you know it."

He moves to stand but I stop him. "Wait. I may be tired, but I don't want to sleep. I want to hear all about your day. The parts of it I missed. How are you feeling?"

Luke grins before his smirk turns cocky again. "I'm on top of the world, Ace. But before we talk about football, I've got something else to say."

"Oh-kay." I pout, making Luke chuckle before he bops me on the nose.

"Winning the Super Bowl was a dream come true. Something I've been striving for my entire life. I had a one-track mind and I wasn't retiring until I got that ring. I may not be as stubborn as you, but I was more than willing to push my body to the limits and outstay my welcome if it meant I could realize my dream."

I huff out a laugh, picturing a middle-aged Luke running across the field. *So much for not talking about football.* I'd usually call him out for less than this, but I give him a pass for today. "You're amazing, Luke. You set out to achieve a life goal, and you did—"

"Wait, I'm not finished."

"Ooh, sorry." I bite back a laugh. "Go on."

"Thank you. Winning the Super Bowl *was* my life goal. My dream. But when we won, the first thing I wanted to do was see you. Yes, I loved celebrating with the team, but I realized my thoughts had shifted to include other goals. Other dreams. And you and Juliet are a huge part of that."

He stands up and it may be the low light, but I swear he looks nervous. "You know, I've never once dreamed about getting married," he begins, catching me off guard. "I never wanted to be a husband and I never wanted a wife."

My brows furrow and Luke smiles, his nerves seemingly dissipating.

"Hold your disgust until I'm finished," he says, his smile lighting up the room. "I never once dreamed of any of that, but I dream of being married *to you.* And before you say anything,"—he reaches forward, covering my mouth with his hand, anticipating my remark—"before you argue, I don't mean our online marriage of convenience. I want to see you walk down the aisle while I struggle to hold back the tears. I want to say all the sappy things people say to each other in their vows. I want our daughter in a cute little dress throwing ridiculously expensive flowers at our friends and family as they all whisper about how perfect she is. And I want to take you back to a fancy hotel and fuck you senseless while you wear a white dress telling the world how pure you are. But I only want those things because it's *you*. You sucked me in when I was a kid and that poor little version of me had no idea just how deep you were going to sink your claws. Hell, the adult version of me still had no clue. I wanted to hate you more than I wanted anything else in the world. Football aside. But maybe that should have been a dead giveaway. All that energy wasted on the wrong emotion."

I try to laugh, but my own emotion clogs my throat as tears fall from my eyes. I've never been an overly romantic person, so I had no idea how much I wanted to hear someone profess their love like that. Until now.

"And here I thought you were with me because of our daughter," I joke but my words come out raspy. Luke knows I'm lying. He didn't need to smirk for me to see that, because we both know, I don't think that at all. Never did. He's been all in from the moment I told him I was pregnant. Maybe even before that. I was just too blind to see it. And while I tried to pretend our night together didn't mean anything, it meant *everything*. More than either of us will ever know. It gave us Juliet and, in the end, brought us together.

"Amelia Joy Rosenberg..." Luke says my name like he's scolding me before walking over to his suitcase and rummaging about inside, hiding something behind his back. "Amelia,"—his voice softens—"you have my word that this is the last secret I'll ever keep from you. But I promise, it's a good one." He drops down to one knee and reveals the small box he was hiding, opening it to show me a square-cut diamond engagement ring and a simple white gold wedding band. I gasp as I lean forward, but before I can say or do anything more, Luke continues on. "I plan to spend the rest of my life making you and our daughter happy because I have never been happier than I am with you. No amount of accolades or Super Bowl wins will compare to the joy you've brought to my life. And while I'll always regret the years we lost, I know that they brought us to this moment. To our happily ever after. So, Amelia J Rosenberg, will you do me the honor of officially becoming my wife? I want you to be mine. Forever."

I'm speechless as tears roll down my face. All I can do is nod before flinging myself into his arms.

"I'm going to need you to answer me, Ace." Luke pulls back. "As cute as the blubbering is."

I shove at his hard chest before smiling through the waterworks. "Luke, I have never wanted to sass you more than I do right now," I rush out, my voice wavering. "But I also want to shower you with kisses and show you how much this moment means to me. Thank you for pushing me to see how amazing life could be with you by my side. You and Juliet are my world, and I couldn't imagine my life without you."

"So that's a..." He rolls his hand, encouraging me to get the words out. *Sassing me.*

"Yes." I giggle. "I'd love to *officially* be your wife."

"Good." He nods a few times, pretending he's unaffected as his eyes well with tears.

"Good," I repeat, my heart pounding so hard, I'm sure he can hear it. "Happy now?"

"So fucking happy." He quickly stands and cups my face, pressing his lips to mine, kissing my mouth, my cheeks, my nose, my forehead, making me laugh as more tears fall. "I love you so fucking much, Amelia." He pulls back and grabs the ring box again before kissing my hand and slipping both rings onto my finger.

Words get stuck in my throat as I stare down at my hand. I didn't think much about wearing rings again. But now that I have them on, it feels like a direct connection to my heart.

I'm married to Luke Bennett.

And I've never been happier.

When I don't say anything after another beat, Luke chuckles before kissing me again. "You need to get naked," he whispers against my lips. "Before Angel wakes up again. You're mine for at least the next hour."

"Wrong." I push him back, my hands locked on his biceps.

"Wrong?" He raises a brow.

"Yep. I'll always be yours, no matter what."

Luke's eyes darken before he curls his hand into my hair. "God, I love hearing that. I can't wait to make you my wife again."

He leans forward but I hold him at arm's length, my chest tight with more emotion than I'd usually be able to handle. "This is the real deal, isn't it?" I ask, my eyes flashing between him and Juliet. "We're really going to make this work."

"Absolutely." Luke smiles, the warmth of it coating my skin in goose bumps. "I told you, whatever it takes."

"Whatever it takes," I agree before pulling him down on top of me and wrapping my arms and legs around him.

And for the first time in years, I feel like I've found my place and I don't plan on losing myself again. Not that Luke would ever let me. It's all up from here.

EPILOGUE TWO

LUKE – THREE YEARS LATER

I drop my suitcase next to Amelia's oversized work bag and yawn as I traipse through the house toward the yard. It's not even three p.m. yet but I'm exhausted after attending an away game with the boys last night—my first since retiring—and I'm ready for sleep. At least, I am until I step outside and find my girls relaxing by the pool.

Amelia's wearing the bright yellow two-piece bathing suit I bought her for Christmas last year and Juliet's trying to match her with a yellow suit of her own, making me smile. She's a mini Amelia in every sense of the word except that she looks like me with her dark hair and dark eyes.

Shadow's head whips up in my direction from where she lies beside them, in protector mode, but when she notices it's me, she resumes her relaxing. Gone are the days where she'd run to see me, desperately missing me after my time away. Now, like the rest of us, she worships the ground Juliet walks on. Where Juliet goes, so does Shadow, and I have to admit, I prefer it that way. It makes it that little bit easier to say goodbye whenever I leave the house.

I watch for a few minutes, not quite ready to disturb the silence, my smile widening when Amelia readjusts herself on her towel, rolling onto her back, and her mini me does the same.

A warmth spreads through my chest and I can't help but laugh to myself. This may have been the last thing I ever imagined for my life, but I'm thankful every day that it's what was planned for me.

Shadow looks my way again, as if she's questioning my actions, and if she could talk, I have no doubt she'd call me a creeper. Yes, I'm quietly staring at my family, but after three years it's still hard to believe that they're mine. Her head tilts to the side and I know I have about five seconds to announce myself before she gives the game away.

I quickly make my move, not wanting to miss Juliet's reaction when she hears me.

"I'm home," I announce, opening my arms wide in anticipation.

"Daddy!" Juliet shrieks my name as she jumps up and runs over, launching herself into my chest at the same time Amelia turns to face me, her loving smile making my heart race, just like it always does.

"I missed you, Angel." I spin Juliet around as she giggles. "Have you been looking after Mom?"

"Yes, Dad. I always do. With Shadow."

"Of course. Always with Shadow."

Juliet gives me one more squeezy cuddle then wriggles in my arms until I put her down, so she can run back to Amelia.

"Is it dinner time, Mommy?" she asks, her deep brown eyes lighting up. "You said Daddy was coming home at dinner time."

"Not yet." Amelia laughs. "We just had lunch and the sun's still high in the sky. Dad must be early." She glances my way with a raised brow. "What time is it?"

I check my watch as the time clicks over to three, my smile morphing into a smirk. "It's go time!" I jog over and press a lingering kiss to Amelia's lips, giving her a proper hello before breaking the connection and searching around for her laptop. This is why I'm home. I took an earlier flight so I could be here in time for Amelia's moment. A moment she's pretending isn't a big deal.

"Hi." Her brows rise as she peers up at me, a little flustered. "Is it really that time already?"

"What's go time?" Juliet asks, pouting as her eyes bounce between ours.

"It's time to see what Mommy's been working on." I drop down onto the lounge beside Amelia and slide back as I bring up the website for our friend Grayson's band—Poetic Nightmares—clicking on the link to their new release "Soulless Whisper." Amelia wrote and directed the music video, and the extended eight-minute cut is about to go live.

As the page loads, I angle the screen toward Amelia and Juliet, now perched in her lap, but before it comes to life, it freezes.

"What happened?" Amelia asks, her expression marred in concern, proving that she's been thinking about this moment more than she's let on. Not that she ever had me fooled.

"I think it crashed," I say with a smile, knowing with every fiber of my being that this is going to propel her career into the limelight. I have no doubt she's about to become "award-winning director Amelia Bennett" rather than "Luke Bennett's wife," and I'm more than excited to be pushed into the shadows for her.

"It's a brand-new laptop." Amelia frowns. "Is it still under warranty? What a time—"

"The laptop didn't crash, Amelia." I laugh, bopping her on the nose. "The entire website did. Poetic Nightmares are one of the biggest bands in the country right now. Fans have been counting down the seconds until this release. It's huge."

"So we can't watch it?" She pouts just like Juliet did and I have to bite back my smirk.

"Give it a few minutes and I'm sure someone will illegally upload it somewhere."

"What? I'm not watching it illegally." Her face scrunches before she folds her arms over her chest, and a second later, Juliet does the same as she tells me off.

"Daaad."

"I'm kidding." I chuckle, shaking my head, already imagining Amelia and Juliet ganging up on me in the future. And I have to admit I love it. "If we were the average viewer, we'd have to wait until they fix the site. But lucky for you, Gray sent me a link to their internal version this morning. We can watch it now."

"Will this affect them in any way?"

"Not at all. It's a good thing. Sort of. As long as they get it back up as soon as possible."

"I'm nervous." She buries her face into Juliet's hair as I type in the new link, and I don't need her to tell me what she's nervous about for me to know. She's not talking about the site crashing; she's worried about her work. I wasn't joking when I said Poetic Nightmares was the biggest band in the country, and with that comes a lot of responsibility and pressure for Amelia—self-imposed pressure, because Grayson and his band are the most laid-back guys I've ever met.

No matter how much we tell her it's going to be amazing, she won't believe us until it actually happens.

After Amelia took a year off with Juliet, we hired a nanny for a few days a week so she could start working again. She didn't want to go back to full-time work, but wanted to flex her creative muscles, and when Preston's song "Wicked Style" became huge, just like he said it would, he approached her to direct his next music video. Using *her* idea. Full pay this time. Including a writing credit.

And it took off. From there she was approached by bands all around the world, but the biggest win was when she connected with Grayson. After that, her career grew in line with my retirement and I'm now a stay-at-home dad, which I love. I still support the team, and with Thomas coaching, I try to get to all their home games, but my life is shifting. Football will always be in my blood, but it doesn't hold as much value as it once did. My heart belongs here.

"You have nothing to be nervous about," I say and I mean it. "I may have snuck in my own viewing of the final cut on the plane." I wince as Amelia's eyes widen until she shakes her head with a laugh. She expects most of my antics these days. "It's phenomenal, Ace. I'm so proud of you. So much so that I had to stop myself from shouting about it to my fellow passengers. I've got to say, it's much better than that quasi docudrama you did about some football team," I joke.

That quasi docudrama that went on to make millions of dollars for our ex-owner and even won a reality TV award. That should have propelled Amelia to stardom, but she distanced herself from the project after reporting Jake to the police. While he no longer worked for Brighton Productions, they were still all questioned and it dragged their name through the mud, creating a bit of bad blood between her and the producers.

"Wasn't that you, Daddy?" Juliet crawls on top of me before bopping me on the nose, just like she saw me do to Amelia.

"Yeah, Angel. That was me. Before you were born. Are you ready to watch?"

I've just hit play when Shadow jumps up and runs to our back door, making us all turn to find Lainey stepping out. Juliet's the next to run but when Amelia moves to stand, I pull her back down.

"Nope. You didn't jump up for me."

"I see you plenty. Are you jealous of your sister?"

"Never," I lie as I watch Juliet and Shadow smother her with love.

"Thomas said you caught an earlier flight," Lainey calls out. "I came to take Juliet and Shadow to the park."

It wasn't enough for Lainey to steal my dog on the regular, she now steals my daughter too. But in this instance, I'm not going to argue.

"Can I go, Dad? Can I go?" Juliet runs back over and clasps her hands together like she's begging us. Amelia did that as a joke once and now Juliet uses it for everything. As if it wasn't already hard enough to say no to her.

"Yeah, you can go. But it's daddy-daughter day tomorrow, okay?"

"Okay, Daddy."

Amelia heads inside to help Lainey with Juliet's bag and I lie back on the lounge, my heavy eyes drifting closed. Random images play through my mind, but before I have a chance to sleep, Amelia's back. She clears her throat as she stands over me, staring down at me with her perfect little pout, her hands on her hips as though she's about to scold me.

"Was I not supposed to say yes?"

"No, that's fine. But you weren't supposed to watch the music video without me."

"I know." I cringe. "But I couldn't stop myself." I sit up and wrap my arms around her waist, pulling her on top of me, chuckling when she squeals. "Do you want to watch it together now?"

Amelia bites her lip and her eyes twinkle with mischief. "Actually." She pauses, trying to hide her smile. "Since I've already seen it a million times, I'd rather just wait to see how it goes."

I burst out laughing and shake my head. "So you just wanted to make me feel bad?"

"Yep." She winks before moving to get off me, not that I let her get far before pulling her back down.

"How does it feel to be the famous one in our marriage?" I ask, bouncing my eyebrows.

"Stop." She shoves me away and rolls onto the lounge next to mine. "That's never going to happen."

"It better. I'm not making any more money, so one of us has to." That's not entirely true—I have a few endorsements in place—but they'll eventually run out.

"Again. Stop." Amelia laughs. "We have plenty of money. And if one day we don't, we could sell this oversized house that we don't need."

"Yet."

"Yet?"

"Yeah, I'm thinking we should fill it with ten kids. Maybe more."

"You're dreaming," Amelia scoffs, knowing I'm joking, but I love this house, regardless of size. "Two will be plenty. Juliet already walks all over you. You'd be drowning with ten."

"Fine." She's got a point. My angel can do no wrong. "We can stop at two." I bite back a smirk as she tucks her hands behind her head, closing her eyes, looking more relaxed than I've seen her in a while. She's been nervous about the music video, and I'm guessing that now that it's out in the world, and she can no longer change it, some of the built-up tension has left her. Which reminds me...

"I'm sorry you missed therapy today. I won't make a habit of going to away games. I just wanted to see Thomas's first—"

"What? No. You're allowed to have a life, plus I... ah... didn't miss it."

"You didn't? Did you give in and call my parents?" My parents are amazing with Juliet, but they're the type of grandparents that believe in spoiling their grandchildren, and while I will admit I spoil Juliet, there's a huge difference. She always comes home feeling sick after too much sugar when she's been with them. They're good in small doses.

Amelia huffs out a laugh, and then shocks me with her answer. "No, I gave in and called *my* mom."

"Wow."

"I know."

"And?"

"She was great. She took Juliet to that fairyland park near my appointment and Juliet won't stop talking about it. Mom was relaxed and happy. She even mentioned a new man in her life."

A genuine smile lights up my face. After Juliet was born, Amelia decided to start seeing a therapist to talk about her family and well...me. It really helped her work through the feelings she'd held on to since she was younger, and she's been working on rebuilding her relationship with her mom. I was hesitant at first, but after Jake was arrested for harassing Amelia, his relationship with her dad came to light, and her mom was devastated that she'd been a part of it. Turns out, when Damien found out Amelia was pregnant, he showed up at the Brighton Productions office and that's where he met Jake.

The asshole—Damien, I mean—has some kind of addiction to causing trouble. That's the best way to describe it. It's not specifically about money, although he did demand it from the news outlets when he sold his story, but it's more than that. It's almost like self-sabotaging behavior but threefold because he likes to sabotage the lives of the people he loves too. It's destructive behavior that I want far away from my family.

"I think she's in a better place," Amelia continues. "It was always going to take time for her to move on from Damien—we knew that. Even after she found out what he'd done. But she hasn't mentioned his name recently, so here's hoping she's finally putting that time in her life behind her."

When Juliet was a few months old, we agreed to let Alice see her on the condition that she never took photos and didn't talk to Amelia's dad, or anyone else, about any of us. It took a while to trust her, but I think Amelia's right. She seems to have changed.

"That's great to hear and you seem a lot happier about it."

"I am. It's like a weight has lifted. But it's not Mom or the therapy that's truly made me happy."

"Oh, yeah?" I raise an eyebrow as Amelia sits up and crawls over to my lounge, straddling my lap.

"Yeah. There's this guy. He's smart and handsome and...rides a motorcyc—"

She squeals as I flip her over, cutting off what was about to be a blatant lie. We've been together for three years and she still loves to sass me any chance she gets. It keeps things interesting and makes me love her a little more each day.

"You hate motorcycles."

"No, I don't." I stare at her deadpan until she laughs. "Okay, I don't love them. But this guy—" I cut her off again, pressing my lips to hers in a bruising kiss, careful to keep my weight off her.

She mewls against my mouth as she wraps her hands around my neck, her fingers dancing through my hair. "Who's the guy?" I ask, my lips brushing hers before I suck her bottom lip and cup her neck with my palm.

"Hmmm," she moans as her head falls back, and I can't help but laugh, knowing the sass is long forgotten.

"I was just saying I love you," I lie jokingly, readjusting myself to glide a hand up her leg, my fingers wrapping around the string of her bikini.

"Yes," she rushes out breathlessly when I kiss a path down her throat, sucking the heated flesh into my mouth. "I love you too."

Pulling back, I stare down at her as she sucks in a breath, her hooded eyes gazing lovingly into mine. This woman is my world. Always has been. And I almost fucked it all up.

But never again.

We may have a shared past that I'm not proud of, but our story is only beginning. And if they ever make a movie about our life, Amelia won't be the director—she'll be the star while I'm merely the supporting actor.

Amelia once told me I was born to make her laugh. She was ten at the time, but even then she had it all wrong. I was put on this earth to love her, and I plan to spend the rest of my life making her happy.

And teasing her.

Because life would be boring without her sass.

And the truth is...I wasn't made just for her and she wasn't made specifically for me... We were made for each other. As equals. It just took us too goddamn long to see it.

Dear Bennett Family Diary,

Life couldn't be better. I finished my career with two Super Bowl wins and the biggest retirement send-off anyone could have asked for. Amelia's killing it with her music videos and short films. She's going to take on the world any minute and I can't wait for her time in the spotlight. And Juliet...my angel...is the light in our lives, keeping us busy in the very best way.

But the icing on the cake...We're having another baby. Juliet is going to be a big sister. Our second little angel is due in five months. I'm destined to forever be surrounded by girls, and while Reed once said it was poetic justice, I couldn't be happier. They own me and I wouldn't want it any other way.

So like I said... Life is good. But there's so much more to come and I'm ready for the chaos.

Bring it on.

Luke

Thank you for reading Luke and Amelia's story.

WANT MORE LUKE AND AMELIA? You can read the moment Luke gives in to Amelia on her knees in this BONUS STEAMY SCENE available when you sign up to my newsletter.

Read it here https://BookHip.com/FXFDANS

And if you're not ready to leave the San Francisco Storm world, Delicate Storm, Easton and Paige's story, is now available on Amazon and Audible.

Keep reading for a sneak peek

CARELESS STORM

A right person / wrong time sports romance

Blair Stevens' thought she had it all — until one devastating moment shattered her world.

Seven years ago, Blair shared a secret love and a future with her brother's best friend, Zane Fitzpatrick. But fate sent them spiraling in opposite directions.

Now she's drifting through life, dating Zane's biggest rival, while he's the NFL's infamous bad boy, making headlines for all the wrong reasons.

Just when she begins questioning everything, Zane reappears, looking at her like no time has passed. And despite her efforts to keep her distance, Zane's unwavering support begins to reignite the strength she thought she'd lost forever.

As the undeniable pull brings them closer together, they're forced to face something bigger.

Because it turns out, Blair's not the only one who's broken. And the only way forward is to face the past... together.

FIERCE STORM

A forbidden, age gap sports romance

He's her boss, her brother's future father-in-law and her best friends dad. She's twenty years younger than him and the one woman he can't get out of his head.

What happens when they give in to temptation?

Find out when the final Storm book releases in June 2026

AVAILABLE NOW ON AMAZON, KINDLE UNLIMITED AND AUDIBLE

ALSO BY KATHERINE JAY

SAN FRANCISCO END GAME SERIES

Beautiful Storm (Luke and Amelia)

Delicate Storm (Easton and Paige)

Reckless Storm (Reed and Hayley)

Careless Storm (Zane and Blair)

Fierce Storm (Salvatore and Keeley)

HOLIDAY ROMANCE

Mistletoe Mail (Mason and Jenna)

SYMPHONY OF SOUND DUET

The Sound Of Silence (Jesse and Willow)

The Sound Of Forever (Jesse and Willow)

HEARTSTRINGS SERIES

When Nothing Else Matters (Dylan and Summer)

Still Here Without You (Joel and Delilah)

It Had to Be Us (Logan and Dani)

Truly Madly Deeply Mine (Wes and Lucy)

A Sky Full Of Stars (Thomas and Lainey)

Ain't No Sunshine - Novella (Nate and Cory)

ALL OF KATHERINE'S BOOKS ARE AVAILABLE ON AMAZON AND
KINDLE UNLIMITED

DELICATE STORM
SNEAK PEEK

PAIGE

I bite back a smile and turn to face the front of the plane, grabbing the airline magazine from the pocket, mindlessly flicking through the pages.

I try hard to stay still, but before long, my legs are bouncing while I tap my fingers on my knees, and barely a minute passes before my window-seat hottie groans.

"Okay. Fine. I'll bite."

"What?"

"Are you traveling for business or pleasure?"

Huh? My brows furrow, but with his arresting gaze boring into mine, waiting for a response, I don't question him again. "*Neither*. I'm moving to California for...a change of scenery. What about you?"

"I was visiting a friend." He's quick to answer, and it's safe to say that small talk is not his thing.

"Visiting a friend," I repeat. "In New York? I wonder if I know them." He stares at me deadpan as if to say "seriously" and I laugh. "What? It's possible."

"I was in Scotland. This is my connecting flight."

He speaks with no emotion while my eyes light up. "Scotland? *Wow*. I've never been but I hear it's beautiful." I smile and picture the vast green landscape I've seen in movies, until a shiver runs through me when I think of the weather. "It's cold, right? Was it cold?"

"It was fine."

"Fine?"

"If it was cold, I didn't notice." *Interesting response.*

"What sights did you see? Anything you'd recommend?"

Window hottie tenses and the frustration is clear in his posture, but he releases a breath and continues amusing me. "I spent the week breaking shit."

"Breaking shit?" My voice rises, giving away my excitement at that prospect. I would love to break shit right now.

"Yep. It was needed."

"In Scotland?"

"Yep," he repeats, popping the *p*, and I find myself watching his lips until they purse, snapping me out of it. Again.

"You know you can do that here, right?" I know that because I've done it. *Maybe it's time to do it again.*

"Break shit? I do. My ex does it all the time."

His ex what? Oooh. I laugh out loud though I'm not sure he meant that to be funny. "I meant you could break shit for a release. Assuming that's what you were doing. You know... You could crush a truck, smash a glass, destroy dinnerware."

"Destroy dinnerware?" He raises an eyebrow and frowns. "Like a plate?"

"Sure. Or a bowl." I shrug and I think I see the hint of a smile, but I don't draw attention to it, though a small part of me makes it my mission to see a full-on grin before we land.

"As I said...my ex was good at that."

"*Wait.* I thought you meant that metaphorically. Like she breaks hearts or promises."

My new friend huffs out the smallest of laughs—if you could even call it that—and folds his arms over his chest, leaning back into his seat to create some distance between us.

"Nope." He gives me nothing else, so I quickly move on.

"I find it's better to do it in a controlled environment," I say though I'm not sure he cares.

"That's definitely a wiser move," he humors me by answering. "Tell me. Have you ever destroyed dinnerware?"

"No."

"I see."

"I smashed a truck," I deadpan, staring into his eyes, trying not to smile.

My response catches him off guard, and I hold my breath as his lips curl into a genuine smile. *Yes.* I knew I could do it. Biting back my victorious laugh, I raise a brow and wait for his response.

"A truck? Was that in a controlled environment? Or did you take a baseball bat to an ex's pride and joy?"

I burst out laughing until the image of that works its way into my mind and my happiness fades. *If only.*

"I wish it was option B. God knows he deserves it. But alas,"—I put on a grin—"it was option A. And let me tell you, it's incredibly satisfying. But I guess you know that already. What did you destroy? Do you have any photos?"

"Photos?"

"Of your wake of destruction?"

"Ah. No. I'm not really a photo guy. Do *you* have photos?"

"Of the truck? Definitely. Loads of them. Sometimes I look at them to remember that high. It's only second to..." I trail off. While it doesn't seem like the gorgeous man beside me has any idea who I am, I'd prefer not to get too personal. Instead, my gaze moves to the food cart as it makes its way toward us. "Thank God. I'm starving. What about you? I'll bet, being the big guy that you are, you're always hungry. Am I right?" He stares at me like I'm crazy, and I'm confused until I replay what I said, barking out a laugh. "Never mind. I didn't mean that as a negative—"

"It's fine." He reaches out toward me but then seemingly changes his mind. "I didn't take it the wrong way. And you're right. I'm often hungry."

"Good. How about I grab us lunch?" I joke, bouncing my eyebrows, hoping for another smile. But instead, I get a quasi-nod snort huff thing which I think might be a suppressed laugh. Either way, I take it as a win.

Delicate Storm is available on Amazon, Kindle Unlimited and Audible. Read it here.

ABOUT THE AUTHOR

Katherine lives in Australia with her hubby, two kids and a mind full of characters. She spends her days partaking in role play, building fortes and dancing, while her nights are spent reading and writing.
Katherine writes emotional and angsty romance with love that's worth fighting for and characters full of heart.
For more information visit:
https://www.katherinejayauthor.com

If you want to stay up to date with all things Katherine Jay, com and join her Facebook reader group - The Angsty Lovers Playlist - for fun, exclusive content and sneak peeks. Or sigh up to her newsletter here or via her website.

Are you following Katherine of social media? If not, you can find her on Instagram, Facebook and TikTok.